"We offer stories ...
stories to produc ...
both dark and ...
*dedicated to Eros, that capricious God of love
and desire. And to the sirens, for somewhere
in this wide world they're still singing."*

—from the Introduction

- In a New York City penthouse, a grandmother
  with lusty appetites meets a different kind of
  animal in **Tanith Lee**'s sensational update of
  "Little Red Riding Hood" . . . *WOLFED*

- A client who is more than she seems turns the
  tables on a gigolo with tasty bedroom talents in
  Neil Gaiman's delicious . . . *TASTINGS*

- A young man's boldness wins him a boon of the
  Faerie Queen—and more than he bargained for
  beneath the bedsheets—in **Delia Sherman**'s
  bawdy Elizabethan romp . . . *THE FAERIE
  CONY-CATCHER*

- A high school boy has an irresistible erotic effect
  on the young girls—and women—in a small
  upstate town in **Joyce Carol Oates**'s unforgettable
  portrait of burgeoning sexuality . . . *BROKE
  HEART BLUES*

SIRENS
AND OTHER DAEMON LOVERS

"Worth a second read, or a third, or fourth."
Folk Tales

Also edited by
Ellen Datlow and Terri Windling

BLACK HEART, IVORY BONES
RUBY SLIPPERS, GOLDEN TEARS
BLACK THORN, WHITE ROSE
SNOW WHITE, BLOOD RED

EDITED BY
ELLEN DATLOW
AND
TERRI WINDLING

MAGICAL TALES

OF LOVE AND SEDUCTION

SIRENS

AND OTHER DAEMON LOVERS

An Imprint of HarperCollins*Publishers*

This is a work of fiction. Names, characters, places, and incidents are products of the authors' imagination or are used fictitiously and are not to be construed as real. Any resemblance to actual events, locales, organizations, or persons, living or dead, is entirely coincidental.

EOS
An Imprint of HarperCollins*Publishers*
10 East 53rd Street
New York, New York 10022-5299

First Eos paperback printing: November 2002
First HarperPrism paperback printing: October 1998

Eos Trademark Reg. U.S. Pat. Off. and in Other Countries,
Marca Registrada, Hecho en U.S.A.
HarperCollins® is a registered trademark of HarperCollins Publishers Inc.

Printed in the U.S.A.

10 9 8 7 6 5 4 3 2 1

This book is for Robert Gould and Jamie Webb,
with love on a very magical occasion, November, 1997.
—T.W.

Thanks are due to Tappen King & Beth Meacham (who may not even remember inspiring the idea for this book many years ago), and to the folks who generously provided research material for the introduction: Ellen Steiber, Alan Lee, Brian & Wendy Froud, and Alice Scott. Thanks also to our agent Merrilee Heifetz, and our editor John Douglas.

CONTENTS

INTRODUCTION

A *siren*, according to the *Oxford English Dictionary* and modern usage of the term, is a woman with an irresistible allure, dangerous to men. The word comes from the sirens of Greek mythology: beautiful bird-women, dangerous and desirable, feared for their fatal beauty yet propitiated for their oracular wisdom. Daughters of the river Achelous and Terpsichore (the muse of choral song), they were once the virginal handmaidens to Demeter's daughter, Persephone—until the girl's abduction to the Underworld by the dark god, Hades. Then the sirens shape-shifted, flocking to the island Anthemoessa, where their famous beauty took on a dark aspect and a deadly power. Nesting on a pile of human bones, the sisters sang to the sun and rain; their song had the power to calm or to stoke the winds . . . and to inflame men's loins. This music was irresistible, luring many a sailor to their shore—where he'd pine away without food or drink, unable to break the sirens' spell. Odysseus filled his shipmen's ears with wax to save them from this terrible fate; Orpheus drowned the sirens out with the music of his lyre to save the Argonauts. Yet in some stories, the men who lost their lives at the sirens' bird-claw feet died blissfully, ecstatically, in a state of sexual enchantment. . . .

In this collection, you'll find the sirens' daughters (women whose dark allure is bound with magic, myth, and mystery), daemon lovers, faery seducers, and all manner of lovers be-spelled. Animal brides and wicked wolves step from the woods of old folk tales; ghosts, spirits, and phantastes emerge from the shadows of the human psyche. These are tales of sexual magic—not only overtly erotic stories (although you'll certainly find those here), but also stories about the power of Eros, the power of sensual love.

Such tales are rooted in a mytho-erotic tradition as ancient as myth itself, for among our oldest stories are explicitly sexual and bawdy ones, found in oral traditions and ancient writings from all around the world. Many of the earliest stories concern the amorous adventures of deities and other supernatural beings—most famously in the Greek tradition, where Zeus pursued nymphs and maidens with abandon, where sexual jealousies were rife among the gods, and where divine erotic energy was worshipped in the form of Eros, god of love. Eros was one of the first of the gods, born from Chaos with Tartarus (although later tradition made him the son of Aphrodite by Zeus.) He is pictured as a cruel, mischievous winged boy who carries two kinds of arrows in his sheath: the golden arrows of love and the leaden arrows of aversion. Unlike the simpering winged Cupids in our present-day greeting card imagery, Eros was a god both revered and feared, for he had the power (said Hesiod) to "unnerve the limbs and overcome the mind and wise counsel of all gods and all men." Less well known than Eros is his brother, Anteros, the god of returned love, who punished all those who refused to return the love that they'd been given. Aphrodite herself was a goddess of love, as well as of beauty and marriage; she symbolized love of a higher nature than the capricious passions imposed by her son. Dionysis, the god of wine, was associated with the lower carnal passions. Dionysian rites involving great quantities of wine and riotous processions of sileni (drunken woodland spirits), satyrs (goat-men of insatiable lust), and bacchantes (participants in sacred orgies) were highly popular during the four fertility festivals dedicated to this god of pleasure.

In Egyptian myth, Atum is said to have made the world by masturbating, creating a god and goddess who then made love to produce the earth and sky. (The two had to be forcibly separated to give the world its present shape.) In Maori myth, the Rangi gods were born from the lovemaking of Nothing and the Night, crawling into a dark world made of the space between their bodies. In the earliest of the *Upanishads* of India, atman (the Self) caused itself to divide into two pieces, male and female. In human shape, these two copulated to make the first human men and women; in the forms of cow and bull they copulated to make cattle, and so forth, until the world was populated. In many of the oldest mythological stories, a mother goddess (Ishtar, Isis, Cybele, etc.) is partnered by a male sexual consort who dies each winter and is reborn each spring, symbolizing the seasonal cycle of nature's renewal in forest and field . . . as well as the ancient idea that the phallus "dies" after orgasm, only to rise again with renewed potency. In Celtic lore, the wild Green Man of the wood (depicted as a male face disgorging vegetation from the mouth) has his female counterpart in the Sheela-na-gig, a female figure disgorging vegetation from between swollen vulva lips—a potent symbol of the mythic connection between human sexuality and the fecundity of the earth. (In a sexual rite found in cultures the world over, and still quietly practiced by some today, couples made love in freshly sown fields to insure a good autumn harvest.) Cousin to the Sheela-na-gig carvings found in old churches in Celtic countries are the carvings of female figures found near the doorways of shrines in India, seated with their legs apart to expose the vulva, or yoni (a sacred symbol of the feminine half of the double-sexed divine.) It was (and remains) customary to lick a finger and touch the yoni for luck; as a result, the carvings have been worn into deep, smooth holes with the passage of time.

In the East and the West alike, mytho-eroticism is found across a wide spectrum of stories both serious and humorous—from myths of "sacred sexuality" (sexual pleasure as a divine cosmological force) to bawdy tales about the follies engendered by rampant carnal appetites. It is in the later category that Trickster makes his appearance, a wicked gleam in his eye and a tell-tale bulge beneath his breeches. Trickster is a paradoxical creature who is both very clever and very foolish, a culture hero and destructive influence—often at one and the same time. Hermes, Loki, Pan, and Reynardine are all European aspects of the Trickster myth; others from around the world include Maui of Polynesia, Legba and Spider in African lore, Uncle Tompa in Tibet, and the shape-shifting foxes of China and Japan. Trickster is a particularly powerful presence in the legends of Native American tribes, where he takes the form of Crow, Raven, Hare, or Old Man Coyote. Coyote tales in particular are often sexual, scatological, and very funny—tales of seduction (usually foiled), rape (which usually backfires), and all manner of sexual tom-foolery: penises that sail through the air to reach their intended target, farts and turds with magical powers, gender switches or impersonations involving animal bladders disguised as genitalia, and other tricks intended to appease a gluttonous sexual appetite. The Asian shape-shifting fox Tricksters are darker and more dangerous, seeking sexual possession of men and women in order to feed upon the vital life force which maintains their power.

Trickster tales bridge the gap between the great cosmological myth cycles and folk tales told 'round the fireside—for Trickster is equally at home in the house of the gods (as Loki or Hermes) and in the woods with the fairies (as Phooka, Puck, or Robin Goodfellow.) Turning from mythological stories to humble folk and fairy tales, we find that the overwhelming force of Eros is still a common theme. The woods of Europe, the mountains of Asia, the rain forests of South America and the frigid lands of the Canadian north are all filled with fairy creatures, nature spirits, and other apparitions who bewitch, beguile, and entice human beings into sexual encounters. The fairy lore most people know today comes from children's books or Disney animations, and so the popular image of fairies is of sweet little sprites with butterfly wings, sexless as innocent children. Yet our ancestors knew the fairies as creatures of nature: capricious, dangerous, and well acquainted with the earthly passions. Folklore is filled with cautionary tales outlining the perils of faery seduction, reminding us that a lovely maid met on a woodland path by dusk might be a fairy in disguise; her kisses sweet could cost a man his sanity, or his life.

The Irish glanconer, or Love-Talker, appears in the form of a charming young man—but woe to the woman who sleeps with him, for she will pine for this fairy's touch, and lose all will to live. The Elfin Knight of Scottish balladry seduces virtuous maidens from their beds; these girls end up at the bottom of cold, deep rivers by his treacherous hand. The leanan-sidhe is the fairy muse who inspires poets and artists with her touch, causing them to burn so brightly that they die long before their time. The woodwives of Scandinavia are earthy, wild, and sensuous—yet their feminine allure is illusory and from the back their bodies are hollow. Nix and nixies are the male and female spirits who dwell in English rivers, heartbreakingly beautiful to look upon yet very dangerous to kiss—like the beautiful bonga maidens who haunt the riversides of India, the čacce-haldde in Lapland streams, and the neriads in the hidden pools and springs of ancient Greece. Mermaids, the descendants of the sirens, sun themselves by the ocean's edge and sing their irresistible song; sailors who lust for them are drawn into the waves and drowned. Mermen and selkies (seal-men) come to shore to mate with human maids . . . but soon abandon their pregnant mortal lovers for the call of the waves.

When we look at older versions of stories we now consider children's tales (Sleeping Beauty, Little Red Riding Hood, etc.), we find they too have a sexual edge missing in the modern retellings. In the earliest versions of Sleeping

Beauty, the princess is wakened from her long sleep not by a single respectful kiss but by the birth of twins after the prince has come, fornicated with her passive body, and left again. In "animal bridegroom" stories older than the familiar version of Beauty and the Beast, the heroine is wed to the beastly groom *before* his final transformation; by the dark of night he sheds his animal shape and comes to her bed. "Take off your clothes and come under the covers," says the wolf to Little Red Riding Hood. "I need to go outside and relieve myself," the girl prevaricates. "Urinate in the bed, my child," says the wolf, a wicked gleam in his eye—and only then does she know it is not Grandmother beneath the bedclothes. These were not tales created for children; they were tales for an adult audience—for listeners and readers who knew that the passions of princes are not always chaste; that beautiful girls might grow up to marry beasts; and that lecherous wolves can lurk in the woods or dress up in women's clothes. (Indeed, so ribald were the old fairy tales that one of the earliest publications of them—Straparola's *The Delectable Nights*—brought charges of indecency from the Venetian Inquisition.)

For centuries, men and women have drawn upon the wealth of sexual imagery to be found in folk tales and classical myths to create fine works of erotic art—in painting, pottery, sculpture, drama, dance, lyric verse, and prose. This legacy comes down to us in beautiful works of ancient poetry: from Anakreon of Ionia ("I clutched [Eros] by the wings and thrust him into the wine and drank him quickly"), from Sappho of Lesbos ("I am a trembling thing, like grass, an inch from dying"), from Catallus of Verona ("She fondles between her thighs, attacking with long fingers whenever she hungers for its sharp bite"). We find an equally vivid sexuality in the verse of the women poets of old Japan, like Onono Komachi ("When my desire grows too fierce I wear my bedclothes inside out") and Izumi Shikibu ("How deeply my body is stained with yours . . ."). Ou-Yang Hsiu ("Behind the crystal screen, two pillows: on one, a hairpin fell . . .") and the "Empress of Song" Li Chi'ing-Chao ("I hold myself in tired arms until even my dreams turn black") created the celebrated love poetry of China in centuries past. In India, the delicious mytho-erotic tradition found in stories of Shiva, the dancing Goddess, and Krishna's amorous exploits is beautifully evoked by numerous poets including Jelaluddin Rumi, whose verses became ecstatic dances for the whirling dervishes ("When lovers moan, they're telling our story, *like this* . . ."), and the Indian princess Mirabai, whose gorgeous, passionate poems were addressed to Krishna, the Dark One ("At midnight she goes out half-mad to slake her thirst at his fountain . . .").*

In the West, a repressive influence dominated the arts as Christian society sought to distance itself from the earthy sexuality of the older animist religions. As a result, we have only a paltry store of erotic poetry and sensual prose from the fourth century onward (compared to India, China, and Japan, where sexuality continued to be perceived as a natural force and not a cause for shame). Yet by using symbols drawn from pre-Christian myth and folklore, Western artists and writers found an important outlet for erotic imagery. We see this particularly in the luminous art of the Italian Renaissance, where Christian devotional works sit side-by-side with mythic works of a distinctly sensual nature — such as Botticelli's voluptuous nymphs and pagan goddesses; Michelangelo's "Leda" (Leda's rape by Jupiter in the form of a swan); and Raphael's secret frescoes for the bathroom of Cardinal Bibiena in the Vatican (based on erotic stories drawn from Greco-Roman myth).

In Western literature, eroticism is firmly entwined with

---

*For complete transcriptions of these and other erotic poems from ancient times to the present, seek out *The Erotic Spirit*, an excellent and informative anthology edited by Sam Hamill, Shambhala Publications, 1996.)

myth and fantasy in works by some of the greatest writers of the English language. We find it in the beguiling faery enchantresses of Malory's *Le Morte D'Arthur;* in the men and women be-spelled by sexual glamour in the *Lays* of Marie de France; in the sexual violence and intrigue of Spenser's *Faerie Queene;* in the amorous antics of the fairy court in Shakespeare's *A Midsummer Night's Dream*, as well as the darkly magical sensuality of *The Tempest;* in the sexualized denizens of fairyland in Pope's *The Rape of the Lock;* in the dangers of fairy seduction found in the ballads of Sir Walter Scott as well as the poems of Byron, Keats, Blake, Tennyson, and Yeats.

In Victorian England, folk tales, fairy lore, and Arthurian symbolism enjoyed an explosive popularity at the same time that sexual expression was most repressed in polite society. Fairy paintings by Fuesili, Noel Paton, and J. A. Fitzgerald fairly drip with an eroticism which would have been banned from respectable galleries if the nudes painted so lusciously had not been given fairy wings. Aubrey Beardsley, on the other hand, never courted respectability; this young man's distinctive illustrations for *The Rape of the Lock* and other fantasies were overtly and deliberately erotic, full of languid women, lewd fairies, and satyrs sporting enormous phalluses. Rossetti's mythic Pre-Raphaelite ladies, with their pouting red lips just waiting to be kissed, were attacked in the Victorian press as lewd and immoral images (albeit these paintings merely look quaintly romantic to us today). *Goblin Market*, the famous fairy poem by Christina Rossetti (sister to the painter), was ostensibly a simple story about the dangers of eating goblin fruit—yet it reads as a heated metaphor for the sexual seduction of innocent young girls. The "fairy music" composed for the harp—a popular fad in Victorian times—also had distinctly erotic overtones; these composers enjoyed the celebrity accorded to pop stars today, and flushed young women would sigh and swoon during their performances. Richard Burton's translation of the magical Arabian stories of *The Thousand and One Nights* also brought erotic tales to the Victorian public in the form of fairy stories. Burton's frank (for the times) translation caused a publishing scandal; nonetheless (or because of this) the book went on to become a best-seller, and a fad for Orientalism joined the popularity of Victorian fairy lore—a distinct thread of magical eroticism running through them both.

In the early twentieth century, the Celtic Twilight writers continued to give a covert erotic touch to works drawn from folklore and myth, such as the Irish fairy poetry of Yeats ("Our cheeks are pale, our hair is unbound, our breasts are heaving, our eyes are agleam . . .") and the opium-dream prose of the Irish fantasist Lord Dunsany. But as the century progressed, fairy lore was relegated to the nursery (much like furniture that has gone out of style, as J.R.R. Tolkien has pointed out), and thus was stripped of all but the most tenacious elements of sensuality. To find magical eroticism as fin-de-siecle fairy lore became passe, we must turn instead to the Surrealists, whose dreamlike imagery often drew on the symbolism of mythic archetypes. Particularly notable in this regard are the stories and paintings of Leonora Carrington and her close friend Remedios Varo, both of whom had a keen interest in magical esoterica. The paintings of Max Ernst, Dorothea Tanning, and Salvadore Dali also display vivid, haunting, deliberately disturbing mytho-erotic elements. Loosely connected with the French surrealists was the Parisian writer Anais Nin, who went on to become one of the best-known writers of literary erotica in this century. The stories published in *Little Birds* and *Delta of Venus* (some of which have a dreamlike, magical flavor) were written in New York when Nin was one of a circle of writers (along with Henry Miller) producing erotica, paid by the page, for the delectation of an anonymous Collector.

As Surrealism, too, faltered with the change of fashions

after the second World War, magical erotica became harder to find . . . unless one looked at its darker manifestation: the vampire's kiss. From Hertzog's film *Nosferatu* to *Interview with the Vampire* by Anne Rice, the erotic element inherent in vampire tales surely needs no explication. While it is not the intent of this book to delve into eroticism in horror fiction (a vast subject all on its own), vampire tales seem to cross that elusive line between works of fantasy and horror, holding an irresistible appeal even to readers who traditionally avoid the latter (perhaps because of the close connection of vampires in traditional lore with the seductive, soul-sucking creatures who haunt the woods of the Faery Realm). As the century closes, and the field of literary fantasy enjoys a popular resurgence, we find that the magical tales which have a sensual or erotic edge still tend to hover close to that fantasy/horror divide, combining the symbols of myth and folklore with the tropes of Gothic horror. Angela Carter's brilliant fiction, for instance, is sensual, sexual, magical and very dark—such as *The War of Dreams*, a voluptuous work of modern surrealism, and *The Bloody Chamber*, which brings adult eroticism back into fairy tales. (*The Company of Wolves* is a film based on some of the stories in the collection, with an excellent, rather Freudian screenplay written by Carter herself.) Tanith Lee's *Red as Blood* is a collection of adult fairy tales retold in a similar vein, rich in sensuality and devilishly dark in tone. Sara Maitland's *The Book of Spells*, Robert Coover's *Briar Rose*, and Emma Donoghue's *Kissing the Witch: Old Tales in New Skins* are three more superb variations on this theme. Anne Rice has also eroticized fairy tale themes (with an S&M twist) under the pen-name A.N. Roquelaure: *The Claiming of Beauty, Beauty's Punishment*, and *Beauty's Release*.

With the ubiquitous pairing of sexuality and violence in our modern culture, it is more difficult to find eroticism when we stray from the dark edge of the fantasy field . . . and yet a few "high fantasy" books exist containing lush, sensuous imagery—such as Ellen Kushner's *Thomas the Rhymer*, a deliciously adult retelling of the Scottish ballad of that name; Patricia A. McKillip's *Winter Rose*, a passionate reworking of the ballad "Tam Lin"; Delia Sherman's *The Porcelain Dove*, a subtle and elegant exploration of sexual mores during the French Revolution; Robert Holdstock's *Mythago Wood*, an earthy, tactile, deeply mythological tale set in an English wood; and Midori Snyder's *The Innamorati*, an exuberantly lusty saga based on old Italian myth. Beyond the genre shelves, we find sensuously magical works by the Magical Realist writers—such as Gabriel Garcia Marquez (*Love in the Time of Cholera*); Laura Esquivel (*Like Water for Chocolate*); and Alice Hoffman (*Practical Magic* and *Second Nature*). *Pleasure in the Word: Erotic Writing by Latin American Women*, edited by Margaritte Fernandez Olmos and Lizbeth Paravisini, contains Magical Realist works among other gorgeous selections of poetry and prose. In poetry, a number of writers have used folkloric themes to sensuous effect, including Anne Sexton, Olga Broumas, Bill Lewis, Liz Lochhead, and Jane Yolen. In the visual arts, Brian Froud explores the sexual nature of fairy lore (*Good Faeries/Bad Faeries* and *Lady Cottington's Pressed Fairy Book*); while painters like Paula Rego and Leonor Fini portray starkly erotic, psychological symbolism drawn from fairy tales. "Doll art" is an unusual area in which to look for eroticism, since dolls, like fairy stories, are thought to be the exclusive province of children; yet in the annual *Dolls as Art* show at the CFM Gallery in New York one finds phantasmagoric imagery with deeply erotic elements by sculptors such as Wendy Froud, Monica, Richard Prowse, and Lisa Lichtenfels.

In both the literary and visual arts, fantasy is used as a potent means to express the inexpressible, to evoke archetypes, to provoke the Gods, to cross over known boundaries into the unknown lands beyond. Erotic art, like fantasy, is a realm the "serious" artist is not encouraged to travel or linger in. But fantasists learn early to ignore such limiting rules and boundaries, preferring to follow the beguiling creatures who beckon them into the woods.

"Regarding her whole self as an ear," writes Toni Morrison (in the novel *Tar Baby*), "he whispered into every part of her stories of icecaps and singing fish, the Fox and the Stork, the Monkey and the Lion, the Spider Goes to Market, and so mingled was their sex with adventure and fantasy that to the end of her life she never heard a reference to Little Red Riding Hood without a tremor."

In the following pages we offer stories mingling sex and fantasy, stories to produce a tremor or two, stories both dark and bright. These are tales dedicated to Eros, that capricious God of love and desire. And to the sirens, for somewhere in this world they're still singing. . . .

TERRI WINDLING, *September 1997*
Devon, England

My Lady of the Hearth

Storm Constantine

 The most beautiful women in the world have a cat-like quality. They slink, they purr; claws sheathed in silken fur. In the privacy of their summer gardens, in the green depths of forests, I believe they shed themselves of their attire, even to their human flesh, and stretch their bodies to the sun and their secret deity. She, the Queen of Cats, is Pu-ryah, daughter of the Eye of the Sun; who both roars the vengeance of the solar fire and blesses the hearth of the home. Given that the goddess, and by association her children, has so many aspects, is it any wonder that men have ever been perplexed by the subtleties of females and felines? Yet even as we fear them, we adore them.

When I was young I had a wife, and she was a true daughter of Pu-ryah. It began in this way.

When my father died, I inherited the family seat on the edge of the city, its numerous staff, and a sizable fortune. The estate earned money for me, administered by the capable hands of its managers, and I was free to pursue whatever interests I desired. My mother, whom I barely remembered (for she died when I was very young), had bequeathed her beauty to me: I was not an ill-favored man. Yet despite these privileges, joy of the heart eluded me. I despaired of ever finding a mate. Thirty years old, and romance had always turned sour on me. I spent much of my time painting, and portraits of a dozen lost loves adorned the walls of my home; their cold eyes stared down at me with disdain, their lips forever smiling. It had come to the point where I scorned the goddess of love; she must have blighted me at birth.

It was not long past my thirtieth birthday and, following the celebrations, my latest beloved, Delphina Corcos, had sent her maid to me with a letter, which advised me she had taken herself off to a distant temple, where she vowed to serve the Blind Eunuch of Chastity for eternity. Her decision had been swayed by a dream of brutish masculinity, in which I figured in some way—I forget the details now.

The banners of my birthday fete still adorned my halls, and I tore them down myself, in full sight of the servants, ranting against the whims of all women, to whom the security of love seemed to mean little at all. The letter in all its brevity was lost amid the debris. I dare say some maid picked it up in order to laugh at my loss with her female colleagues.

Still hot with grief and rage, I locked myself in my private rooms and here sat contemplating my hurts, with the light of summer shuttered away at the windows. Women: demonesses all! I heard the feet of servants patter past my doors, their whispers. Later, my steward would be sent to me by the housekeeper, and then, after hearing his careful inquiries as to my state of mind, I might consider reappearing in the house for dinner. Until then, I intended to surrender myself entirely to the indulgence of bitterness.

In the gloom, my little cat, Simew, came daintily to my side, rubbing her sleek fur against my legs, offering a gentle purr of condolence. She was a beautiful creature, a gift from a paramour some three years previously. Her fur was golden, each hair tipped with black along her flanks and spine, while her belly was a deep, rich amber. She was sleek and neat, loved by all in the house for her fastidiousness and affectionate nature. Now, I lifted her onto my lap, and leaned down to press my cheek against her warm flank. "Ah, Simmi, my sweet angel," I crooned. "You are always faithful, offering love without condition. I would be lucky to find a mistress as accommodating as you."

Simew gazed up at me, kneading my robes with her paws, blinking in the way that cats show us their affection. She could not speak, yet I felt her sympathy for me. I resolved then that my time with women was done. There was much to be thankful for: my health, my inheritance, and the love of a loyal cat. Though her life would be shorter than mine, her daughters and their children might be my companions until the day I died. Many men had less than this. Simew leaned against my chest, pressing her head into my hand, purring rapturously. It seemed she said to me, "My lord, what need have we of sharp-tongued interlopers? We have each other."

Cheered at once, I put Simew down carefully on the floor and went to throw my shutters wide, surprising a couple of servants who were stationed beyond the window, apparently in the act of gathering flowers. I smiled at them and cried, "Listen for my sorrow all you like. You'll not hear it."

Embarrassed, the two prostrated themselves, quaking. I picked up my cat and strode to the doors. "Come, Simew, why waste time on lamenting? I shall begin a new painting." Together, we went to my studio.

I decided I would paint a likeness of Simew, in gratitude for the comfort she had given me. It would have pride of place in my gallery of women. I arranged the cat on a crimson cushion, and for a while she was content to sit there, one leg raised like a mast as she set about grooming her soft belly. Then, she became bored, jumped from her bed and began crying out her ennui. I had made only a few preliminary sketches, but could not be angry with her. While she explored the room, clambering from table to shelf, I ignored the sounds of falling pots and smashing vases, and concentrated on my new work. It would be Pu-ryah I would paint; a lissom, cat-headed woman. Simew's face would be the model.

Pu-ryah is a foreign goddess. She came to us from the east, a hot land of desert and endless skies. She is born of the fire and will warm us, if we observe her rituals correctly. I had no intention of being burned. My brush flew over the canvas and I became unaware of the passing of time. When the steward, Medoth, came to me, mentioning politely that my dinner awaited me, I ordered him to bring the meal to the studio. I could not stop work.

I ate with one hand, food dropping from my fork to the floor, where Simew composed herself neatly and sifted through the morsels with a precise tongue. Medoth lit all my lamps and the candles, and even murmured some congratulatory phrase as he appraised my work. He made Pu-ryah's sign with two fingers, tapping either side of his mouth. "The Lady of the Hearth will be pleased by this work," he said.

I turned to wipe my brush. "Medoth, I had not taken you for a worshipper of Pu-ryah."

He smiled respectfully. "It comes from my mother's side of the family."

I laughed. "Of course. She is primarily a goddess of women, Medoth, but perhaps because she knows the ways of her daughters so intimately, she makes a sympathetic deity for those who suffer at their hands."

Medoth cleared his throat. "Would you care for a glass of wine now, my lord?"

I worked until dawn, given energy by the fire of she whose portrait I made. Simew lay on some tangled rags by my feet, her tail gently resting across my toes. Sometimes, when I looked down at her, she would wake and roll onto her back to display her dark golden belly, her front paws held sweetly beneath her chin. She seemed to me, in lamplight, more lovely than any woman I had known, more generous, more yielding. If I were a cat, I would lie beside her and lick her supple fur with my hooked tongue, or I would seize the back of her neck in my jaws and mount her with furious lust. This latter, inappropriate thought made me shiver. Perhaps I had drunk too much wine after my meal.

As the pale, magical light of dawn stole through the diaphanous drapes at the long windows, I appraised my work. Fine detail still needed to be added, but the picture was mostly complete. Pu-ryah sat upon a golden throne that was encrusted with lapis lazuli. She was haughty, yet serene, and her eyes held the wisdom of all the spheres, the gassy heart of the firmament itself. She gazed out at me, and I felt that I had not created her at all, but that the pigment had taken on a life of its own, and my own heart had imbued it with soul. I had depicted her with bared breasts, her voluptuous hips swathed in veils of turquoise silk. Her skin was delicately furred and brindled with faint coppery stripes. Her attenuated, high-cheekboned face had a black muzzle, fading to tawny around the ruff, then white beneath the chin. Her eyes were topaz. Around her neck, I had painted a splendid collar of faience and gold, and rings adorned her slender fingers. Her claws were extended, lightly scraping the arms of the gilded chair. Behind her, dark drapery was drawn back to reveal a simmering summer night. I fancied I could hear the call of peacocks in the darkness beyond her scented temple, and the soft music she loved so much. Her taloned feet were laid upon flowers, thousands of flowers, and their exotic perfume invaded my studio, eclipsing the tart reeks of pigment and solvent. She was beautiful, monstrous, and compliant. If I closed my eyes, I could feel her strong arms around me, her claws upon my back. No woman of this earth could compare.

Weary but content, I went out into my garden to sample the new day. Dew had conjured scent from the shrubs and gauzed the thick foliage of the evergreens. Simew trotted be-

fore me along the curling pathways, pausing every so often
to look back and make sure I was following. I felt at peace
with myself, at the brink of some profound change in my life
or my heart. Delphina Corcos seemed nothing more than a
thin ghost; I could barely recall her face. Let her deny her
womanhood and seek the stone embrace of the Eunuch. The
day itself was full of sensuality, of nature's urge to procre-
ate. The woman was a fool to deny herself this.

Simew and I came to the water garden, where a low mist
lingered over the linked pools. Simew crouched at the edge
of the nearest pond, her whiskers kissing the surface of the
water. I gazed at her with affection. "Oh, Simew, how cruel
it is we are separated by an accident of species! If you were
a woman, we might walk together now with arms linked. I
might take you in my arms and kiss you."

The fire of the goddess ran through my blood. As the sun,
her father, lifted above the trees to sear away the mist, I spoke
a silent prayer to Pu-ryah, declared myself her priest. Yet, in
her way, she was a goddess of carnality, so how could I wor-
ship her alone, without a woman to help express my devotion?

I pressed my hands against my eyes, and for a while all
the grief within my heart welled up to smother my new-
found serenity. I had riches, yes, and a loyal feline friend,
but I was essentially alone, devoid of a companion of the
heart, with whom I might make love or talk about the mysteries of life.

Then I felt a soft touch upon my arm, of gentle fingers.
Alarmed, I dropped my hands and uttered a cry of shock. I
beheld a young woman, who backed away from me, her
eyes wide. She crouched down before me, utterly naked, her
skin the color of honey, her body hunched into a position of
alertness.

"Who are you?" I demanded, while within me conflicting
emotions made war. My male instincts were aroused by the
surprise of finding a naked girl in my garden, but she was
still an intruder. What was she doing there?

The girl held up her hands to me, and now her expression was pleading. She shook her head slowly from side to side. Her face was small and heart-shaped, utterly enchanting.

"Speak!" I said, "or I must summon my staff to evict you."

The girl's face was puckered with anguish. She shrugged her shoulders in an ophidian motion, which seemed to indicate impatience, then touched her mouth with her fingers. I realized she could not speak.

I reached down and took her forearms in my hands, lifted her to her feet. She did not seem at all ashamed at her state of undress, and I could not help but admire the trim conformation of her body. "Are you lost?" I asked her.

She smiled then and shook her head. It was a fierce smile, quite without fear, and a strange tremor passed through me. She held my gaze without blinking, pushing her long amber hair back behind her ears. Then, she dismissed me from her attention and held out her arms before her, twisting them around as if to examine them for the first time. After this, she shrugged and began to walk away from me. Aghast, I called out and she paused and glanced over her shoulder, before resuming her walk back toward the house. I felt that she knew this place well, but how? I think perhaps it was at that moment I realized Simew was nowhere to be seen. A chill coursed through my flesh. No! I called her name, scanning the trees and bushes, but of course it was my lovely visitor who turned her head to answer the call.

Pu-ryah had heard my prayers and answered them. As I had dedicated myself to her, so she rewarded me. Simew had been transformed into a woman, the most lovely woman I had ever seen. I caught up with her by the cloister that flanked the back of the house, and here took hold of her arm.

"We must be discreet," I said. "The servants must not see you undressed."

She shrugged, as if to imply she would concur with my wishes, but didn't really care whether someone saw her or not. I went into the house before her, and led the way back to my private chambers, checking round every corner beforehand to make sure the coast was clear. In my rooms, I turned the key in the lock, and leaned against the door to gaze upon this magical creature. She stood in the center of the room, looking around in curiosity. Now, the world must appear very different to her. Then she turned her attention upon herself, and began to stroke her body in long, slow movements. She raised her hand to her mouth and licked it. I was entranced by her, my cat woman.

"You can no longer wash yourself," I said. "The human body is far less supple than a cat's."

She gave me a studied look, as to contest that remark. Her mouth dropped open and expelled a musical, feline cry. She was not mute, then. My flesh tingled.

She slunk toward me, her eyes half-closed. I heard her purring. When she was very close, she butted her head against my cheek, uttered a chirruping sound. I seized her in my arms. She wriggled away, still purring, and ran nimbly to my bedroom. I followed her and found her crouched on all fours, on the bed. She turned round in a circle a few times, before collapsing gracefully in a curving heap, peering up at me seductively through a veil of hair. The invitation was unmistakable. I approached her and she rolled onto her back, as was her custom. I reached down and stroked her belly, conjuring louder purrs. Her skin was softly furred by tiny, transparent hairs. I ran my hands up over her firm breasts and she arched her back in delight. Emboldened, I continued this tactile investigation, sliding my fingers down between her muscled thighs. All I found was welcome. Lust overtook me and I tore off my robes. Simew positioned herself on all fours once more, her glistening vulva displayed provocatively, her hands kneading the bedclothes before her. When I entered her, she screeched; her whole body became rigid. Never had coupling been so swift for me.

Afterward, she did the most astounding thing. I watched

in silent amazement as she contorted her body without apparent difficulty and set about washing her private parts with her tongue. Then, she cleaned herself all over, licking her hand to reach more inaccessible areas, unable only to attain the back of her neck. I lay in a stupor beside her, aroused once more by her bizarre behavior. When she came to lie against my side, purring, I laid her on her back and took her that way. Her desire was kindled instantly and she appeared to enjoy the change of position.

Throughout that day, I taught her many tricks of the art of love. The servants came to my doors, but I would not allow them entrance. No doubt they thought I had succumbed to melancholy once more. But then, they must have heard the howls and grunts emanating from the bedroom, and drawn their own conclusions, upon which it is better not to dwell. Simew could not help but sound like a cat when throes of delight overtook her.

How she loved the sexual act. I had always suspected cats were masters and mistresses of carnality, but now, with Simew transformed physically into a human, while retaining feline sensibilities, I had no doubt. She was quite impossible to sate. The more we coupled, the more hungry she became. I remembered that the member of a male cat is barbed, and people say that during feline copulation it is only when he withdraws from the female's body, thus tearing her delicate flesh, that she finds satisfaction. I had no wish to hurt my beautiful lover, but how could I provide her with what nature had denied me? Eventually, her agitation became so great, I put my fingers inside her and raked my nails along the slick flesh. She uttered an ear-splitting howl and lashed out at me, her body bucking. Within her, powerful muscles gripped my fingers and warm liquid flowed down my wrist. Then, as the convulsions subsided, she lay quiet, her eyes half closed, a soft purr rippling from her throat. I felt exhausted.

When I stood up to go to my bathroom, I found my body covered in scratches, welts, and bites. My member seemed to have shrunk back into my body in an attempt to escape my lover's demands.

Weak, I drew my own bath and lay there for some time, blinking in the steam. I had never felt so utterly complete. The sexual urge had been drained from me. I had filled Simew's cup to the full and now my vessel was empty, but the experience had exhilarated as much as sapped me.

I knew that I could not keep Simew a secret, nor did I want to. I had no women's clothes for her and this must be attended to before anything else. As I went back into the bedroom, drying my tender flesh with a towel, I gazed upon her lying amid the tangled sheets, her damp hair spread around her shoulders. She was sleeping now, but for how long? I dared not leave her alone, because Simew was accustomed to having the run of the house. If I locked her in my chambers, it was likely she would awake and then howl at the door until one of the servants came to her aid. Medoth had keys to my rooms. He would no doubt be summoned to let the cat out. It had happened before in my absence. I dared not think about the consequences of that.

In the end, I woke her with a gentle caress and told her we must go out of the house and purchase garments for her. As always, she appeared to understand my every word, although I sensed she was not altogether pleased with my suggestion. I remembered the occasion a previous lover of mine had bought her a jeweled collar, and the manner in which that gift had later been found shredded under the dining table, its expensive gems scattered by playful paws.

I dressed her in one of my own robes, using sashes to create a suitably fitted garment. Simew growled a few times as I made her hold out her arms to assist my adjustments. I bound up her hair as best I could, then led her from my chambers. Medoth had clearly been lurking nearby, and now came forward to hear my orders. Without explaining the presence of the oddly dressed female at my side, I demanded my carriage be made ready for a trip to town. Discreet as ever, Medoth bowed and obeyed my word.

The trip was not without its awkward moments. The proprietress in the dress shop we visited seemed to accept my story of a visiting relative having had an accident with her luggage, but unfortunately Simew was unable to behave in the way that women usually do while purchasing clothes. The noises she made, the attempts to bite from her body the gowns she found most offensive, plunged the staff of the establishment into silent horror. I laughed nervously and explained she had an hereditary affliction of the mind. At length, the proprietress suggested frostily that we take one set of garments now and that the rest might best be examined and tried on in the privacy of my home. Someone from the shop would be sent round the following day. I understood her desire to get rid of us, because several other customers had already vacated the premises in alarm at Simew's behavior. Spilling coins from my purse into the tight-lipped woman's hands, I agreed readily with her suggestion and Simew and I fled the shop. She was dressed now in a simple gown of soft green fabric, and wore emerald slippers on her feet. The outing had been a trial, but at least my lover was now dressed.

In the carriage on our way home, I tried to explain to Simew that it might be best if she remained silent in the presence of other people. Clearly, I had a lot of work to do with her regarding etiquette and good manners.

The story I concocted for the servants was that Simew was a distant cousin of mine, who had arrived in the night, having escaped a brutal father. I could do nothing but provide sanctuary, and indeed had even extended my services to offering her marriage, so that she would be forever safe from paternal threat. The servants were all stony-faced as I told them this story, and it was Medoth who ventured to tell me my cat was missing. I think he guessed the truth at once, because Pu-ryah was his goddess, but he did not voice his suspicions to me.

So the transformed Simew became part of my household. I decided that once I had trained her enough to be presentable in company, we would be married and all of my friends in the city would be invited. To the servants, I repeated the story that Simew—who I now called Felice—had been ill, because of the treatment she'd received from her father. Her mind was slightly damaged, but it could be cured and patience and love were the medicines she must receive. Because she was still essentially Simew, it didn't take long for the household to learn to love her. Everyone became conspirators in my plan to transform this wild girl into a young woman of society. To her, I think it was all a game. She was playing at being human and thought it was hilarious to ape our behavior. She learned to laugh, and it was the most thrilling expression of joy any of us had ever heard. It brightened every corner of that vast house; she was like an enchanted light buzzing through its halls and chambers. No one could have overlooked her catlike habits, but they were prepared to tolerate and then to change them.

The portrait of Pu-ryah was hung in the main hall, and Simew would often stand before it, staring into that feline face, as if remembering with difficulty the days when she had looked the same.

One of the strangest things about Simew the woman was her incomparable clumsiness. As a cat, she had always seemed a little heavy on her feet, and no fragile things had ever been safe in her presence, but now she seemed unable to enter a room without knocking something over. At dinner, wine glasses were spilled with regularity, quite often onto the floor. Medoth arranged that a servant equipped with a pan and brush was always stationed near the door. We got through so much glassware and crockery that eventually I bought Simew a set of her own, crafted from gold. These, she could not break by accident. It took a while to teach her to eat using cutlery. She found that these implements simply delayed the consumption of food and would sometimes lash out at me and growl, when I pointed out a young lady of breeding would never eat food directly from her plate without even the agency of fingers. "Simew," I murmured one night, with fraying patience. "You are here to be my wife. The Lady herself has arranged it. I'm doing all I can to keep my side of the bargain, please oblige me by keeping yours."

Then, she laughed and shrugged. "All right," she seemed to say, but there were still lapses.

Neither could she take to immersing herself in water to bathe. The shrieks and clawing that occurred when we tried to enforce it became too much, and eventually we had to compromise. At morn and eve, her personal maid would clean her body with a damp sponge. This she tolerated— just. The maid was often scratched.

It was also difficult to accept Simew's gifts, which invariably she brought up from the cellar or in from the grain store. I would hear her muffled chirruping as she made her way to my studio, and then she would fling open the door with a dramatic gesture of her arms. A mouse, or even a rat, would be hanging from her mouth. It was worse when they were still alive. Her eyes would be shining and she'd run to me and drop her prey at my feet. I suppose she expected me to eat it with gratitude. It took some weeks to rid her of this habit, and I ached to see the sadness my disapproval conjured in her eyes.

She loved perfume though, and I indulged her craving for it. Scent was like a religious tool for her. She never wasted it, nor mixed aromas but, after her bathing routine, chose with care which perfume to wear. This she would apply with economy to her throat and wrists, lifting her hand to her nose to take little, contented sniffs from time to time throughout the day. It was an adorable habit.

At night, she would be waiting for me in my bed-chamber, clothed only in delicious scent, purring softly in her throat, kneading the pillows. She rarely offered herself to me submissively now, but grabbed me bodily and threw me down onto the bed to begin her pleasure. I taught her technique perhaps, but she taught me something more powerful—the instinctual sexual drive of an animal. I realized that cats had their own beliefs and that sex was very much a part of their devotion to their spiritual queen. They had a language we could not understand, that functioned nothing like a human tongue, but it *was* language. In time, during our lovemaking I too began to make the sounds and Simew displayed her approval with purrs. Pu-ryah was always very close to us in our bed-chamber.

Simew the cat, the house mourned. The housekeeper decided she must have been stolen or killed, and I went along with this idea, but my grief could not have been that convincing. Perhaps no one else's was either, for as time went on I have no doubt that more than one of my staff suspected my new love's origins and then passed their suspicions around, but we all had to pretend.

Eventually, I decided that Simew was ready to present to society. The household was put into a frenzy by the preparations for our grand marriage. My friends already knew I was betrothed to a mysterious distant relative, and more than a few had been most insistent about meeting her—especially the women—but I had remained steadfast in my refusal. "She has been very ill," I said. "She cannot yet cope with social occasions."

"I have heard," one lady remarked at a soiree, "that she was locked by her brute of a father in a cellar for years on end. Shocking! Poor dear!"

I inclined my head. "Well, that is an exaggeration of her trials, but yes, she has suffered badly and it has affected her behavior."

"How dreadful," another murmured, touching my hand. "You are so good to take her under your wing in this way." I could not say that had I possessed wings, it's unlikely I would still have been there to accept their sympathy.

I do not know what my friends expected when they finally met "Felice," but I know the experience amazed them.

Our nuptial banquet took place on an autumn evening. During the day, we had undergone a quiet wedding; a priest from Pu-ryah's temple had come to the house to officiate at a ceremony that had been written especially to accommodate my bride's inability to speak.

In the early evening, Simew's maids dressed her in a splendid gown of russet silk. Her hair was twined with autumn leaves of gold and crimson and I adorned her neck and wrists myself with costly ornaments of amber, topaz, and gold. She appeared to be as excited as any of us at the prospect of being introduced to my friends.

I waited downstairs to receive our guests as they arrived, while Simew underwent the final primpings and preenings in our chambers. I wanted to present her once everyone had gathered in the main hall. I wanted them to see her descend the stairs in the caressing lamp light.

Ultimately, the hour arrived. My friends were clustered in excitement around the stairs, and I signaled one of the maids to summon the new mistress of the house. I continued to exchange pleasantries with the guests and it was only when the assembly fell silent that I knew Simew was among us. I turned, and there she stood at the top of the stairs. I shall never forget that moment. She was the most radiant, gorgeous creature ever to have entered the hall. My heart contracted with love, with adoration. She stood tall and serene, a half smile upon her face, and then with the most graceful steps slowly descended toward the company. I heard the women gasp and whisper together; I heard the appreciative, stunned murmurs of the men.

"May I present my wife," I said, extending an arm toward her.

Simew dipped her head and glided to my side. She smiled warmly upon the gathering and together we led the way in to dinner.

Bless my love—she behaved with perfect decorum as the meal was served. Nothing was tipped over or broken; she ate modestly and slowly, smiling at the remarks addressed to her. Those sitting nearest to me lost no time in congratulating me on my fortune. They praised Simew's beauty, grace, and warmth.

"You are a lucky fellow," one man said with good-natured envy. "All of us know you've nursed a broken heart more than once over the past few years, but now you have been rewarded. You've earned this wondrous wife, my friend. I wish you every happiness." He raised his glass to me and I thought that I must expire with joy.

The meal was all but finished, and Medoth was supervising the clearing of dessert plates. Soon, we would all repair to one of the salons for music and dancing. Simew loved to dance; I was looking forward to showing off her accomplishment.

Then, it happened. One moment I was conversing with a friend, the next there was a sudden movement beside me and people were uttering cries of alarm. It took me a while to realize that Simew had not only vacated her seat in a hurry, but had disappeared beneath the table. For a second or two, all was still, and then the whole company was thrown into a furor as Simew scuttled madly between their legs down the length of the table. Women squeaked and stood up, knocking over chairs. Men swore and backed away.

Again stillness. I poked my head under the tablecloth. "Felice, my love. What are you doing?"

She uttered a yowl and then emerged at full speed from beneath the other end of the table, in hot pursuit of a small mouse. Women screamed and panicked and, in the midst of this chaos, my new wife expressed a cry of triumph and pounced. In full sight of my guests, she tossed the unfortunate mouse into the air, batted it with her hands, and then lunged upon it to crack its fragile spine in her jaws.

"Felice!" I roared.

She paused then and raised her head to me, the mouse dangling, quite dead, from her mouth. "What?" she seemed to say. Tiny streaks of blood marked her fair cheek.

At that point, one of the ladies vomited onto the floor, while another put a hand to her brow and collapsed backward into the convenient arms of one of the men.

I could only stare at my wife, my body held in a paralysis of despair, as my guests flocked toward the doors, desperate to escape the grisly scene. Presently, we were left alone. I could hear voices beyond the doors, Medoth's calm assurances to hysterical guests.

"Simew," I said dismally and sat down.

She dropped the mouse and came to my side, reached to touch my cheek. I looked up at her. She shrugged, pulled a rueful face. Her expression said it all: "I'm sorry. I couldn't help myself. It's what I am."

And it was, of course. How wrong of me to force human behavior on the wild, free spirit of a cat.

The news spread rapidly. I told myself I did not care about the gossip, but I did. For a while, I was determined not to abandon my position in society and attended gatherings as usual, although without my wife. I felt I should spare her any further humiliation. Whenever I entered a room, conversation would become subdued. People would greet me cordially, but without their usual warmth. I heard remarks through curtains, round corners. "She is a *beast*, you know, quite savage. We all know he's an absolute darling to take her on—but really—what is he thinking of?"

I was distraught and blamed myself. Simew should have remained a secret of mine and my loyal staff. I should have kept her as a mistress, but not presented her publicly as a wife. How could I have been so blind to the pitfalls? We had never really civilized her. I know Simew sensed my anguish, although I strove to hide it from her. She fussed round me with concerned mewings, pressing herself against me, kissing my hair, my eyelids. The staff remained solidly behind

her, of course, but she was not their responsibility; her behavior could not affect them. The terrible thing was, in my
heart I was furious with Simew. Public shame had warped
my understanding. I suspected that she knew very well what
she'd done at the marriage feast, but had wanted to shock, or
else hadn't cared what people thought of her. She had despised them, thought them vapid and foolish, and had acted
impulsively without a care for what her actions might do to
me. My love for her was tainted by what I perceived as her
betrayal. I wanted to forgive her, but I couldn't, for I did not
think she was innocent. I made the mistake of forgetting
what she really was.

One night, she disappeared. The staff was thrown into tur-
moil, and everyone was out scouring the gardens, then the
streets beyond, calling her name. I sat in darkness in my
chambers. I had no heart to search, but sought oblivion in
liquor. Steeped in gloomy feelings, I thought Simew had
gone to find herself a troupe of tomcats, who like her had
been turned into men by the imprudent longings of cat-
loving women. No doubt I, with my over-civilized human
senses, could no longer satisfy her. She would return in the
morning, once she thought she'd punished me enough.

But she did not return. Days passed and the atmosphere in
the house was as dour as if a death had taken place. I saw re-
proach in the faces of all my servants. Dishes were slammed
onto tables; my food was never quite hot enough. One
evening, my rage erupted and I called them all together in
the main hall. "If I don't see some improvement in your du-
ties, you are all dismissed!" I cried. "Simew is gone. She is
not of our world, and I am not to blame for her disappear-
ance. Her cat nature took over, that's all."

They departed silently, back to their own quarters, no
doubt to continue gossiping about me, but from that night
on, some kind of normality was resumed in the running of
the house.

After they had left, I went to stand before the portrait of

Pu-ryah, resolving that in the morning, I would have it taken down. I heard a cough behind me and turned to find Medoth standing there. I sighed. "If she is a mother, she is cruel," I said.

Medoth came to my side. "You put much into that work, my lord. Some might say too much. It has great power."

I nodded. "Indeed it has. I thought I could brave Pu-ryah's fire, but I was wrong, and now I am burned away."

"Your experiences have been distressing," Medoth agreed. He paused. "Might I suggest you make a gift of this painting to the temple of the Lady? I am sure they would appreciate it."

"Yes. A good idea, Medoth. See to it tomorrow, would you?"

He bowed. "Of course, my lord."

I began to walk away, toward my empty chambers.

"My lord," Medoth said.

I paused and turned. "Yes?"

He hesitated and then said. "One day, you will miss her as we do. She only obeyed her nature. She loved you very much."

I was about to reprimand him for such importunate remarks, but then weariness overtook me. I sighed again. "I know, Medoth."

"Perhaps you should acquire another little cat."

I laughed bleakly. "No. I don't think so."

I did see Simew again. After some years had passed, she came back occasionally, to visit the servants, I think. Sometimes, I found fowl carcasses they had left out for her in the garden. Sometimes, alone in my bed late at night, I would hear music coming from the servants' quarters and the joyful peal of that unmistakable laugh. To me, she showed herself only once.

It was a summer evening and dusk had fallen. I went out into the garden, filled with a quiet sadness, yet strangely content in the peace of the hedged walkways. I strolled right to the end of my property, to the high wall that hid my domain from the street beyond. It was there I heard a soft chirrup.

A shiver passed through me and I looked up. She was there, crouching on the wall above me, her hair hanging down and her eyes flashing at me through the dusk. She was clothed, I remember that, in some dark, close-fitting attire that must be suitable for her nocturnal excursions. Where was she living now? How was she living? I wanted to know these things, and called her name softly. In that moment, I believe there could have been some reconciliation between us, had she desired it.

She looked at me with affection, I think, but not for very long. I did not see judgment in her eyes, for she was essentially a cat; an animal who will, for a time, forgive our cruel words and unjust kicks. A cat loves us unconditionally, but unlike a dog, she will not accept continual harsh treatment. She runs away. She finds another home.

My eyes filled with tears and when I wiped them away, Simew had gone. I never married again.

The Faerie Cony-catcher

Delia Sherman

In London town, in the reign of good Queen Bess that was called Gloriana, there lived a young man named Nicholas Cantier. Now it came to pass that this Nick Cantier served out his term as apprentice jeweler and goldsmith under one Master Spilman, jeweler by appointment to the Queen's Grace herself, and was made journeyman of his guild. For that Nick was a clever young man, his master would have been glad for him to continue on where he was; yet Nick was not fain thereof, Master Spilman being as ill a master of men as he was a skilled master of his trade. And Nick bethought him thus besides: that London was like unto the boundless sea where Leviathan may dwell unnoted, save by such small fish as he may snap up to stay his mighty hunger: such small fish as Nicholas Cantier. Better that same small fish seek out some backwater in the provinces where, puffed up by city ways, he might perchance pass as a pike and snap up spratlings on his own account.

So thought Nick. And on a bright May morning, he packed up such tools as he might call his own—as a pitch block and a mallet, and some small steel chisels and punches and saw-blades and blank rings of copper—that he might make shift to earn his way to Oxford. So Nick put his tools in a pack, with clean hosen and a shirt and a pair of soft leather shoon, and that was all his worldly wealth strapped upon his back, saving only a jewel that he had designed and made himself to be his passport. This jewel was in the shape of a maid, her breasts and belly all one lucent pearl, her skirt and open jacket of bright enamel, and her fair face of silver burnished with gold. On her fantastic hair perched a tiny golden crown, and Nick had meant her for the Faerie Queen of Master Spenser's poem, fair Gloriana.

Upon this precious Gloriana did Nick's life and livelihood depend. Therefore, being a prudent lad in the main, and be-thinking him of London's traps and dangers, Nick consid-ered where he might bestow it that he fall not prey to those foists and rufflers who might take it from him by stealth or by force. The safest place, thought he, would be his cod-piece, where no man nor woman might meddle without his yard raise the alarm. Yet the jewel was large and cold and hard against those softer jewels that dwelt more commonly there, and so Nick bound it across his belly with a band of linen and took leave of his fellows and set out northwards to seek his fortune.

Now Nick Cantier was a lusty youth of nearly twenty, with a fine, open face and curls of nut-brown hair that sprang from his brow; yet notwithstanding his comely form, he was as much a virgin on that May morning as the Virgin Queen herself. For Master Spilman was the hardest of task-masters, and between his eagle eye and his adder cane and his arch-episcopal piety, his apprentices perforce lived out the terms of their bonds as chaste as Popish monks. On this the first day of his freedom, young Nick's eye roved hither and thither, touching here a slender waist and there a dim-pled cheek, wondering what delights might not lie beneath this petticoat or that snowy kerchief. And so it was that a Setter came upon him unaware and sought to persuade him to drink a pot of ale together, having just found xii pence in a gutter and it being ill-luck to keep found money and Nick's face putting him in mind of his father's youngest son, dead of an ague this two year and more. Nick let him run on, through this excuse for scraping acquaintance and that, and when the hopeful Cony-catcher had rolled to a stop, like a cart at the foot of a hill, he said unto him,

"I see I must have a care to the cut of my coat, if rogues, taking me for a country cony, think me meet for skinning. Nay, I'll not drink with ye, nor play with ye neither, lest ye so ferret-claw me at cards that ye leave me as bare of money as an ape of a tail."

Upon hearing which, the Setter called down a murrain upon milk-fed pups who imagined themselves sly dogs, and withdrew into the company of two men appareled like honest and substantial citizens, whom Nicholas took to be the Setter's Verser and Barnacle, all ready to play their parts in cozening honest men out of all they carried, and a little more beside. And he bit his thumb at them and laughed and made his way through the streets of London, from Lombard Street to Clerkenwell in the northern liberties of the city, where the houses were set back from the road in gardens and fields and the taverns spilled out of doors in benches and stools, so that toss-pots might air their drunken heads.

'Twas coming on for noon by this time, and Nick's steps were slower than they had been, and his mind dwelt more on bread and ale than on cony-catchers and villains.

In this hungry, drowsy frame of mind, he passed an ale-house where his eye chanced to light upon a woman tricked up like a lady in a rich-guarded gown and a deep starched ruff. Catching his glance, she sent it back again saucily, with a wink and a roll of her shoulders that lifted her breasts like ships on a wave.

Nick gave her good speed, and she plucked him by the sleeve and said, "How now, my friend, you look wondrous down i' the mouth. What want you? Wine? Company?"—all with such a meaning look, such a waving of her skirts and a hoisting of her breasts that Nick's yard, fain to salute her, flew its scarlet colors in his cheeks.

"The truth is, Mistress, that I've walked far this day, and am sorely hungered."

"Hungered, is it?" She flirted her eyes at him, giving the word a dozen meanings not writ in any grammar. "Than shall feed thy hunger, aye, and sate thy thirst too, and that right speedily." And she led him in at the alehouse door to a little room within, where she closed the door and thrusting herself close up against him, busied her hands about his body and her lips about his mouth. As luck would have it, her breath was foul, and it blew upon Nick's heat, cooling him enough to recognize that her hands sought not his pleasure, but his purse, upon which he pushed her from him.

"Nay, mistress," he said, all flushed and panting. "Thy meat and drink are dear, if they cost me my purse."

Knowing by his words that she was discovered, she spent no time in denying her trade, but set up a caterwauling that would wake the dead, calling upon one John to help her. But Nick, if not altogether wise, was quick and strong, and bolted from the vixen's den 'ere the dog-fox answered her call.

So running, Nick came shortly to the last few houses that clung to the outskirts of the city and stopped at a tavern to refresh him with honest meat and drink. And as he drank his ale and pondered his late escape, the image of his own foolishness dimmed and the image of the doxy's beauty grew more bright, until the one eclipsed the other quite, persuading him that any young man in whom the blood ran hot would have fallen in her trap, aye and been skinned, drawn, and roasted to a turn, as 'twere in very sooth, a long-eared cony. It was his own cleverness, he thought, that he had smoked her out and run away. So Nick, having persuaded himself that he was a sly dog after all, rose from the tavern and went to Hampstead Heath, which was the end of the world to him. And as he stepped over the world's edge and onto the northward road, his heart lifted for joy, and he sang right merrily as he strode along, as pleased with himself as the cock that imagineth his crowing bringeth the sun from the sea.

And so he walked and so he sang until by and by he came upon a country lass sat upon a stone. Heedful of his late lesson, he quickly cast his eye about him for signs of some high lawyer or ruffler lurking ready to spring the trap. But the lass sought noways to lure him, nor did she accost him, nor lift her dark head from contemplating her foot that was cocked up on her knee. Her gown of gray kersey was hiked up to her thigh and her sleeves rolled to her elbows, so that Nick could see her naked arms, sinewy and lean and nut-brown with sun, and her leg like dirty ivory.

"Gie ye good-den, fair maid," said he, and then could say no more, for when she raised her face to him, his breath stopped in his throat. It was not, perhaps, the fairest he'd seen, being gypsy-dark, with cheeks and nose that showed the bone. But her black eyes were wide and soft as a hind's and the curve of her mouth made as sweet a bow as Cupid's own.

"Good-den to thee," she answered him, low-voiced as a throstle. "Ye come at a good hour to my aid. For here is a thorn in my foot and I, for want of a pin, unable to have it out."

The next moment he knelt at her side; the moment after, her foot was in his hand. He found the thorn and winkled it out with the point of his knife while the lass clutched at his shoulder, hissing between her teeth as the splinter yielded, sighing as he wiped away the single ruby of blood with his kerchief and bound it round her foot.

"I thank thee, good youth," she said, leaning closer. "An thou wilt, I'll give thee such a reward for thy kindness as will give thee cause to thank me anon." She turned her hand to his neck, and stroked the bare flesh there, smiling in his face the while, her breath as sweet as an orchard in spring.

Nick felt his cheek burn hot above her hand and his heart grow large in his chest. This were luck indeed, and better than all the trulls in London. "Fair maid," he said, "I would not kiss thee beside a public road."

She laughed. "Lift me then and carry me to the hollow, hard by yonder hill, where we may embrace, if it pleaseth thee, without fear of meddling eye.

Nick's manhood rose then to inform him that it would please him well, observing which, the maiden held up her arms to him, and he lifted her, light as a faggot of sticks but soft and supple as Spanish leather withal, and bore her to a hollow under a hill that was round and green and warm in the May sun. And he lay her down and did off his pack and set it by her head, that he might keep it close to hand, rejoicing that his jewel was well-hid and not in his codpiece, and then he fell to kissing her lips and stroking her soft, soft throat. Her breasts were small as a child's under her gown; yet she moaned most womanly when he touched them, and writhed against him like a snake, and he made bold to pull up her petticoats to discover the treasure they hid. Coyly, she slapped his hand away once and again, yet never ceased to kiss and toy with open lip, the while her tongue like a darting fish urged him to unlace his codpiece that was grown wondrous tight. Seeing what he was about, she put her hand down to help him, so that he was like to perish e' er he spied out the gates of Heaven. Then, when he was all but sped, she pulled him headlong on top of her.

He was not home, though very near it as he thrust at her skirts bunched up between her thighs. Though his plunging breached not her cunny-burrow, it did breach the hill itself, and he and his gypsy-lass both tumbled arse-over-neck to lie broken-breathed in the midst of a great candle-lit hall upon a Turkey carpet, with skirts and legs and slippered feet standing in ranks upon it to his right hand and his left, and a gentle air stroking warm fingers across his naked arse. Nick shut his eyes, praying that this vision were merely the lively exhalation of his lust. And then a laugh like a golden bell fell upon his ear, and was hunted through a hundred mocking changes in a ring of melodious laughter, and he knew this to be sober reality, or something enough like it that he'd best ope his eyes and lace up his hose.

All this filled no more than the space of a breath, though it seemed to Nick an age of the world had passed before he'd succeeded in packing up his yard and scrambling to his feet to confront the owners of the skirts and the slippered feet and the bell-like laughter that yet pealed over his head. And in that age, the thought was planted and nurtured and harvested in full ripeness, that his hosts were of faerie kind. He knew they were too fair to be human men and women, their skins white nacre, their hair spun sunlight or moonlight or fire bound back from their wide brows by fillets of precious stones not less hard and bright than their emerald or sapphire eyes. The women went bare-bosomed as Amazons, the living jewels of their perfect breasts coffered in open gowns of bright silk. The men wore jewels in their ears, and at their forks, fantastic cod-pieces in the shapes of cockerels and wolves and rams with curling horns. They were splendid beyond imagining, a masque to put the Queen's most magnificent Revels to shame.

As Nick stood in amaze, he heard the voice of his coy mistress say, " 'Twere well, Nicholas Cantier, if thou woulds't turn and make thy bow."

With a glare for she who had brought him to this pass, Nick turned him around to face a woman sat upon a throne. Even were she seated upon a joint-stool, he must have known her, for her breasts and face were more lucent and fair than pearl, her open jacket and skirt a glory of gemstones, and upon her fantastic hair perched a gold crown, as like to the jewel in his bosom as twopence to a groat. Nick gaped like that same small fish his fancy had painted him erewhile, hooked and pulled gasping to land. Then his knees, wiser than his head, gave way to prostrate him at the royal feet of Elfland.

"Well, friend Nicholas," said the Faerie Queen. "Heartily

are you welcome to our court. Raise him, Peasecod, and let him approach our throne."

Nick felt a tug on his elbow, and wrenched his dazzled eyes from the figure of the Faerie Queen to see his wanton lass bending over him. "To thy feet, my heart," she murmured. "And, as thou holdest dear thy soul, see that neither meat nor drink pass thy lips."

"Well, Peasecod?" asked the Queen, and there was that in her musical voice that propelled Nick to his feet and down the Turkey carpet to stand trembling before her.

"Be welcome," said the Queen again, "and take your ease. Peasecod, bring a stool and a cup for our guest, and let the musicians play and our court dance for his pleasure."

There followed an hour as strange as any madman might imagine or poet sing, when Nicholas Cantier sat upon a gilded stool at the knees of the Queen of Elfland and watched her court pace through their faerie measures. In his hand he held a golden cup crusted with gems, and the liquor within sent forth a savor of roses and apples that promised an immortal vintage. But as oft as he, half-fainting, lifted the cup, so often did a pair of fingers pinch him at the ankle, and so often did he look down to see the faerie lass Peasecod crouching at his feet with her skirts spread out to hide the motions of her hand. Once she glanced up at him, her soft eyes drowned in tears like pansies in rain, and he knew that she was sorry for her part in luring him here.

When the dancing was over and done, the Queen of Elfland turned to Nick and said, "Good friend Nicholas, we would crave a boon of thee in return for this our fair entertainment."

At which Nick replied, "I am at your pleasure, Madam. Yet have I not taken any thing from you save words and laughter."

" 'Tis true, friend Nicholas, that thou hast scorned to drink our Faerie wine. And yet hast thou seen our faerie revels, that is a sight any poet in London would give his last breath to see."

"I am no poet, Madam, but a humble journeyman goldsmith."

"That too, is true. And for that thou art something better than humble at thy trade, I will do thee the honor of accepting that jewel in my image thou bearest bound against thy breast."

Then it seemed to Nick that the Lady might have his last breath after all, for his heart suspended itself in his throat. Wildly looked he upon Gloriana's face, fair and cold and eager as the trull's he had escaped erewhile, and then upon the court of Elfland that watched him as he were a monkey or a dancing bear. And at his feet, he saw the dark-haired lass Peasecod, set apart from the rest by her mean garments and her dusky skin, the only comfortable thing in all that discomfortable splendor. She smiled into his eyes, and made a little motion with her hand, like a fishwife who must chaffer by signs against the crowd's commotion. And Nicholas took courage at her sign, and fetched up a deep breath, and said:

"Fair Majesty, the jewel is but a shadow or counterfeit of your radiant beauty. And yet 'tis all my stock in trade. I cannot render all my wares to you, were I never so fain to do you pleasure."

The Queen of Elfland drew her delicate brows like kissing moths over her nose. "Beware, young Nicholas, how thou triest our good will. Were we minded, we might turn thee into a lizard or a slow-worm, and take thy jewel resistless."

"Pardon, dread Queen, but if you might take my jewel by force, you might have taken it ere now. I think I must give it you—or sell it you—by mine own unforced will."

A silence fell, ominous and dark as a thundercloud. All Elfland held its breath, awaiting the royal storm. Then the sun broke through again, the Faerie Queen smiled, and her watchful court murmured to one another, as those who watch a bout at swords will murmur when the less-skilled fencer maketh a lucky hit.

"Thou hast the right of it, friend Nicholas: We do confess it. Come, then. The Queen of Elfland will turn huswife, and chaffer with thee."

Nick clasped his arms about his knee and addressed the lady thus: "I will be frank with you, Serenity. My master, when he saw the jewel, advised me that I should not part withal for less than fifty golden crowns, and that not until I'd used it to buy a master goldsmith's good opinion and a place at his shop. Fifty-five crowns, then, will buy the jewel from me, and not a farthing less."

The Lady tapped her white hand on her knee. "Then thy master is a fool, or thou a rogue and liar. The bauble is worth no more than fifteen golden crowns. But for that we are a compassionate prince, and thy complaint being just, we will give thee twenty, and not a farthing more."

"Forty-five," said Nick. "I might sell it to Master Spenser for twice the sum, as a fair portrait of Gloriana, with a description of the faerie court, should he wish to write another book."

"Twenty-five," said the Queen. "Ungrateful wretch. 'Twas I sent the dream inspired the jewel."

"All the more reason to pay a fair price for it," said Nick. "Forty."

This shot struck in the gold. The Queen frowned and sighed and shook her head and said, "Thirty. And a warrant, signed by our own royal hand, naming thee jeweler by appointment to Gloriana, by cause of a pendant thou didst make at her behest."

It was a fair offer. Nick pondered a moment, saw Peasecod grinning up at him with open joy, her cheeks dusky red and her eyes alight, and said: "Done, my Queen, if only you will add thereto your attendant nymph, Peasecod, to be my companion."

At this Gloriana laughed aloud, and all the court of Elfland laughed with her, peal upon peal at the mortal's presumption. Peasecod alone of the bright throng did not laugh, but rose to stand by Nicholas' side and pressed his hand in hers. She was brown and wild as a young deer, and it seemed to Nick that the Queen of Elfland herself, in all her female glory of moony breasts and arching neck, was not so fair as this one slender, black-browed faerie maid.

When Gloriana had somewhat recovered her power of speech, she said: "Friend Nicholas, I thank thee; for I have not laughed so heartily this many a long day. Take thy faeric lover and thy faerie gold and thy faerie warrant and depart unharmed from hence. But for that thou hast dared to rob the Faerie Queen of this her servant, we lay this weird on thee, that if thou say thy Peasecod nay, at bed or at board for the space of four-and-twenty mortal hours, then thy gold shall turn to leaves, thy warrant to filth, and thy lover to dumb stone."

At this, Peasecod's smile grew dim, and up spoke she and said, "Madam, this is too hard."

"Peace," said Gloriana, and Peasecod bowed her head. "Nicholas," said the Queen, "we commence to grow weary of this play. Give us the jewel and take thy price and go thy ways."

So Nick did off his doublet and his shirt and unwound the band of linen from about his waist and fetched out a little leathern purse and loosed its strings and tipped out into his hand the precious thing upon which he had expended all his love and his art. And loath was he to part withal, the first-fruits of his labor.

"Thou shalt make another, my heart, and fairer yet than this," whispered Peasecod in his ear, and so he laid it into Elfland's royal hand, and bowed, and in that moment he was, in the hollow under the green hill, his pack at his feet, half-naked, shocked as by a lightning-bolt, and alone. Yet before he could draw breath to make his moan, Peasecod appeared beside him with his shirt and doublet on her arm, a pack at her back, and a heavy purse at her waist, that she detached and gave to him with his clothes. Fain would he have sealed his bargain then and there, but Peasecod begging prettily that they might seek more comfort than might be found on a tussock of grass, he could not say her nay. Nor did he regret his weird that gave her the whip hand in this, for the night drew on apace, and he found himself sore hungered and athirst, as though he'd been beneath the hill for longer than the hour he thought. And indeed 'twas a day and a night and a day again since he'd seen the faerie girl upon the heath, for time doth gallop with the faerie kind, who heed not its passing. And so Peasecod told him as they trudged northward in the gloaming, and picked him early berries to stay his present hunger, and found him clear water to stay his thirst, so that he was inclined to think very well of his bargain, and of his own cleverness that had made it.

And so they walked until they came to a tavern, where Nick called for dinner and a chamber, all of the best, and pressed a golden noble into the host's palm, whereat the goodman stared and said such a coin would buy his whole house and all his ale, and still he'd not have coin to change it. And Nick, flushed with gold and lust, told him to keep all as a gift upon the giver's wedding-day. Whereat Peasecod blushed and cast down her eyes as any decent bride, though the goodman saw she wore no ring and her legs and feet were bare and dusty from the road. Yet he gave them of his best, both meat and drink, and put them to bed in his finest chamber, with a fire in the grate because gold is gold, and a rose on the pillow because he remembered what it was to be young.

The door being closed and latched, Nicholas took Peasecod in his arms and drank of her mouth as 'twere a well and he dying of thirst. And then he bore her to the bed and laid her down and began to unlace her gown that he might see her naked. But she said unto him, "Stay, Nicholas

Cantier, and leave me my modesty yet a while. But do thou off thy clothes, and I vow thou shalt not lack for pleasure."

Then young Nick gnawed his lip and pondered in himself whether taking off her clothes by force would be saying her nay—some part of which showed in his face, for she took his hand to her mouth and tickled the palm with her tongue, all the while looking roguishly upon him, so that he smiled upon her and let her do her will, which was to strip his doublet and shirt from him, to run her fingers and her tongue across his chest, to lap and pinch at his nipples until he gasped, to stroke and tease him, and finally to release his rod and take it in her hand and then into her mouth. Poor Nick, who had never dreamed of such tricks, was like to die of ecstasy. He twisted his hands in her long hair as pleasure came upon him like an annealing fire, and then he lay spent, with Peasecod's head upon his bosom, and all her dark hair spread across his belly like a blanket of silk.

After a while she raised herself, and with great tenderness kissed him upon the mouth and said, "I have no regret of this bargain, my heart, whatever follows after."

And from his drowsy state he answered her, "Why, what should follow after but joy and content and perchance a babe to dandle upon my knee?"

She smiled and said, "What indeed? Come, discover me," and lay back upon the pillow and opened her arms to him.

For a little while, he was content to kiss and toy with lips and neck, and let her body be. But soon he tired of this game, the need once again growing upon him to uncover her secret places and to plumb their mysteries. He put his hand beneath her skirts, stroking her thigh that was smooth as pearl and quivered under his touch as it drew near to that mossy dell he had long dreamed of. With quickening breath, he felt springing hair, and then his fingers encountered an obstruction, a wand or rod, smooth as the thigh, but rigid, and burning hot. In his shock, he squeezed it, and Peasecod gave a moan, whereupon Nick would have withdrawn his hand, and that right speedily, had not his faerie lover gasped, "Wilt thou now nay-say me?"

Nick groaned and squeezed again. The rod he held pulsed, and his own yard stirred in ready sympathy. Nick raised himself on his elbow and looked down into Peasecod's face—wherein warred lust and fear, man and woman—and thought, not altogether clearly, upon his answer. Words might turn like snakes to bite their tails, and Nick was of no mind to be misunderstood. For answer then, he tightened his grip upon those fair and ruddy jewels that Peasecod brought to his marriage-portion, and so wrought with them that the eyes rolled back in his lover's head, and he expired upon a sigh. Yet rose he again at Nick's insistent kissing, and threw off his skirts and stays and his smock of fine linen to show his body, slender and hard as Nick's own, yet smooth and white as any lady's that bathes in ass's milk and honey. And so they sported night-long until the rising sun blew pure gold leaf upon their tumbled bed, where they lay entwined and, for the moment, spent.

"I were well-served if thou shoulds't cast me out, once the four-and-twenty hours are past," said Peasecod mournfully.

"And what would be the good of that?" asked Nick.

"More good than if I stayed with thee, a thing nor man nor woman, nor human nor faerie kind."

"As to the latter, I cannot tell, but as to the former, I say that thou art both, and I the richer for thy doubleness. Wait," said Nick, and scrambled from the bed and opened his pack and took out a blank ring of copper and his block of pitch and his small steel tools. And he worked the ring into the pitch and, within a brace of minutes, had incised upon it a pea-vine from which you might pick peas in season, so like nature was the work. And returning to the bed where Peasecod lay watching, slipped it upon his left hand.

Peasecod turned the ring upon his finger, wondering. "Thou dost not hate me, then, for that I tricked and cozened thee?"

Nick smiled and drew his hand down his lover's flank, taut ivory to his touch, and said, "There are some hours yet left, I think, to the term of my bond. Art thou so eager, love, to become dumb stone that thou must be asking me questions that beg to be answered 'No?' Know then, that I rejoice in being thy cony, and only wish that thou mayst catch me as often as may be, if all thy practices be as pleasant as this by which thou hast bound me to thee."

And so they rose and made their ways to Oxford town, where Nicholas made such wise use of his faerie gold and his faerie commission as to keep his faerie lover in comfort all the days of their lives.

Broke Heart Blues

Joyce Carol Oates

John Reddy, you had our hearts.
John Reddy, we would've died for you.
John Reddy, John Reddy Heart

"THE BALLAD OF JOHN REDDY HEART"

 There was a time in the village of Willowsville, New York, population 5,640, eleven miles east of Buffalo, when every girl between the ages of twelve and twenty (and many unacknowledged others besides) was in love with John Reddy Heart.

John Reddy, sixteen years old, from Las Vegas, Nevada, was our first love. You never forget your first love.

And where John Reddy wasn't exactly our first love (for after all, our mothers must've loved our fathers first, when they were young, in that unfathomable abyss of time before our births—and certain Willowsville moms were in love with John Reddy Heart) he supplanted that first love, and its very memory.

Our fathers despised him. We knew better than to speak of John Reddy Heart in our fathers' presence.

John Reddy Heart.

* * *

That winter it came to be known that the head custodian of Willowsville Senior High, Alistair, whose last name none of us knew, whose dislike of us as spoiled rich kids shone in his whiskey-colored eyes, was arranging for John Reddy Heart and his girl Sasha Calvo, whose parents refused to allow them to date, to meet surreptitiously in the school basement where Alistair had a windowless, overheated, cozy office squeezed between the mammoth furnace and the hot water tanks. Alistair's most urgent responsibility was to check the pressure gauges on the furnaces when they were in operation—"Without me, the whole friggin place *goes*." He spoke with mordant satisfaction, snapping his fingers. Surely Alistair would have lost his job if he'd been caught arranging for Sasha Calvo to slip down the basement stairs from the east, sophomore wing of the school, make her way along a shadowy corridor to his cave of an office to which John Reddy would have come, eagerly slipping down the basement stairs from the west, senior wing of the school. There was said to be music playing, a radio turned low. A shaded forty-watt bulb. Shabby yet still colorful carpet remnants laid on the concrete floor, curling up onto the walls to a height of several inches. And Alistair's old sagging cushioned sofa. "Oh, God. A throbbing *womb*." We were uneasy, anxious, seeing the lovers below us, oblivious of us and of danger. How famished they were for each other—kissing, embracing, their hands clutching at each other's bodies. No time for words, only murmurs, groans, choked cries. Their lovemaking was tender, yet passionate. Possibly a little rough, bringing tears to Sasha's beautiful eyes. As, at the foot of the basement stairs, smoking his foul-smelling pipe, Alistair stood watch. "S'pose Stamish comes down? What's Alistair gonna do?" Some of us were convinced that John Reddy and Sasha met like this only a few times; others, that they met every weekday afternoon through the winter and spring. For these were the only times they could meet, we reasoned—the Calvos guarded Sasha so closely. In our dull rows of seats, in our classrooms on the floors above, the red second hand of clocks in every classroom, positioned uniformly above the blackboard, ticked urgently onward. "What're they doing now, d'you think? *Now?*" "Do you think they do it bare-assed? Or some quicker way?" "Shit, John Reddy wouldn't do anything *quick*." Boys, aroused and anxious, tried to hide their gigantic erections with notebooks, or textbooks, that occasionally slipped from their clammy fingers and clattered to the floor. Girls, short of breath as if they'd been running, a faint flush in their cheeks, dabbed at their eyes with tissues and sat very still, feet flat on the floor and legs uncrossed. Our most innocent, unknowing teachers like Madame Picholet and Mr. Sternberg were observed mysteriously agitated, a glisten of sweat on their brows. The *throb! throb! throb!* of furnaces was reportedly felt as far away as the music practice room on the third floor of the annex. In Mr. Alexander's fifth-period physics class, always a drowsy class, dazed eyes blinked rapidly to keep in focus. "Excuse *me*? Is this class *awake?*" Mr. Alexander inquired in his hurt, chagrined way, staring at us with his hands on his hips. "Peter Merchant!—How would you approach this problem? Petey Merchant's physics text crashed to the floor. His cheeks flushed crimson. Yet there were those, among them Verrie Myers, who vehemently denied that John Reddy and "that Calvo girl" were lovers at all. Nor had she believed that there'd ever been a baby—"That's *sick*." In time, Verrie's view prevailed. More disturbing tales were being spread of John Reddy on those evenings when his windows were darkened down on Water Street, when the girls of The Circle, or any other girls who sought him, discovered he was gone. At such times John Reddy was cruising in his funky-sexy Mercury in Cheektawaga, Tonawanda, Lockport, or downtown Buffalo, restless and looking for action. Often he was seen with a glamorous girl, or an adult woman, pressed up close beside him, head on his shoulder and fingers, though not visible from the street, caressing the inside of his thigh. John Reddy had gone out with Mr. Stamish's youngest, pretty secretary Rita, that seemed to be a fact. Scottie Baskett came to school pale and haggard and stunned by an experience he could bring himself to share only with his closest buddy, Roger Zwaart, and that after several days: Scottie had returned home a little early from swim practice to discover his own mother, her hair damp from a shower, in slacks and a sweater clearly thrown on in haste, no bra beneath, and, of all people, John Reddy Heart!—"In my own house. He was there laying tile, supposedly, in our guest room bath. Farolino's truck was out front, I don't pay much attention to what my folks do so I was surprised to see it there, but, okay, I walk in, and there's—*John Reddy.* 'We're laying tile in the guest room bath,' Mom says. She's trying to sound cool but she's trembling, I can see her hands. Her face is all pale— no makeup. And you never see my mom without makeup. They must've heard me come in so John's hammering away innocently in the bathroom like somebody on TV and Mom's like rushing at me in the kitchen, her boobs bobbing, asking if I'd like a snack? chocolate milk? buttercrunch cookies? like for Chrissake I'm ten years old and fucking *blind.*" Two days later, Art Lutz had a similar experience, re- turning home after school to discover John Reddy on the premises, and "my mom acting wound-up and hysterical, saying 'We're having these beautiful new cabinets put in, Art, see?—aren't they beautiful?' and there's John Reddy on a kitchen stool hammering away, in a sweaty T-shirt and ripped jeans, his prick practically hanging *out.* And fuck- smell all over the house like steam from a shower. He looks at me with this shit-eating grin and says, 'How's it going, kid?' and I realize I got to get out of there fast before I get violent. So I slammed out again, climbed into Jamie's car and floored 'er." Bibi Arhardt was wakened in the middle of the night by gravel thrown against her second-floor bedroom window. Frightened, she knelt by the windowsill without turning on the light and saw, below, the figure of a man, or boy, signaling impatiently to her. "Though I couldn't see his face clearly, I knew it was him—John Reddy. And there was the Mercury out on the street. At once, I had no will to resist. I knew it might be a mistake, but—" Bibi hurriedly dressed, and slipped out a side door into the night, which was a bright moon-lit gusty night smelling of damp, greening earth—for it was late March by this time, and the long winter was ending. There came John Reddy, his eyes burning, to seize Bibi in his arms and bear her, feebly protesting, to his car. In silence they drove to Tug Hill Park which was larger, more desolate and wild than Bibi remembered. How many hours passed there, in John Reddy's car, Bibi could not have said; how many hungry kisses passed between them; how many caresses; how many times, with gentleness and sweetness, yet control, John Reddy made love to her, bringing her to tears of ecstasy—"It wasn't like you would think! It wasn't like you would imagine any guy could *do*." A few nights later, in her bedroom on the second floor of the Zeiglers' Georgian colonial on Castle Creek Drive, Suzi, though wearing Norm Zeiga's onyx signet ring on a chain around her neck, was wakened by a sound in her bedroom and looked up to see a tall figure standing over her bed—"I was too scared to scream. I seemed to know, even before he knelt beside me, and kissed me, who it was. 'Don't be afraid, Suzi, I won't hurt you,' John Reddy whispered. 'And if I do, forgive me.' " Evangeline Fesnacht came to school pale, moist-eyed, strangly silent. When Mr. Lepage tried to engage her in their customary witty banter, as the rest of us looked on, Evangeline sighed, lowered her gaze meekly and made no reply. "Have I, Miss Fesnacht," Mr. Lepage said in a voice heavy with sarcasm, "a rival for your thoughts this morning?" In the back seat of his brother's Dodge Castille, as Art Lutz kissed her eagerly with his opened mouth, and awkwardly tried, with his left hand, to unhook her bra beneath her sweater, Tessa Maypole burst into guilty tears, saying, "Oh, Artie, I can't. I can't. I'm in love with someone else, it wouldn't be fair to you." Lee Ann Whitfield, our fat girl, was observed in the school cafeteria pushing around, on her plate, a large portion of macaroni-and-cheese, with the look of one who has lost her appetite, or her soul. Ritchie Eickhorn noted in his journal, under the new, heady influence of Pascal *We yearn for eternity—but inhabit only time.* Miss Flechsenhauer noted with suspicion an unusual number of girls asking to be excused, with "cramps" or "migraine," from gym, swim class, team practice. "What is this, girls, an epidemic?" Miss O'Brien, our school nurse, a chesty, dour woman with a perpetual sinus snuffle, noted, with suspicion, an unusual number of girls requesting Bufferin and Midol and to be allowed to lie, with heating pads on their lower abdomens, on cots in the peaceful, darkened infirmary. "What is this, girls, an epidemic?" John Reddy Heart was said to have been seen at nine A.M. Sunday church service at the United Methodist church on Haggarty Road. "But nobody goes *there*, who would've seen him?" John Reddy Heart, as spring progressed, was looking, at school, more and more exhausted, as if he no longer slept at night. His eyelids drooped as our teachers droned on; he was having trouble, it seemed, staying awake in his classes. His left eye was bloodshot and leaked tears. His jaws were sometimes stippled in tiny cuts from careless or hurried shaving. Some mornings, he didn't shave at all, evidently. His longish hair, separating in greasy quills, exuded a frank, pungent odor, sharp as that of his body. Girls swooned if they passed too close to him. It was known to be particularly dangerous to pass too close by John Reddy on the stairs: Several sophomore girls nearly fainted. In fourth-period English, Miss Bird, leading a discussion of Robert Frost's "After Apple Picking," stared at John Reddy Heart, who was gripping his textbook and frowning into it as if the secret of life might be located there, in a few teasing lines of poetry;

she sniffed his scent, and for a long embarrassing moment lost the thread of her thought. We'd realized for some time, uneasily, that Miss Bird no longer wore her hair skinned back from her face in that unflattering style but curled and fluffed out, "feminine" in the way that women are "feminine" in late-night movies of the Forties. Her small, pursed lips were a savage red. Her slightly bulgy brown eyes, fixed on John Reddy, who may have been glancing shyly up at her, appeared to be shifting out of focus. "Miss Bird? I'll open a window," Ken Fischer said quickly, leaping to his feet. "It's kind of stuffy in here." For a precarious moment— "I held my breath, oh, God, she's going to faint!"—Miss Bird swayed groggily in her spike-heeled shoes. Then she smiled wanly at Ken, touching the back of her thin hand to her forehead, and the sinister spell was broken. Yet the following morning in Mr. Dunleddy's biology class, where John Reddy sat in his prescribed corner, first row, extreme right, Sandi Scott, usually so poised and droll, astonished us by bursting into tears in the midst of a recitation of the steps of mitosis: " 'Prophase'—'metaphase'—'anaphase'— 'telophase'—Oh, God, it's so relentless! So *cruel*." Mr. Dunleddy, short of breath even sitting, overweight by fifty pounds, who would be the first of our teachers to die, a few years later, of a stroke at the relatively young age of fifty-six, stared at the weeping girl with middle-aged eyes of dolor and regret. That night, Evangeline Fesnacht typed the first line of what would become, eventually, after numerous metamorphoses, her first published novel ("wild, dithyrambic, dark, riddlesome") *I woke from a dream so vivid I would search the world for its origin—in vain*. Ritchie Eickhorn noted in his journal *We inhabit time but remember only "eternal moments." God's mercy*. Dexter Cambrook impulsively called Pattianne Groves. He was flooded with excitement as with an intoxicant in his normally calm veins—"My acceptance just came from Harvard!" He waited with sweaty palms, pounding heart for Pattianne's kid brother to call her to the phone and asked her point-blank if she'd go with him to the senior prom and was met with, after a moment's startled silence, "Oh, Dexter? Did you say—Dexter? *Cambrook*? Oh, gee, thanks. I mean, that's so thoughtful of you, Dexter. But I'm sorry, I guess I'll be going with—" Verrie Myers and Trish Elders, closest friends since kindergarten, who, in recent weeks, had scarcely been able to look at each other, each feeling a deep physical revulsion for the other, found themselves walking swiftly, then breaking into a run, like foals, onto the vividly green playing field behind the school. Each girl grabbed the other's hand at the same instant. Their uplifted faces were luminous, radiant. Their eyes shone. We watched, a haphazard and unknowing trapezoid of (male, yearning) observers, one of us from a second-floor window of the school, another from the parking lot and the third as he was leaving the building at the rear, as the girls in maroon gym shorts and dazzling-white T-shirts ran, clutching hands; at that moment the sun burst through the storm clouds, and a diaphanous rainbow appeared in the sky, near-invisible, an arc of pale gold, rose, seablue shimmering over open fields beyond Garrison Road—"like a wayward, tossed-off gesture of God" (as Ritchie Eickhorn would one day observe). It was John Reddy Heart toward whom those girls were running, we knew. Yet we were resigned, not bitter; philosophical, not raging with testosterone jealousy. *He won't love them as we love them. One day, they will know.* Unknown to any of us, John Reddy Heart was having, at that very moment, a near-encounter with an "older woman." Sexually rapacious, stylishly dressed Mrs. Rindfleisch, Jon's problem mother (a "nympho mom" we'd been hearing lurid rumors of since we were all in sixth grade), her hunter green Mazda parked crookedly, idling at the curb, hurried swaying into Muller's Drugs to pick up a prescription (for Valium: Mrs. Rindfleisch described herself as a pioneer of state-of-the-art tranquilizers in Willowsville in those heady years) and nearly collided with a display of hot water bottles, staring at the tall, rangy classmate of her son's, what was his name, the Heart boy, the boy with the astonishing sexy eyes. Mrs. Rindfleisch heard her husky voice lift lyrically, "John Reddy! Hel-*lo*." She somewhat surprised herself, cornering a boy Jon's age who so clearly wanted to escape. (What was John Reddy doing in Muller's? Some of us speculated he was stocking up on Trojans for the weekend, he must've run through rubbers like other guys run through Kleenex.) John Reddy appeared startled that Mrs. Rindfleisch knew his name. Or maybe it was the lilt of her voice, her gleaming predator-eyes and shiny lipsticked lips. He must not have recognized her, though he and Jon had been on the varsity track team together and she'd come to a few meets, eager to see her son excel and proud of him even if, most times, unfortunately, he didn't, and she wasn't. "Well, um, John—lots of excitement imminent, yes?" Still he regarded her blankly. "I mean—the end of the school year. The end of—high school. Your prom, graduation. Such a happy time, yes?" Politely John Reddy murmured what sounded like, "Yes, ma'am." Or possibly, "No, ma'am." Mrs. Rindfleisch queried brightly, "And will your family be attending your graduation, I hope?" John Reddy shook his head, pained. "Why, that's too bad! No one?" Mrs. Rindfleisch moved closer, emanating a sweet-musky scent like overripe gardenias. She tried not to lick her lips. "Why don't you join us, then? I'm hosting a lavish brunch that day. Family, relatives, friends, scads and scads of Jon's classmates—your classmates. Will you join us? Yes?" Not looking at the woman's heated face, John Reddy mumbled he might be busy that day, but thanks. Flushed with her own generosity, Mrs. Rindfleisch said, "Well, John Reddy, know yourself *invited. Chez* Rindfleisch. Any time. In fact—" Her second Valium since lunch—or was it her third?—had just begun to kick in. That delicious downward sensation. Sliding-careening. A spiraling tightness in the groin. In the juicy crevices and folds of the groin. She had a quick, wild vision

of how her pubic hair (not graying for the same shrewd reason the hairs on her head were not "graying" but shone a
fetching russet-red) would appear to John Reddy Heart's
staring eyes, flattened like italics glimpsed through the pink
satiny transparency of her panty-girdle and believed it was a
sight that would arouse him; she laughed, effervescent.
Teeth sparkled. Asking the edgy boy if, um, would he like to
join her in a Coke? a cup of coffee? a beer? a slice or two of
zingy-hot pizza with all the trimmings? next door at The
Haven or, better idea, her car's right outside, ignition already
switched on for a quick getaway, they could drive to Vito's
Paradiso Lounge on Niagara Boulevard, no trouble there,
him being served. "What d'you say, John Reddy? Yes?" But
John Reddy was mumbling, not meeting her eye, "Ma'am,
thanks but I gotta go, I guess. Now." Mrs. Rindfleisch was
astonished to see her hand leap out, as long ago that very
hand might've leapt out to forestall her swaying, toddler-age
Jonathan from falling and injuring himself, now it was a
beautifully maintained middle-aged hand, manicured,
Revlon-red-polished nails scratchily caressing the boy's
hairy forearm, brushing against the boy's taut groin, she saw
a flicker of—what?—helpless lust in his face?—or childish
fear?—"Ma'am, thanks, *no*." Quickly then he walked away,
about to break into a run. Mrs. Rindfleisch stared after him,
incensed. How dare he! What was this! As if everyone didn't
know the brute animal, the lowlife fiend, sexy boy! As if she
hadn't one of her own, a handsome teenage son, at home!
Watching John Reddy exit Muller's as if exiting her life,
steadying herself against a rack of Hallmark greeting cards.
His lank black greasy hair was long enough for her to have
seized into a fist, and tugged. God damn she should've. The
way he'd insulted her. A hard-on like that, practically popping out of his zipper, and cutting his eyes at her, sending
her unmistakable sex-messages with his eyes, staring at her
breasts, at her (still glamorous, shapely) legs in diamond-
black-textured stockings, then coolly backing away, break-

ing it off, teasing like coitus interruptus, the prig. Like all of them, God-damn prigs. Tears wetted Mrs. Rindfleisch's meticulously rouged cheeks. Tears wetted Mrs. Rindfleisch's raw-silk champagne-colored blouse worn beneath an aggressively youthful heather suede vest ideal for mild autumn days and nights. She stumbled in her high-heeled lizard-skin Gucci pumps to the door, or what appeared to be the door; she'd forgotten—what? Some reason, some purchase to be made, she'd come into Muller's for, what was it, God damn who cares, that beautiful boy was slipping through her outstretched fingers *like my very youth, my beauty, you wouldn't believe how lovely I was, my perfect little breasts so bouncy and so free-standing, just hated to strap myself into a bra.* Oh, but there he was, waiting for her—on the sidewalk—he hadn't stalked off after all—no: It was her son Jon, glowering Jonathan, he'd sighted the Mazda crooked at the curb, motor running, left-turn signal crazily winking. "Oh, Jesus, Mom, what the hell are you *doing?*" this boy yelled, grabbing at her arm, and Mrs. Rindfleisch, who was crying screamed, "You! You and your dirty foul-minded 'John Reddy Heart'! *Don't any of you touch me.*"

Wolfed

Tanith Lee

 Under the glittering cliffs of skyscrapers, in the tangled night wood of neon, concrete, glass, and steel that calls itself New York City, he strayed from the path, and went into a little bar.

He was twenty-six years old, six foot four in height, and he weighed around one hundred and seventy-two pounds. He had the kind of face sometimes seen on celluloid, but once, that very year he thought he might make it as an actor, the middle-aged woman in the casting office had said to him, "Oh, honey. You're just too good-looking. That blond hair and those *black* eyes—be warned. You'll have a bad time here." She then suggested something else. And when he did that, she was very generous, both with her surprisingly pretty body, and with the wad of bills he found later in his car. It was this that started him on his present career, the one he should have been pursuing right now, since he was down to his last twenty. So maybe the bar was a fine idea . . . or not. Really, it was the girl. She was the reason he came in. And she was not the sort of girl to be of any use. Because she wouldn't *need* him, not at all.

As he sat down on the chromium stool at her side, practiced, he took her in, through the low, cave-dim light. But practice had not prepared him. He liked women a lot. Their voices, their bodies—oh, yes, those—their clothes and how they wore them. Their cosmetics even, jewelry, lingerie— everything about them. And this one—

She had a burnished hood of claret-red hair, matched neatly by her velvet gown, which being tight, backless, and nearly frontless, gave him an exquisite view of several rich curves, and a faultless pearl-cream skin.

Then, imagine a deer in the wood who is truly a wicked— but beautiful—witch in disguise. That was her face. She had no makeup but for the black kohl around her eyes and on her lashes, which looked real and a full inch long, and the ripe scarlet on her full, smooth lips. No jewelry, good or cheap, on her slim arms, at her long, delicious neck, or in the lobes of her alabaster ears. However, where her shorter-than-short skirt rode up, just above the black lace of her long-legged stocking-tops, he noted a garter with a golden rose. And five years of having to do with gold, though seldom in the way of owner-ship, suggested the golden rose, like her lashes, was quite real.

He did not speak, but he saw from his vision's corner, that she had turned to frankly study him. Perhaps she liked the look of him. Most women did. Suddenly she laughed, a great laugh, appealing, not too loud, not ugly, and *not* irri-tatingly coy. Lashes, gold, laugh—all genuine?

He turned, too, and gazed at her full on.

Oh, yes.

Her teeth were white, and her eyes the shade of green found in Han jade. She smelled faintly, warmly, of some smoky flower, perhaps not of the earth. Was that the catch— she was an *X-Files* alien?

"Thank you for laughing at me."

"I'm sorry."

"No, I liked it."

"Why?"

"It means I've amused you. And I didn't even have to tell a joke."

She smiled now, and raising her glass—of some green

cocktail less convincing that her Han-green eyes—she said "I laughed because you're so handsome."

"Oh, I see."

"Do you?"

"Well . . . maybe. Shall I do it at you?"

"If you want."

The few other customers were far off along the room, but now a waiter was floating down the bar counter, and the girl signaled, and he floated right over.

He knew now she would buy him a big drink, and she did, and when it had been served on its little white paper coaster, she said to him, "Will you tell me your name?"

"Sure. It's Wolfgang. But you'll believe I prefer to be called Wolf."

"So we don't gang up on you," she said.

"Yeah, that's it. And I guess they call you Red," he added, guessing that he doubted that.

"Rose," she answered.

She leaned a fraction toward him, and the white fruits of her breasts moved gently in the red velvet, just enough that he understood she had on no brassière, and probably no underclothes at all, apart from the stockings with the garter.

"Rose," he repeated. He let her hear it, that he was aroused. From the warm fragrance of her, the darkening of her eyes, he was suddenly recklessly banking on the fact that she was, as well. You had to take a chance sometimes. But you had to be careful, too. There had been that girl in Queens who looked like five million dollars, and turned out to have a habit, and a worse habit—which was a knife.

"Are you hungry?" said Rose.

"I'm always hungry." He paused. "Not always for food."

"Me neither," said Rose.

Wolf glanced at those other customers. No one was looking at Rose, or himself, they were all lost, as most persons were, in their own involving lives. Just as well, perhaps, for she had put her slim white hand now on his crotch. It was the mildest, almost, you could say, the most *tactful* caress. But he came up like a rock against her.

"You're interested," she said.

"My. You can tell."

"I'm so glad. Because you're perfect, Wolf."

"That's nice."

"I hope so."

"What," he said, as she removed her cruel, tender little hand, "did you have in mind?"

"Well, you see, it's not really for me." She watched him, watched his face change down, cool an iota. "No, this isn't some trick, Wolf. It's just, you see, I promised to take my grandmother something."

"Your *grandmother*."

Rose laughed, differently now. This was exuberant, even coarse, and yet, she could get away with it entirely. Muscles rippled lightly under red velvet dress and white velvet skin. Despite all his years of experience, he wanted badly to pull her close, and open his mouth, let out his tongue against her ear, her throat, to taste the heat of her under her succulent sheath, and then he would like—

"It sounds unattractive, I know. But it isn't. *She* isn't. Grandmothers aren't always elderly anymore. I'm nineteen, and my grandmother—Ryder, that's her name—is just, well, in her early forties."

"That doesn't sound like it's legal."

Rose shrugged.

"Or quite truthful," he amended, sternly.

Rose picked up a little ruby purse, and slid out of it a small photograph. She held this out. When Wolf took it from her, he saw it showed a most beautiful, lion-maned woman, in a skin-tight leotard. Not young, but nevertheless voluptuous, limber, strong, and highly enticing.

"This is Grandma?" he said.

"That is she. And honestly, Wolf, the picture hasn't been retouched."

"You'd swear that on your mother's life?"

"Can't. No mother, now. I'd swear it on mine."

Wolf emptied his glass. The girl raised her hand and the waiter stirred. Wolf said, "Maybe not. I don't want you to waste your money."

"I haven't. Look, we'll take a cab over there. Go up, and see. I know, when you meet Ryder, you'll want to go in . . . if you take what I mean."

"And if not?"

"No hard feelings. Make some excuse to her—wrong floor, wrong apartment. If you come straight back down, well, I'd wait around a while, and let's say two hundred dollars for your wasted time. How's that?"

"You guessed. Aw shucks."

Rose leaned forward again. For a blissful moment, as she adjusted one crimson pump, he caught, in the scoop of neckline, the peek-a-boo flicker of an icing-sugar-pink nipple. The colors didn't clash at all. And then her soft lips were on his, and her narrow tongue darted in and out—and was gone.

"I did so want to give her something lovely for her birthday," said Rose. "And you are, Wolf, lovely as lovely is."

The elevator had gold inside, not solid this time, but not bad: gold-plated.

When he alighted, and rang the gold-plated bell, her intercom came on. "Is that you, honey?"

Ryder's voice was low and sweet—and dangerous.

Wolf said, "I guess not."

"Oh," said Granny's intercom. "Then what?"

"Rose—sent me up."

"Rose did? Do I know a Rose?"

"She says she's your granddaughter."

"Oh, that Rose. Okay."

The jet-black shining door opened wide, and showed him an enormous reception area, with black and white marble underfoot and on the walls, golded mirrors, a skylight set with milky glass shot by red jewels that threw down rosy blood-drops all over everything. There were no other furnishings, and just two engraved glass doors, opening somewhere else, presently closed. You couldn't see through the engraving, not properly. But inside it looked fairly impressive.

He had been let straight in and he hadn't yet seen Granny, in case he had to back off nicely if he didn't care for her. But then, anyway, the elevator was a private one and this was the penthouse suite, so it would be kind of unlikely he had taken the wrong route, or made any mistake at all.

Just then the glass doors were pushed decisively open.

And there stood—Granny.

"What a wonderful voice you have," said Granny. "Trained, yes?"

"I was an actor."

"Not anymore? No more acting?"

"Not on a stage."

She grinned. She had perfect teeth, the teeth the best sort of predator would have. Which was about right. She definitely did exude the aura of a lioness. Even a lion. Almost as tall as Wolf, in her high-heeled slippers, and with a mane of gleaming platinum-to-silver hair, she wore otherwise a completely transparent robe, tied tight to her tightly muscular waist by a thin rope of Cartier gold. She was muscular all over, the way a dancer is, and maybe she was a dancer. On the muscles had been smoothed a satin padding of flesh, and over that a lightly tanned skin like honey. Her breasts were heavy, but edible. The urge to weigh them in the hands was overwhelming. And she had done just what they did in books, gilded her nipples. Under her round and muscular belly, which gave a little ripple even as his eyes irresistibly went there, a sort of little *wave* to him, her bush was of the same metallic effect as her mane.

She gave a kind of kick with one long, long, *long* leg. That was like a horse. But no, she was simply kicking out of the way a champagne cork lying on the mosaic—it *was* a mosaic—floor.

"My birthday party," she explained. "They drank and drank. They all brought me presents, so I couldn't turn them out. Would you like to finish the Dom Perignon? A couple of bottles still half full, I think, and I don't drink alcohol on weekdays. It would be a kindness."

"I guess I can force myself."

"Then come on in."

She turned and moved away. Her bottom was a stimulating sight. Yes, a dancer must be it—perhaps with a giant snake, winding and coiling about her amber body, caressing, slipping, its incredible muscles matched by her own.

The room was about two blocks big, with carpets on the walls that might have come from ancient Persia, and a single statue in bronze, of a girl holding up a dish, and in the dish lavish fruit: oranges, peaches, grapes—the proper stuff of an epic lust scene.

Had Rose already called up? She must have told Granny that she would like *this* present. Or why else had Granny come to the door clad fit to wake the dead?

She was returning with a large, sparkling crystal goblet about a foot long, somewhat the way he was feeling in a particular part of himself right now, and full of bubbling silvery-golden something.

"Wolf—that's right, is it?"

Rose had called.

"Yes, ma'am."

"My name is Ryder. I don't look a day over forty-three, and I'm not."

She deserved an accolade, though she probably received them always. "You don't look more than thirty-three to me." She didn't, or not by very much. And though she had expression lines by her mouth, which was large and marvelously shaped and had the faintest gilded glisten on it, and by her eyes, which were as dark as his own and also gilded—they were of the variety of line that made you want to deepen them through laughter, and through loud cries that had nothing to do with sorrow or dismay.

"The trouble is," said Ryder, putting her hand lightly on his shoulder, huge eye to eye with him, her slight, clean breath just blowing over his lips, scented by silk, musk, and savannah, "I didn't know about you when I took the two herbal tablets. They're terrific. They make you sleep for six hours. It's been a tiring day. I calculate I have about forty minutes before those pills work. Do you think we could find something to kill forty minutes?"

Interestingly, her personal bathroom was even bigger than the two-block sitting room. And in the midst of its Grecian glacier of tiles and friezes, its ten- and twenty-foot emerald-colored plants that thrived on heat and steam, lay a very special jacuzzi of ink-black marble.

"I love to get wet," said Ryder. Then she added, "Do you mind short hair?" And drew off the mane, just as she had discarded her transparent robe and golden tie. Her own hair was also silver, a thick short fur over her head leading into a serpentine coil along her neck. This way, she looked more cat-like, more chancy even than before.

She stepped down into the tub, and lay along a marble ledge just under the water. There were a pair of black marble nymphs here, too, naked and glowing. Ryder lifted her arms and wrapped her hands loosely around their hips.

"Come in."

So far, the water moved only gently, and through the little liquid thrills, her breasts, lifted by her arms, golden nipples glinting, bobbed and trembled as the water came and went. The way the water ran, he noticed, the nipples were getting particular attention. That must feel good, and obviously the ledge had been arranged for exactly this position and this treatment.

He took off his clothes, and Ryder watched him through

half-lidded eyes. He could see she was pleased with him, very pleased. She wriggled her legs as he descended into the pool, and a spray of delicate cool-warm drops hit the surface of his chest and thighs, sprinkling like diamonds his already enormous erection.

"You're a little ahead of yourself there," she said.

He laughed.

The water was at a clever temperature, warmed enough to be comfortable but cool enough to brace. He eased onto the ledge beside her, and bent to her mouth. They kissed, tongues entwining like the serpent dance he had visualized, while his left hand and the water played over and over her big cushiony breasts, and her hard little nipples eagerly nosed after his fingers, wanting to be tickled. She made a deep luxurious moaning sound, again and again into his mouth.

When he lifted his head, a soft flush was on her face, making her look younger than ever. She pulled him over and on top of her, his penis lying delightfully trapped between their bellies, quivering uncontrollably with its own life.

Ryder polished his back with her hands, and slid them into the groove between his buttocks. She, too, began to play, while the water lapped with its own caress, creating a melting fire that trickled ever more strongly through into his loins, and until she had drawn out of him in turn a murmur of tortured pleasure. But he was now so hard that pleasure was stealing close to pain. He eased himself away from her.

"Step back off the ledge, but stay close," she whispered. "Kneel facing me, where the groove is. Trust me, you'll like it there. The water does something—special. Custom built." He did what she said, and as he knelt on the smooth marble between her legs, she glided them up onto his shoulders, and her hands clasped firmly on the black stone nymphs. The speed and direction of the water intensified at once. It became insistent, *skillful*. It was probing at him in exactly the most apt of places, bubbling around and around his balls, and stroking, fierce, rhythmic, at his stem, while at the hugely engorged tip of him there began a ceaseless, miraculous suction, like that of the most amazing and cunning and unavoidable mouth in the world.

He said, ". . . Ryder—"

"Oh, Mr. Wolf," she gasped. Her calves slid on his back. "Will you eat me?"

As the wicked water deliriously stroked and taunted and urged him, he bent into the wet sweet core of her vulva to kiss her better and better. Her hair here was coarse and aromatic as summer grass. Her clit was small but totally erect, standing up to him like a pearl on fire. He licked her, licked her, to the tempo of the inescapable ecstasy chasing up and down along his spine, mounting like architecture in his groin, and felt the long quivers of a glorious complementary agony vibrating through her legs as he clasped her jerking hips in both his hands.

She lay spread before him, and he glimpsed her as she writhed, panting, clinging, and squeezing at the nymphs as if she were drowning, so that the jets of water they controlled were increasing, going wild, roiling over the maddened gems of her nipples, and working upon his penis like five or six desperate tongues and one starving loving mouth. He could feel Ryder's tension churning and swollen beneath his grasp, banked up against her clit as if behind a dam, galloping in her vagina, the whole golden pulsing hill of her pelvis.

Her eyes were fluttering. Her vulva was fluttering.

And he had only moments left to him.

She heard him groan aloud, and she breathlessly teased like a naughty little girl, "Oh, he's starting to come—he can't resist—he's going to, he's going to come—" but then her breathing and voice broke entirely in her first soaring scream.

A spasm as huge as the whole skyscraping tower that contained him shook Wolf to his roots. He roared, arching against her, smothered in her, even as the lights exploded, frantically, gaspingly, swirling and slapping with his tongue on and on upon that burning orgasmic pearl of hers, to hear her screaming, so the marble room rolled and boomed like a bell, and her golden heels beat against him like the drums of paradise.

To his amazement, when he was only fourteen, Wolf had learned that there *was* life after orgasm. Heaven knew how.

He had to admit he was sorry, however, that Ryder had had to go and sleep off her two herbal sleeping capsules. There were lots of things they could have done, after an interval. Instead she had left him the run of her apartment, all the rooms excluding her bedroom, dressing room, and the bathroom with the fascinating jacuzzi.

So he wandered a while through her studio, which was indeed equipped for dancing and exercise, and also partly as the most economical, effective—she proved it—and *female* gym he had ever seen. He viewed the study, the swimming pool of chartreuse water in the conservatory, the music and book library with a piano and a music system that had spread gold-rimmed speakers all through the apartment, the *computer* room—small, yes, but *astounding*—guest rooms, eating rooms, roof garden, three more bathrooms out of *Spartacus* or *Jupiter's Darling*, and so on. And . . . so forth.

The kitchen was the tiniest room. Even so, it had everything the health- or diet-conscious—or even the simply greedy and thirsty—could wish for.

Ryder was opulent, but trusting. Which was warming. Wolf had always had his own code and behaved well, which he had not always been credited with. A meeting of social graces.

He ate some smoked salmon and some creamy chicken, a poppy-seed bagel, and a salad of dark green cress, frilly lettuce, and yellow tomatoes. He finished the first of the three half-empty bottles of champagne.

It was back in the sitting room that he found her note. It was to him, and he didn't know when she had written it. Possibly, even before he had arrived at the apartment.

Wolf, once we part, I'll be out, dead, for six or seven hours. So I'll see you tomorrow, if you care to stay over. (The guest rooms have everything.) Meanwhile, I think Rose may be coming back, around midnight. She's been very sweet to me, and I'd like to be really sweet to her, too. I'm not actually her grandma. You may have guessed. That's a little—how shall I say?—joke. Did you like Rose, too? I hope you did. I'm sure you did. You have, I think, excellent taste. Yum. So, let me tell you what Rose really likes. Get ready:

Wolf read on. He raised an eyebrow, recalled he was not on camera, raised both eyebrows.

He laughed again. "Oh, boy."

Then he sat down to consider.

Twenty minutes later, at ten fifty-one precisely, he strolled into the second dressing room that led from the closed bedroom of his sleeping hostess.

It was like stuff he had seen backstage and in the caravans of the movie lot. Only a good deal more generous, and expensive to the point of being fabulous, the essence of *fables*.

At least two hundred gowns. At least a hundred and fifty wigs. All of them beautiful, the most realistic, the most exclusive. And in drawers, when he opened them, smiling and already aware of something else, all the pure Indian and Chinese silk, and handworked lace, all the patterned and mist-sheer stockings, garter belts, waspies, buttoned gloves, that any woman of that turn of mind could have conjured. All the makeup, too, every lip-paint, blusher, mascara, shadow, tint, texture, contour, highlight . . . A Garden of Eden for any girl who liked these things.

Or any man who liked them, too.

It had been a revelation, the first time. The rich girl in

Idaho who, in her long white house, had dressed them up together, saying, when she had finished painting him, lacing him, putting on his costume, "Well, just look at you." "I'm way too tall," Wolf had commented, staring at himself, or rather at this new *herself* in the mirror. "Sugar, I just don't think," said the rich girl, "that anyone'd mind that. The hell of it is, you're prettier than *me*."

Not since then. Not quite. Though now and then . . . just flirting with a pair of panties, hose, softly silicone-padded bra.

He liked women. The look and feel of them. He liked making love to them. He liked what they wore, their perfumes, and the unguents they stroked on to their faces and over the curves of their breasts. And the stockings they drew up their legs, and the lisping of the silky stuff over their bodies. Once or twice, just . . . once or twice. He dreamed of it. She, and he, also a she.

Apparently, it was just this very thing that turned Rose on. A slim, handsome man, disguised—as a woman.

He was erect again. He was thinking of Rose now. Rose all freely moving and warm and white and spilling over in her red dress, and the stocking-tops, and the garter, and he, Wolf, perhaps in that one, there, the black number. Because it was a fact, the garments that fitted Ryder's big firm body, would fit him just as neatly.

He'd need that bathroom with its razor for guests and its creams and glosses. He'd need some more champagne, too. And it was already eleven. He would have to hurry.

But then, the actor is expert at changing costume fast, and everything else that goes with it.

Rose let herself into Ryder's apartment at a quarter past midnight. The lights were low, and the softest music was playing. As she opened the two glass doors into the vast sitting room, Rose called quietly, "Ryder? It's me, are you around?"

"I'm afraid she's dead," said a low, light, husky voice from the couch.

"*What?*" said Rose.

"Sorry. I mean she's dead to the world. Herbal sleeping tablets."

"Yeah," said Rose. "And who are you?"

The tall, beautiful woman on the couch re-crossed, with an electric rasp, her sheerly stockinged legs, revealing, as she did so, the long black tongue of a garter belt, under the black satin hem of her dress. Her hair was a mane of foaming black curls, just lit with a streak or two of silver. She was big, but slender, her stomach flat, her breasts, under the high-necked gown with its collar of black sequins, rather small. Her face was truly something, smooth as bone china, with a crimson mouth and somber velvet eyes.

"Who am I? You can call me—Nana."

"Oh, *Nana.*" Rose smiled. She leaned right down to adjust her pumps, and as she did so, she put her hand against her bosom, so that only the upper swell of her breasts was visible. She tossed her claret hair. "My," said Rose, "what big eyes you've got, Nana."

"Research shows," said Nana, idly, standing up and bringing the champagne, "that the larger your eyes are, the better you can see."

"Really?" Rose took the glass, and extracted a few sips. "And does research tell me why you're wearing my grandmother's French perfume?"

"It tells *me* she's not your grandmother. Way too young."

"True. It's our joke, hers and mine. When we met, you see, she said, Now, Rose, stop that—I'm old enough to be your grandmother. Now you understand. So, tell me why the perfume?"

"Because she left it for me, in the guest bathroom. Along with the nail polish."

Rose observed the nails of Nana. " 'Savage Sunset,' " deduced Rose. "Like the lips. Blood red. Mmm. Have you been biting and clawing? Have you been *eating* someone?"

"I admit, I like to eat women."

"Poor, helpless, older women, all alone in their humble homes."

"And little girls in short red dresses."

"Oh, Nana, what big teeth you have."

"Forget about the teeth. Look at the tongue."

Rose lowered her eyes.

Nana, in her high black heels, now towered over her. Rose swayed toward Nana, pliant, almost confiding.

"Do you know, Nana, there's this bulge—just *there*. Yes, just where I have my hand. Are you pleased to see me?"

"Extremely pleased."

"Yes, you do seem pleased."

Rose slipped her hands around Nana's buttocks and massaged them and pulled them inward. She rubbed against the mysterious bulge in Nana's satin groin, back and forth, back and forth.

Nana tilted back her head and closed her eyes.

Nana was feeling very near the edge again.

It had started as she shaved herself and creamed herself, and it got more and more as she dressed in the cool shivery silk and it slithered and shivered all over her, and kept on slithering and shivering and slithering, teasing at her, and then the warm, tactile silicone padding of the brassière rubbed on her nipples, her male nipples, which were the nipples of none other—what a shock!—than Wolf. And by the time the stockings were hooked to the garter belt, it was with enormous—enormous being the absolutely right word—difficulty that Wolf packed his rampant and colossally aroused penis into the satin and lace modesty pouch.

"If you keep on at that, Rose, I'm not going to be able to hold on to myself—"

Rose shook her head with surprise, and ran her arms all up him, all up Nana, and lifting herself up his body, by some magical acrobatic feat, somehow lifted up Nana's skirt as she came, and wriggled down the pouch, so out popped the gigantic rearing waving almost howling snake, red-hot to bursting. And supporting herself on his shoulders, while Wolf-Nana held her up by his hands cupping the smooth round little curves of her bottom, Rose sank on to the snake, absorbed it deep within her divine recesses, and so began to dance.

"Oh, Nana—how big—how *big*—"

Wolf pushed hard against and into her. He must think of other things. Not silk, not being danced upon. Not her wonderful enfolding vagina, that had him now as if it would never let him out. And not—*decidedly* not—about the white breasts rising up now from the neck of the dress, blinking their two adorable shy pink eyes at him, going in again, creeping up again, *appearing*, vanishing, and creeping up—

Think about the wood.

Think about the city.

Think about the stars.

But the wood is all thick and twinkling with white, half-naked young women, their breasts playing hide-and-seek, their naked bottoms filling the hands, and their legs wrapped tight around the waist where the corset is, and the silk, and the brassière above, tweaking him innocently so two ravenous little stars ignite there, and Rose is throwing back her head, her neck is arched, her breasts rise like two moons, first with a faint flush, and then with her nipples all bare and upright, and he is going to, again—going to—

Think of the moon.

The moon is a *breast*.

Think of—think—of—the subway—

A tunnel, lined with wet eager velvet—*clinging, surging*—the train is—*coming*—

Think—

"Oh, Wolf—*faster*—"

He is on the couch—did they fall?—and she is on top of

him, and he is thrusting and thrusting her home upon him, with his hands on her bottom, and her dress is just a red rope around her middle, and her breasts tickle his lips, and he is nuzzling them, and now she is gasping, and now giving a little sound nearly like the start of the first word of a sentence—Oh, come, Rose, come, oh, come into the garden, Maud—oh, Rose, Rose, come before it's too late—

And then she comes.

She makes a noise like laughter, and she shudders all over, again and again, and he sees her, shuddering, laughing in ecstasy, her breasts and her hair, and he rushes her body up and down the length of him, and tingles and rills and impossible yawns of unbelievable pleasure tumble up his spine and across his blood and through his penis, until he detonates, in what must be the fireworks display of the century, but, alas, all invisible inside her.

In the early morning light, punctual as a clock, after her six or seven hours, Ryder wakes up and joins Rose and Wolf-Nana, and they shower together and eat a small but healthy—and nourishing—breakfast, and go back to bed, which is Ryder's bed, all lambent with her scent and the size of Central Park. And here, the two women praise all Wolf-Nana's virtues, which are many, and play games all over him, until in the end, in a knot of limbs and hair and laughs and shudders and spasms and shrieks, they are coming together, and coming apart, and coming and coming and coming.

And perhaps, being so well-suited as they are, at the top of that cliff in the city wood, they *will* live happily ever after.

Ashes on Her Lips

Edward Bryant

Here is what happened so many times later on.

Naked and sweaty, chest thick with curled dark hair, muscles taut and finely delineated, he whirled her across the bedroom. It was the season of heat, and this was an old, old dance. Nicky or Carl, Tad or Paulie, whatever his name was, the man was a late spring blossom of color and passion, testosterone and promise.

"Here," Chiara said. "Right here." She felt almost unable to speak. His superheated breath brushed aside the hair on the back of her neck.

"Not the bed?"

"Not yet," she answered. "Soon. For now, right here." She gripped the edge of the smooth cherrywood vanity with tight fingers, the tips already tempted to slide with sweat. She felt his arousal as hotly, tightly, vividly as she registered her own.

Then Chiara reminded herself to tell him what she truly wanted.

"Use the box," she said, voice low, breath ragged. "Now. Like I told you."

He reached past her right shoulder and opened the container. He clumsily extracted a substantial pinch of the iridescent gray powder inside and lifted it to her waiting mouth. Her lips and tongue took it smoothly off his hand.

Chiara turned sinuously, dropped to her knees facing him, and took a fair length of him into her mouth. She imagined she could feel him absorbing the heat of pliant lips, the insistent wrap of her tongue, the slickness and slightly abrasive texture as she anointed his hard penis with the mixture of saliva and grit.

On her feet again now, she turned back to the vanity, her eyes meeting his in the beveled mirror.

"Do it now," she said. "No more waiting."

Using strong fingers to spread her, he slid up high and taut inside.

"It feels—"

She ignored his words and flexed tight around him.

"You feel—"

She reached down with one burning hand and cupped his balls.

He finally found the word he apparently groped for. "—fine!" he said, slamming up against her. He hesitated for just an instant, resting, before sliding back into the aggressive, escalating rhythm she knew he would generate.

"Don't stop," she said. "Do it, baby. Just do it."

He did—for as long as she wanted.

After a time they were both so slick with the heat, it was hard to stay inside her.

She found another way to squeeze, and that was enough to trigger the explosive pyre that consumed them both.

Later he said, as they all did, "When can I see you again?"

Chiara hated that question, because she already knew the answer.

Once upon a time, in a life far away, there was a woman and a man who loved each other, and there was the gargoyle box. It had been a gift to him from a mutual friend named Todd— the girl with a boy's name, Chiara called her—the woman whose gifts had always seemed to arrive at a time appropriate to change the recipient's life. "Or at the very least,"

Chiara's lover once said, "to give me a fucking clue."

The gargoyle box had originally come from an obscure gift shop at Disney World, but neither held that circumstance against it. When Chiara had first spied the box on his desk, she had coveted it with all her being. But the present was his.

Later, when the bone disease had begun to crumble him away from the inside, he had hung on to the box, even though, in the potlatch phase of his decline, he gave away most of his clothes, the books, the music, the art, all the rest of what he termed the "really neat things" he had accumulated over a lifetime.

The gargoyle box crouched in its accustomed position on the external drive beside the computer monitor. The box itself was rectilinear, carved from some variety of smooth gray-greenish stone, a mineral bearing a most unusual patina.

"It feels like flesh." Chiara had marveled when she first ran her fingertips along the carved patterns inlaid within the sides. "Flesh that's hard." She couldn't help but laugh at his smile when she said those words.

He took them both, gargoyle box and woman, into the bedroom.

"I'll show you flesh that's hard," he said, curling powerful hands around her upper arms and drawing her slowly and deliberately toward his own body. Just before her breasts would have touched his chest, he dipped his head and touched first the right nipple, then the left, with the tongue Chiara always felt was itself a highly tumescent organ.

She knew what he was going to do. She still gasped, let her arms pivot together from the elbows, brought her hands down so her strong fingers could wrap around the inches of hard flesh she sometimes joked about as *his tongue gone south*. When she'd first told him that, he had cocked one eye and said, "Should I then imagine you referring to my tongue as *my penis gone north*?"

"Whatever," Chiara said. "I was never very good with directions."

They both laughed. Then their collective breath quickened. It always did.

But after this one time, as both of them lay across the bed, skin sheened with salt and heat, limbs akimbo and plaited, passions still humming like a dynamo switched into standby mode, he said, "Just don't let any of this ever go west."

Chiara drew back her head slightly so she could look at his eyes and made a small sound of curiosity. Somehow his voice had sounded both resigned and wistful.

"Going west," he said, "that mythic thing."

"Oh," said Chiara. "Right. Like dying."

"Yes, a *lot* like dying."

The box itself. It resembled an ancient and elaborate sarcophagus covered with erotic carvings in relief. It was not obvious, nothing like the crassly amusing coffee mugs covered with giraffes copulating, or alligators wound into complex arabesques of reptilian sexuality. When eyes beheld the gargoyle box, they followed, for a while, the sinuous lines as the human sense for patterning gradually turned shapes into limbs, the limbs into linked bodies.

But, as he pointed out to Chiara, the linked bodies never quite slipped into stereotypical form. Sexual images? Well . . . maybe. Sensual? Indisputably. Pornographic? Perhaps . . . with imaginative leaps.

"Use *intuitive* leaps," he said one night, holding the box up against the diffused light from the Tiffany torchier.

"Evel Knievel leaps?" She teased him, nestling close behind, rubbing, stroking, trailing her fingertips down his chest.

"You don't have to span a canyon," he said, laughing. "Just that old chasm of disbelief."

Chiara was silent for a few moments. "Don't leave me," she said.

He did not laugh at all. "Why are you saying that?"

She didn't answer for a much longer time. Finally she picked careful words. "You used to tell me everything about doctor's appointments. It was a pain." Chiara hesitated. "Now you tell me almost nothing, or else when you do, I feel like I'm getting a completely laundered version. That's far more excruciating."

He set the gargoyle box on the bed table and shoved it to the edge of the lamplight. "I'm sorry," he said, and she could hear the regret in his voice that said he was telling the absolutely literal truth. "I haven't been altogether forthcoming."

"Be that now." She cupped his face with her fingers, leaned toward him intensely, gazed into his eyes. They were lighter than hers. In this diffused light, they looked almost green. The light always changed them; sometimes green, sometimes brown, other times hazel. She said he had the eyes of a chameleon. Or a shapeshifter.

"All right," he said. He did something he rarely did before launching words at her. He took a deep, deep breath.

Later, she cried herself to sleep.

What perched *on* the gargoyle box was not the standard, garden-variety dog-faced boy with wings, as he sometimes described other gargoyle art. This gargoyle was feline, with a lithe, muscular body crouched atop the lid in an aggressively watchful attitude. The reptilian wings spread at precisely the appropriate angle to provide the perfect handle for grasping and lifting the lid.

Winged and fanged, the cat looked the part of the fearsome guardian.

"No vermin will come close," her lover said. "No bugs need apply." He laughed. "No mice, no rats, no takers to confront such a creature. She's one fierce beastie. They're all afraid."

"I hope so." Chiara shook her head and let her fingers wander over the obscure curves of the seductive stone. "This one—" She felt she could almost prick fingertips on the creature's teeth. "She's only interested in bigger game."

He nodded seriously. "It's tough to outmatch a gargoyle. That's why they've got the guardian job."

Chiara nodded slowly, with gravity. "Can she protect us both?"

"Up to a point, I expect." He shook his head with sudden violence as though coming abruptly awake from a reverie. "Hey, what do I really know about gargoyle specs?"

"You convinced me." She let her lips mold to the curve of a high cheekbone.

Time passed, seconds ticked off loudly by the tail-switching black Felix wall clock.

"What point?" Chiara said.

"What point what?" He blinked and drew a little away from her. He had been staring raptly into the cat gargoyle's hard eyes.

"The point when she won't protect us anymore."

"*Can't* protect us," he said. "It'll come as a surprise. We'll know the time."

Chiara leaned close and tight into one sheltering shoulder. Her hair, abundant and silky when she untied it, tickled his nose. Close up, he focused on the vein of startling silver that only emphasized the sheer ebony remainder.

Unbidden, his hands rose, strong fingers caressing and barely discernibly tightening around her throat, generating a band of intense heat around her.

She shuddered—but not with fear.

"I'm not the expert," he demurred. "I've just read a little about this."

"Then who is?"

He hesitated. "It's going to sound pretentious, but experience is the master."

"We've taken care of each other for a while now," she said. "Bad times, lots of good times, times when I didn't know what to think of you."

"You too," he said. "Tears and laughter, all of it." He reached out to touch her hair. "We never abandoned each other."

"We never will." She realized it sounded more like a question than an affirmation. "Will we?"

"Never," he said. "I'll never willingly leave you."

Chiara said nothing more for a while, using action as a substitute. His words made her wetter than the late humid August. Nothing would stop her. Not tonight. She took him then, there in the office.

It was her time to practice mastery, sitting astride him and controlling everything: depth, angle, frequency.

Chiara raised herself just enough, almost too far, so she nearly lost him. His tip brushed those hot slick lips like a lover's lazy touch across her mouth. Illness, she reflected, had little diminished his reaction to her body.

He moaned.

"Shhh," she said.

But she herself screamed when he bucked his hips up as she descended firmly around him.

The gargoyle watched them like a feral sentinel, a wild creature only marginally more benign than its human masters.

The cat gargoyle became their constant nocturnal companion. Chiara had the odd feeling the creature was almost sufficient to constitute the third party in an exotic *menage à trois*. Her lover laughed at that.

One night he said, "So. What should I keep in the box?"

Her gaze flickered like the firelight. She spoke boldly. "In the pussy box?"

He laughed with delight. "The gargoyle box."

"That's what I was thinking of."

"Liar," he said.

Chiara nodded. "Prick," she answered, grinning.

"Exactly." He considered things for a moment. "It's too big for paper clips."

"And it's too wet. They'd rust."

"Elevate your mind."

"I'll elevate *something*," she said.

"The gargoyle box—" he gamely persisted.

"It's big," she agreed. "It'd hold a quart at least."

"What comes in quarts in a home office?" he said, sounding puzzled.

"Not *what*," Chiara said. "*Who*."

"There are times," he said, "when I think the name *Chiara* surely derives in a truly loose sense from the word *incorrigible*."

"And you love that."

They stopped discussing the gargoyle box. Their mutual attention sidled into a whole new climatic zone.

"I know *who* I love."

They both did.

"I haven't been with you nearly enough," Chiara said.

"Nor I with you." The words glowed like coals.

They flickered.

"Just for a while longer . . ." Her words sounded forlorn, and that was the last time they did so.

They made love with the passion and heat of cats mating. But it was not a quick thing. Their voices were without human words, crying out, rising and falling like feline screams until exhausted silence fell.

The echoes persisted stubbornly.

She slipped away when he left.

That's far too circumspect. More precisely, she ran when he died.

When she came back, she discovered he'd left a note, weighted beneath one corner of the gargoyle box.

"It's not the idea of dying I mind," he had said on more than one occasion. "I just don't want to be there when it happens."

Neither did she.

Chiara returned to the house and hesitated outside, watching all the lights in the first floor blazing. The upper story was dark. A paramedic gave her a note that had been left for her on the bed table.

It read: "I stole the line about dying and being there from Woody Allen. Give credit where credit's due. But I hope you'll give me credit too, sweetie. I love you."

It was unsigned. It did not require his name.

"I love you too, darlin'." Chiara cried for a long, long time.

And for a far longer time, it seemed to her, she lived by herself in the empty house with the gargoyle box. She moved it to the table by the bed. She went to sleep staring at the cat creature.

Nights fell around her, silent and cold.

There was no funeral and no burial. She permitted neither.

Then came the morning when the telephone rang. She ignored it. Ten minutes later, when it rang again, Chiara didn't answer. She covered her ears with the pillow as the answering machine picked up the message.

Two hours later, the lawyer showed up at the door.

He kept his well-manicured index finger pressed to the bell until she answered.

All the while, the stone box kept silent company with her.

When what now remained of her lover was returned to Chiara, it reminded her of Chinese takeout. At least that's what the white shiny-stock cardboard box resembled.

She unfolded the lid and contemplated the contents. When she stirred with one tentative and delicate forefinger, she discovered the bits of bone.

Chiara withdrew her finger and stared at the dusty patina that filled in the whorls of her fingertip. The rose glow of the Tiffany lent everything a sensual radiance.

The time seemed appropriate, so she talked to him.

Chiara talked far into the evening.

Eventually—and not to her great surprise—he answered.

I guess we ought to discuss our relationship, he said.

She smiled. "I always thought it was forged in heaven."

Even now?

"We fought sometimes," she said. "We had misunder-standings. A few times we hurt each other. But we learned to talk it out. Each of us cared enough to work for what we wanted."

I miss you, he said.

She didn't have to say anything. It was in her sudden tears. "Can we stay together a little longer?" she said.

I think so, the equivalent of his voice said, sounding wistful. There's a way.

"I'd like that," she said. "Tell me."

Then . . . , he began to whisper, you know what you need to do.

Yes, she did, but she had to think about it a while longer, denying herself food, drink, sleep. But she was a quick study. She required only a brief parching stint in the wilderness of her own soul to reach a conclusion.

Yes, she knew what she had to do.

And more, she *wanted* to do it.

She bought smooth stones, alleged to be, if not outright magical, at least highly spiritual, from a Boulder, Colorado, woman named Chalice. The surface of the stones was veined with a blue mineral.

Chiara used the stones to grind the bone fragments from the take-out box into a fine powder. Then she sat at the kitchen table under a bright light, her largest facial mirror set out on the checked cloth. She used the spare sharp X-Acto blades from the tool drawer to divide the powder into a finer dust. Some dispersed into the air with the quick, birdlike motions she employed.

She thought the cloud particles looked shiny, almost glowing in the light from the overhead.

"*So* beautiful," Chiara murmured. She knew who that really described.

Some of the dust settled on her lips. She flicked with the moist tip of her tongue. The ashy residue tasted—she wasn't sure at first—a little of salt, with a hint of something much richer.

Chiara licked her lips again, eager now.

She abruptly saw herself as if from another's eyes, toiling in dirty work clothes with the sharp blades, the mirror, the powdered remains. Chiara laughed at the image and offered a silent half-serious prayer that the police were not somehow watching.

This would be a tough one to explain.

She finished powdering the bone and mixed it back into the contents of the box. Then she put away the smooth stones. Chiara realized she was humming, and her lips curved around the companion lyrics:

"Fee, fie, foe, fum . . ."

Tonight she did not feel alone.

Not one bit.

The gargoyle box bided time patiently, watching over Chiara and the men she chose.

Rick or Roddy, Steve or Lance, whatever his name was, his body was younger than hers. She thought about that briefly, a little regretfully, and then put it out of her mind. Rick or Roddy had been a tennis pro. Steve or Lance worked out well and regularly. His muscles were toned, the definition as clearly delineated as a USGS topo map.

Good territory, she thought.

Chiara surveyed him from where she lay back on the Olmec print comforter. He was ready, clearly so. She watched and appreciated the rigid jut, the involuntary quiver of anticipation.

He smiled down at her and settled himself on the bed. He reached to part her legs and she was instantly rolling onto her side, and then to hands and knees.

"No," she said. "Not for a minute yet. Remember? Indulge me."

"Right," said Rick or Roddy. Slowly, knowing she watched avidly, he raised one hand to his mouth, then licked the inside of his beefy fingers. He used that hand to reach for the gargoyle box on the bed table. He carefully lifted the lid and set it aside.

Fingers dipped lightly into the powder inside. He transferred that dusting first to the head, then the shaft of his penis.

"Enough?" His voice was hoarse as he started to pump with his hand the length of his shaft. "This is kind of strange."

"But you like it," Chiara said.

He looked doubtful at first, but then nodded. "Yeah, I like it."

"Then it's enough." Chiara moved her head, eyes fixed on his, knowing she was all *too* ready now. Waiting any longer was totally out of the question. "Come here," she said.

He didn't have to part her legs now. She did that well and smoothly on her own, feeling the air on moist flesh as knees, thighs, vaginal lips divided at her own urging.

The man descended into her as she arched to meet him.

He moaned. "Oh, Christ, so goddamned deep . . ."

"You can go deeper," she said. "I want that. I can take you deeper." Fingers digging hard into the corded muscles in his rear, she pulled him into her.

"That powder," he said. "It's like goddamned Spanish fly. It's not helping my self control."

"Don't worry, baby," she said. "It doesn't have to. I came as soon as you entered me. You'll make me come again before we're done."

He said nothing, just uttered eloquent, inarticulate sounds as he slammed into her again and again.

"That's it," she said, "harder, baby."

"Now!" he said. "Now, now, now, *now*!" Heat shot into her, sleeted through her. She thought she felt sexual exit wounds glowing with radiation like a nuclear test site.

After a while, she turned back into the shelter of his arms and said, "That was wonderful. I loved it."

"Me too." The man seemed to hesitate before speaking again. He toyed with her breasts, bringing the nipples erect as small stones. "Chiara, you think maybe we'll ever get, well, really serious?"

"You want to?" she said.

He slowly nodded. "I gotta admit, I've never been with a woman like you."

"You're very sweet." In the half-light, she thought she could see him blush.

"I mean it," he said.

She nodded sleepily and kissed him on the lips.

Really serious? she thought.

Chiara knew she would leave him in the morning, or the morning after. She would never see him again.

Night followed night, month after month, man after man, the Rickies, the Robbies, the Randies. The gargoyle box made them all momentary possibilities.

But the store of powdered desire was depleted. The night Chiara had dreaded eventually arrived.

She sat crosslegged on the bed in the room that had given her so much solace, the implements of that comfort spread out around her. Chiara gazed down into the emptiness that now mostly filled the open box.

She rested her palm lightly on the cool, sharp-veined stone wings of the creature on the lid.

The voice whose source she could never quite see whispered close to her ear: Love, I think it's finally time.

She slowly nodded. "I was never unfaithful," she said fiercely. "I've loved only you."

I know. But we're both on courses that no longer cross.

She wet her finger with her tongue and lowered it into the box, picking up the final vestige of powder.

I'll miss you very much, he said.

She tried to smile. "I'll miss you too."

Silence stretched, bent, flexed in its supple way.

What will you do? he said.

Chiara dipped the tip of her tongue, caught the last bit of ash. "Have you no faith in me?"

I have every faith, he finally answered. But I'm still a little jealous.

I am too. She didn't say that aloud.

What will you do?

When she spoke, her eyes were as wet as the rest of her had become. What will I do? she thought.

The taste was bitter and salt, sour and sweet on her tongue. It brought back everything. She had to swallow before she could speak.

"Well, darlin'," she said. "I guess I'll just have to fall in love again."

The pain stung there, sharp and sudden as a blade; then it was gone.

And so was he.

Mirrors

Garry Kilworth

He found himself in an exotic city, in an oriental country, but was not quite sure which city or which country. Having taken the sleeping pill, he had been bemused when awakened from a deep pool of sleep to be told the plane had developed engine trouble and they had to make an emergency landing. The airline had driven the passengers from the airport to a hotel, where a room had been provided. It was the Hilton. One might be in a Hilton in Bangkok, New York, or Amsterdam: They all had similar interior plans, similar decor. The hotel was no indication of where he was. Nor was the staff, who simply looked *oriental*. They might have been Korean, or Thai, or Vietnamese: Walt was no great traveler and could not separate these nationalities from one another. In an American city he had once mistaken a Filipino maid for Chinese.

So, here he was, wandering streets encrusted with neon lights—red, blue, pink, opal—each sign like pouting lips begging him to enter the establishments they advertised. There were bars, night clubs, nude theaters, dancing palaces, houses of erotic fantasy . . . his mind had stopped on that one, fixed on it. Houses of erotic fantasy! This was a new one on him. At first he had decided he would not go inside one, but simply think about it further in a bar. But sidestreets and backstreets and a long narrow alley had led him to one of these houses of fantasy which unlike the others seemed to be trying to hide itself, down below the street. The sign bidding him to enter was level with his knees and the steps under the sign led down to a basement.

Should he go inside? Did he have time before the aircraft was repaired? Sure, he had the whole night. Perhaps all of next day too! He was lost anyway. It would be necessary to call a cab to get back to the hotel. There was no way he could find it himself. Especially not in the dark.

He descended.

"How much?" he asked the man standing at the open door. "How much for an erotic fantasy?"

"What one?" came back the reply. "Ordinary, Special or Extra-special?"

"Will traveler's checks do? American dollars?"

The man smiled. "Of course."

"Then I want the best."

"Extra-special—four hundred dollar."

"Four hundred?" cried Walt.

The man laid a slim-fingered hand on Walt's sleeve and moved conspiratorially closer, as if about to reveal a sacred trust.

"Listen, mister—you never have something like this again. Four hundred very cheap for this. She very beautiful woman. What happen if you say no? You go home. You sit in chair by fire and make regrets. You tell yourself you would pay *one thousand dollar* for chance like this again."

He let these words sink in, then he added, "Maybe you just want Ordinary or Special—but not so good. I tell you mister, you not want your autumn years to be filled with sadness. Extra-special is best of best."

Walt knew his own true nature. He knew his own weaknesses. In the past he had bought toys for more than four hundred. That mountain bicycle for a start. That had cost him five-fifty and he hardly ever used it. The chance of an experience like this did not come twice in a lifetime. He really had no choice.

"I'll take the Extra-special."

The man was effusive.

"You make good choice. This wonderful adventure. Very fantasy. *Very erotic.*" The man did a little shimmy with his hips and smiled one of those enigmatic smiles that only Orientals can seem to produce. "I guarantee you never have nothing like this before in your life. You not forget this night for a thousand years."

"I should live so long," replied Walt, dryly.

Walt had never been with an oriental woman. In truth he had not had sex for quite a time, not since his marriage to Jody had broken up a year ago. This would be quite a new experience for him. He believed he liked diminutive females. They appeared to be more submissive. That might not have been true, but it seemed so. Jody had not just been a muscular five-feet-eight. She had also been a work-out freak. When her arms gripped him around the back of his neck, and legs locked behind him, her heels driving him into her, he had felt as if he were in some kind of medieval vice, a fucking-machine built to pummel men's genitals to pulp. He had felt manacled. No need for handcuffs or leather straps: Jody had been a human bondage device all by herself!

He was led through narrow winding passageways, the walls lined with red-and-gold-flocked wallpaper, to a wooden door. The man turned and smiled as he produced a large iron key. The door was opened and Walt pressed gently inside.

"Woman come in a moment. She pretty. You like her."

"I'd better," said Walt, staring around him.

There was a musky perfume coming from somewhere. He discovered holes in the sides of the bed and guessed they were vents. The aroma was powerful and intoxicating, with some kind of an aphrodisiac quality. He felt himself being aroused. Walt had heard of certain foods and drinks doing that, but not a fragrance.

The room was weird by his standards.

He inspected the bed, which was large with black satin sheets.

Each side had a huge round red pillow with a hole for its center.

The headboard was carved with a painted rain forest scene. There was a red monkey motif following the oval shape of the bedhead: mischievous-looking creatures with round quizzical mouths, linking tails. Snakes slid in and out of stylized undergrowth. There were tigers in there somewhere, half in and half out of shadow. Magnolia trees stood leafless and bare, with dark-red cupola-shaped buds on the tips of their branches. Succulent pitcher plants, with deep mysterious recesses, grew from mossy banks. Vines entangled and wound their way throughout the whole scene, binding all the individual beasts and plants together. Incongruously, right in the center of the headboard there was a long railway train entering a deep tunnel.

When he studied the picture closer he could see death in there too.

There were the symbolic skulls, obvious to any culture. He noticed that these were arranged in casual piles with exactly four skulls to each heap. There were shapes of pale light which might have been severed hands scattered throughout the undergrowth of the jungle, secreted in pockets of dead leaves. White flowers and white feathers decorated the floor of the rain forest. Rib bones curling out of rotten logs were hung with hair-moss, dripping with a substance that might once have been human skin.

Necrophilia?

"We're having none of that sort of thing," he murmured to himself, half-jokingly. "She'd better be alive when she comes in here."

It was then he turned his attention again to the walls, floor, and ceiling.

It was all mirrors, mirrors everywhere: on floor, ceiling, and all four walls.

Reflections of the bed went into infinity in all directions. When he stepped further into the room, a thousand-thousand Walts went with him, like a curved line of soldiers. When he stood still, he was the hub of helicopter rotary blades made of Walts, which whirled gracefully away into light years beyond. It was while he was thus experimenting with the simulacra that he was aware of another presence. She suddenly appeared by his side in the mirrors, startling him.

"Did you just come in?" he said, looking at the closed door. "I didn't hear you enter."

"I am very quiet," she said, smiling.

She was an enchanting, delicate young woman whose very form and beauty took his breath away. He was not just astonished but shocked by her loveliness. He felt inferior to such a woman. She could not possibly want to stay in this room with a clumsy oaf like him. If she did, there must be something wrong with her, something hidden and perhaps vile.

"Are you—well?" he asked.

"Yes, thank you," she breathed, misunderstanding him. "I am perfectly well, thank you very much."

Her breath smelled of oranges and mint, as the words came out of her mouth like invisible bubbles. Suddenly, he did not care. She could be riddled with horrors for all he worried at that moment. He knew this was his one chance to have such a woman, for he would surely never get another. There were drums in his loins. Heavy metal music coursed through his thighs and belly. This was happening to *him*. Two hours ago he had been just another seedy passenger on a plane. Now he was a king with the most exquisite concubine in the land. He watched as she removed her scant clothes to reveal small breasts with brown tips, a smooth flat stomach with a neat dark triangle below it. Walt swallowed hard and began trembling.

"Shall I—shall I undress now?"

Once Walt had stripped himself, she took his clothes and put them in a box under the bed, as if they were tainted things. Then she lay beside him on the bed, where he was studying himself in the ceiling mirror, his erection somehow larger and more formidable in this looking glass.

Thousands of curved penises went sweeping away in a crescent, like a palisade of sharpened stakes on a medieval battlefield, ready to pierce the chargers of rash knights. Then her rosebud mouth was on his breast and he could feel the dry silkiness of her breast beneath his armpit. A lump came to his throat. He began to cry soft tears. He did not know why. They just came from somewhere deep inside and flowed down his cheeks. She licked the tears from his eyelashes, saying they were deliciously salty.

Then, when she reached for him down below, he felt her fingernails graze his abdomen.

"Ouch," he said, looking down.

"Sorry," she replied, smiling.

But he was astonished. He had not noticed before now, but her fingernails were about an inch long, and very sharp. Her hands were like those of a goddess from some dark jungle religion. If she wished she could pierce his skin with those claws. It was not a thought that rested lightly on his mind.

"Good God," he said. "Don't you ever cut those?"

"My people believe it is beautiful to have long nails," she explained in a disappointed voice. "You not like them?"

"I—well—they just look a little dangerous, that's all."

But then, looking down on her, he forgot about the nails.

They made love not just once, but three times in the next two hours. This was remarkable enough, since Walt was normally a once and then roll over and go to sleep man. But even after the third session he was still ready to go again. He guessed it had something to do with that smell of musk.

Then he found the gun.

He had thrust his hand under his pillow accidentally during a moment of passion to find a pearl-handled revolver there. He whipped it out to study it. It was an automatic, manufactured in Japan, an exact copy of one of the Colt .38 models. On checking it he found it loaded. A magazine of twenty-seven rounds. Having been a sergeant in the army, he knew how to use it. Its presence in the room gave him concern.

"What's it doing here?" he demanded to know. "Why?"

"Sometimes in the past we have had robbers," she explained. "It is for your own protection, in case we are attacked."

"Are we likely to be?" he questioned, alarmed, thinking of Chinese triads, or Burmese bandits, or even Indonesian pirates. He did not know where he was. It could be any of them. Perhaps even Cambodian rebels looking for hostages? "I don't like this—where are my clothes?"

Slim long-nailed hands restrained him, pressed against his hairy chest, forcing him back down on the bed with their sheer daintiness.

"You must not worry. It is all in the past."

"Are you positive?"

"Yes."

Her small buttocks somehow worked themselves underneath his hands. The gun was back under the pillow. He was fondling crevices again, finding his potency amazingly fresh. Never had such energy coursed through his body before this night. Jody would have at first been delighted, then not so delighted, then finally weary of him. He always suspected she pretended a high sex drive in order to humiliate him. He could have used this newly discovered potency to destroy her domination over him.

Where had it been when Jody was at her most demanding? It had not been her fault. It had not been his. It must have been the fault of the time and place. He should have thought of mirrors before. It was, after all, simply narcissism taken to extremes. It was fun to watch.

He found, after a while, that he enjoyed her mirror image better than the flesh and blood. If she was lovely in life, she was superlative in glass. They tried many different positions and he adored the reflections which tumbled away from him in all directions. Superb forms, equal to those produced by any sculptor he cared to name. Poetry in moving images. He preferred the silence to words or music. This was art. This was profound. This was the sport of angels . . .

"Hey!" Alarmed, he sat up quickly. "Did you see that?"

"What? What have you seen?"

He stared into the right hand wall. He could have sworn . . . but it was impossible. He was surely drugged by that heavy narcotic called *sex*.

"It doesn't matter," he said, resuming what he had been doing, what she had been doing to him. "I'm seeing things."

But then it happened again and he was sure this time.

"I did see it," he cried, pushing her away. "That—that . . ."

It was the hundredth, no, perhaps even further back than that, about the hundred-and-fiftieth reflection of himself and the girl. This distant set of reflections had been doing something different. Walt and the woman had actually been in one position, and this particular couple, out of the thousands before and after them, had been in another! Surely that *was* impossible. Unless there was some sort of flaw in the mirror. But wouldn't that affect all the images? He tried to decide whether it worried him or whether he was merely intrigued by this strange phenomenon. Eventually he decided on the latter. Maybe it was because he was sated. Overload? His mind was playing tricks on his eyes. Yes, he was seeing things. It might be interesting to go with it, allow himself to be swept along with the illusion.

He lay back again and she eased herself on top of him.

Walt's eyes scanned the mirrors, watching for the one rebel image to appear. All around him were couples locked in the shape of a reversed T. Wait! Yes, there. One pair on the far wall, way back down the line, had flipped over with the man now on top. Walt stared in fresh amazement as this movement fanned out from this single couple. Forward down the line the images began riffling, running down toward him like a row of dominoes. Flip, flip, flip. It was a fantastic sight. He had seen computer images do this, but these were simply mirrors. Then the line reached him and his consort.

He suddenly felt himself being flipped over. Their sexual roles were instantly reversed. He was now on top of her.

At the same time as this physical miracle took place he had an orgasm that was like a massive jolt of electricity rushing through his loins.

"Jesus!" he yelled. "Arrrggghhhh! Christ!"

The sweat poured from his naked body. He had never felt anything like this before, not even his first time over that gravestone at the back of St. Peter's church. His head ached from the absolute pure passion of the moment. Semen gushed from him in a torrent. And yet afterward he did not feel drained of desire. There was still a river of raw lust rushing through him. Her hands were all over him still, rousing him again, bringing him to a new and superhuman state of sexual excitement.

"Again!" he cried. "Let's do it again. Did you feel it too? You must have felt it. I heard you yell. You loved it, didn't you? Christ I feel randy. I'm ready for half-a-dozen of those. I bet it's better than any drug. What do you say—let's go for another one, eh?"

She smiled at him with small even teeth. Then she worked her contortions to form the two of them into a new interlocking puzzle. Her body was fantastic. Walt thought she must have bones of rubber the way she was able to arch her back, put her legs under her own arms, bend her waist that way. Eagerly he stared into the mirrors around him, searching for that one set which would herald an unbelievable orgasm.

Yes, there it was, on the ceiling.

"Here it comes," he yelled in excitement. "Here it co . . . aaarrrrhhgggg—oh, GOD, GOD, GOD, GOD . . ."

The small three-letter word was appropriate. He was having the orgasms of a young god. The world was not just moving. It was spinning at ten times its normal speed, hurtling through space a thousand times faster than usual. He held her small naked body to his as if they could fuse together, meld, merge. She let out a high tinkling laugh. Incredibly she was enjoying it as much as he was. Oh, he knew that hookers faked it all the time, that they were good at making the right noises at the right moment, but he could *tell* she was luxuriating in it—not wildly like himself, but sensitively. It was as if she were enjoying a glass of fine champagne in a hot bubble bath.

"Again?" she said, laughing.

Thrice more they were manipulated by the couples in the mirrors and each time it got better and better. Finally Walt did not think he could stand another one and he suggested they have a cigarette. He went to the box under the bed and found his packet of Camels. He lit one, but she refused, with a little shake of her head. Walt shrugged and lay back on the bed, puffing away contentedly. Four hundred dollars? Christ, this had been worth a million. Fantastic experience. Jody would have been proud of him. Or perhaps not? Maybe she would be jealous. That thought was very pleasing to him, since he was the one who had been dumped.

He lay there in a state of bliss, studying a thousand-thousand Walts with lit cigarettes, all in equal states of bliss. He arced his red-ended cigarette through the air, made designs as might a child with a sparkler. The Walts all copied him, faithfully, their lit cigarettes tracing figures of eights, centripetals, and other pretty shapes.

Beside the Walts lay the beautiful oriental women, resting like lilies on black satin sheets. Their arms were by their sides, limp and lovely. Their mouths slightly open, revealing a hint of white teeth between the cupid's-bow lips, their eyes closed.

Suddenly, as he stared, there was a tiny movement amongst one of the images down the curving line. The stirring of a butterfly. The flutter of a moth.

What *now*? He frowned. He was enjoying his cigarette.

A search of the couples revealed nothing at first and then he saw her, way, way back down the long sweep of oriental beauties.

She had opened her eyes.

He glanced quickly at the real woman beside him, to see that her own eyes were still tightly closed. He looked back at the woman in the distance. So, this one was staring out at him from her place in the line, way out in space somewhere. So what?

Then he saw that the Walt beside her was unaware of her changed state. That should not be, for he—the *real* Walt— was certainly aware.

The next move made Walt start with horror. The distant female image had used those long sharp fingernails at the end of a flattened palm. Her hand was like a knife with a serrated blade. In one swift movement she had slit the throat of the man beside her. Blood spurted up in a fountain, dousing the cigarette. The reflection of Walt made a motion as if gargling and pressed his hands to the gaping wound. To no avail. The blood gushed between his fingers, splashing on the black satin sheets.

And her face was twisted in an ugly triumph, as if she had just performed a great duty for herself. She stared out gleefully at the real Walt. It was horrible to witness the savage joy in her expression. It was as if she hated him with a primitive passion, a loathing nursed by ten thousand years of servitude.

He watched horrified as his dying image, deep inside the mirrors, reached out wildly with blood-blinded eyes, seeking a hold on his murderess, only to find its fingers groping between her open legs, scrabbling for a grip on the sparse hair of her vagina. Desperate fumblings, unable to get a hold on that elusive female center. It was her magnet, yet now she used it to repel what she had once attracted. His hand fell back, clawed at his terrible wound, which opened like a second mouth crying for pity.

She threw back her head and silently laughed.

All this happened within the tiniest fraction of a second.

Then, inevitably, all along the line the women began slitting the throats of the unsuspecting Walts, one after another, slash, slash, slash, slash, slash, with the same reactions, the same twist of the female features. The blood and gore rushed down toward him like a swiftly burning fuse. In that instant he knew he was going to die. When the line of murders reached the end, the nearest reflections, the woman beside him would wake and then slit his throat with her scissor-sharp claws.

Down the line came that sweep of slashing hands on the end of white arms, like a sea wave surging down a long curved bay.

"NO!" he screamed.

Instead, he reached under his own pillow and found the automatic pistol. In the next moment, before the line of arms reached his bed, he shot the woman beside him twice in the chest. She did not even open her eyes. There was the faintest of grunts and then she flopped over the edge of the bed, to strike the glass floor with the sound of a dead fish hitting a slab of marble.

Walt sat there trembling, the gun still gripped tightly in his fist. At any moment he expected the door to be flung open. There would be oriental men wielding meat cleavers tumbling into the room. They would see the dead body and set about him, hacking him to pieces, leaving him bleeding from a thousand cuts. In his mind he could feel the cold bite of the choppers and butcher's knives now, biting into his vulnerable flesh. Bile rose to his mouth, as the terror of a horrible death washed through his stomach.

He had twenty-five rounds left in the automatic. He

waited in abject misery, wondering how he had got into this mess, and how he would ever get out of it.

No one came.

He waited for at least ten minutes, before breaking down and sobbing, burying his face in one of the pillows.

Then he suddenly got angry. Red, misty rage swamped his brain. He sat up quickly. What the hell was all this? They had set him up, somehow. He was a patsy. They had used him to murder a woman whose name he did not know. What would he say to the police? The whole story was so fantastic the cops would laugh at him. Yet it was possible, with modern technology, to arrange something like this. The mirrors could be screens, displaying pictures they picked up through hidden cameras. Once the computers behind the screens had the images, they could do what they liked with them. All right, he had experienced unbelievable orgasms, but those could have been drug-induced, using that fragrance which pervaded the room at all times.

He stared again at the terrible mirrors and another thought came to him.

Maybe it was more devious still!

He remembered they could often hide prying eyes behind them. He finally saw through their whole filthy deviant scheme now. There was an audience behind those mirrors, paying to watch him make love to, then murder a young woman. Voyeurs of sex and death. The owners were using him to supply their jaded customers, those men who had seen and done everything, with a new excitement, a new experience. He imagined drooling customers watching openmouthed as he and the woman frolicked on the bed, cried out in ecstasy, desire overflowing. Then the spectacle of the murder, the weapon blasting, the bullets striking flesh, the fear on the face of the murderer, the subsequent show of remorse. They probably loved every twisted minute of it: their voyeurism satiated with visions of fornication and blood.

Well, this was Walt Jones they were dealing with, not some namby-pamby from the suburbs of Suckerville. He was not going to lie down for this kind of deception. He was going to make them pay in more than money.

"You bastards!" he shrieked. "You bloody bastards!"

He began firing then, at random, the bullets shattering the mirrors all around him, above him. Walt imagined the terrified audience behind those mirrors, running for their lives as he pumped rounds into the walls and ceiling. He felt a barbarous achievement as the mirrors crashed all around him, the shards falling on his bed, slicing and piercing his naked body. It was raining glass and he did not care whether one of those dagger-sharp shards pierced his heart or not. He felt he really deserved to die with the woman. Those monsters had forced on him the role of executioner for their own anomalous cravings and he had failed to see how they were manipulating him.

Finally, he was out of ammunition, the mirrors all broken.

He shook his head. Fragments like diamonds fell from his hair. Bits of mirror lay all around him, reflecting parts of him: an eye, a tooth, a foot. Debris of his lust, his hunger for secret pockets of flesh. He wondered what made a man risk all to simply merge with woman for a few moments of high pleasure. How deep-seated was the desire to perform the futile act of procreation simply for itself?

Blood seeped from his wounds, staining the bedsheets. He leaned over to look at the body of the woman. There was a need to know she had not been mutilated. Some subconscious impulse to make sure her previously unblemished form had not been further disfigured by the falling segments of mirror, some of them shaped like scimitars.

She was gone. Her corpse was gone. The space on the floor where she should have lain was simply covered in splinters of glass.

Looking around him at the walls and up at the ceiling, he

could see no evidence of hidden recesses from which people might have viewed.

"What?" cried Walt, distressed. "What is this?"

Frantically he began searching through the shards, thinking the woman's body might be underneath. As he moved the broken slices of mirror around he discovered parts of her shattered image still captured in the glass. Sobbing hysterically, he began to piece her together again, like a puzzle—a pretty brow here, a small breast there, a piece of thigh—and gradually he began to reform her. She was cracked of course, a flawed image, but she remained just as beautiful under the faults and fissures.

Once he had her complete face, she opened her eyes, looked out at him, and smiled a sweet smile.

"Oh, God!" cried Walt. "You're still alive in there."

At that moment the door began to open. A high wind suddenly rose from nowhere. Glass began swirling, whirling around the room in a blinding blizzard. Faster and faster flew the shards, until it was as if he were in the vortex of some mighty storm, whose snowflakes were deadly slivers of obsidian. He put his arms around his head to protect himself from the hurricane, but the blast around him did not touch. It showered debris against the bare walls and ceiling. As the fragments flew into the walls and ceiling, they refitted like a self-making jigsaw, until finally the wind died and the mirrors were all back in place, with not a crack to be seen.

"Christ help me," moaned Walt.

Gradually he unfolded his arms, uncurled himself from the fetal position. Looking down he saw that his earlier wounds had miraculously healed, that there were no cuts or abrasions. It was as if he had never been lacerated in the first place by the falling glass. He was clean in every part.

An oriental man walked in, smiling. The same man Walt had met earlier. He had a drink in his hand. Giving it to Walt he looked around him and his grin grew broader. He shook his head, looking about him.

"All over so soon? You finish quick. You want to go again? Only two hundred dollars this time. Extra-extra-special. Only two hundred. You want?"

Walt whimpered and hugged his knees to his chest.

Midnight Express

Michael Swanwick

Excuse me. This can't be right.

Yes?

According to this schedule, we arrive at Elf Hill Station at 8:23 P.M. and after a half-hour layover, the train departs exactly two hundred years later.

Quite right.

But that can't be!

Is this your first time on this route?

Yes, my company is expanding into new markets. I'm a commercial traveler. I used to cover Indiana and Illinois.

Well, that explains it. I take it this is your first visit to Faerie? No previous travel experience in the Noncontiguous Territories—Grammarie, Brocielande, Arcadia, et cetera?

Well . . . no, but I've done a lot of traveling, and I've got an excellent record. I won the Daniel L. Houseman Sales Cup three years running.

Most impressive. An obviously intelligent man such as yourself, then, should have no trouble comprehending the chronologically liberated nature of the *night lands*, as we like to call them.

I beg your pardon. Chronologically liberated?

That's what I said. You'll have noticed that physical travel here is particularly dreamlike, that an hour can be spent rushing furiously past a small pond, that a hundred miles can go by in the wink of an eye. That's because you journey not only physically but temporally—back, forth, sideways in time. Much of the governance of the Territories is managed in that way. Which is a good thing, given how fey most of the officials of Oberon's court are. I doubt they could deal with matters in a more straightforward manner.

Phew! You'll pardon me for feeling dizzied. Things don't work that way where I come from.

That's not entirely true. There are owls.

Owls?

Owls are continuously flying back and forth through time. It's their nature. That's why they have that short labyrinthine name: the circle, the recomplication, the straight line. It's also why they're nocturnal. Ambichronology is so much easier when nobody's looking.

Then that's why it's still night, even though we've been traveling so long?

I said that you were intelligent! To differing degrees, it's always night here. Don't worry about Elf Hill. You'll make up the time later. Or earlier—fourth-dimensional grammar is so boring, don't you think? I trust you have a Baedeker. You'll want to study it carefully.

I see, I will. Well. That clears things up quite a bit. Thank you.

You're welcome. Do you like my breasts?

I—yes, they're quite lovely.

You may touch them if you wish. Yes, like that. Mmmmm. Both hands, please.

They're amazingly soft and . . . warm, aren't they?

It's the fur. You haven't said anything about my nipples.

They're beautiful too. And pink. Startlingly so.

All my leathers are pink. Look at the pads of my paws. Exactly the same.

Wow! Those are some claws.

Three inches long. Needle sharp. Retractable. They can

slice through steel. They can gut a man from crotch to sternum in less time than it takes to say it. You took your hands away.

I wouldn't want to get, ah, overly familiar with you.

I'll let you know if you're getting fresh. You're not entirely unattractive, you know. For a mortal.

Really, I'm nothing much. Just a commercial traveler. Nobody special.

I feel myself strangely drawn to you.

I can't imagine why.

A woman—well, a female, at least—has certain needs. Desires. No, needs.

I'm sure I don't know what you're talking about.

You have noticed that I'm female, haven't you? And beautiful. God's own lioness, a poet called me once. Isn't that lovely? It's a pity what happened to him.

I think I'd better leave.

I think you'd better not. I think you'd be well advised to stay. In fact, I don't believe you'd be able to leave if you wanted to. If you get my meaning.

I—I'm afraid I do.

Good. You should take off your suit.

Yes. Perhaps I should.

I'll lock the door. So we're not disturbed.

Who—what—would dare disturb *you?*

You'd be surprised. Slowly, little mouthful, slowly! Don't just throw off those clothes. We've got all the time we need; night lasts forever here, remember. Oh, now that's quite nice. You must work out every day. Now the trousers. My! You're a big one. I hope that's not painful to you. I promise to take good care of it. Afterward I'll ask you a riddle.

Why?

It's just my nature, I'm afraid. I'd spare you if I could. But let's not think about that now. What would you like to do first?

I'm not sure I should.

I beg your pardon.

It's just that it . . . well, it would be bestiality. Wouldn't it?

It's only bestiality if *I* am a beast. Do you think me a beast?

I . . . I don't know.

Good. That's the way it should be. It would be impertinent for you to presume one way or the other. Now let's see, how shall I begin? I think I'll just—mmmm. And then—ahhhh. You like that, don't you?

Well . . .

There's no need to be coy. Nobody's taking notes; this is completely off the record. Bring your mouth here. Kiss me. Yes. Now lower. Lower. There. Yes. The other one too. Oh, that's quite nice—what you do with your hands. Yes, I like that. Lower.

My God, you're so . . .

Yes, I'm a hairy bitch all right. Keep doing that. I'll just stretch around like this and . . .

Watch it with those claws!

Sorry. I'm passionate by nature—Mediterranean, you understand. Here, I'll lick away the blood. Now isn't that better?

Yes.

Oh, my! I feel quite carried away. I think I'd like to—

None of that, now!

Tsk. What's life without a little risk? Here. I'll just run my tongue up the side, and then . . . You liked that, eh? The way I closed my lips about the tip?

My God, yes.

Let's see how much of that monster I can take in my mouth at once.

That's . . . oh, yes, that's fine, that's . . . *Whoah!*

Did I hurt you?

No, I, I'm just startled is all. I wasn't expecting—

What use are such fine sharp teeth as mine if they're never used? I didn't actually break the skin anywhere, did I? No, I didn't think I had. It's not the sort of thing I'd do by accident. Come up here, you. Yes, bring your face to mine. Now we kiss. So you can taste yourself in my mouth and I can taste myself in yours. Let the flavors mingle. That's what's called the alchemical marriage. It can be harnessed to work magics.

Like what?

Well, I'll admit I've never actually done it myself. There was never anything I wanted at that particular moment more than what I could easily arrange for myself with materials on hand.

I could think of a few things.

Really? Then tell me, what would you like to have *right now?* Be honest. What is it you really want most? Diamonds? A gold Rolex? A Mission-style hacienda with central air, in-ground heated pool, and a tennis court?

I'd . . . like your mouth again. You know. What you were doing before.

Oh, wise little monkey! And here's your reward for choosing so well.

Ahhh. This is wonderful. This is so good. I could do this all night.

Be careful what you wish for. Remember where we are.

What do you mean?

Time is malleable in the night lands. Here, desire is a primal force—it's entirely possible to be so caught up in some action that it lasts all night. And remember, night here lasts forever. Literally.

Oh.

I like how hairless you are. It's so perverse. I'm going to crouch over you. Like this. With my front paws on your shoulders. It's exactly the posture a lion takes before tearing open its prey. Do I frighten you?

A little.

Good. You should be frightened. I'm not at all human, you know. Do you enjoy what I'm doing with my tail?

Very much.

How gallant. Now I'll just drag the tips of my breasts across your . . . Sir! What an impetuous creature you are. Not that I dislike it, mind you, I—yes, that's good. That's nice. But just lean back down for a moment and let me place you inside me. There! Ahh. Yes. You can continue what you were doing now.

What I was doing? Do you mean you want my mouth *here?* Or maybe you'd like my hands to squeeze you *here?* Or would you like me to place my fingers . . . *here* and do . . . *this?*

Oh, my. So many decisions to make. Demonstrate those choices for me again, would you? Ahhh. Mmm. Oh! Well, I must say they're all . . . diverting. I believe I'll take the lot.

You'll have to choose. I can't possibly do them all at the same time.

You can't? How tiresome. In that case, I'll just . . . *throw you down!* And ravish you! Yes! You're helpless now. I can do anything I want with you.

I'm not as helpless as all that, you know. I'm not helpless at all. Let me show you a hold I learned in varsity wrestling. I just place one hand here and the other there, and—voila!

Yes, yes, tumble me around! Tumble me around! Take me from behind now. Here, I'll crouch down low and raise my haunches high. Do you like this? Do you think it's sexy?

More than words can express. Sexier than anything I've ever imagined. What are those lights?

Fata morganas. Ignore them. Just keep—ahhh, yes. Like that. They're just excess magic grounding itself. Our passion creates little eddies in the time-flow. Ooh. Harder. You don't need to be delicate with me. I admit they're pretty to look at, though. The lights, I mean.

Lights? What lights?

I forget. I—ah! Oh, but you're—ah!

You like this, eh? You do? You want me to keep going?

I'll kill you if you stop. Ah! Oh, but that's—ah!—nice.

Then I'll continue. It wouldn't be very gentlemanly of me to refuse a lady what she wants.

Ah! Ah! Ah! Ah! Slam it home! Slam it home! Ahhhhhh, ahhhhhh. Oh, what a sweet little monkey you are.

Hey—the cushions!

Hmmmm? Did I do *that?* Well, no matter, we'll just flip them over. And you. Poor thing, you're not finished yet.

Well . . .

Here. Let me just roll you over, and—comfy? Good. Now I'll run my tongue down your abdomen, and . . . Oh, are my breasts in your way? No, I can see that they're not. That's very nice, by the way. I'll put one paw here, and the other here, and then I'll bring my mouth up to . . .

Ahhh. That's so . . .

Hush. Let me just . . . mmmmm. And . . . mmmmm. You're a lot closer to coming than I thought you were. Here—I'm going to shift myself around, and guide you inside me. Ahh. Isn't that better? Don't try to answer me. I'd be terribly insulted if you could.

I, I . . .

That's more like it. Incoherent with passion. Now. Long, even strokes. I want you deep inside me when you—oh, my.

Oh god, oh god, oh god, oh god.

There. There, it's done. Are you happy, sweetmeats? Was it good for you?

My god, yes.

Good. Because now I have to ask my riddle.

Why are you putting your paws there? Don't you think you should retract your claws?

It's only a technicality. First I ask the riddle. Then you answer it. Correctly, I hope. Because if you answer it wrong, I'll rip the family jewels right off that precious little bod of yours.

But that's terrible! I'd be a . . . I'd bleed to death!

Well, yes, but I'd like to think I'm worth it. Are you ready?

No!

I'm going to ask you a second time, and it won't matter what you say. But the third time, if you say no . . . well, remember what I said about some things lasting forever. Not all primal experiences are pleasant, after all. Are you ready?

Can't we just—?

No. Third time's the charm, now. Ready?

I suppose so. As ready as I'll ever be.

Here's the riddle: What walks on two legs and enters four-legs with his third leg to make a beast with six legs and—sometimes—two backs?

Oh, but that . . . it's . . . you're talking about the two of us. What we just did.

There. You see? That wasn't so difficult after all, was it? Of course, *I* get to choose which riddle to ask, and I'm feeling particularly fond of you at the moment. So I'll just retract my claws and . . . Why, you bad thing! You're hard again. So you like a taste of danger, do you?

Well, that and . . . how shall I put it?

Delicately, I trust.

A certain . . . a touch of . . . perfume in the air.

Oh, that! Well, I am feline in nature, after all. When I'm in heat, I stink of it. But right now, I'd better see to your needs. That looks so terribly, terribly swollen. Would you like me to take care of it?

Oh, yes.

Then I will. And afterward, I'll ask you another riddle. You'd like that, wouldn't you?

Mmmmm.

This could take all night.

No Human Hands to Touch

Elizabeth E. Wein

When Medraut stepped off the merchants' ship I had not seen him since Artos, his father the high king, had taken him from me at ten. I knew him now by his hair and eyes; but he was an exotic in this wintry archipelago of islets where my brother the high king has banished me. His dress was foreign, his face and hands burnt to copper in the African sun and on the sea, and his hair was so sun-bleached that it was as blindingly and unnaturally fair as it had been in his babyhood. He had been a slender and shapeless child; now, at five-and-twenty, he was taller than my husband. It seemed to me that he must have trained his body to match his will, until they had become alike in their iron surety.

He kissed me formally when he greeted me, and held my hands in his own.

"My child." I welcomed him. "You have changed a great deal since I sent you off."

"Godmother," he answered warmly, "but you are exactly the same, and all as beautiful as I remember."

Since I had seen him I had borne two more children, five in all, not counting those not carried to term. My husband, King Lot of the Orcades, flung words like hag and crone in my face when he wanted to hurt me. Yet I had never known Medraut to say a thing he did not believe to be true.

He sat by me as we feasted him on his first night back in the home of his childhood. He shared a plate with me. His left hand rested quiet and still upon his thigh, while he broke his bread and handled his meat only with the right. He did it deftly, and without making a show of it; I only noticed because I was fascinated by the curious beauty of his long, dark hands. My own hands had grown thin and wiry over the years of birthing and cutting and healing and killing; they were now lean and taut as a man's. Medraut's hands were like replicas of my own, but larger, stronger.

"Have you hurt your hand?" I asked, and touched his left very lightly. "You do not use it."

"It is only habit. It is very rude to eat with your left hand in Aksum."

I clasped his fine fingers beneath mine. He tolerated this patiently, but did not return the endearment. His first ten years had taught him to beware my attention.

"How long were you ambassador there?" I asked.

His look turned suspect a moment. It was exactly the expression he had worn at seven, apprehensive that he was about to endure another humiliating catechism: Why do I have you beaten in place of my husband's sons, Medraut? Why do I place the fault at your feet when you did no wrong? Why is it meet that the high king's bastard should wait on King Lot's children?

Now I laughed at his look, very gently. He joined me, laughing at himself, suddenly at ease; or attempting to be. His hand lay still beneath mine.

"I was in Aksum a little longer than three years," he said. "Which of these young men are my cousins?"

He called them cousins, not brothers or half-brothers, for it is a secret that I am his mother. He had been taken from me when he was born and then, after an occult series of maskings to hide the truth of his birth, given back to me a little later to "foster" for his father the high king. It would have been profanity to allow the people to know that the high king's only child was born of incest. Medraut had never heard the truth from me.

"I think I can guess Gareth and Agravain," Medraut continued, "but I don't recognize Gwalchmei at all. Agravain's hair is so like yours."

"And Gareth's like yours," I said.

He shot me a swift, startled frown. So: He knew what I meant. How could he not, with my eyes and my hands and my cool, collected glance? But Artos must have told him.

"Gwalchmei has more of his father's look than mine," I added calmly, as though nothing had passed between us in that moment of subtle testing and recognition. "There he is, at the opposite end of the other long table. And Gaheris is on his right. Gaheris is devoted to him."

"Artos wants to offer them all places in his court," Medraut said.

Perhaps he meant it only as a polite and honorable invitation. It was sheerly threatening. Well, I thought, so he declares his loyalty.

"And you," I said gently. "Have you a place there?"

"Always," he said warmly, reverent and unguarded.

I felt the same surge of jealousy and hatred that I had known when he was a child. It made me want to strike him, as it always had. What a spirit he had had then, how he had endured my dominion over him in silent stoicism, how he had clung pridefully, quietly, to the knowledge of who his father was, and to the hope that Artos would rescue him from the northern hell that was his childhood. And here he was back within my grasp, his loyalty confirmed, himself no longer a child.

"Neither Gaheris nor Gareth was born when I left," said Medraut lightly. "I have been away longer than it seems."

I had striven so to create him, this living weapon against my brother. I remembered the seduction and the labor, the intrigue and the exile, and felt myself haggard with age and strain. I thought I had lost him.

"Medraut," I said, "stay with me a while before you return to your father in Camlan."

His idle hand turned suddenly over. The long, beautiful fingers folded around mine in apology. He could have crushed my hand.

"I can't stay here."

The seven-year-old I had fought with and beaten and solaced regarded me through the poised and guarded gaze of the young man. He looked down at our thin hands entwined and smiled ruefully. "I only came because I did not think I would have another chance to see you. But I am bound for Camlan. I have been doing too much. There's nothing for me here. I need to act. I need to learn."

He had been important in Aksum. He had been feared and loved and admired as an administrator, and for his skill as a warrior and a hunter. He had taken great cats of strange and wild strains on the African plains, and brought me gifts of lion and leopard skin.

"You could learn much from me," I said.

He looked up. It was like staring at my own gray eyes in a glass to look into his calm and shuttered gaze. "How much do you mean that, I wonder," he said. He had never been anyone's fool. "You have always kept your knowledge jealously concealed."

"I have only ever wanted one apprentice," I said. "I have been waiting."

"Waiting for me?" He laughed. "You never told me so. Do you mean to say that in thirty years you have taught no one else any of your physician's skill?"

"And lose my reputation as a sorceress?" I said playfully. "I am revered for it."

"And abhorred, some would say."

"You are as bold with me as you ever were."

He was silent a moment. "I did not mean to be rude. But I feel as though I am being tempted not for my good will, but to your own purpose, Odysseus ensnared by Circe."

I laughed lightly. "The traveler and the witch."

"You suckled me on Greek legend," he made excuse. "And the old stories have been much on my mind in my journeys, seeing the famous places for myself."

"I did not suckle you," I corrected gently. "But I am glad you remember the stories. You do not really fear me, do you?"

"Of course not," he answered swiftly.

"Then stay here," I said. "Prove to me your courage. I have much to teach you."

I felt like one who wants to trap and cage a little bird, and after years of waiting and luring and baiting finds that she must do no more than hold out her hand, and the finch lands on her finger and does not fly. You scarcely dare to move. It rests on your hand whole and free, foolishly trusting and infinitely courageous. It will never be more beautiful.

"I'll do it," he said.

My pig of a husband had long since ceased to share a bed with me. I think by now he must have guessed that the only thing that stopped me lacing his ale with aconite was my brother's threat to have me executed for regicide if he heard rumor that Lot had died unnaturally and in my presence. "Well, you've a new toy now," Lot said to me at the end of the evening. "Perhaps this season you won't find it necessary to drug all the townsfolk at the Lammas festival."

"You are idle as I am."

"Take a lover," my husband said.

"None of your fawning retainers is to my taste. Let you rut like a wild boar, without choosing, the nearest thing on heat. I can better satisfy myself."

"Then do so," Lot said cruelly. "Wait much longer to choose a man and none will have you. Go to bed, old woman."

Easy, easy, easy to twist the knife.

That night I stood still and aching in the antechamber of

my empty apartment and thought of my dearest bid for power: of my brother the young king, over twenty-five years ago, and how barren a life he had then condemned me to. It was an old and stale ache. So I had a new toy, as Lot said, something to amuse me during the short days; but the northern nights would ever be as long. Years ago, on such a night, I would have had a handmaid sleep with me, for warmth and for the semblance of companionship. But now I hated my ladies-in-waiting for their careless youth and petty beauty, and for knowing they would rather have my husband's favor than my own.

I let fall my mantle and stood before the dressing table. Silvered glass and polished bronze mirrors in many lengths held my frame and face for my inspection, and I reflected bitterly: I am still beautiful. The lines of my belly have changed, my face is thinner. But my skin is smooth, my breasts are full, my eyes are a clear color between smoke and slate . . . My teeth are better than any of my stupid servants'. How can it be possible that the lines around my eyes and the spotting on my hands have marred me so much?

I sat naked in the taper light before the gentle and truthful mirrors and slowly pulled the brooches from my hair. A waterfall of fire, a shower of gold rain. So must have Danaë looked when the god Zeus poured himself inside her . . . I combed my hair about me with one hand to watch the gold rain in the mirrors, the other hand beginning to move between my legs. This was an old and sweet fancy for me, the rape of Perseus's mother; how lonely it must be to have Zeus for a lover, no lips to kiss, no human hands to touch.

I glanced at my own hand in the mirror: and saw instead my son's. There it was, in a peculiar instant of illusion, the same spare masculine beauty, the hard, strong lines. I held the hand still, staring, enchanted.

What would it feel like, I dared to guess in that hot, strange moment, what would I *think*, to hold Medraut's long fingers crushed and cocooned inside my thighs like this?

The secret dream brought a sudden, startling pleasure that drowned the thought of taboo.

Medraut sent word to his father that he would stay with me throughout the coming year, and I began his tuition. I was pressed to keep apace of him. Secure in my degree of expertise, I had forgotten how quickly one learns when one is new to knowledge. He made me feel young and vigorous, intelligent and alluring, not the sorcerous old mother spider that my husband made me out to be. I liked teaching him. I liked arguing with him. I did not tell him that I dreamed of his hands.

Never mind that Medraut had been Britain's ambassador to one of the world's greatest civilizations. He was modest and moderate, and made no complaint at sleeping on the floor of Lot's hall with the rest of our retainers. But after a month he retreated to the cot in my surgery. I granted him this privilege. I tested him often and harshly, and felt that this little privacy I could give him was a fair exchange for his being woken hours past midnight to minister at a birth, or to have to help put out a brush fire and then tend burns on the shepherds and slaughter dying sheep for the next day and a half without sleep. Our court grew used to Medraut's being there; my young sons liked and admired him, although Agravain was envious of the attention I gave him. My hand-maidens adored him.

"Your long-legged Teleri is annoying me," he commented during his second month in the Orcades. "She is very persistent."

"Then bed her," I said lightly. "She is very pretty."

"I have a friend in Africa who would not like it," he answered in the same light tone.

"No woman in this court will expect you to keep faith with a girl four thousand miles away for very long."

"All the same, I am not going to lie with Teleri."

"Has she suggested it?"

"Suggested!" The word came out in a short burst of laughter. "Well, she has not spoken of it exactly, but she has twice tried to climb into bed with me."

"I'll punish her for you, if you like," I said.

He set down the vial he was scouring and gave me his sharp, serious frown. "Don't do that. She's done nothing wrong."

"Don't complain of it to me if you don't want me to end it," I said. "I have little sympathy with such shallow affairs."

"You might try scolding her before you have her beaten," he said shortly.

One evening in his third month he told me he was going with Gwalchmei and Agravain and a few other young nobles who wanted to join the fishermen of our capital in their yearly seal spearing. They would be gone a month, boating and camping in the far reaches of the islands and the skerries. Medraut was a passionate huntsman; he missed the strange and dangerous challenges he had known on the plains of Africa.

"You will be whaling next, and off northward to the Ice for a season," I protested.

"I couldn't afford so much time. I am only here for a year," he said. And I could not help feeling that he said it to assert his independence, and that he knew it would incense me.

"You'll learn nothing in a year in any case," I said, and instantly regretted that I should stoop to so petty a retort.

Sometimes I think I have already learned too much," he answered distantly, his voice unaccountably bleak.

"Why, Medraut!"

"I do not like your methods. I do not like the way you use me, or the way you use other people. I do not like the way you punish your servants with purges and sedatives. I do not like to know it is happening, and to have to keep it as your secret."

"Then leave."

"I only thought to hunt with the sealers for a little while, and so you tell me to leave!"

"You will not find lost nerve for this work out in the far skerries."

He glared at me through narrowed eyes. His blue-gray gaze looked black in the dim light of the oil lamp.

"I've not lost my nerve."

"Prove it."

He was silent a moment, then said, "Why must you make a test of every little thing?"

"Because you would cross me in so many little things, and I am unsure of you. I do not want to waste my time on your instruction if you are not going to see it through."

"I am your pupil," he said slowly, "but I am not your apprentice. I am not bound to you. I am no longer even your foster child. I am hunting with the sealers for this month, Godmother."

I lay awake hours into the night in irrational panic, thinking that I should go mad if I should lose him so soon. I knew it would be folly to forbid him to go; well, as he said, I could not forbid him. But if I made him regret the decision later on, he might as easily leave in anger then. Nothing bound him. Even my husband was afraid of me, but I had nothing with which to bind Medraut.

I thought, finally, that I must give him my blessing and let him go on his voyage, that it was the only answer he would respect, and a risk that I must take. And still unable to sleep, I felt that I must tell him now.

It was dark, too dark to see him when I entered the chamber where he worked and slept; I did not need a light to find my way around these rooms. I sat on the edge of his cot and lightly stroked his hair, to wake him.

"Teleri?" he said, and reached out a hand which touched my leg. "You are overdressed this time."

I was wrapped in a gown and mantle, of course, having been walking in the cold halls of my husband's holding.

That Medraut should mistake me for one of my handmaidens amused me. I grasped his hand and held the palm to my face, that he should know me.

But he did not. He let me hold his hand there against my throat and chin, cupping my jaw. He said gently, "Get out of my bed. I do not want you any more tonight than I did last—"

His fingers and palm were cold. Their light touch sent gooseflesh across my shoulders. How could he not know me—

Truly, truly, I was only trying to shock him into recognition, but I drew his hand down inside my gown, and then suddenly I was reeling with the insanity and sheer delight of his taut, long fingers at once disdaining and tempted by my failing body. He thought I was Teleri—his sure hand held by me reluctantly a moment against my breast, and still he thought I was young. I shivered with bottled laughter, delighted by this game.

"Get out of my bed," he said again, his voice harder this time, more irritated and less patient.

How reluctant are you, I wondered, and drew his hand lower down my body.

God, his *hands*!

I was at once besotted with the flattery in their blindness, and blind myself with their cool, burning touch.

Again he hissed at me to leave, and added, "You are lovely, you are arousing, you are all you wish to be. But Teleri, I'm tired, I'm short of temper, and you are not the lover I would choose—"

I shook with laughter. I could scarcely contain myself, but I knew that if he heard my voice the game would be over. In the dark, groping, I bent to kiss him somewhere along his naked ribcage.

"Out!" he hissed. I could not bear that I did not know exactly how excited he was, and reached down to feel the taut rod between his legs. Aroused, indeed.

At this crude invasion of his privates he lost all patience with me, and threw me out of his bed.

No one who knew me would have dared such a thing.

I sat for a moment shaken and trembling in an undignified heap on the floor; then hooked vicious fingernails into his back, which he had turned on me in an exaggerated gesture of dismissal, and tore open his shoulder.

His hand locked around my wrist in a grip of iron, hard and fast. He dragged me up from the floor and back into the bed, and pinned me so between hard knees. His face close to my ear, with one hand hitching up my robes, he hissed in dreadful quiet, "Do you want me so much? Do you really think you want me so much? Do you think I love *kindly?*" And then he pinned me further with an elbow cruelly pressed against my throat, and as I gasped for breath, he in all fury plunged his lean, hard body into mine.

I screamed silently, strangled by his elbow, unable to warn him of the fearful thing he was doing.

"You're not Teleri!" he gasped hollowly, enjoying none of this, concentrating on his retributive abuse of me. "Who are you?"

I could scarcely breathe, so how could I speak? I had come to give my son permission to leave me and ended in being raped by him—the thought made me wheeze with choking and hysterical laughter. Suddenly, as suddenly as the livid anger had taken him, he stopped his cold, punishing ploughing of me and let go of my throat. He whispered again, "Who are you?"

"You know who I am," I gasped.

"Aiee!"

He made a choking noise something like a muffled scream, and struggled frantically to untangle our cleaving bodies.

"Beast," I flung at him, accusing and wounded as a green girl.

"I!" he cried. "I! You tear my back to ribbons, and call me a beast! Have you any idea what pain—"

"Have you?" I snapped.

That silenced him for a moment, reminding him of his uncharacteristic and mindless brutality. He bent over me still, awkwardly, trying not to touch me, trembling.

"You have not said who you are," he whispered. "Tell me yourself."

I had not ever meant for such a thing to happen. But I, of all, ought to have known that it could: I, who bore him by my brother; I, who had suckled him on Greek myth, as he said.

"You know who I am," I repeated.

His voice was full of horror. "I did not know. I did not know!"

"You did not know me," I said, nearly as shaken as he, "but you knew what you were doing."

"This is what happened to my father," he said through his teeth.

"No," I said coldly. "I invited him. You forced me."

"You deceived me!"

"I deceived Artos, as well," I said. "But your father would never use any woman so ruthlessly as you have used me." I shivered, scarcely able to believe what he had done. "You are not like your father."

"No," he said, still speaking through clenched teeth. "I am like you." He hovered over me, close but not touching me, intimate but not invasive. Caught in the nightmare of his own fury and recklessness, he added in a fierce, icy whisper, "I am not so easily toyed with as my father. I might desire more of you."

I am sure he meant it only as a threat; but I realized then that I had him trapped, that the finch was mine forever, if I took this to its logical conclusion.

"Do you?" I asked.

He wrenched at my hair in frustration.

"So, so, so." I touched his wiry hand, and then lightly ca-ressed his hair, calming him in the same warning and as-sured way I would have calmed him as a child. It was automatic, and eerie in how surely it worked on him. "Medraut, don't hurt me."

He let go of my hair with a soft sigh. "I was not thinking. I am not thinking. I don't know what to do."

"Don't try to think." I twined an arm around his neck to draw him down to me until his mouth was breathing hotly against mine, and then he lost all reason, and we clung and kissed frantically. I could not stop shaking, nor could he cease his choking sobs, until he tore our mouths apart and moaned, "What am I to do?"

"You need not do anything. Nothing has come of it. Let go of me, and I'll go back to my chamber and you'll go back to sleep—"

"*Nothing has come of it!*"

"Not unless you finish what you began," I said softly. "Is it true that you cannot love kindly? Show me. You owe it me."

"I will not *finish*! I was wrong, I acted evilly—"

"Must I command you?" I said in a voice that he surely knew not to challenge.

He gave a wordless cry of disbelief and said in baffle-ment, "You cannot want this!"

"What do you fear?"

"The wrath of the gods," he answered swiftly.

"You said I was beautiful."

"Yes, but . . ." He sighed. "And arousing, as I said. I am lost."

"Come," I said. "You are not Odysseus. There are no gods that care. Prove to me your courage."

A long moment of absolute stillness, and then his whis-pered assent.

"I'll do it."

He moved inside me slowly and sweetly, tentative this

time, exploring rather than invading. It was as though he expected the act of incest to be different, somehow, from the same act with any other woman. And when we were entwined softly and comfortably and he began to accept that indeed he was not about to be struck down by a blow of lightning, he murmured at my ear, "Godmother, have I grown too old for you to begin to suckle me?"

"Do it, do it," I murmured in return.

"This is madness," he said, and laughed, and closed his mouth over my breast.

He would not know until too late how thoroughly I had caged him. I would clip his wings, and train him to sing at my command, and pinion him if he tried to fly.

I was thinking only of how I should triumph over my brother by this act, but I had not realized how sweet it would be to have Medraut as a lover.

I say we were lovers, but love—I think I do not know what love is—I have trained all my sons to revere me in some cross between fear and devotion. What binds Medraut to me is deeper and harsher even than that, though, tempered with his clear-sighted understanding for what I am and why I do the things I do, and tainted with the lust that brought us to quivering ecstasy in each other's arms for nearly two years. He always thought of our love as tainted. He could not ever put aside the knowledge that what was between us was a universal evil, an immortal sin; and still he took me to his bed.

All of it, all of it comes back when I think of him: child and man. How once, when he was six, he had been made to kneel all night on one knee at the foot of my bed, naked and with his head bowed, because he had dared to contradict me. Again, twenty years later, his silver head between my legs, his hungry mouth and tongue in the secret places of my body, his long and gentle fingers. How he would look up at me then, with the eager, half-frightened expression I knew so well from his babyhood: Have I pleased you, Godmother, is it enough, will I not be punished this time? He would by day hunt fiercely, work in the fields, drive himself as hard as he had ever done; and then he would come to me for instruction. How much of yourself, of your soul, are you willing to barter for today's scrap of arcane information?

"Kiss me and I'll tell you."

Sometimes I said it lightly. Sometimes he did it. More often the exchange was unspoken; what I give you today, you will pay me for tonight.

"This will cost you a great deal . . ." I could feel myself smiling as I spoke. And his eyes would narrow and his hands would clench, but every now and then he would smile too:

"A small price to pay."

I forgot that I was in exile. I forgot that I was aging. I forgot I had a husband; I forgot my other sons. Even, for a time, I forgot that I was training Medraut to go back to his father with his loyalties shifted and slanted.

Out of respect for the man who had fostered him Medraut did not habitually sleep in my bed, but otherwise we made no attempt to hide our affair. No one knew the truth of Medraut's birth, as I have said, and I doubt anyone would have dared raise question even if it had been known. The court was growing to fear Medraut even as they feared me, out of guesswork, out of self-interest, because we were so close. We ate together. We combed each other's hair. We worked in consultation.

But still we battled. I could tell of so many battles, so many little ways in which we teetered between tenderness and spiteful torment of each other. Never had I dreamed of an apprentice or lover so diligent, so passionate and craving, and yet so difficult to manage. I threatened him, made love to him, and hurt him. I cozened him. I coddled him. What a way to learn to minister to the afflicted.

He came storming into my apartment at daybreak one morning. He still affected foreign dress in the first year he lived with us, and in the gray dawn light of my antechamber he seemed very alien and unappeasable. But he spoke calmly and directly. "Godmother, I want no more of your tuition if I must come by it in waiting upon poisoned children."

I find it difficult to answer such directness. One feels so sly, one wants to laugh, one wants to lie. To acknowledge or deny the accusation is to accept that one has done some kind of evil.

I said, "Tell me this story."

"If you have wondered where I was tonight," he said, "I have spent the last half day ministering to my old nurse's grandson, who has been vomiting himself inside out after sharing his evening bread with Gaheris and Gareth. He had not eaten anything else since before noon. Neither of your sons suffered—"

"How can you possibly know what Fercos had eaten between noon and supper?" I said, but I meant the question as a test, not a defense.

"I don't," said Medraut shortly. "But I know what poisoned him, and how it may be administered."

"You will not know the symptoms if you do not see it happen," I said.

"Then poison your own children," he snapped.

"Medraut," I said, and laid a hand on his shoulder, to make him sit down. "Do you mean that?"

He looked up into my face. His expression struck me to my very core: the frightened, stubborn look of rebellion that he had given me as a boy, so sure that he was right, so afraid of what I might do to him.

"No," he said. "I would not see Gareth suffering as Fercos did last night."

"Agravain, then," I said softly.

"Not even he," said Medraut immediately, peevish with suspicion.

"Then you have a choice," I said, turning my back to him. I played with the face paints on the dressing table, watching my hands in the mirrors.

He said nothing, suspect, waiting.

"Quit me now," I said, "or I will visit these tests on your own body."

He was silent for so long that it grew lighter while I waited for his answer. I did not insult him by repeating or rephrasing the challenge. One chance: one answer only.

"I'll stay another year. I'll do it," he said.

"Will you? Or will you come asking for solace and mercy as you do now?"

"I'll do it!"

"Prove me this."

"Ah, my God," he growled. "What must I do?"

I turned to look at him, my hands behind my back. His face was set in a familiar grimace of bleak, defiant determination.

"Give me your hand."

For a moment he did not move. Then he nodded once, and held out his right.

"Your other hand," I said mildly, which ought to have warned him.

His eyes never left mine. He held out his left hand, palm up. He was calm; the hand I held now was relaxed; but I saw the twitch in his jaw as he braced himself against the unknown blow.

The blade I used was so thin, so keen, that I do not think he at first felt anything. Then he lowered his eyes to stare at his wrist. A slow glance at me, then down again at the bloody slash that scored his inner forearm.

He lost precious seconds and a good deal of blood in registering how seriously I had hurt him. Then he snatched at the wrist with his other hand, choking off the pumping vein, raising his forearm above his head. It was expertly done, but it was not enough, and he lost another few precious seconds before he realized that. Now in utter calm, as if there were no hurry, he stood up and reached for the tongs in the brazier. No longer expert, but anyway efficient, he sealed the wound with a glowing coal, and laid the tongs down, and fainted at my feet.

I knelt trembling at his shoulder to examine his arm, but he had done the trick; he had saved himself. The first coherent thought that came to me after that was that he would never get the bloodstains out of his white linen *shamma*. And I was meanly glad of it, because the leopard skin that covered the floor was ruined also, and I hated and envied Medraut's African dress as the badge of his freedom.

He lay profoundly insensible for perhaps twenty minutes, and awoke bewildered and pathetic. He lifted his arm languidly, and stared at the seared skin, and let the arm fall. "God, what a mess."

I was kneeling at his head like a harpy.

"You will need to change your clothes," I said.

"I think I will pass out if I try to sit up."

"There will be no hunting for you for a few days," I said softly. "Are you thirsty? You will need to drink."

He hesitated. "Would you help me now?"

"For a fee."

He lay flat on his back on the ruined leopard skin he had given me, his body drained of blood and his burnt arm blistering, and spoke with patient resignation: "Come. I'll drink of you." The languid hand reached up to touch my knee. "Here, you must ungirdle yourself, this time. I have not the strength to wrestle with your skirts."

"If I say you must?" I murmured, but gathered my skirts aside.

"I'll weep with frustration. You would not have me weep, would you?"

"Not if it distracts you." And now my legs were free, and he turned his head toward me and parted his lips.

"Come nearer," he whispered. I threw one leg across his chest, so that his pale head rested against the inner thigh of my other leg, and laying my hands on the top of his head I pressed his mouth against and into the soft, wet slot where he had started life—

—I knew, I knew that eventually I must give him up, but I never, ever tired of this. And he had said he would stay another year.

Medraut did not tire of it, either. The long winter nights, which had always seemed endless to me, were no longer time enough. But as our liaison continued and grew increasingly cruel and complex, his mind began to rebel more and more against his tireless body. He mourned the betrayal of his unwitting love in Africa. Though he had agreed to it, he so resented my testing new medicines on him that he experimented against it, and countered me with skill and untold intuition. Somehow I kept the upper hand, and had my way of him, but the damage to his body began to show itself in his weariness, in a slight faltering of his hands.

"Come here," I said to him one night early in his third summer in the Orcades, as he cleared away the herbs we had been grinding.

He came, and knelt at my side.

"Give me your hands."

He did not look at me. I held his hands lightly in my own, gazing in wonderment at their spare grace, their taut strength, their harsh beauty.

"I hate for you to be so submissive," I said softly.

"I am only obeying you in deed," he said. "In spirit I defy you, and all this business."

"You defy me!" I scoffed. "You lust for me."

"I hate you."

"Medraut, you are cruel."

He leaned against my knee, and I stroked his hair. "Godmother," he said, distractedly, "I do not understand why I am made to desire you so."

"You choose to."

He sighed, miserable beneath my fingertips. "Our lovemaking would be evil even if we were strangers. We are so hurtful to each other. As it is—"

"It has always been your choice. You have always been free to end it, free to go. I am the one who is imprisoned in this place. You called me Circe on your first day here, but I am more like Calypso, alone on my island, waiting for a lover."

"Calypso!" He gave a short bark of laughter. "Godmother, you are more like Medea, who slew her sons, or Jocasta, who married hers—"

"Jocasta never knew what she was doing," I said quietly. "I have known all along. As have you."

"I must stop this," he said. "I am destroying myself."

"You are an idiot to use the narcotics the way you do. You are becoming addicted to the poppy."

He blazed at me, "I am addicted to you."

The following night I could not wake him when I came to his bed. He was utterly unconscious, sunken in a sleep deeper than sleep. For a few moments I feared for him, and then knew that he had done this to himself. Poppy again, perhaps, or nightshade. I could smell nothing in his breath but the faintest trace of wine, which was not so unusual. He had been careful. He had been exact. I had taught him well.

I said nothing, the next day, when I found him hollow-eyed and clumsy at his work, but that night I fed him a stimulant that would both keep him awake and punish him if he tried to counter it. No fool, he was on his knees over a bucket trying to vomit when I came to him, bringing up nothing, shaking with strain. I sat on the floor and took him by his trembling shoulders, and drew his head down into my lap. He clutched at me blindly, gasping, defeated again.

"You must wait it out," I told him, and let my hands move idly over his hair while he sweated and sobbed and the poison ran its course.

When he had recovered enough to speak he repeated indistinctly, his face muffled against my belly, "I hate you."

"Do you so?" I said sadly.

"You deal with me as coldly as if I were a bird, a fish—"
I laughed.

"Tear out the hook and throw the creature back. You will bait it again when it is older and more worth your while. Its torn face will have healed by then. It is only a fish."

I bent over him, and said softly at his ear, "Little fish, do you know what bait I used on you tonight?"

He was quiet a moment, then said slowly, "I thought it must be foxglove and water hemlock."

"I have only taught you a fraction of my own knowledge," I said, and gripped his hair to pull his head up a little. "I will not be crossed by you, Medraut. You cannot best me at this game.

"Now touch me," I ordered icily, and let go of his hair. He sank his face against my thigh, staring bleakly across the floor at nothing. His right hand still clutched at the skirt of my gown; but with his left he sorted through the linen folds until his long fingers found the inside of my thigh, and then I had to snatch at his hair again to brace myself at the untold pleasure his hands lit in me.

He winced as I pulled at his hair, and gasped aloud: "Do you think Jocasta used her son so?"

"Medraut," I murmured, "Do not call me Jocasta, or I will let you borrow my brooches and you can put your own eyes out with them, and end this yourself, as her son did. Touch me!"

It was the last for a long time. The following day he dealt himself injuries more complete, more ugly, more evil, than any hurt I had ever done him.

They told me he was dead. And, God, I knew him so intimately by then that all I need do was glance once at his eyes to know he lived, but in the instant when three hysterical househands came reporting his death to me, I believed it. That instant in itself was his revenge, the dart he had aimed at me. That instant, and the time it took me to come to his side—seconds of unheard of nightmare for me, which he paid for, of his own volition, for the next three months.

He looked as close to death as any living thing could seem. His face was set in an agonized snarl, his teeth bared and his jaw clenched, and the rest of his utterly ruined body was set so tightly that he was still gripping his hunting knife in his right hand—they had not been able to pry it from his iron clutch. The other hand was crushed, the fingers so dreadfully mutilated that they only rested on, but could not grip, the broken shoulder he was trying to protect. But his gaze blazed purely triumphant when I knelt at his side in shock and grief. Nothing of pain in the dark blue eyes, nothing of fear. There was only victory.

He caught me wordless. I knelt by him and found myself mirroring his grimace. Never had I been so betrayed, never had I been so deeply wounded, never had I been so angry. I knelt with my hands hovering over this broken thing that had been my work of art, not knowing where to begin, what to touch, how to mend it.

Speechless, I asked him in a gesture of my hands: What, why?

His eyes blazed defiance into mine. His lips curled back, barely, and he croaked at me: "I do not need your brooches."

Then I, awash with grief and hatred, gathered my skirts and turned from him, so that I could find a place alone and mourn his ruined body in dignity.

They had gone stag hunting, on foot, with spears. They told me this later; it wearies me to tell it over again. He had been first, and had set upon the stag with his hunting knife alone. There was no reason for it. He had acted in pure fearless and witless pride, to challenge himself, to prove it could be done. He had been trampled in wrestling it to the ground, and torn by its hoofs nearly as soundly as he himself had stabbed at the wild beast; and when he finally finished with it and cut its throat, his legs were caught beneath the dead and crushing weight of its massive body. His own body had become such a wreck that we could not tell where all the damage had come from, or how it could possibly have happened.

I worked over his crushed hand for so long that my eyes began to burn, and my head to ache. I must have sat there for half a day trying to piece his fingers back together. Others came and went around me, waiting on me, bringing me clean linen and thread and new salves, and the occasional cup of wine; and Medraut drifted in and out of ken, sometimes aware of me, sometimes not. The fourth time my physician Huarwar advised me to rest and let him spell my watch a while, I sent them all from my sight, and sat finally alone with my broken son and my worthless, bootless skill. Medraut, deep in his self-induced fever, said clearly, "Godmother, you lied to the high king's messenger."

Twenty years ago, nearly twenty years ago I had punished him for saying that.

"Child," I said, as I had said then, "You will not cross me—" And I snapped apart the fractured bone I had just set.

It woke him. He stared at me in full comprehension, and utter disbelief. His other arm was bound at his side; the shoulder was broken. His legs were bound to heavy splints. There was nothing free but this hand, which I held between my own.

"I will teach you to cross me—" I spoke through my teeth, and broke apart another balanced fracture.

He gave a soundless scream, neck arched in agony, gasping for air. He looked as though he were drowning. The fish hooked one final time—

I began to weep, now, myself, as I finished the work he had begun, methodically twisting and cracking the bones in his hand beyond any hope of repair.

I know, I know, how ugly a vengeance this was. I am sorry I did it. But even in my regret I am selfish. I am not sorry that I punished Medraut; I am only sorry that I so thoroughly destroyed the hand I loved so well. I still dream of his hands. They are whole, in my dreams.

I bound and bandaged the hand in its wrecked state, and it took Medraut three days of begging and pleading and threatening Huarwar, and the others who tended him, before he was able to convince them to go against my ordinance and remove the bindings. When they discovered what I had done they banished me from his side for over a month. Oh, they could not have stopped me seeing him if I had insisted, but he never asked for me in all that time, and I felt I must wait.

He never did send for me, but he overruled my exile at last. I came to his bedside one afternoon like a visitor to a convalescent in a monastery. For all my anger I ached at seeing how helpless he was still; he had not attempted to walk since his legs had been broken, the shattered shoulder was not strong enough to bear his weight when he tried to raise himself up on one elbow, and the hand, the hand—

"They cut your hair," I said.

"Fever."

I leaned over and ran my fingers through the short and tangled mane. The lightness of it made him look like a child. "Don't," he said, wincing away from my touch.

I drew back a little. "I used to plait it for you," I said.

He tried to shrug, then uttered bitterly, "But usually I had to plait it myself, and that would be difficult now."

"Yes," I said slowly. "That is true. Is the hand healing?"

"As may be," he muttered.

"Let me see."

He held it out to me in defiance, stubbornly battling fear. I carefully undid the bandages and removed the splints. He held very still as gently, gently, I tested the tendons, felt the setting bones, examined the newly healed scars.

"Your hands are beautiful," I said at last.

"I had been vain of them," he whispered.

"The scars will fade in time," I said. "Who reset the last three fingers?"

"I did."

"That was bravely done," I said, and bent again over the hand, in admiration. "I taught you well. Those fingers are straight and whole as they ever were, except that they do not bend."

"You tore the tendons," he said bitterly. "The joints were ruined beyond repair."

I let his hand fall back onto his chest, but did not let go of it.

"I could have done that to your wrist, which I set also," I said softly, "Or your legs."

He closed his eyes and drew a sharp, haggard breath. I saw the shiver go through him. "Why didn't you?" he said.

"Medraut, you are the most beautiful and splendid lover I have ever had. And you are my son. I could not cripple you."

"Your lover and your son," he repeated in quiet. "You have crippled me."

There was one time, still before Medraut was able to walk, when I thought I would go mad with knowing that he lay so close to me day in, day out, and that I could not hold his powerful and comely body pulsing inside mine yet one more time. When I came to him, as ever, he could neither deny nor hide how quickly his passion for me kindled; but it was a strange and sad thing to find his frame and form so changed with illness, and I wish I had not forced him. Pitiably cautious, he held his arm carefully away from our bodies as we pressed against each other in this last lovemaking, too fearful of jarring his damaged hand to lose himself in desire.

It was well into October before he could walk any distance, and he came to me then to tell me he was leaving. I turned from the dressing table where I was seated before the candles and the mirrors, and asked him when.

"Tomorrow morning. I will take passage to the mainland with one of the fishermen."

"It's too late to travel to Camlan this year."

"I won't stay."

He did not say it, but I could well imagine that he was thinking: I would rather freeze to death in a snowstorm in the Caledonian highlands than risk another winter of suffering and slaving at your hands.

I closed my eyes, and sighed deeply.

"You are polite and gracious as ever to dare to bid me goodbye."

"Well, Godmother," he said in a quiet voice, "I can scarcely bear to think of leaving you. But even Odysseus left Calypso at last."

He could have called me so many evil names, and chose Calypso. Calypso, the sea nymph, the lover. Calypso, who let Odysseus go his way at last. I bowed my head against my hand, leaning on the dressing table, and could not answer him. He stood gazing at me, unmoving, his sound right hand gripping the back of a chair, because he was still unsteady on his feet.

The silence was complete. One of the tapers guttered on the iron tine that held it, and I put it out by crushing its flame beneath two outstretched fingers. I held my hand still like that for a few moments, fingertips resting in hot wax, but did not flinch, as if somehow Medraut's words were burning into me as well, through the quenched flame.

I folded my hands in my lap and raised my head.

"Well, I think we should bid one another goodnight, then."

I stood up and began putting out the candles one by one, dousing all their flames between my fingers or beneath the palm of my hand, and then began killing the lights in the oil lamps with the same self-destructive vehemence.

Medraut said gently, "Godmother, you will hurt your hands," and took them in his own, the hands I had crippled. "Now stop," he said. "Just stop."

I turned my face to his, and he let go of my hands.

"You truly mean to go."

"I must," he said.

I raised my hand, and he flinched. Still he flinched.

But all I did was to kiss the tips of my soot-blackened fingertips and touch his lips with them.

"All right. Good night."

"Goodbye."

"Good night now, and goodbye in the morning."

I do not understand why I should feel so betrayed and abandoned now that he has gone. Have I not sent him off to do my bidding, trained him in poison, tutored him in the art of fear? Have I have not twisted and torqued his stubborn loyalty to his father with a tormented loyalty to me: his father's sister, his mother, his lover?

I still dream of his hands.

Attachments

Pat Murphy

 My brother's wife Adelaide pours me a glass of cider and smiles at me sadly. I love my brother's wife, and that's the problem.

The year is 1874 and I am sixty-three years old. I am playing chess with the learned Dr. Ruschenberger while my brother, at my side as always, tells dirty jokes to the doctor's assistant. My brother's laughter—braying, foolish laughter—rumbles against my side as I contemplate my next move. He calls to his beautiful wife for another glass of whiskey.

The doctor glances up from the chessboard and looks past me, frowning. "Your brother is drinking rather much," he says very softly. My brother, who is laughing at another of his jokes, does not hear.

I continue studying the chessboard. "This is his house," I say. "And he does as he chooses. He is certainly not willing to listen to advice from me."

This is my brother's house. His wife is pouring his whiskey. Two of his daughters are in the kitchen, washing the dinner dishes. His youngest sons are sitting on the porch, whittling and smoking. Just a few miles away, my wife Sarah Ann and my youngest children are in my house. In two days, my brother and I will go there and I will be mas-

ter for a time. But now I am in my brother's house and my
brother is drinking more than he should.

Dr. Ruschenberger shakes his head. Many, many years ago,
my brother and I visited the doctors at the Philadelphia College of Physicians, hoping that with their advanced surgical
techniques they might sever the flesh that binds my brother
and me together. We are linked at the chest by a band of flesh
as thick and strong as a man's arm. It is a living connection,
warm and pulsing with blood. Cutting that link might have
killed us—or might have left one dead and the other alive and
separate. In the end, we did not try the experiment.

At the time, Dr. Ruschenberger was a young man, just
learning his trade. He's older now, as are we all. Every now
and then, while traveling on business, he comes to visit us.

"Your brother is growing drunk, but you still seem quite
sober," Dr. Ruschenberger observed.

I nod. "His drinking does not affect me."

"Strange." He is gazing at my brother, who is telling another joke. "I've warned your brother that excess drink is
harmful to him," he says in a low voice. "That paralysis of
his right side—the drinking aggravates that, does it not?"

I move a bishop. "Indeed it does. But telling him not to
drink is like telling a fish not to swim." I look up from the
board and meet the doctor's concerned eyes. "There is little
point in trying."

Perhaps, I think, my brother will drink himself into a stupor. That would be for the best. But I don't tell the doctor my
thoughts.

I look up from the chessboard to see Adelaide, sitting by
the fire and working on her needlepoint. The firelight shines
on her face and I remember the first time I saw her, many
years ago.

"Which one do you want?" my brother asked me in Thai,
jerking his head toward a pair of women who stood near the
fiddle player. "The tall one or the short one?"

A young farmer standing a few steps away glanced over at us, then looked away, scowling. I frowned at my brother. "We must mind our manners," I told him softly in Thai.

With the profits from our time with P .T. Barnum, we had purchased a farm in this small North Carolina town. For the past year, we had worked hard on the land—and worked equally hard to become part of the community. Initially, the local people were wary of us. Not only were we a curios-ity--two men linked to make one—but we were foreign as well. It had been kind of our neighbor to invite us to this party, a celebration of his daughter's wedding. I did not want to offend him or the other townspeople.

"Tell me—which do you want?" my brother insisted. His voice was loud. He had been drinking and he would not be put off.

I glanced across the barn. The two young women were standing near the fiddle player, tapping their feet in time to the music and watching half a dozen couples dancing a Virginia reel. The tall one was laughing. "I favor the tall one."

"Good enough, then," he agreed. "Let's go."

"What do you mean?"

"We'll ask them to dance."

"We can't   "

But it was too late. He had already started across the barn and I had to accompany him. I could plant my feet and re-sist, but that would only start a quarrel. I did not want to fight with my brother here, in front of all these strangers.

"Good afternoon, ladies," my brother said in English. "You look lovely tonight."

He introduced us and the taller woman laughed. "We know who you are," she said. "You're famous."

"You have the advantage of us," my brother said. "You know who we are but we don't know who you are."

"Sarah Ann Yates," said the taller woman. "This is my sis-ter, Adelaide."

"I heard about you," Adelaide said softly. "You bought the Johnson farm."

"Indeed we did," my brother said. "We're neighbors."

The song came to a close. The dancers clapped for the fiddle player. A few couples headed for the cider keg at the side of the dance floor.

"It's fine music, isn't it?" my brother was saying to Adelaide. "Perhaps you and your sister would care to dance?"

I smiled at Sarah Ann, feeling shy but having no choice.

Adelaide glanced at the dancers, then back at my brother. "It seems rather awkward . . . ," she murmured

My brother answered before I could speak. "My brother and I can manage anything any other men can manage."

"Oh, let's give it a try," Sarah Ann said, smiling. She placed her hand on my arm and my brother took Adelaide's hand.

As children, living in a bamboo but on the river, my brother and I had learned to swim, working together and co-ordinating our movements. When we began appearing on stage, we had learned to tumble and somersault, always aware of the connection between us. Compared to that, dancing was easy. We had to modify some of the steps and it confused the other dancers at first. They moved back to give us room when the call came to swing your partner, since we took twice as much space to swing as an ordinary couple, but we managed.

When the fiddler's tune came to an end, we stood beside the dance floor and my brother told the sisters about our travels across America, about our tour of Europe. I was always aware, as we talked, of the warmth of Sarah Ann's hand on my arm. When we stepped outside for a breath of air, Sarah Ann kissed me on the cheek, a sweet and fleeting touch.

That was decades ago. We were young men then. Now we are old.

It is Dr. Ruschenberger's move. While he studies the chessboard, I listen to my brother tell the doctor's assistant about the other prodigies in P.T. Barnum's show: the wild woman, the fat lady, the hermaphrodite who had the breasts of a woman and the genitals of a man. He is describing their bodies to the young man in graphic detail—the hair on the wild woman's belly was as thick and curly as the dark locks that covered her pubes; the fat lady's breasts were immense, each twice the size of a man's head; the hermaphrodite had a penis as well as a vagina.

Adelaide's eyes are on her sewing. She is ignoring my brother's talk. She is silent and beautiful in her serenity. I study the chessboard, listening to my brother tell of the time that he convinced a New York tart to join him in bed, paying double, he said, because she would do double duty. He laughs. "And indeed she did. I had her as many times as two men. But my brother wouldn't have her at all. Just lay there and slept, not interested at all."

The doctor moves a rook and I turn my attention to the chessboard. "Check," the doctor says. Then, a few moves later, "Checkmate."

The doctor and his assistant take their leave when the clock on the mantle strikes eleven, riding away to the inn in town and leaving us alone.

My brother is tired—his body is slumping, tugging on the flesh that binds us together. I glance at his face—slack-jawed, one eye drooping half-closed. He frowns at me. People say we look alike; people call us identical. I can see some resemblance, but so many differences as well. I would never curl my lip in such an insolent and unattractive expression; I would never narrow my eyes in such a malicious gaze.

When the surgeons were preparing to cut the band of flesh that joined me to my brother, Sarah Ann was the one who stopped the operation. She and her sister had traveled by train to Philadelphia, two farm girls in the big city.

We were on the operating table when Sarah Ann stormed into the College of Physicians, dressed in her Sunday best and shouting in the voice she used to summon hogs to feeding. "You can't do this! You'll murder them both! You can't." Adelaide trailed in her wake, as always, following obediently.

The College of Physicians was no match for Sarah Ann. The distinguished head of surgery threw up his hands when she said she would accuse him of murder if he attempted the operation. She threw herself into my arms and swore that she loved me as I was, that I did not have to change for her, she would marry me as I was. While Sarah Ann shouted, Adelaide stood quietly at my brother's side, watching her sister's hysterics.

That afternoon, my brother asked Adelaide to marry him and she accepted. We married the next day. I don't believe that I ever directly asked Sarah Ann to marry me. But after she said that she would marry me as I was, it was understood that I would marry her. There was no more discussion of that matter. So we had a double wedding.

I don't know when it was that I fell in love with Adelaide. Perhaps it was on her wedding night. My brother and I had drawn straws to determine who would celebrate his wedding night first and my brother had won. So he would spend the night with Adelaide; the next night, I would spend with Sarah Ann.

I remember my brother's wedding night better than my own. The lantern burned with a steady light on the bedside table. Adelaide was leaning over to blow out the flame when my brother said, "Leave that. I want to see you naked."

He was smiling lasciviously. As he spoke, he was unbuttoning his own shirt, fumbling with the buttons on either side of the thick strip of flesh that joined us. He dropped his shirt on the floor and loosened the tie that fastened his pants.

Adelaide stood in the light, her hands clasped before her, her eyes cast downward. My brother stepped toward her, and

I was pulled along. He unbuttoned her dress, exposing the lace of her chemise. He groped at her breasts drunkenly, cupping one in each hand, then leaned forward and rubbed his face upon them, nuzzling the nipples through the thin fabric.

"Husband," she said, her voice soft. "Get into bed, and I will come to you.

My brother kicked off his pants and we sat on the edge of the bed together, then we swung our legs up and lay down.

Adelaide had her back to us. She had taken off her dress and wore only the chemise. The lantern light shone from behind her, revealing her body through the fabric—the soft curve of her waist, the gentle swell of her hips.

"Take that off and come to me," my brother demanded.

I lay still on the bed, watching as she lifted the chemise over her head and stood naked in the lantern light. She turned and the light shone from behind her, casting her breasts into shadow. My brother was fondling himself; I could feel an echo of his touch, like a ghost hand touching me, arousing me. With his free hand, my brother reached out and grasped Adelaide's arm, then pulled her toward him. As she came onto the bed, she glanced at me and I looked away, trying to give her what privacy I could.

I could smell her scent, delicate as night-blooming jasmine; I could hear her breath catch as he roughly pushed his hand between her thighs. I could imagine that my own hand felt the tickle of pubic hair, the slippery wetness of her.

She cried out when he penetrated her: a high note, like the alarm call of an exotic bird. He moved his hips against hers, and the note repeated, a sweet song of pain and pleasure. My brother grunted beneath her, and I closed my eyes, feeling the rush of his lust. My hand moved of its own accord and I stroked myself, echoing his thrusts. I could not help myself. But I made no sound; I kept my hips still.

My brother groaned like a boar servicing a sow, a base animal sound. And he moaned as he came with a rush, flooding her with his semen.

When it was over, my brother's breathing grew steady. He slept, drunken and sexually sated. I watched the lantern light flicker on the ceiling of the hotel room. The straw tick mattress rustled as Adelaide stood to blow out the lantern. In the moment before darkness came, I saw that her cheeks were wet with tears.

"Adelaide," I whispered in the darkness. "Are you hurt?"

"No," she said softly. "Not really."

"Why are you crying?"

She was silent for a moment.

"Tell me, Adelaide. I'm your brother now. Tell me why you are sad."

"My mother wept at the wedding. She is sorry that I am moving away.

"Not so far away," I told her. "Just a few miles."

"A few miles. So far. I've never been so far from my family." A moment of silence. "You can't understand how far that can be. You are never more than a foot away from your family."

I could feel my brother's heart beating, through the flesh that joins us. "That is not always a good thing," I said.

"At home, I always knew what they were doing. I could hear my mother in the kitchen when I was falling asleep. I could hear my brother's snoring from the next room. Sometimes it bothered me, but now I miss it. I could hear my sister, beside me in the bed."

"I will do my best to snore for you, sweet sister-in-law," I said, "if that will make you feel at home."

"You are a sweet brother to me," she said, her tone lighter.

I remained awake after Adelaide fell asleep, listening to the steady rhythm of her breathing and my brother's snores. I wondered what it would be like to be so far away that I could not hear my brother's breathing, not feel his heart beating in rhythm with mine. I could not imagine it.

The next day, before my wedding night with Sarah Ann, my brother and I drank toast after toast with people who had come to wish us well. I was not accustomed to drinking and I was drunk by the time the others left. I vaguely remember joking with Sarah Ann as I pulled her dress over her head. I remember seeing my brother grinning at her naked body. She laughed as she tossed a corner of the blanket over his face to hide his staring eyes. I pulled her onto me, driving myself into her, overcome with my own animal nature.

"Let us go to bed, my husband," Adelaide says. The children have already gone to bed and she does not speak to me. My brother and I quarreled yesterday. He wants to buy more land and I think we already have more land than we can handle.

We began by talking about land, but in the end, it went beyond that. He had been drinking again and I lost my temper. I told him he was a fool and a parasite and he told me I was a coward. I told him that he had no soul and he told me that I had come into the world with my head tucked between his legs—that was the story our mother had always told. "Your head was between my legs when we were born, and I've protected you ever since," he said. I said I would not sign my permission to buy the farm that adjoins mine, and he has not spoken to me since. He would be angry with Adelaide if she spoke to me. So she does not speak, though she acknowledges me with a glance.

Adelaide walks to the bedroom ahead of us, holding the lantern to light the way, her dress pale in the yellow light. My brother is clumsy in his drunkenness, and it is all I can do to keep us upright as he stumbles down the hallway. He curses under his breath, but he does not address me.

He is watching his wife's hips sway as she walks ahead of us. Though she is old, though she has given birth to many children, she is still slender and lovely. Her beauty is not just a beauty of the body, but a beauty of the soul. I think about the soft touch of her hand and I know my brother is thinking about that too. But he is too old and too drunk to act on his desires.

We undress and lie down in the large bed that my brother and I built many years ago. In the dim light of the lantern, I watch Adelaide unbutton her dress and hang it from a peg on the wall. In her thin cotton chemise, she sits on the stool by the dressing table and reaches up to take the pins from her hair. Such a familiar gesture, the same since she was a young girl. Her hair, still thick and brown, tumbles down around her shoulders and she begins to brush out the tangles.

My brother is already snoring, sedated by whiskey and talk.

"Adelaide," I whisper. "How are you tonight?"

"I am well, my brother-in-law," she says softly. She glances at her husband. His head is thrown back; his mouth is open.

"I wrote you a poem yesterday," I tell her. "When I was watching you peel potatoes for the stew."

"A poem about peeling potatoes?" She laughs. "How can this be?"

"You are beautiful when you peel potatoes. The sunlight was shining on your hair and your hands were so graceful that I would rather watch you peel potatoes than see the finest dancer in New York take a turn on the dance floor."

Every evening, when my brother is asleep, we talk like this.

"You are a foolish man, my brother-in-law."

"I am foolish only for you." I pat the bed beside me. "Sit here on the bed," I say. "Let me brush your hair." She blows out the lantern. A beam of moonlight shines through a gap between the curtains. In the moonlight, I brush her hair and whisper to her, telling her of how beautiful she is. I whisper my poetry, foolish poetry, appropriate only for the flower-scented darkness. Love poetry to my sister-in-law. Her hair is warm beneath my hands.

"Lie beside me," I say.

She glances at my brother, still snoring. "Just for a moment," she says.

"He won't wake," I reassure her. "Just let me hold you."

Sometimes, on nights like this when my brother is drunk and asleep, she will lie beside me for a while, letting me feel her body next to mine. I gently pull her close. Sometimes, she welcomes my touch, but tonight she is tense, afraid that my brother will wake up.

"I want to be alone with you," I murmur. It is an old story; an impossible request.

"We are alone," she whispers back.

But I know better. Though my brother sleeps, I can feel his heartbeat through the bond that joins us.

After a moment, Adelaide brushes her lips across my cheek in a ghost of a kiss and slips out of bed, moving to the other side to lie beside my brother. When he wakes in the morning, she will be by his side.

If this were my house, Sarah Ann would be sleeping by my side. Sarah Ann has grown up to become a strong-minded practical woman who has no time for poetry. She gives me warmth and comfort, and I feel affection for her, but it is nothing like the love I feel for Adelaide.

Adelaide doesn't love my brother. I am sure of that. How could she love such a man? She is beautiful and sensitive; he is bitter and crude. I fall asleep at last, listening to Adelaide's breathing and wishing that I could, just once, sleep with her at my side.

I wake in the night to a sudden silence and I lie in the darkness, staring at the ceiling. Something is wrong. Something has awakened me.

I can hear Adelaide's soft breathing. Other than that, the room is quiet, so very quiet that it seems to me the silence itself has awakened me. Something is missing. For a moment, I don't know what it is.

Then I know. A sound that had always been beside me is gone. I cannot feel my brother's heartbeat, the rhythm that always beat a counterpoint to mine. I cannot hear him breathing.

I call his name softly, but there is no answer. I push myself up on an elbow so that I can twist my head to look down at my brother, an awkward position made even more awkward by my brother's stillness.

The moonlight falls in a white stripe across his face. His eyes are open and staring. His mouth is agape. He is gone.

"Adelaide," I call, my voice breaking. "Adelaide!"

She shifts, turning toward my voice. "What is it?" she murmurs, her voice thick with sleep. "What is the matter?"

I can feel the chill of his body next to mine. I don't know how it is that she can't hear the silence that fills the room, pressing down on us. I lie back down, so that my mouth is near my brother's ear. Such a strange thing, to feel only one heart beating. "You are a fool," I whisper to my brother. "You are an animal, a parasite without a soul." He does not respond. He is gone.

"My brother is dead," I say to Adelaide, and for a moment I can say no more.

I feel her sitting up in the bed, moving slowly. "Dead?" she murmurs, her voice fearful. She is sitting up now. "How could that be?" But she is drawing away from his lifeless body, even as she denies that he is dead.

"I'll send one of the boys for Dr. Ruschenberger."

I shake my head, knowing that the doctor would do no good. Already, I can feel the chill of my brother's body sucking the warmth from mine. I can think of only one thing that can warm me.

"It is too late for doctors," I say. "Come lie beside me."

She hesitates.

"My brother is dead. You are a widow. Come lie beside me."

At last, she gets out of the bed and walks around to my

side. She lifts the blanket and slides into bed beside me. Her body is warm against mine. I put one arm around her neck. I cannot embrace her; my other arm is pinned in place by the weight of my brother. But her warm body presses down on me, chasing back the cold.

I want to make love to my brother's wife, my brother's widow, the beautiful Adelaide. "You are so beautiful," I tell her. There are tears on her cheeks as I pull her on top of me, feeling her soft thighs part for me as they have parted for my brother. I have dreamed so many times of this moment and in my dreams I had always feared that my brother would wake up, aroused by my movement, by the surge of my love for Adelaide. But he cannot wake up. Though Adelaide is on top of me, I am alone. I close my eyes and remember that long ago wedding night when the beautiful young Adelaide came to our bed.

I feel young again. I feel that things have been set right at last. I am alone with Adelaide and she is mine. She cries out when I penetrate her—so high and sweet. She is hot and wet, squeezing me tight, taking me in. Such a warm place, so welcoming.

As I come, I feel the heat leave my body. The chill is spreading from my brother's body. Though I press closer to Adelaide, I can feel the flesh that binds me to my brother tugging on me, pulling me down.

Adelaide is crying quietly. Why are you crying? I want to ask her. Does she cry for my brother? Does she cry for me? But I have no energy for words. I kiss her goodbye and I lie back on the bed, knowing that I will not be alone for long.

In the Season of Rains

Ellen Steiber

> . . . Wild cats will meet hyenas there,
> The satyrs will call to each other,
> There Lilith shall repose
> And find her a place of rest
>
> —ISAIAH 34:14

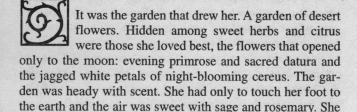 It was the garden that drew her. A garden of desert flowers. Hidden among sweet herbs and citrus were those she loved best, the flowers that opened only to the moon: evening primrose and sacred datura and the jagged white petals of night-blooming cereus. The garden was heady with scent. She had only to touch her foot to the earth and the air was sweet with sage and rosemary. She had lived in deserts for many generations now, and for more years than even she could count she had longed for that first garden.

So she appeared in his. He heard the noise out back behind the house, and was sure one of the cats had gotten out or a rabbit in. He opened the screen door and strained to see into the shadows. He listened more carefully. The crickets who'd fallen silent when he stepped onto the porch began singing again.

He did a quick mental inventory of cats. The old tom was asleep in the living room; the tiger stripe in the kitchen, eating. Which meant it was the little black female.

"Seena!" he called. He'd named her for an ex-girlfriend. Like the woman, the cat demanded great affection and endless indulgence, but over time the cat had proven more endearing.

And more responsive. He called her again. It was unusual for her not to answer.

Something moved inside the garden gates. He stepped into the yard, surprised as always by the softness of the summer night. He rarely came out to the garden after sunset. He'd water at dawn before work, and do the occasional weeding and trimming on weekends.

The garden hadn't been his idea at all but a legacy from another girlfriend, Cassie, who couldn't stand the sight of his barren yard and had decided to do something about it. It made him uncomfortable, actually, that Cassie had worked so hard on his land. Still, it had made her happy at the time and he'd ignored the premonitions of obligation as long as he could. Eventually, after she put in the star jasmine and the gardenia, but before she could plant the wisteria that was meant to wind round the trellis, he broke it off. She was giving him gifts he could never repay, and it had to stop before he fell too deeply into her debt. So he told her it was over and he sent her from his house and her garden. He still missed her sometimes. Cassie was a sweet one. But it was cleaner this way. He had no regrets. And now he had a garden that bore the imprint of one who loved the earth and knew how to work it, one who knew how to coax life from the desert's parched ground.

He heard the sound again. It was an animal but not Seena, he decided. Whatever it was, was wearing some sort of bell. He called the cat again and was answered by a woman's laughter, low and throaty and mocking.

She came toward him and he honestly couldn't tell if she was walking or dancing or floating above the ground. She moved slowly, her body swaying lightly as though the evening wind moved through her. She had long, glossy black hair that shone in the moonlight and a body that was too full to be fashionable—high, full breasts, a long waist with a round stomach, and stocky, muscled legs. She wore a white gauzy skirt tied just above her pubic bone, and he realized that what he'd thought were bells were tiny golden disks sewn to the skirt. Brighter disks hung from her ears and from the bangles on her wrists. She was barefoot, bare-chested, bare-armed, and she faced him without shame or surprise.

"Who are you?" he asked. When she didn't answer, he tried his first language, Spanish. "*Quién es?*"

"I came to enjoy your garden," she replied. Her English was accented, an accent he didn't recognize.

"You didn't answer my question," he said.

She smiled. "I've told you what you need to know." She gestured to the garden. "Did you plant it?"

"No," he admitted. "Except for the birds of paradise."

She regarded the delicate plants with scorn. "They're not doing well. You bruised them when you planted them, and then you gave them too much water. The poor things are waterlogged."

He didn't doubt his senses. He was a scientist, trained to make accurate observations. He rubbed his forehead, knowing full well that this was real and yet unable to make sense of it.

"Who are you?" he asked again.

"How long has it been since you've lain with a woman?" she countered. "It's been a while, hasn't it? Nearly half a year. And you wake up hard and frustrated and you tell yourself it's better that way. Easier."

"I think you'd better leave," he said quietly. He remembered that he hadn't heard any kind of vehicle approach. "If you don't have a ride, I'll call you a cab." He stared at her dark nipples. "I'll even lend you a shirt."

"Your generosity is overwhelming, Enrico."

His name wasn't anywhere on the outside of the house or the mailbox.

She reached a hand toward him and the scent of the datura became stronger. "I want to show you something," she said.

She took his wrist in strong, cool fingers and despite the heat of the summer night, the coolness went through his body like snowmelt poured through his veins.

He pulled away from her, chilled, unsure of what it was he'd just touched. A gust of wind bent the branches of the jasmine, tumbling tiny white stars toward the ground.

She stepped deeper into the shadows, and the golden spangles clicked together softly. "Here," she said, pointing to the garden path where it was arched over with cassia branches. "Lie down."

He was getting hard and he had a horrible feeling that she knew it. "You are one strange lady," he said.

"Not a lady," she told him. "Never that. Lie down, Enrico, and let the earth give you her gifts."

He wasn't used to taking orders from women, but he was too curious to refuse this one. He knelt then laid himself down, descending into a layer of air woven through with the scents of the garden. He hadn't known the rich tapestry of smells. Rosemary overlaid with cassia, the musk of sage intertwined with the nectar of honeysuckle.

He looked up at her and swore for a second that behind her back two large dusky wings were rubbing together. No, it was a trick of the shadows.

He held out a hand to her. "Come down here with me."

"You like to invite women in," she said. "And then to make them leave again. It's a rhythm with you, no?"

He felt the hairs on the back of his neck rise. She'd spoken with Seena's exact inflections.

"You won't have to ask me to leave," she promised. "I never stay."

Overhead, a screech owl winged through the night, and he remembered something his grandmother had told him. His *abuelita*, who'd grown up in a tiny mountain village in Mexico, was as superstitious as they came. "The owl brings death, Enrico," she'd say. "When you see the owl, you must pray to *la Virgen de Guadalupe*. Then only she can help you."

The woman was standing by his side now. She moved one hip and her skirts brushed the ground, then his chest. The tiny golden spangles were like thin disks of ice against his bare skin. It was impossible, he told himself. The temperature was in the nineties. Nothing could stay so cold in the summer night.

"You're chilled," she observed.

He took it as his way out. "I must be coming down with something," he said, and got to his feet. "I'd better go in."

The laughter again. "What about your little cat?" she asked. "Don't you want to find her?"

Somewhere to the north lightning flickered in the skies, and the scent of creosote began to fill the air. The skies were unusually dark, the desert stars hidden behind a mass of cloud cover. There would be a storm, he knew, quick and hard and loud. The female cat was terrified by thunder. Astrid, another ex, was a therapist who had told him in no uncertain terms that the young cat suffered from an anxiety disorder related to noise.

"The cat will be fine," he told the woman.

"That she will," the woman agreed.

He started toward the house, aware that he was leaving a cat to a storm and a half-naked woman in his yard, aware that it was high-summer in southern Arizona and he was colder than he'd been after being stranded for hours in a Montana ice storm. He would not try to puzzle out who she was or how she'd known the things she had, for all of it was impossible.

He went into the room that he'd made into a study and sat down at the computer. The map of the watershed was still on the screen. He studied flood plains, diverted water courses from their natural routes, and "protected" banks, lining them with steel and concrete to prevent erosion. Long ago, he'd realized that it was the land that needed protection from the developers and engineers, and that there was something perverse and futile in all the shoring up and redirecting of streams. Not that he let it stop him. He was good at what he did, he made good money, and he found pleasure in the numerical equations that defined the flow of water, the drainage of soil, and the momentum of a given flood. Now he worked a set of equations, allowing the familiar discipline to calm him. There was great comfort in knowing one's variables and being able to manipulate them with precision.

Lightning flickered again, followed by a shudder of thunder. He counted the number of seconds between them. Twenty. The lightning was approximately four miles away. Close enough to fry a hard drive. He saved the map of the watershed, and disconnected the computer and printer. Then he made himself a cup of hot tea. He was still freezing, probably running a fever. He'd take two aspirin and go to bed.

The wind rose in a high whine, almost a cry, then dropped again, pulling the storm down from the skies. Needles of rain hurled themselves against the house, then sank into the earth. He heard one of the blue wooden shutters blow open and slam back against its frame.

The cat, he thought. She was still out there.

He started toward the porch to call her in, then stopped as he reached the screen door. What if the woman was still in the garden?

There is no woman, he told himself. But he could not make himself step outside. He called the cat from the porch. He called for a good three minutes. And when she didn't answer, he went back into the house, shut off the lights, and got into bed.

He lay there, conscious of the hollow next to his hip where Seena liked to lie. Every night, seconds after he got into bed, she'd curl up beside him. This was the first time in the year since he'd gotten her that he'd gone to sleep alone. He missed her warmth. He made himself concentrate on the sounds of the wind and rain, and let the storm lull him to sleep.

She had told him that she wouldn't stay. She didn't bother to mention that she would also return. But she knew he would wonder and when his fear had waned, he would secretly hope. And so she would let him hope for seven nights, until the moon waxed from a bone-white semicircle to a full silver sphere.

He didn't let himself think about her at first. He was disturbed only by the fact that the female cat hadn't come in for breakfast that morning, nor was she there when he'd returned home from an afternoon of meetings. He wondered if she'd found a way over the garden fence or perhaps burrowed beneath it. He hoped she hadn't been too badly frightened by the storm. And that she'd managed to keep herself safe from the roaming bands of coyotes. She was a smart little animal, he reminded himself. Cats were, after all, natural survivors.

That evening, just to be sure he sweated out any toxins from the previous night's strange malaise, he ran six miles. He returned home slick with sweat and reassured by his own strength. A blinking light in the study caught his attention. He pushed the answering machine's PLAY button and a woman's voice spoke, "Enrique, it's Liora. I just got back into town, and I've brought you a souvenir . . . ."

Liora was an Israeli archeologist, doing research for the university. They'd met on campus last fall when both of them cut out early from a mind-numbing faculty meeting. He'd gone out with her only a few times before they made love, after which he'd explained quite clearly that he didn't do commitment, ever. He was always honest with them; it was for their protection, really. She had met his announcement with a sleepy yawn and then explained that she would be working on a dig in northern Mexico for the next six months. He hadn't really expected to hear from her again. Now he welcomed the idea of seeing her, a real, flesh and blood woman, one who happened to be very good in bed. The perfect prescription to banish last night's crazy fever dream. Sometime during the day he'd decided that the problem was he'd simply gone too long without sex.

Liora declined the invitation to come to dinner at his house. Instead they met two nights later at a coffeehouse near the university.

She sat at a table in the far corner, making notes in a small spiral-bound notebook, her thick, black hair gathered in a silver clasp at the back of her neck.

She glanced up when she saw him approach and smiled. *"Holá, Enrique, cómo estás?"* she said. Liora's family were Sephardic Jews, originally from Spain. She spoke Hebrew, English, Greek, and Spanish, with English being the only language in which she had a noticeable foreigner's accent.

"Okay," he replied, sitting across from her. "How was Mexico?"

"Good," she said, accepting his decision to conduct the conversation in English. "Actually, better than good. The dig is going well. We're finding even more than we'd hoped." She was wearing a faded blue denim shirt, her skin dark against it. A thick silver hoop hung from each ear.

"Finding," he echoed. "Does that mean you're going back?"

She nodded. "The rains. We had to take a break. There's serious flooding right now." She gave him a wry smile. "The people in the villages there could probably use your help, though I doubt they could afford you. . . . Have you been busy?"

He told her about the summer grad classes he was teaching, about his various consulting jobs. How he'd built detention basins for flood waters by redesigning the local golf courses.

She found this very funny. "I see," she said. "We must make the desert safe for rich, white suburbanites."

He was finding her both irritating and compelling. He would feel much better when he had her slim, muscled body lying beneath his own. He touched the back of her wrist, then took her hand.

He turned it over and stroked the underside of her forearm. "The moon isn't up yet," he said. "Is there any way I could persuade you to go look at the stars with me?"

"Where would you want to do that?"

He named the range of mountains that bordered the western edge of Tucson. "You can't see the city lights from there, so the stars are really bright." He glanced at his watch. "We could drive there in twenty minutes."

Her dark eyes studied his, and he noticed the fine lines at their edges. Too many days under the suns of too many deserts. She'd worked in the Sinai and the Kalahari and on the blazing slopes of Mediterranean islands. The Sonora was just the latest in a string of hot, dry lands whose secrets she sought to unearth.

"You never struck me as the star-gazing type, Enrique. I think this is a not-very-well-disguised invitation to fuck."

There was no anger in her voice, so he played it a little further. "And that's not an invitation you'd want to take me up on? As I remember, our bodies liked each other."

"They did, but not tonight." She glanced at her watch. "I promised to help one of the undergrads catalog pottery shards."

He released her arm. "Oh, that sounds fascinating."

Her dark eyes danced with amusement. "Uh-huh."

"Is this why you called?" he asked. "So you could tell me about pottery shards?"

"Enrique, calm your ruffled ego. I told you why I called. I brought something back for you." She reached into the large woven bag on the seat next to her and drew out an oddly shaped object wrapped in a Mexican newspaper. "I found this in one of the *mercados*. It had your name on it."

She placed the gift firmly in his hand, left money on the table to cover their coffees and tip, then stood up. She was wearing a short black skirt that revealed long, tanned legs and sandals that laced round her ankles. He got up to follow her out, remembering what it felt like to have those legs wrapped around him, pressing against his back, clasping him to her.

She stopped just outside the cafe's door. "The clouds keep building," she said, looking up at the dusk skies. "We wouldn't have seen any stars anyway." She reached up to kiss him lightly on the mouth. "*Ciao*, Enrique."

She left him standing on the street, holding her gift. He was so annoyed it didn't even occur to him to open it until he was back in his truck. Then he tore open the newsprint wrapping. He was holding a small stone carving of a voluptuous, high-breasted woman with talons for feet. And an owl's wings folded behind her back.

He was in a mood by the time he got home. He did not like dates with women that did not end in bed. And tonight he'd wanted Liora. Wanted her badly.

What was that all about? he asked himself. Was meeting for coffee the opening move in a new flirtation or the close of an old one? Did she really just want to give him that strange little lump of stone? He resolved to call her the next day and find out.

The wind was up again and sheet lightning creased the western sky. The night had the heavy feel of a dry storm, of a rain that wouldn't break. Still, he could hear thunder over the mountains, so once again he called the young black cat. Though she'd been gone nearly four days, he found he couldn't give up on her. This time he made himself go out into the garden. He took a flashlight, searched the shadows. The cat wasn't there, but under the cassia bushes the ground glittered with round, golden spangles.

He knelt to pick one up. It was made of a light metal, the weight of aluminum but the color of ancient gold. Had it fallen from her skirts the other night—or had she returned? The idea pleased him, and for the first time he let himself wonder what would have happened if he hadn't bolted. He pocketed the golden disk, imagining how he might have taken her there under the cassias, what it would have felt like to be inside her. If opportunity presented itself again, he wouldn't let himself get scared off by a case of the chills. And he wouldn't let her get away so easily. He turned as he sensed a movement beyond the garden fence, but his light picked out only the form of a very large jackrabbit.

The sound of the phone ringing brought him back into the house. He heard his mother's voice and decided not to intercept the machine. He listened as she left a message telling him that his *Tiá* Carmen had taken sick in Mexico City and she was going to stay with her for a week, and would he please pay a visit to his *abuelita* while she was gone. His grandmother, who'd had a series of strokes, had been in a nursing home for the last year. She was partially paralyzed and barely spoke. She spent her days waiting for aides to change her and feed her, put her in the wheelchair, then back into the bed. He didn't visit her often because it saddened him. He preferred to remember the *abuelita* who made the finest tortillas he'd ever tasted and a *mole* sauce that was heaven, who went to church every morning and lit candles to the Virgin every night. He didn't know who it was he was supposed to be visiting in the wheelchair. He did not call his mother back.

He worked instead, reading through a developer's plans to re-direct a wash away from an eastern tract of the desert.

He studied the topographic map of the flood plain and the

builder's blueprints. Then he began to work the numbers, losing himself in the elegance and surety of the calculations.

His sleep was broken that night by a cat's blood-curdling scream. He sat bolt upright in bed, knowing it was Seena. He heard it again, louder and closer this time, and he knew with certainty that she was fighting for her life.

A coyote must have her. Or a bobcat.

Still caught in the heaviness of sleep, he forced himself out of bed. He stumbled out of his bedroom and stopped halfway down the hall. The two male cats were blocking his way, both of them arched and hissing.

He walked toward them slowly, then drew back as the tiger stripe swiped at his bare legs, drawing a clean line of blood.

Swearing softly, he knelt to face them. "What the hell's got you so frightened?" he asked.

He stood up and again tried to pass, but the old tom went after him, closing its teeth around his ankle so fast it made his stomach lurch—and stopping just short of puncturing his skin.

"Okay, okay," he said. Gently, he stroked the tom's head and the side of its jaw, until the animal released his ankle. His bone ached where the cat's teeth had gripped him.

"You've both gone *loco*," he told them. "What am I doing living with crazed cats?"

Their eyes glittered in the dark hallway. He could feel a low growl coming from the tom.

"Relax," he told them, his hands raised in surrender. "I'm going back to bed. But in the morning, I expect you both to behave."

He started back to the bedroom, wondering what had gotten into the animals and why on earth anyone would put up with it. He'd all but forgotten about Seena. Until he flicked on the bedside lamp and saw her sitting on his bed, contentedly washing her face as though she'd never been gone.

*   *   *

The phone woke him the next morning. He glanced at his alarm clock. It was seven, exactly. Usually he was up by six. Without opening her eyes, the little female cat rearranged herself so that her head pressed against his hip. Then he remembered. He'd overslept because of that nonsense with the cats.

"Welcome home," he murmured, running a finger down the cat's nose.

The phone rang for the third time. He rubbed his eyes and put the receiver to his ear.

"Enrique Ortiz?"

"Yes?" He didn't recognize the voice.

"This is Evelyn Mitchell at the Desert Hills Home. I'm sorry to disturb you so early. I'm calling about María Terésa Hernadez. Your mother listed you as next of kin."

María Terésa . . . *abuelita*. "My grandmother, she's—"

"She had another stroke, Mr. Ortiz. Several hours ago." The woman's voice reminded him of a television reporter's, frighteningly well practiced in the art of delivering devastating news. "Your grandmother has suffered additional loss of movement on her right side but she *is* conscious. We were hoping you would stop by today. Dr. Donovan thinks it might be beneficial for her to see a member of her family."

He was sitting up now, staring at the receiver as if it were a rattler who'd struck him.

"Mr. Ortiz?"

"Yes."

"Can you come in today?"

He groaned and tried to recall what it was he had planned. He had eight and ten A.M. classes to teach, followed by a lunch with the developer, and then an on-site visit to the wash that was being diverted. Then he'd planned on calling Liora, taking her to dinner, bringing her home. . . .

"Mr. Ortiz?" Evelyn Mitchell was relentless.

"I have a lunch meeting at twelve-thirty," he said. "I'll try to stop by after that, though I can't stay long."

He could hear Ms. Mitchell penciling him in to whatever appointment book lay open in front of her. "That will be fine, Mr. Ortiz. I'll try to ensure that Dr. Donovan is available."

"I'm sure you will," he told her, and hung up.

The smell of the nursing home hadn't changed: urine and age and tasteless steamed food all blended together with a thin wash of antiseptic. He bypassed the patient information desk and walked down the spotless hall to his grandmother's room. He was carrying a bunch of carnations he'd picked up at a nearby supermarket.

It was still hard for him to believe that she was the one who was ill. All through his childhood, whenever he was sick, it was his *abuelita*, not doctors, whom his mother called. *Abuelita* would sit beside his bed and explain that being sick meant that your *alma*, your soul, was a little lost. Even fear, she'd say, could shake the soul from a body. So what they had to do to make him well was to call it back. He remembered being wide-eyed with wonder as she explained that his soul had not traveled far—it hovered near his pulse points: his wrists, his temples, his throat, his heart. Solemnly, she would touch these points, calling his *alma* back into his body. She would then supplement this therapy with candles and incense, soups and fruits and herbs, hot compresses and her omnipresent prayers to *la Virgen*. Her cures had never failed him.

The door to her room was open. His grandmother sat in a wheelchair, a thin crocheted blanket wrapped around her shoulders. When had she gotten so small and wizened and gray? She used to be so round. He remembered sitting next to her in church as a boy, leaning into the soft warmth of her body.

"*Abuelita*. It's Enrico."

There was no movement or response. Her eyes, he noticed, seemed focused somewhere beyond the room.

He leaned forward and kissed her cheek. "I brought you red flowers," he said in Spanish. Red was her favorite color. "Do you want me to put them in water?" He did not ask her how she was feeling. That would have been absurd.

He busied himself filling a drinking glass with water and attempting to arrange the long, green stems inside it. He put the carnations on the night stand where she could see them. When she'd first come here, his mother had brought her one of the tall votive candles, with a decal of the Virgin on the red glass. She never even got the chance to light it. An aide informed them that the nursing home forbade candles.

He sat down on the neatly made bed. "They told me you had another stroke last night."

A trickle of saliva ran from the corner of her mouth. He grabbed a tissue and dabbed at it gently.

"Are they treating you okay here? . . . Can you hear me at all?"

His grandmother's only response was to continue to drool.

"Mama's in Mexico with *Tía* Carmen," he told her. "So it's just going to be me visiting for a while. Is there something I can get you? Something you want?"

As far he could tell, she didn't even know that he was in the room with her. He laid his fingertips against her wrist, as she would have done for him. But he detected nothing beyond her heartbeat.

He glanced at his watch. He'd been here fifteen minutes. He'd stay another ten and then he really had to take a look at that wash.

He sat with her in silence, listening to the hum of the air-conditioning system, to the sound of medication carts being wheeled down the hall. Neither Dr. Donovan nor Ms. Mitchell appeared, and he had no desire to seek them out.

When the twenty-five minutes were up he got to his feet.

"I've got to go now," he said. "But I'll be back later this week, okay?"

He was halfway to the door when she spoke. *"Te . . ."* Her voice was weak and slurred.

"Qué?" he asked. *"Digamé, abuelita."* He tried in English, "What? Tell me."

She never once looked at him, but she struggled to speak. *"Te . . . te . . . ten miedo,"* she said at last, her voice a whisper.

He listened for more, but there wasn't any. He waited another five minutes, until he was convinced that it was all she would say. He wondered if she were sensing her own approaching death. If her soul had been shaken loose. What she'd struggled so hard to say was: Have fear.

He stroked her cheek. *"No miedo,"* he told her, and kissed her once again before leaving.

"You related to her?" A voice stopped him as he walked down the hall.

He turned to see a tall, black woman dressed in a nurse's white uniform. A blue cardigan hung from her shoulders.

"I'm her grandson," he answered.

"I haven't seen you here before," she said pointedly. "What's your name?"

He told her.

"Guess you're not him."

"Who?"

"Yesterday afternoon, I went in to give her her medication. She was in a state. Very agitated. Kept repeating, 'Elbooho, elbooho, elbooho.' I didn't know what she was talking about. I checked her elbows—nothing. So now I see you coming out of her room and I think, maybe his name is Elbooho."

He shook his head. "Sorry."

The woman gave him a long look. "Uh-huh," she said.

"What?"

"Nothing," she said. "Guess I can't tell a grown man he ought to come around and visit his grandma more often, now can I?"

"Point taken," he told her. "You're very subtle."

She finally smiled at him. "It's my talent."

It was not until he was halfway across town, driving toward the wash, that he let his grandmother's words run through his mind. He thought about the way she'd phrased it. She hadn't meant that she had fear, he realized. It was a command, a warning, perhaps even for him. An even odder thought occurred to him. Maybe elbooho wasn't the name of a person. Maybe it was two words: *El búho.* The owl.

The wash was at the very edge of town, in the foothills of the Rincons. The area was still rural—dirt roads, a few houses, mostly cactus and palo verde and a few soft green mesquite bosques hidden in the folds of the land. It was slated for two different developments that would include houses, a strip mall, and a small industrial park.

He drove down a wide, graded dirt road that had once led to a ranch, then took a smaller road, branching north. He parked the truck beside the wash, surprised to see a dust-covered jeep a few hundred yards away. He hadn't expected company.

Curious, he stepped out of the truck and glanced up and down the wash. The owner of the jeep wasn't in sight, nor were there footprints in the soft, sandy soil. The channel was fairly deep here, and the banks and even the middle of the wash were covered with green, a thick growth of acacia, desert broom, scrub oak, and mesquite. A striped lizard skittered across the sand and disappeared behind a rock.

He knelt to check the soil sediment, then began walking upstream to see if the banks were stable, to see where the erosion was going. He glanced up as he heard a low rumble of thunder. It was still early in the afternoon, and full white clouds were rising from behind the Catalina Mountains to the north. The clouds were already a good deal larger than they'd been when he'd left the nursing home half an hour ago. Another storm was building.

He stopped walking as he saw her. This time she was

wearing loose khaki shorts and a black, sleeveless T-shirt. Her hair hung in a single, heavy braid. She was kneeling in the wash, brushing gently at the soil.

"Ah," he said, "just the woman I was hoping to meet up with. *¡Qué casualidad!*"

Liora shaded her eyes to look up at him. "Not a coincidence," she corrected him. "The State Historical Commission hired me to do some sampling."

"Let me guess. We are standing on the site of a prehistoric Native American village. Or better yet, a sacred burial site."

"If we are, your developer doesn't get to divert the wash," she said, rising to her feet.

He stared at her, aware of the sheen of sweat on her arms and chest, of her eyes being nearly as black as her hair and of both being darker than the faded cotton T-shirt. "Maybe I ought to wait on my report until you tell me whether or not you're going to stop the project."

"I'd like to," she said. "It would give me great pleasure to prevent you from destroying the wash. Unfortunately, I can only tell them what I actually find." She gave him a perfectly friendly smile. "Why don't you leave me to my work and then we can both file our reports?"

He shook his head and walked closer to her until he stood only a few inches away. "I'm not going anywhere until you explain that little gift you gave me."

She gazed at him calmly, making no attempt to explain. Once he had been able to pull her toward him simply by letting her see the desire in his eyes, knowing that it was matched perfectly by the desire in hers. The current between them had been so strong, he'd understood what it was to be an iron shaving in the presence of a magnet. Then it had been impossible to be with her and not take her into his arms.

He let the past go, intent on the present. "Did you find it on one of your sites?"

"I don't give away artifacts," she told him. "I told you, I found the carving in a market."

"Where?"

"She's actually from my part of the world, Jerusalem."

"You said it was a *mercado*."

"That's because you wouldn't have understood if I'd used the Hebrew. But it was in the Old City, lots of tiny dark stalls, a market more similar to Mexico's *mercados* than to say . . . Safeway or Kmart or—"

"I get your point," he said. "I thought you were working in Sonora, Mexico. When did you get back to Israel?"

"I went home for a visit." Liora folded her arms over her chest. "Enough of the third degree, Enrique." The thunder rumbled again and her eyes went to the tops of the mountains. The clouds were massing now, their undersides a dark gray. "We don't have long before the rain breaks," she said.

He couldn't help himself. His hand closed on her upper arm. "I want to see you again."

She pulled out of his grasp easily. "Look, my schedule is very tight—"

"So is mine," he said. "But I'll make time for you."

Something different entered Liora's eyes, a flicker of interest perhaps. "Enrique, what did you do with the gift I gave you?"

"It's in my truck. On the front seat."

"Where you left it after you unwrapped it."

"Is that a problem?"

She met his question with a gaze that was impossible to read. It made him uncomfortable, needlessly defensive. "It's perfectly safe," he assured her. "I'll show you—"

She knelt again at the spot where she'd been working and began to make notes on a pad. The wind was rising now. Tendrils of her hair pulled loose from the braid and brushed her cheek.

He watched her, wondering what he'd done wrong. Had he offended her? No, he decided, she was just playing the game. She liked being pursued, and she was well worth pursuing.

He knelt beside her. "You know what I've always wanted to do? I've always wanted to make love outdoors during a storm." He nodded toward one of the large mesquites farther up the wash. "Perhaps . . . under that tree."

Liora didn't look up from her notes, but a smile hovered at the corners of her mouth. "Didn't your mother ever tell you not to play in washes? She didn't tell you *la llorona* would get you?"

La llorona, the wailing one. He hadn't thought of her in years. The spirit who haunted the washes, a Latino Medea, grieving the children she'd murdered, and searching for others to take in their stead.

"Not my mother," he told Liora. "My *abuelita*. Every time the wind rose, she was sure it was *la llorona* calling for me."

Liora's black eyes bored through him. "Like now?"

His grandmother's healings were one thing, her stories quite another. Even as a child, he'd been skeptical of them. *La llorona* was no more real than the bogey man or Santa Claus. But here in this wash with the clouds darkening and the wind keening through the trees . . .

"Maybe she is calling you," Liora said. She tucked the pad into her pack and stood up. "You're the hydrologist. You ought to know it's not a good idea to hang out in a wash with rain coming." She started toward her vehicle. "It sweeps things away, Enrique."

"Thank you for explaining that," he said curtly. The last thing he needed was an archeologist lecturing him about floods.

He caught up with her as she reached the Jeep. "You didn't give me an answer," he said. "How about going out? Just until you return to Mexico?"

"You'd like that, wouldn't you? A relationship with a pre-arranged date of termination. Clean, finite. Saves on all those messy break-ups."

"Why are you twisting around my words?" he asked, exasperated. "I'm not trying to insult you. I'm just trying to ask you for a date."

"It's not a good idea," she said.

"Well, if it's such a bad idea, then why did you bring me 'a gift' all the way from Jerusalem? Why'd you bother to call at all? Is this some kind of payback?"

"For what?" Liora asked, seeming genuinely surprised. "You and I had a fine time together."

"That's what I thought." He was going to ask if she was teasing him, but the calm in her eyes told him that she wasn't. "So . . . why the souvenir?"

"You've seen her, haven't you?" Liora asked.

The chill was back, racing through him like a disease. They were still in high summer. Since nine this morning, the mercury had hovered near 103. And he could see goose bumps on his arms. He forced himself to speak normally. "Why do you say that?"

"You're the perfect candidate."

It was all he could do not to shake her. "Liora—"

"I can't tell you everything," she said, cutting him off. "If I did, you wouldn't believe me. But the statue, it's meant as a warning of sorts."

"A warning," he repeated blankly.

"She is very ancient. The Babylonians called her *ardat lili*, the 'maid of desolation' . . . not so dissimilar to *la llorona*."

"My grandmother isn't even dead yet and she's haunting me," he muttered.

"The ancient Hebrews called her Lilith, the word for screech owl. They said she was Adam's first wife, even before Eve. They said that she would not submit to Adam's will, and so she fled from the Garden of Eden to a cave on the shore of the Red Sea. There she mated with demons and gave birth to all the evil spirits in the world."

Enrique stared at her wordlessly. The last thing he'd expected was biblical fairy tales.

Liora went on, "According to Hebrew legend, she was a shape shifter, who often took the form of a cat or an owl.

And like *la llorona*, she was a baby killer—though she was typically said to take children in the first week of life. Right up through the Middle Ages, the Jews regularly used amulets that invoked the angels to protect their children from her. She is also known as a night demon and a seductress, who preyed on men who slept alone, who possessed them and drove them mad. She—"

"Why are you telling me all this?" he broke in.

"You wanted to know about the statue."

He shook his head, weary of explanations. "Forget the goddamned statue. Just tell me whether you'll go out with me."

"I can't," Liora said. "You're not for me anymore, Enrique. You already belong to someone else."

That night Enrique found himself unable to sleep despite the sound of a soft, steady rainfall. Liora's oblique answers taunted him. Her inability to explain anything worth explaining annoyed him. And her refusal to see him stung his pride and made him play out mental scenarios in which she confessed her stupidity and begged his forgiveness; and he then graciously made love to her all night long.

At one that morning, having tossed and turned since ten, he got up and turned on the computer, hoping that crunching numbers would lull his brain into a state of relaxation. The three cats sat on his desk while he worked, clearly pleased that he was finally acknowledging the joys of being nocturnal.

At two he went back to bed. The soft rain had intensified into a downpour. He drifted off only to be startled awake by a deafening clap of thunder. At two-thirty, he ignored the rains, strode out to his truck, grabbed the statue and its newsprint wrappings, and brought the whole soggy mess into the house and set it on the kitchen table with a *thump*.

He glared at it for a few moments before taking the funny little statue out of its newspaper cocoon. A bird woman.

Great. What was he supposed to make of that? He looked at it back and front, examined it top to bottom. Disgusted and more exhausted than ever, he gathered up the tattered newspaper to toss.

Which is when he saw it. A thin strip of yellowed paper in the very bottom of the wrappings, and on it, written in bright, red ink: *Set me as a seal upon thine heart. . . .*

He studied it, surprised. Obviously, Liora's cool disinterest was a ruse. Clearly, she'd meant for him to find this; that was why she'd been so pissed that he'd left the thing in the truck. She wanted him, after all. She just couldn't come out and say so. And he'd almost thrown it away.

Mystified but pleased, he turned off the kitchen lights and was about to return to bed when he decided on a little extra insurance, just to make sure he slept this time. He reached into one of the cabinets for a bottle of tequila.

His hand closed on the glass bottle and he pulled it out of the cabinet. He reached for the cap and realized it wasn't a bottle at all. Turning on the kitchen light, he saw that he held a red glass votive candle. A decal of the Virgin of Guadalupe graced its front, a fiery sacred heart its back. It was the same candle his mother had brought his grandmother. She'd stopped by his house after the nursing home ordered it removed. She'd said that *abuelita* wanted him to have it.

He shook his head, set the candle on the counter, and once again rummaged for the tequila. The bottle was half empty. Nearly a year ago Lupita, another ex, brought it to him as a gift. She claimed tequila was medicine, that it opened the heart. What he'd found was that Lupita didn't like making love without it. The tequila buzz dissolved her Catholic-school inhibitions. Two shots and she was all over him, her body swaying to some inner music. Three shots and she began murmuring about love and after the fifth, she had a positive gift for the scatological. On one such high, she'd told him in revelatory tones that the outline of his balls and the shaft of his erect penis combined to form the shape of the sacred heart. Ultimately, though, Lupita had been a good Catholic girl who wanted a husband and babies in white baptism gowns. He'd explained that he wasn't the marrying kind, then had promptly taken up with both Madeleine and Gwen to prove his point.

He opened the half-empty bottle and swallowed. He felt the golden liquid burn its way through him, then swallowed several more times, letting the liquor melt him into ease. Ten minutes later, he felt sure he would finally sleep. He turned toward the bedroom, then on impulse turned back.

Feeling foolish but too drunk to care, he struck a match and lit the votive candle. A tiny yellow flame danced inside the red glass.

"You know I don't believe in you," he told the Virgin. "But my *abuelita* does. So maybe you'll help her out, okay?"

It rained without cease all the next day and the day after. The washes ran high on the first day. By the afternoon of the second, they began to flood. Roads were blocked off and a bridge washed out. The city traffic became a tangle of detours. The Rillito River, normally a dry wash, had risen so high that people were canoeing and swimming their houses, and one of the riverside university buildings was in danger of joining them in the drink. Enrique found himself doing crisis management, assessing the damage to the riverbank, consulting on the repair of the bridge, assuring assorted politicos that the city of Tucson would not be swept away, and even doing an inane forty-second TV interview that somehow took an hour to tape.

It was dark by the time he got finally home from the TV station. The rain was still falling. His driveway was a sheet of mud. Inside the house, the cats greeted him impatiently, demanding their dinner. The kitchen glowed with a dim red light. The votive candle was still burning. He turned on the overhead, took care of the cats, and found himself staring at the candle. *La Virgen de Guadalupe*, the Virgin Mary who had miraculously appeared in sixteenth-century Mexico as a pregnant, dark-skinned Indian woman. She was depicted as she'd been for the last four hundred years: wearing a blue cloak scattered with golden stars, standing on a crescent moon upheld by an angel, and surrounded by a spiky golden halo.

He nuked himself a frozen dinner in the microwave, listened to phone messages (Liora hadn't left one), and made a brief call to the nursing home. His grandmother's condition hadn't changed.

Seena rubbed up against his ankles, plaintively crying to be let out into the garden. He turned on the porch light and let her onto the porch. The rain had thinned to a drizzle.

"Are you sure?" he asked. "It's wet out there." The cat replied with a definite affirmative. He shrugged and opened the screen door. "It's your fur," he told her.

He waited through the tedium of the evening news, only to find that his interview had been cut for a report on the sighting of a black jaguar roaming the outskirts of the city. Jaguars were extinct in Arizona, though there was a remote chance one had wandered up from Mexico. It was typical that they'd bumped his interview for a highly doubtful rumor. More storm hysteria.

Two hours later he called Seena in. She made a guttural sound in response but did not come to the door.

Resigned, he stepped outside. As there'd been no need to water, he hadn't gone out into the yard in days. The garden, he saw, had been transformed by the rains. The sage was taller than he was. The grapevine so thick and heavy that it was snaking along the roof, blanketing the porch screens, the kitchen and bedroom windows, and wrapping around the western edge of the house. The datura had climbed all the way up to the top of the fence, covering it in white blossoms; a hibiscus he hadn't even remembered being there was wound with pink flowers; and a carpet of purple verbena covered even the garden paths. Just beyond the gates a chorus of coyotes began their eerie harmonies. It reminded him uncomfortably of the night he'd seen that woman, the night the cat had disappeared.

"Seena!" he called again. He was embarrassingly relieved when she trotted right up to him. He scooped her into his arms and took her back into the house, making sure to lock the sliding glass door. He locked the other doors, then turned in for the night. He fell into a deep sleep at once.

He never knew what woke him. Not thunder or lightning or coyotes or the cats. It was curiously quiet for a summer night in the desert. Even the crickets were silent.

Thirsty, he got up and padded into the kitchen for a glass of water. The votive candle was still flickering, burned nearly halfway down, the Virgin gazing at him with compassion.

"And a good night to you," he told her as he finished his water. It was beginning to seem like she was the only woman he was actually having a relationship with.

He started back to bed when he thought he heard something on the porch. He switched on the porch light and peered through the sliding glass door. The wicker rocker was rocking and the porch swing swaying, as if both had invisible occupants.

It's the wind, he told himself. But he was not certain enough of that to be able to go back to bed.

He unlocked the glass door and walked onto the porch. It was the wind, rising again, rippling through the leaves of the grapevine, carrying the scents of orange tree and honeysuckle, washing him in the garden's perfume. He hadn't put on a robe, but he stepped outside anyway, drawn by something he couldn't begin to name.

She stood beside the Rose of Sharon, waiting for him to register her presence. He was naked, exactly as she wanted him, and comely. And his garden made her very happy. It reminded her of that first garden, awash in the sweet mix of scents that she had known when she first came into the world.

Enrique found himself moving tentatively, aware of being barefoot on land that had long been the province of scorpions, black widows, rattlers, and a host of other venomous creatures. The desert, he'd always known, was searingly beautiful and far from benign.

The night was soft and warm and heavy. Humidity from the rains still hung in the air despite the winds. Thick patches of cloud scudded across the full moon, concealing it, then gliding on and revealing it again. And so the light kept changing, there one moment, gone the next. He couldn't make his eyes adjust; every time they did, everything changed again and he found himself unable to see. Yet he was becoming more sure by the second that he was not alone in the garden. She'd returned and was waiting for him.

Thunder rumbled through the skies followed by a white streak of lightning, forked and branched, like a map of a streambed illuminated in the sky.

He walked along the soft dirt path that ringed the outer edge of the garden, then spiraled to its center. He spun, alarmed, as he felt something behind him, and then felt the fool, realizing it was only the soft fronds of the cassias blowing against him, tickling his naked buttocks.

He stopped walking as he reached the hibiscus. He could swear Cassie hadn't planted one. And he certainly hadn't. Had the tree grown from seed? The clouds slid over the moon again, plunging him into darkness, and when the moon cleared she was standing in front of him. She was dressed exactly as she had been before—in nothing but bracelets and earrings and the sheer skirt made of tiny golden disks.

"Enrico," she said. Although her upper body remained still, her hips began to sway, the metal disks clicking against each other in a rhythm that rose and fell with the soughs of the wind.

"I—" He didn't know what to say to her.

A light rain began to fall. He ignored it, his eyes on her hips, her waist, the round, full breasts. He reached a hand out and touched the side of her neck. He felt the pulse inside her, warm and even.

The clicking of the golden disks stopped. She took his hand from her neck and touched it to one of the hibiscus's pink flowers, now furled against the night. "Rose of Sharon," she said. "There were endless rose of Sharon in the Garden—pink, white, yellow, purple, even a blue—and I was so fond of them." When he didn't respond she explained, "I thought they would go well in your garden."

He found his voice at last. "I want you."

"Of course," she said. "And I want you—and if you had half the sense of a jackrabbit, that would send you running in the opposite direction."

"No," he said. "I promised myself I wouldn't run from you again."

"More's the pity," she said softly. But she took his hand and led him to a place where the verbena grew thick and green over the brown earth. And she drew him down next to her.

She touched one hand to his collarbone and trailed her fingers to his groin. " 'Behold thou art fair, my beloved, yea, pleasant . . . our bed is green.' "

The word *beloved*, uncomfortably close to love, nearly snapped him out of it. "Wait—" he began. "I don't know you—"

"And you don't love me," she finished, amused. "Relax, Enrico. It's just a line from an old poem." She bit down gently on his chest and for a split second, lightning turned the night sky white, and it seemed to him that she was not biting his chest at all but sinking her teeth deep into the center of his being. And as she did he thought he heard his grandmother's voice, calling on the edge of the wind, *"El búho, Enrico, ten miedo!"*

He forced himself to sit up, to hold her at arm's length. She rocked back on her knees. "What is it?" she asked.

He shook his head, unable to explain. At last he said, "Would you turn around for a minute?"

She gave him a questioning gaze but did as he asked. He wove his hands through the fall of black hair and sighed with relief as he found them: shoulder blades. Normal, human shoulder blades.

"Okay," he said.

She turned back to him, her eyes sharp in the moonlight. "What were you searching for?"

"Wings," he said to his own surprise; he found it impossible to lie to her. "I thought maybe you were an angel," he joked.

"No," she said. Her tongue circled his nipples. "Angels aren't to my taste."

"That's good." He pulled her into his arms and tugged on the waist of her skirt. The golden disks fell from her body. "Mine either."

The rain became heavier, but he didn't notice. All he knew was her. She smelled of amber and musk. Her body fit against his as if she'd been made for him. Each breast exactly filled one of his hands. He traced the curve from the small of her back to the fullness of her butt, and she made a sound that was almost a purr of pleasure. Her skin was so soft that he actually believed she was vulnerable.

He licked her body. She tasted like the juice of the cactus fruit, tart and sweet. He made her lie still while he drank her, and what streamed inside her tasted like the desert itself, a nectar of sun and wind and all the life that fought so hard to survive there, subtle and strong and infinitely precious.

She suddenly twisted away from him as he drank.

"What's wrong?" he asked.

"Let me," she said. And then she was kneeling by his side,

taking him into her hands, then her mouth; his cock and his balls, the very center of him, inside her.

She knew exactly how close he was to coming. So she took her mouth from him, let the rain baptize his cock, and then she straddled him, lowered herself over him, opening to him, enclosing him and yet somehow keeping herself maddeningly out of reach. He couldn't touch the center of her. He arched his hips, held her close, thrust into her. She danced above him and he knew that it was she who controlled his every sensation. Every shudder, every moment of pleasure and release he felt because she gave it, she allowed it. She taught him a rhythm that was all her own. She was fiercer than any lover he'd ever known. She wouldn't let him hold back. She took everything from him. It went on forever and it was over too soon. She taught him what it was to be truly lost.

After, she lay in his arms, the rain rinsing the sweat from their bodies. She was murmuring something in a language he didn't recognize. "What?" he murmured drowsily.

"That poem again," she said. " 'My beloved is mine and I am his. He feedeth among the lilies. Until the day break and the shadows flee . . . .' "

He stroked her cheek. "There are no lilies in this garden. Just about everything else but—"

"This will do," she said. She reached up and plucked a large, white flower from the plant behind them, then brushed it across his mouth.

Seconds later his lips began to feel chapped and then to sting. He licked them. No taste but a scent he recognized. "What the . . . datura?"

She nodded. "Sacred datura. I've always loved it."

He pulled away from her angrily. His lips were blistering. "Did anyone ever tell you it's toxic?"

Again, she nodded, blithely unconcerned. "Some say datura is poison. Others say, it gives you vision."

He cupped his hands, hoping for enough rain water to rinse his mouth. It wasn't necessary. The burning sensation stopped as a wing brushed his face.

He glanced up, confused. She was kneeling in front of him. The clouds freed the moon and in its light he saw that she had changed. The long hair was gone, her head covered in what looked like a cap of glossy black feathers and her feet curved into talons. She had no arms, but long, black wings.

"Who are you?" he asked, forcing his voice to remain steady.

"That depends on how you meet me," she replied. "As I came to you, I'm called Lilith. But you've had other names for me."

The wing brushed his face again. The feathers that covered her head became finer, thinning into silky black fur. She sat on her haunches, her arms straight in front of her, and as he watched, the edges of her body blurred and rounded. The fur covered her skin completely and she became a small, very familiar black cat.

He backed away from her, until his back was pressed against the garden gate, its wire cutting into his skin. "No," he said. "I won't believe that."

The wing brushed his face, lingering over his eyes, then Seena was gone, and in her place he saw a jet-black screech owl.

"Owls aren't black," he said, desperately trying to hold onto reality.

The owl stared at him with burning golden eyes and extended a monstrous black wing.

"No!" he screamed.

He covered his head, tried to dodge, but the owl's wing found him, brushed his eyelids closed, and when he opened them he was no longer in the garden.

He lay on the bank of an arroyo, inches from a river of flood water that was flowing fast and cold, absorbing a cool, light rainfall. He was still naked, and he could still smell her scent all over him.

He forced himself to his feet. His head was pounding. His throat was raw. His entire body ached. Somewhere close by, a lone coyote called and the pack answered with a shrill harmony. He rubbed his throbbing temples, trying to banish a thought completely at odds with what he knew from years immersed in science: that the coyotes were calling down the rains.

The clouds and the winds were still playing games with the moon. He waited for a moment when he could see and tried to orient himself. Even at night, he could usually identify at least one of the four mountain ranges, know which way was north. Tonight rain veiled the mountains.

The coyotes sent up another round of calls. For animals who usually kept a safe distance between themselves and humans, they were much too close. He began walking along the edge of the arroyo. He'd follow the water until he recognized a landmark.

He hadn't gotten five yards before he slowed. The moon was swathed with clouds again, and he couldn't see it, but he sensed something directly ahead of him.

A furious scream rang out and he stumbled backward as something ripped into his shoulder. In a flare of lightning he saw his attacker. He hadn't believed it earlier, couldn't believe it now. He was staring at a coal black cat, its body thicker, larger than a mountain lion's, its ears flattened, crouched to spring. His hand went to his shoulder and came away slick with blood. He felt his stomach churn. There was no skin left.

The coyotes shrieked, even closer, and the jaguar whirled to face them. A coyote, fully the size of the jaguar, edged toward the cat and howled a challenge. In the moonlight its fur was tipped with silver. The jaguar launched itself at the coyote and the two met in a fury of screams and howls. Enrique stood, transfixed, knowing the battle impossible, these creatures belonging to a world that no longer existed.

"They are mine, Enrique." Lilith's hands snaked out from behind him, pulling him against her breasts and thighs. "This night belongs to me."

He turned to face her and for a foolish moment felt reassured. She was a good half foot shorter than he. How could any man be afraid with a small, voluptuous woman in his arms?

Then she was gone, as were the coyote and the cat, and he would have thought it all a dream except that the earth shook with thunder and the sky opened. The rains streamed down, drenching him, drilling into the exposed flesh of his shoulder.

You have got to get out of here, he told himself. But he stood, paralyzed, unable to make his body obey.

And then the landscape strobed white and he saw her.

Not Lilith. But a tall, thin woman wearing a long, black dress and a black shawl. She stepped toward him, and pure terror returned movement to his body. He edged backward toward the wash. He didn't have to hear her cries or see her desiccated face to know who she was. She was exactly as he'd imagined her as a child, her fingernails so long they curved and gleamed like polished tin, her eyes burning red fire. She cried out to him, and her voice seemed to be the coyotes' song, then the jaguar's scream, then wind itself carving the face of the land. She was grief become madness and she would take all in her path. Her hands stretched out, reaching for him.

He risked a quick glance over his shoulder. He stood inches from the edge of water. He knew the soft earth beneath his feet would not hold. The waters were rising swiftly, nearly even with the top of the arroyo. They were going to take him, the ultimate irony, a flood-control engineer drowned in the floods.

Lightning flared and the black owl winged above him, enfolding him in the shadow of her wing, enclosing him in a desert transformed from familiar home to unrecognizable terror. And for the first time since childhood, he prayed to the Virgin, *"Dios te salve María, llena eres de gracia, los señores contigo . . . ."* asking her mercy before giving himself to the floods.

He woke in his garden. The rains had stopped. A thin red line of dawn sketched the tops of the eastern mountains.

He lay on wet, soft earth. Lilith stood over him, her spangled skirt glinting softly in the gray light. "You're lucky, Enrico," she said. "You asked for help and it was given. The night didn't take you, after all."

Lucky was not the word he would have chosen. His shoulder felt like it was on fire. He knew he ought to get it cleaned, bandaged, but he was weak with exhaustion and probably blood loss. He couldn't even imagine moving.

She knelt beside him, her fingertips tracing the line of his throat. " 'Many waters cannot quench love, neither can floods drown it.' " She smiled at the question in his eyes. "Yes, that poem again. But also what was tonight. Give thanks that you are the grandson of a *curandera*, Enrico. Know that it was her love that saved you." He flinched as she touched his ripped shoulder. "Though you will have a scar to show for it."

She ran her hand through his hair, as a mother might caress a small child. "So what shall I do with you?" she mused. "Take your mind? I've done that before, to others. It is no great feat to drive a man to madness."

Her hand dropped to his penis. She stroked it once and he was instantly hard, too sick to move but aching for her. Even after all that had happened, he still wanted her.

"Take your cock, of which you're so proud? Yes, I could leave you unable to ever fuck another woman, but that seems unfair since you gave me pleasure. And I won't take your first-born, though I've done that too."

She scared him. Thoroughly. And yet he found himself saying, "Just make love to me again."

"No, Enrique, the time for that is over." Her fingertips

pressed against his right temple, then his throat. "So what happened to your soul?" she asked. "How did you lose it so completely? I think you must have given it away."

He blinked, too dazed to respond.

She touched the center of his chest. "Your heart." Her voice was a whisper. "You've kept it closed for so long— even the ones you loved, you wouldn't let in. So now, know that it is safe. Know that it will never open again for another. It is mine for eternity." She kissed him lightly on the lips. "You will remember me, Enrico. I will be there in your dreams. You will see me in every storm. 'The only peace you know, you shall find in my eyes.' "

He watched transfixed as she lifted her hand and a fine red streak of light danced between her palm and his chest. Her hand touched his skin again and went deeper, as if she held his beating heart in her hand.

" 'I set my seal upon thy heart,' " she whispered.

He reached for her, but the owl's wing brushed the length of his body, closing his eyes once again. He felt her lips press against his.

" 'Turn to me, my beloved.' Now you will always turn toward me."

He opened his eyes, tried to do as she had asked, but she was gone. He was alone in the garden. A shrill cry called his gaze to the sky. Above him a black screech owl flew west, away from the dawn.

Bird Count

Jane Yolen

It was his wings I fell in love with first: feathers soft, wimpling; the strong pinions flexing. They weren't white or yellow, but somewhere in between, like piano keys after years in a dark room.

I dreamed those wings around me. I dreamed them against my breasts.

I dreamed them between my legs. But I never dreamed they could hurt so, the shafts scraping against my shoulders and back, leaving a deep imprint on my skin, as if I—and not he had worn the wings.

When I saw him first, he was only a speck against the sky. I was by the fire tower at Mount Tom, one of the early risers for the annual hawk watch. I was there because my lover, Lewis, was an obsessive birder who thought nothing of spending hours in the field making lists that only he would ever care about or actually see.

Trying to hold on to a relationship that had nothing to recommend it but inertia and obsession, I had bought myself a pair of vastly too expensive field glasses. I would rise each weekend morning before dawn to accompany Lewis on his passionate activity—he saved his passion for birds alone. I had become a martyr to ornithology, a bird widow, even though I knew little about the birds we watched and cared less. I only wanted to get Lewis's attention. He wasn't much, but he was all I had at the time. And at thirty-two, *time* was the operative word.

My biological clock wasn't just ticking; it was sounding like a Geiger counter in an old sci-fi movie.

The thing about Lewis was that even when we were together I was alone. Or rather Lewis was alone and I was just some *thing* that happened to be occupying space near him. It wasn't that he didn't notice me; he didn't notice anyone. If he was hungry, he ate whatever food appeared before him. If his laundry needed doing, he knew that the universe would somehow, mysteriously and wonderfully, get it cleaned. Before me there had been Lewis's mother to deal with the mundane world.

I was the intern on call when his mother had coughed gently, said "Take care of my boy," and died. Thinking she was talking about a minor child, I worried as I went out to the waiting room, afraid who I would find there. I was quite unprepared for Lewis, but relieved to find him an adult.

"Mr. Snowden," I said, "I am afraid that your mother has just passed away."

He seemed less shocked then confused, saying simply "She can't have." But his tone was not one of denial; rather he seemed put out with her, as if she had just gone on a trip without telling him.

And then he smiled a dazzling smile at me, and in all seriousness added, "I'll need a white shirt for the funeral and I don't know how to iron."

So when my shift was over, I went home with him, did his shirts, and stayed. He was quite simply the most beautiful man I had ever seen and I, while not technically a virgin, was so focused on my medical career I hadn't had much experience with men. Beauty in a man shook me, entangled me in a way for which I was unprepared.

When I say beautiful, there is no other word for it. He had a shock of dark hair that fell uncut—unless I cut it—over a clear, broad forehead. His eyes were like dark almonds and about as readable. He had a straight, perfect nose, skin that had the kind of ermine edging that is on a blackberry leaf—soft and slightly fuzzy to the touch. His ears, shell-like, were velvety and made to be touched, caressed, blown into. He was lean and well-muscled, but never had to work at it, so he did not have that false sculpting that men have who only develop their tone in a gym. And most important, he was totally unaware of his beauty. It was like his clothing—there for covering. I must have tried to write dozens of poems about him those first weeks with him, which was odd because I had never written anything before other than critical essays for school.

Even when his beauty lost its power over me, I stayed—and this will sound bizarre and slightly shocking, but is true nonetheless—because he smelled like summer, moist and hot and beckoning. He was not in fact any of those things. He was more winter than summer, arctic really. But he smelled as if he could be cultivated and might even blossom in time if only I could find the right tools.

So I stayed.

Which is how I found myself frequently on birding expeditions: tracking down errant wheatears along the stone abutments at the Quabbin Reservoir, chasing after odd rarities at feeders in Hadley and Montague, looking through snowstorms for an elusive snowy owl, spending a whole day and night driving Lewis around the Northampton meadows on the Christmas bird count. Of course he did not know how to drive. The universe supplied drivers.

As for why he stayed with me, there is no mystery in that. I was as comfortable for him as his furniture. He did not expect his furniture to up and move away. Nor did I.

Until.

Until the hawk watch when something extraordinary happened. And only I seemed to have noticed it.

A bird as big as a man, a man with wings, came down

from the sky and took me in a feathery embrace. And only then, after I had been well and truly fucked by some other-worldly fowl, did I begin to understand real beauty.

I do not expect you to believe me. I expect you will say I had been drinking. Or smoking funny cigarettes. I expect you to say I was hallucinating or dreaming or having an out of body experience. I expect you to say the words "alien abduction" with a breathy laugh, and suggest I was having a breakdown.

I was not. I was awake that day as I am at this moment. The morning was still and chill. I had dressed warmly, but evidently not warmly enough for I could feel the cold through my chinos, like a light coating of ice on my thighs. My earlobes were numb.

Lewis was with the ardent birders high up on the fire tower. I was down below, my field glasses in my hand, thinking about my caseload and praying that my beeper would signal me to make an early and unanticipated visit to the hospital. My relationship with Lewis had reached the point where I could not just leave without a summons, but I spent a lot of time praying that one thing or another would demand my time away from his side.

I heard a noise. Not my beeper, but a kind of insistent high-pitched cry. When I looked up, I saw this speck in the sky hurtling toward me. I put my glasses to my eyes, twisted the focus, and then dropped the glasses on the ground. $2,500 worth of Zeiss and I simply let it fall from my hand without thinking. But I was too shocked to notice. What I had seen was not possible. How quickly it moved was not possible. I scarcely had time to raise my hands to ward off the thing when it was hovering over me, the wind from its wings literally taking my breath away so that I could not have screamed if I had wanted to.

No one else seemed to have noticed anything wrong and I, even as I was stunned by the quickness of the bird-thing, wondered how that could be. The best birders in Western

Mass were crowding the high platform of the fire tower: Gagnon and Greene and Stemple and the rest. They were taking notes and talking hawks and comparing counts from the year before. At any one moment, eight or nine pairs of eyes were scanning the skies over the valley. Those birders missed nothing. *Nothing!* Yet not a one of them had seen what now landed in front of me, scarcely a yard away.

For a long moment I stared into the bird-thing's eyes. No, not a thing. A man. He had the fierce beaked nose of a hawk and a feathery brow, white and black and brown intermixed. His eyes were yellow; his mouth a generous gash. He was naked except for the feathers that curled around his genitals, that encircled his nipples, that streaked across his flat stomach and bare chest like ritual scars. His wings arched and beat back and forth and we were both caught in the swirling winds from them. I could scarcely stand up to those winds, even thought for a minute I might be swept off the mountain, even hoped I might so that he could rescue me and take me off into the air with him. I felt drunk with the thought.

He stood still for another long minute, with only those wings beating. Then he moved his shoulders, up and down, turned away from me and opened his wings even wider, then turned back. The feather-scars on his chest rippled like little waves, the white feathers like foam on top of the dark. His long, black hair stuck straight up in front like a cock's comb and he was deadly serious as he stared at me. Then suddenly he threw his head back and crowed. Not like a rooster or any other bird I could name. But it was certainly some kind of triumphant cry.

Then he pumped those wings again and took off into the air and was gone.

I was stunned. It took me a while to realize that he had been doing a mating display. And by the heat in my face, by the burning between my legs, by that odd sensation in my stomach that was part nausea and part longing, I know I had responded to it as he had meant.

There was a sudden odd clatter above me as the birders descended the iron stairs. I reached out to one of the railings. *Cold iron*, I thought. *Proof against fairies*. I tore off my glove, touched the icy metal. But it did nothing to banish the picture in my head of that glorious creature—man, bird, whatever. It did nothing to discourage the flush on my face, the weakness in my groin.

"We're going for coffee," Lewis told me, "You can go on to the hospital. Dave will get me home." And they walked on by me without another word, going down the path, leaving me to follow as best I could with shaky knees and a head full of odd ideas.

I did not go out birding with Lewis the next morning before hospital rounds because I did not dare. And, quite frankly, because I thought it would mean being disloyal to Lewis. I had spent the night dreaming of the bird man, the hawk king. I had even fantasized about him while Lewis and I made love. Normally I just kept my eyes open and watched Lewis, who goes through the mechanics of lovemaking with his eyes closed, without a single change on his beautiful face. This time I closed my eyes—not that Lewis would have noticed the difference—and fancied he had wings and feathers on his chest. It made my breath come quicker, and I climaxed as soon as he entered me, which was unusual enough for him to open his eyes and say, "Something's different." Lewis likes things to be the same.

"Pre-menstrual," I said.

"Oh," he answered. And that was all.

He went off birding with his friends and I lay in bed thinking about nothing. Or trying to think about nothing. Burying my face in the feather pillow. Trying to remember if any of my close relatives had recently gone mad. Then I got up, took a long, leisurely shower, and dried myself in front of the window. Not that anyone could see me. The bathroom overlooked an old abandoned tobacco field. The house was surrounded by trees.

I saw many specks in the sky, some easy to identify, some too far away for casual naming. But nothing that fell to earth like a feathered star.

So I put on my terry-cloth robe and made myself a cup of coffee, went out onto the deck to drink it, though the morning was even colder than it had been the day before. I was hoping, you see, for something. I was trying to keep alive the belief that I was *not* crazy. I was afire, giving off signals I suppose. Pheromones, they're called. I put my head back and tried to imitate the sound the hawk man had made right before diving to earth. "Kreeeeeeccc!" I cried. But I was embarrassed to call out very loudly even though the nearest house was about a quarter mile away. "Kreeeeee!"

I turned to go back into the house when I heard something above me, looked up, and saw the speck, my feathered hallucination, falling out of the sky to my feet. I opened my arms to him and, without more foreplay than that, he embraced me with his wings, the shafts scraping my back, and then thrust himself in me. First from the front, a hot searing pinning, leaving me still weak with desire. Then he turned me around, pushed my robe up, and mounted me from behind. The feathers of his breast emblazoned themselves on my back, sticking into the raw scrapings his wings had made. I felt the pain and yet it was sweet, too, as if I were growing wings.

Then he lay me down on the cold boards and did it twice more, front and back, and I was hot and wet with him and cried, a sound more like the call of a loon than a hawk, throaty and low. He gave me love bites on the neck and shoulder and buttocks.

Then he stood, shook himself all over, pumped his wings, which covered me with wind, and fled into the sky with that defiant, triumphant cry.

I lay on my back, my robe half around my waist, till I shivered with the cold. When I got up at last, I found a feather he had dropped on the deck. Whether it was from our lovemaking or after, when he had given that odd shaking, I didn't know. I held the feather so tight, the shaft made a mark on my palm.

I went back inside and took another long shower, called in sick to the hospital, and went to bed. I dreamed the hawk man fucked me over and over and over, and as I dreamed, I ran the feather across my breasts and over my stomach and between my legs. The dreams were so real, I had an orgasm each time.

When Lewis came home, he didn't seem to notice anything, not my flushed face, not the marks on my back and neck and arms. He heard me when I said I thought I was pregnant. He insisted he wanted to marry me. He did not understand when I moved out.

I live now on the top floor of the highest building in Springfield. An aerie, I call it. I have made a bassinet and lined it with down. I am a doctor, I will know how to attend to my own delivery. I do not trust anyone else, for my child might look like his father. I am not certain that the attending physicians at Cooley Dickinson are ready for a baby born with pinfeathers. I have practiced lullabies, especially the one about the baby in the treetops. It seems right, somehow.

I am alone now. But that does not matter. I am sure the hawk man will come back next season. One thing Lewis taught me: The big hawks mate for life.

And so do I.

So do I.

A Wife of Acorn, Leaf, and Rain

Dave Smeds

Jordan Welles waited in his study, glad to spend a Monday at the mansion. The paneled walls and heavy bookcases insulated him, holding at bay the purposelessness that clutched at him at work. Downtown was a universe away. Among the century-old rooms, the vast garden, and the wooded acres stretching toward the shore, he could concentrate on the goal that surmounted all others.

Here, the Outsider could visit, as he could not in the city, with all its metal and trappings not of nature.

Jordan stared down into the box at the items he had placed within it. A negligée. An evening dress. High-heeled shoes. A makeup kit. A diary with its lock removed. He resisted the temptation to turn the box over and restore the contents to their places around the house. Though he would be getting everything back within a few days, it hurt to be deprived of these mementos.

He was adding articles to the accumulation when the housekeeper appeared in the open doorway.

"Your visitor has arrived," she said. A faint twitch of her mouth hinted at the disapproval he knew she must be feeling.

"Very good, Mrs. Cory. I'll meet with him here."

She vanished, reappearing only briefly as she escorted the guest to the room.

The Outsider was taller than Jordan, as his kind often were, and slim to the point of emaciation. Fair-skinned and fair-haired, he paradoxically conveyed the impression he was standing in shadow. A human inexperienced in the effects of the glamour might have, after the fact, remembered him with the aspect of a Sicilian or Spaniard. A Mediterranean teenager, Jordan thought, body hair atypically sparse, with a distinct flavor of androgyny.

The visitor shrank away from the metal lamp at the end of Jordan's desk. He tucked his head farther beneath the hood of his robes and hid his hands within the sleeves, retreating from the hostile emanations of the house, encasing himself in layers of chestnut and sorrel.

"You've found someone for the job?" asked Jordan.

"Indeed."

Jordan had already learned his guest was a creature of few words. That was just as well, given the unnerving tendency of his speech to echo. All that mattered was that he could deliver what he had been asked to acquire.

"She'll need these," Jordan said, gesturing at the box on his desk. He also picked up a thick manila folder and extended it, declining to make contact as the material slid from his grip.

The Outsider glanced in the folder. Photos of Véronique flashed momentarily into view. He grunted approval at the thick sheaf of biographical notes.

"I'd like to add something else," Jordan stated. "Do you have access to a VCR? Can you operate one?"

The being reacted with distaste. "We study all the magicks of your world, as best we can. A way can be found."

"Tapes will make the task easier. They'll provide a means to study physical mannerisms, speech patterns, and so forth."

"If you wish, we will use them."

Jordan opened a drawer and added the half-dozen video-cassettes he found there to the box. He held up the final one, unmarked save for a blue sticker. "This one's especially important."

Jordan paused, then let the cassette settle into the box. He had promised Véronique he would never let anyone see that recording. It was for him, for those times when Véronique couldn't be with him, and occasionally for them to view together. He grimaced at the thought of strange pairs of eyes poring over its images. Did Outsiders feel voyeuristic delight? What of any human who might be brought in to assist in the operation of the machinery?

The visitor lifted the box. He cradled it against his body, apparently able to tolerate the traces of metal therein—just a few tiny screws in the cassettes. "These will help, but the dreams are the key," he said.

"She can do this, can't she?" Jordan asked, almost hoping to be told otherwise.

The other nodded. Taking off his glove, he held out his hand. The index finger grew indistinct. When it came back into focus, it had become thicker and was no longer the same length as the middle digit. It strongly resembled Jordan's own.

The transformation lasted a few moments, then reverted back. The Outsider swayed, blinked, and caught his breath.

"That much I can do with but a smattering of the talent. The one I have arranged to bring is rich in the skills and will have the time needed to prepare herself. A pooka could not do better."

"She'll have to hold the shape for hours at a time," Jordan warned. "As much as half a day."

"She can. Depending on how you dream."

"My dreams have been of nothing but Véronique."

"Then your companion will be Véronique, for as long as you wish her to be."

The visitor restored his glove, turned, and left. Jordan stayed where he was until the being was fully gone, beyond the ability to call him back. During that vigil he wondered if Véronique, wherever her spirit might be, would forgive him.

* * *

The Outsider reappeared on Friday at twilight, a juncture his kind seemed to favor. Jordan had dismissed Mrs. Cory and the other servants, leaving no human witnesses to the arrival of she who was to be his companion.

The guest recommended the lights be dimmed. Jordan agreed, and in stepped . . . Véronique.

The subdued illumination almost preserved the illusion. She was Véronique's height. The body silhouette matched. The clothes and cosmetics were Véronique's own. She would have fooled anyone casually acquainted with Jordan's late wife, but he caught the subtle differences. The woman's skin contained a pallid undertone at odds with Véronique's robust complexion. She wore no jewelry. Her facial features were slightly elongated, the collarbones overly delicate. His wife's pupils had rarely displayed such a deep, black-pool intensity.

But the attempt was as good as he had been promised, and he knew it had the potential to improve.

The male—was it male?—of the pair held out the contract. Jordan had already signed other documents, but until he added this one, the woman standing in front of him was still just a candidate, as was he to her.

Jordan signed.

The male rolled up the parchment in the manner of a scroll and slipped it into a pouch. "Follow my instructions carefully." He produced a cord of hand-woven hemp and a long thorn of dark wood. "Tie one end of the rope to her wrist. Tie the other end to yours. Prick her finger and drip three drops of blood along the leash. Do the same with your own blood. Then recite aloud, 'You are mine.' "

"Is all that really necessary?" Jordan asked.

"She cannot do as you require until the ritual is fulfilled."

"I have to be sure it's what she wants," Jordan said.

The Outsider glanced at his companion, who at last gave up her silence.

"I undertake this bond of my own will."

Her voice mimicked Véronique's. The pitch was high and ethereal, the diction more formal than anything Jordan's wife would ever have used, but the similarities raised hair on the nape of the widower's neck.

"Very well," Jordan replied. "But your word is enough as far as I'm concerned. That and your continuing service." He recalled stories he had heard of such ceremonies, but in those, the cord had been tied around the woman's neck, or her waist. In Bangkok or Saudi Arabia or Japan. This was better, but still enough to bother him, no matter how he believed in the integrity of his own motives.

"The bond will help me," she explained. "I cannot endure this place long without it."

"It is our way," the male added.

Ultimately Jordan did as he was asked, proceeding methodically, checking her reaction throughout. To his astonishment, no sooner had he uttered the final words than the cord vanished. He could still feel the loop over his own wrist, snug but not confining, an invisible presence that neither chafed nor tugged nor restricted his movements in any way. Unless he focused his attention, the fingers of his other hand passed right through it.

"The compulsion is upon her," the male said. "She is yours as long as you will have her. Just as the laws of your people bind you to the terms, the laws of the Sidhe bind her. Let neither of you violate your oaths."

Jordan considered the signature he had placed upon the contract. An oath? He had faith that he would not abuse a single clause, but it was, after all, just an arrangement of words on paper. What the elf had committed herself to seemed alarmingly complete and inviolate, like nothing extant in human culture.

"For the rest of the evening, it is best that you see her as little as possible," added the male. "She is still only a depiction of what you want her to be."

"I understand," Jordan said.

"Good. My part is done. You have been generous in your remuneration. I hope that we can do business again."

"We each had what the other needed," Jordan said. "All ventures should be so clear-cut." For him, it had been a bargain. The acreage he had leased out, valuable as it was to the Outsider clan as a home and refuge, would have remained undeveloped woodland for the foreseeable future. The interim presence of the elves would not diminish its worth.

The intermediary took his leave. Jordan saw him through the window as he reached the edge of the lawns and crossed into the woods. The Outsider relaxed and reached up to clutch a handful of pine needles and shower his head with them. They briefly assembled into the shape of a crown.

Alone with the woman—strange, but he found it difficult to refer to her as an Outsider—Jordan shuffled uneasily from foot to foot, trying to think of what to say.

"You should try to sleep, my lord," she said.

"It's very early."

"Then go to bed. Read. Let yourself be lulled. I will keep vigil, and when you do sleep, I will be ready."

When he had settled into bed, she entered the room in the negligée from the box and sat down in the Edwardian parlor chair beside his bed. He could see her out of the corner of his eye, but he resisted staring and managed not to converse with her.

He thought it would be easier to ignore her once the lights were out, but he was wrong. He could hear her breathing, and it was a measured whisper lacking Véronique's punctuated, often sharp, nighttime inhalations. And in the darkness he was aware of her scent. Essences of woodlands, fallen leaves, freshwater streams, wild grasses.

The middle of the night came and went, bringing drowsiness, but not enough to claim him. Or had he dozed, just for a moment?

The woman left the chair and joined him in the king-sized, four-poster bed. His heart thundered against his sternum. She curled up on her left side, taking a moment to reach out and run the back of her hand gently down his neck. A quintessential Véronique gesture.

Suddenly, he regained the confidence that the plan would work. He lay quietly, believing now that sleep would come, and with it the dreams they both required.

In the morning, Véronique was beside him. No more pale undertone. No more whiff of forest. Hair tousled, late to rouse, she snuggled close. Her breasts were hot where they pressed against his ribs, while her toes exhibited their trademark clamminess and chill despite long hours deep beneath the blankets. She, and everything about her, was just as he remembered.

Tears welled up and poured down his face, a flood withheld since the funeral.

She stirred and opened her eyes. Reaching out, she captured a droplet on her manicured fingernail and murmured, "No, no, no, my love. I'm here." She held him tight, kissing his shoulder.

He sobbed audibly. It was Véronique's voice, down to the last nuance.

Mrs. Cory, to her credit, hid any ambivalence or other emotion she may have felt as Jordan and Veronique gathered on the sundeck for breakfast. The cook, however, remained entrenched in the kitchen, foregoing his customary hello.

The wind teased the waves in the distance. Small fishing boats drifted offshore. Jordan had paid well to own such a view as this.

He had chosen to eat outdoors partly because he believed the elf would be more comfortable here, within reach of oak boughs and immersed in the fragrance of the trumpet vines in the railing. Véronique herself might have preferred the dining nook now that summer was being lured south.

Or perhaps not. The weather had been brisk the morning of his wife's death, and that had not kept them from enjoying the air as they lingered, post-coitally, over coffee and pastries.

This would do as a start. They were neither post-coital nor preparing to catch separate flights from JFK, she aboard an aircraft with a puncture in a hydraulic line. Instead, it was a Saturday, and they could reach for the sort of quiet, insular day he might have had with the real Véronique, had she never boarded that jet.

After the meal, they strolled through the woods east of the mansion. Along the way she slid her hand into his, and he let it stay—the first extended contact he had permitted since the embrace when she had awakened. Again, Jordan had chosen a setting he felt would appeal to the elf, but she gave no hint of relief to be out from within the unliving walls of the residence with all its electrical fields, any more than she had seemed distressed while inside. She addressed herself to their surroundings the way a human would, such as when a squirrel pranced exuberantly up a tree trunk, kindling the smile that had won his heart the first time he had ever seen Véronique.

She filled the excursion with conversation, relating the news she had read in the morning paper as Véronique had a tendency to do. Had she taken that detail of character from his dreams? He hadn't realized how much the lack of his wife's chatter had isolated him. After the funeral, as before, the only parts of the paper he read were the business and sports sections, giving him at best a workaholic's outline of happenings in society at large.

In the afternoon, they climbed into the limousine for a ride along the South Fork to tour wineries. The chauffeur jumped visibly as she called him by name, and was perhaps less attentive to his driving than he might have been, but Jordan forgave him that.

At the third tasting room they selected an expensive late-harvest Riesling. Véronique usually preferred dry whites and reds with a strong hint of the barrel atop the fruitiness, but he knew she would have liked the vintage. His companion drank selectively so as not to become so sated she lost the keenness of taste. Just like Véronique, and unlike elves, who he had heard were gluttonous in regard to alcohol. She wore gloves to avoid touching the metal of the car, but even those were Véronique's own, bought in Paris two winters past.

The divergences mattered less and less as the hours wore on. Just before dinner, a call from his brother in Hawaii drew him from the room. It tortured him to leave her.

"I can't tell you what this means to me," he said as they sat down to the meal.

She didn't reply. He would not have needed to make such a declaration to the former Véronique. He realized he was holding back, reminding himself that this was illusion.

No more. He had called her back from the dead. By now, it was the airplane crash, the funeral, the grieving that seemed unreal.

"Come to bed," she murmured after the main course. "We can have dessert there."

He knew that sparkle in her eyes. It had been bright in courtship and when they were newlyweds. It had not faded.

She was assertive and eager, quickly burning away his nervousness. He knew this body. He was conditioned to respond to it. Just past the brink of middle age, sex was the best he had ever known it to be, because unlike the arrogant young buck he had once been, he knew how to communicate what would gratify him most, and could sense what was wanted in exchange. Knowledge of a partner enriched the passion.

That was why no one but Véronique would do, why in their years together he had not succumbed to adultery, and he a wealthy man who could have starlets and models and golddiggers by the mattressful.

She tasted like Véronique: salt and honey. Slightly on the sweet side the way she was at times. She whimpered in that familiar, inspiring way. Regaining her breath after her first orgasm, she climbed atop him and straddled his face, putting her own mouth to work even as she offered him the chance to bring her to a second peak.

They licked simultaneously, gently and languorously teasing each other to desperation. Sometimes she strained as she engulfed him, as if she wanted to have it all. He had never minded the inability. No other cheeks nor tongue nor lips had ever understood so instinctively what he liked, and the joy she took from it was evident from the sweet liquor coating his own tongue.

When at last she rolled, sighing, onto her back and spread her legs to let him clamber between, he hesitated, wondering if she would feel the same inside as what he knew. Then he breached her, and within her heat and slickness found a homecoming.

He had dreamed vividly of this, night after night, grief fueling the intensity of the imagery. Why should he doubt that this, of all things, would be anything other than what he wanted?

"Don't ever leave," he whispered. Though spent, he was still unwithered inside her.

She squeezed back. With her arms as well. "I'm here, my love. I'm here."

Here. At least until he could bear to let her go.

The clock glowed 3:12 when Jordan suddenly woke. Reaching out, he found the sheets warm beside him, rich with the lingering bouquet of lovemaking, but vacant. No sounds leaked out of the master bathroom, nor any other room in the house.

He rose and went to the French doors that led to the balcony, and pulled aside the draperies. There she was—on the lawn. Her silhouette wavered, occasionally looking like

Véronique, other times taking on a foreign, even unnatural, configuration. Arms too thin, fingers too splayed, neck too long. Too androgynous, as well, though he tried not to think about that.

Transformed, she moved under the trees to the spot where the other elf—the prince?—had fashioned his crown of pine needles. The tree's lowest branch seemed to have reshaped itself since Jordan had last noticed it. It offered the visitor a broad, hammocklike curve, within which she tucked herself and lay her head back, as if exhausted.

She would be back, he told himself. Before dawn, she would return, join him beneath the covers, and peer into his dreams.

He sensed the loop around his wrist. He could tug, and no doubt she would be compelled to join him immediately. The temptation flared, putting a shiver into his lower arm.

Carefully he lay down on the bed, closed his eyes, and tried to be content with what he had.

In the morning, he attempted to forget what he had witnessed in the night. It only distracted him from the quest at hand—to make the most of a resurrection. There were so many little things he wanted to get right, now that he had the chance.

They made love again before breakfast, contorting the sheets until they came loose and nearly slipped from the mattress. She was sleepy and affectionate, per expectations, slow to climax but radiant when it happened.

Breakfast came, and lunch, and then he found himself tied up on the phone.

"We can't stall on this any longer," Jordan insisted to his VP of Finance. "I say interest rates are going up. They'll be up for the rest of the year. Get the loan taken care of before we lose another quarter point."

The short hand of the grandfather clock at the bottom of the stairs completed a circuit before he had convinced himself his executive agreed with him for the right reasons. He tried never to enforce his authority arbitrarily. He had no yes-men working for him.

He found Véronique in the basement gym. She was practicing yoga on a corner of the mat. Other than her location as far as possible from the weight machines and barbells, he was reminded of the many times he had found her here after one interruption or another had stolen away his attention. Even on Sundays.

Air seemed to collect behind his heart. "I'm sorry. I didn't mean to be gone so long."

"It's all right."

"No, it isn't. I got distracted. Coleman means well, but sometimes I think he was born too rich. He doesn't quite have the urgency of someone who had to scramble up the way I did."

"I don't need explanations."

The real Véronique had seldom asked for any, either. She had her foundation work, her friends, her beautiful mansion. Her life.

"I . . ." He hadn't planned this yet, but—"I think we should go to the symphony tonight."

"Anyone we know going to be there?" she asked casually.

That struck at the heart of the matter, all without dropping out of character. "Yes," he replied. There would inevitably be members of his circle of acquaintances at the buffet for patrons. Precisely who could not be predicted, but it would include those who knew of Véronique's death.

"I'm looking forward to seeing them," he added.

They arrived at a fashionable point, not too early but allowing time to mingle. Eyes turned immediately to Jordan's companion. He realized this was inevitable. Even among ladies bedecked in finery and enhanced by everything liposuction, health clubs, and beauticians could offer, Veronique attracted more than her share of admiration.

It was not until late in the feasting that he was approached by a rotund figure in a tuxedo that, despite the expert tailoring, no longer fit.

"Ramsey," Jordan said, offering his hand.

Ramsey's grip was moist, his handshake cursory. He leaned forward, breath heavy with Cabernet. "So, Welles, you've found yourself a foxwife. Been borrowing ideas from old Takahashi?" He thrust his chin toward the buffet table, where Véronique was adding a pair of strawberries to her depleted plate.

"Don't compare me to Takahashi," Jordan retorted, failing in his plans for a calm explanation of the elf's presence.

Ramsey failed to suppress a locker-room chuckle. "Oh. Well, of course. He's *yakuza*. They don't think like you or me. All I meant—"

"Outsiders have rights," Jordan said. "This is all properly done."

"Of course, of course." Ramsey gazed at Véronique again from the straps of her shoes to her pearl necklace—one of the few types of jewelry the elf could tolerate. Jordan suspected antebellum plantation owners had scrutinized their slave women in just such a way.

As quickly as possible, Jordan disengaged from Ramsey and escorted Véronique to their seats in the concert hall.

The musicians played as if inspired, but after the finale, Jordan had to consult his program simply to recall which compositions had been featured.

Jordan made no further arrangements to go out in public with the elf, except to places where they would be perceived as just another wealthy couple taking in the sights. This annoyed him, because it was not a restriction the real Véronique would have tolerated; she had loved socializing. The new Véronique accepted it without comment.

He forced himself to contact his office as little as possible. Monday they loitered at the mansion. Tuesday they spent aboard his yacht, visiting Shelter Island and roaming the Atlantic a bit, beyond scrutiny. Finally on Wednesday he spent three hours downtown.

The lure sank in. Thursday he returned for nearly a full day.

This was not what he had planned when he hired the surrogate, but he told himself the elf needed the respite to shrug off whatever deleterious effects the shapeshifting caused.

His own employees said nothing to him of foxwives or ghost-chasing, and they probably wouldn't, so long as he didn't thrust the evidence right in their faces. He knew they knew. He hadn't told them, but gossip was unstoppable.

She was waiting when he arrived Thursday late afternoon. A kiss and hug, body against his, aroused him as reliably as ever, but he suppressed the urge to take her upstairs that very minute. They had plenty of time to indulge later, in the darkness.

"Let's take the limo out," he said.

"All right," she answered. "That would be nice."

Véronique had loved riding through the countryside with no particular destination in mind. Jordan told the chauffeur to re-create the route taken a few days before the accident.

The elf talked to him, often serving up the same sort of observations his wife had made on the original trip. Had he been dreaming of the ride last night, letting her siphon from him the raw material to mimic the past? No matter. It soothed him, as did the hand she tucked into his palm.

As they came around a bend at dusk, Jordan gazed across a pasture toward a copse of trees and made out a collection of tents. Even at this distance, he could tell none were made of synthetics. No bright colors. The fabric had been hand-woven of natural materials, the poles selected from deadfall rather than shaped industrially. A handful of fey beings stood in a ring, paying obeisance to the setting sun with raised arms and a crooning that just managed to drift into the car through the half-lowered window.

Jordan had forgotten the camp was located there. Perhaps

he had not seen it on the previous excursion. Outsiders tended to be relegated, by their choice or otherwise, into the nooks and crannies of the landscape. The parcel was not unlike the one he had leased to his companion's clan.

The tents slid out of view, but the memory of them nagged. Finally, when it was clear she was not going to comment, he asked, "Is that how you live in your world? Or do you have homes? You know, solid structures?"

"Would your wife have such knowledge?" The voice and physical mannerisms remained those of Véronique, but the elf had emerged, if only to remind him of the role she was supposed to be fulfilling.

"No. But I'm asking anyway."

She leaned back, half-closing her eyes as if gazing over the horizon. "We dwell among the forests and meadows in abodes made of living trees and vines. Bowers for the least exalted among us, palaces for the mighty. The trees shape themselves at our command, and in return we revere and nurture them. They have a kind of sentience possessed by only a smattering of the plants in this realm. To walk beneath the leaves of my home near *Cnoc na Fírinne* . . ." Her voice faded, wistfulness stealing its vigor.

"You'd prefer to be there right now if you could," Jordan said.

"Yes."

"Is it true what they say, that your people were exiled?"

"The details I will not speak of. I and those forced to this side of the gateway angered our Lord and Lady, who believed our actions benefited a scheme of the drows. A year and a day we must pay our penance."

"But you've been here much longer than that already."

"Time flows differently on this side of the barrier. A century and more will pass here before we can return."

"That's awful," he said emphatically. "Though from what I've heard, you're capable of living to see the day."

"We do not age once we are grown, but we are not invulnerable. There is so little in this world that sustains us, and what there is of it is dearly bought. Many of us will die before the exile is complete."

Jordan had read of murdered elves, of suicide. In less than twenty years since the Fall, a third of the tens of thousands who had been banished had already expired, with almost no births to offset the attrition. To him, those facts had been mere statistics, of no greater significance than the number of malnutrition cases in the Third World.

As for the remark about "dearly bought," the deprivation of the Outsiders had been something for him to exploit.

"You ask me of these matters as if they troubled you personally," she said.

"I wanted to learn more about you."

"Are you courting me, then?"

"No," he said quickly. "No, of course not."

"Good. It cannot come to fruition."

The weather turned stormy, as good an excuse as any to sequester themselves in the mansion once more. Jordan placed the weekend before him as if it were another of his projects, concocted a goal, and set about to fulfill it.

"I want you to read aloud to me," he announced after brunch.

"All right," she said. "Read what?"

He deposited a large stack of paper on the coffee table. "I want to hear her words," he said, settling beside her on the sofa.

The stack contained printouts of the archive of email Véronique had sent him over the years. There were scores of letters written during the many separations while he was off on business trips or she traveling from city to city doing her foundation work. His wife had composed them almost as ongoing journal entries, with a depth he was ashamed he seldom put into his replies on the infrequent occasions he answered her by written word. The paper version saved the elf from what were, to her, noxious energies emitted by the computer.

He had reviewed some of the text immediately after the funeral, but hearing the words in Véronique's voice restored the full impact.

"Charles managed to uproot the entire tulip bed," she read from a letter written while he had been in Tokyo for a week, manipulating his way past trade restrictions. "Sometimes he's still such a puppy."

Charles had been a strapping boxer, already elderly at the time of the note. The dog had died five years ago come Christmas week. He had been Véronique's pet from before the marriage, but Jordan had come to love that odoriferous idiot. Yet he had barely thought of him in ages. The note, too, he had completely forgotten, along with the fact that they had always planted tulips by the south entrance, a custom buried with the animal.

"Stop," he said.

The woman paused in midsentence.

"Read something more recent."

She rifled through the stack and pulled out a long missive written at Easter. That letter seemed fresh. Current. Jordan relaxed onto the cushions, only then realizing that he had tightened up.

Véronique's words should not have seemed distant, five years old or not. For them to have that quality meant that these other words, written so recently, would one day be distant as well.

Early on Sunday evening as they were engaged in the fifth long session of delving into the archives, the elf asked if they could pause.

He looked at her straight on for the first time in many hours. At some point, she had changed. A hint of darkness marred her cheeks beneath the eyes. The sheen of Véronique's brunette locks had faded.

"You're suffering, aren't you?" He phrased it as a question, but it was more a statement.

"I apologize. I am failing to meet the agreement." Her voice faltered, almost losing Véronique's pitch and accent. "If we are to be together later tonight, it is necessary that I take a short rest."

"Then do so," he said. He gestured out the window, at the woods.

She rose unsteadily and made her way immediately toward the front door. Along the way, she shucked her clothing, as if even the touch of the costume of the role she was playing overwhelmed her.

Jordan's glance roved over the familiar contours of her back, thighs, and bottom before she fled from his sight. How many times had he stared at the naked features of the body that one was modeled on? It was a sight he could never get enough of. Yet he couldn't help but note that, in every past instance, a naked Véronique meant a Véronique approaching him. Never one running the other way.

For the next several days, Jordan attempted to follow a precise schedule. He went to the office, actively taking up matters which he had been delegating during his period of mourning. At first he felt as though he were still going through the motions, but the routine mattered. It comforted him.

He did not, however, linger overtime. He returned to the mansion before dinner each night. That was his rule. Everything in balance.

The elf met him there. Demonstrating no further stress now that she only had to maintain her human shape for a fraction of the day, she continued to be the wife he had known and loved, save that she was more cooperative, as an employee would be.

It was everything he had contracted for, and everything he had thought was necessary.

On Friday, at the close of the business day, a couple of his VPs suggested drinks at the North Star Pub. He declined, letting them go on without him. A drink sounded great, but not with the old gang. Not yet. Instead, he went alone to the bar at the Hilton.

He hadn't gone out solo in years. He wasn't quite sure what to do with himself, so he stared at the nearest television set.

His eyes glazed over while the news broadcast dragged on. He emerged from his reverie during a segment on the problems rising from an attempt to settle a clan of Outsiders in the Imperial Valley of California. Project supporters had argued that the agricultural setting would allow the elves to thrive, as well as provide them with a means of economic self-sufficiency, but the plan had failed to take into account the need of the refugees for sylvan venues. The only deep shade in the region came from buildings.

"Damn spooks. Can't handle working an honest job," muttered the man at the table nearest to Jordan.

"No one here asked for your opinion," Jordan said.

The man bristled, but fell short of a confrontation, perhaps because the segment concluded with an image of an Outsider collapsed in a field, suffering convulsions for reasons no human physician could fathom. After a few tense moments, the fellow polished off his drink and left.

Jordan considered leaving as well, but he'd barely touched his Glenlivet. Though he could always find more in his liquor cabinet at home, he made it a practice never to rush a single-malt Scotch.

The amber liquid was half gone when a tall, well-dressed young woman ambled by. She stopped.

"That seat free?" she asked.

Jordan shrugged. "Sure."

She joined him. "My name's Angie. You?"

He was going to beg off conversation, but she was straightforward, appealing in manner as well as in body. He gave her his first name.

"What do you do?" she asked.

"A little of everything," he said guardedly. "I work for Welles and Haggard across the street."

"You're kidding," she said brightly. "I'm an attorney. I've done some research on tariff regulations for your firm."

She was not the hustler he had worried she might be. In fact, within a few minutes it was clear that she was the sort of fascinating woman he'd never expect to meet in so serendipitous a fashion. She had come in to rendezvous with a client, but had arrived to find a message canceling the meeting.

She also managed, by the time his glass was empty, to casually refer to a break-up with her most recent boyfriend, and the lack of anyone new in her life.

At that point, Jordan knew he had to say something.

"Angie, I'm a married man."

She glanced at his left hand, biting her lip. He probably should have left the wedding band on, but he hadn't been able to do so since the accident. "I'm sorry," he added, sympathy fueling the sincerity of the comment.

The woman shrugged, giving a wan smile that said his honesty had made her wish even more that he had wanted her companionship. She gracefully withdrew. As her fine, long legs found rest upon a distant stool, Jordan's face clouded.

That night, Jordan relished the sensory details of making love to Véronique to a greater degree than he could ever remember doing, as if recording them for all time. The light caught her curves, shadows deepening her feminine outlines. Her mouth was open and hungry. Her nipples quickened as air struck them, then softened until his tongue restored them to hardness. Her hair traced a feathery path along his skin, a faint touch more subtle than her hands or breasts or pelvis, more subtle even than her mouth. Had he ever noticed that before, amid all the pleasures they had shared?

Lying beside him, she draped a leg over him and ground her crotch against his outer leg, her knee gliding on a layer of perspiration. Her eyes blazed with lust. She squeezed his cock urgently, as if anticipating it inside her. He pressed her back and let his own hand rove, bringing it ultimately down to manipulate her labia. She moaned. His finger slid inside and her pelvis drew up, seizing hold. The moan became a gasp.

She pulled him on top of her, wrapped her legs around his pelvis and, by dint of wriggling, placed him at the brink of penetration. He toyed with her, rubbing the head of his erection against her clitoris.

"Put it *in*." Her words came out in a hiss.

He entered her and pumped furiously. She rocked with him, challenging him to maintain the rhythm, thrashing. Her tension gathered and he knew that when the peak arrived, it would be a massive, lung-heaving release. As would his.

It was stupendous in the way that farewell passion should be, the way it should have been with the real Véronique, if only they had known the last time was at hand.

In the delirium of the aftermath, they lay intertwined. The sweat cooled. Their heartbeats fell to inaudibility. Their breathing returned to an even cadence. Without a word, the woman slipped from the bed and set off toward the door to the stairs.

"You're leaving?" he asked.

"Until the morning." The voice no longer sounded entirely like that of Véronique.

"But . . ."

"I must. It was what you dreamed, my lord."

"When?"

"Last night, and the night before, and the night before. I am compelled." Chin down, reticent, she closed the door behind her.

He rolled to the edge of the bed, intending to rise and follow her, but he never made it past a sitting position. Wisps of memory floated up. Yes, he *had* produced such dreams, hadn't he? As often happened, they hadn't lingered in his daylight thoughts, but in hindsight, he could see the message his subconscious had been whispering.

He lay back, closed his eyes, and waited to see what dreams might arrive this time, with no one but him to see them.

In the morning he excused the household staff, asking them not to return until noon. He found the shapeshifter in Véronique's dayroom. Jordan and his wife always slept together, but she enjoyed having a bedroom of her own in which to house the spillover from her wardrobe and give her a place to retreat to when she needed privacy.

The elf, looking perhaps as much like Véronique as she had ever managed, was carefully packing away Véronique's clothes in their designated drawers and hanging them on their proper hooks, many wrapped in plastic as if they were not to be touched again for a long time, if ever. When that was done, he helped her make the bed—apparently she had slept in it for a portion of the night, though her hair was fragrant with pine. Finally, she removed her nightgown, and put that away as well.

They went outside to the lawn, halfway between the house and the woods. She kissed him. Lightly, reverently, the way Véronique always did upon leave-taking. The way she had kissed him the morning of the accident.

The next step was not easy, but there was an element that made it possible: Unlike the loss of his wife, stolen by a whim of fate, he had a choice now in how he acted. Even that small measure of control made such a difference.

He probed for the ethereal bracelet around his wrist. The more he sought it out, the more tangible it became. The hemp hardened beneath his fingertips, allowing him to work the knot free. Finally it slid loose. The cord hung at her side, visible once more.

"You are free."

She regarded him intently, as if to be sure he would not snatch the noose back up and reattach it once he had had a moment to realize what he had done. Slowly, she pushed the loop off her own wrist, and let the cord drop to the grass. The object seemed so mundane, lying there, surely no part of sorcery or oaths.

"We are both exiles, awaiting the day of our release," she murmured. "Take heart. This is a presage of things to come."

Smiling, light-footed, she scampered across the lawns and into the woods, never looking back. Her shape was already indistinct, transformation initiated.

He turned and reentered the house. Echoes danced up the stairs as the door struck the jamb. The house was empty, save for him. As it had to be.

Tastings

Neil Gaiman

 He had a tattoo on his upper arm, of a small heart, done in blue and red. Beneath it was a patch of pink skin, where a name had been erased.

He was licking her left nipple, slowly. His right hand was caressing the back of her neck.

"What's wrong?" she asked.

He looked up. "What do you mean?"

"You seem like you're. I don't know. Somewhere else," she said. "Oh . . . that's nice. That's really nice."

They were in a hotel suite. It was her suite. He knew who she was, had recognized her on sight, but had been warned not to use her name.

He moved his head up to look into her eyes, moved his hand down to her breast. They were both naked from the waist up. She had a silk skirt on, he wore blue jeans.

"Well?" she said.

He put his mouth against hers. Their lips touched. Her tongue flickered against his. She sighed, pulled back. "So what's wrong? Don't you like me?"

He grinned, reassuringly. "Like you? I think you're wonderful," he said. He hugged her, tightly. Then his hand cupped her left breast, and, slowly, squeezed it. She closed her eyes.

"Well, then," she whispered, "what's wrong?"

"Nothing," he said. "It's wonderful. You're wonderful. You're very beautiful."

"My ex-husband used to say that I used my beauty," she told him. She ran the back of her hand across the front of his jeans, up and down. He pushed against her, arching his back. "I suppose he was right." She knew the name he had given her, but, certain that it was false, a name of convenience, would not call him by it.

He touched her cheek. Then he moved his mouth back to her nipple. This time, as he licked, he moved a hand down between her legs. The silk of her dress was soft against his hand, and he cupped his fingers against her pubis and slowly increased the pressure.

"Anyway, something's wrong," she said. "There's something going on in that pretty head of yours. Are you sure you don't want to talk about it?"

"It's silly," he said. "And I'm not here for me. I'm here for you."

She undid the buttons of his jeans. He rolled over and slid them off, dropping them onto the floor by the bed. He wore thin scarlet underpants, and his erect penis pushed against the material.

While he took off his jeans, she removed her earrings; they were made of elaborately looped silver wires. She placed them carefully beside the bed.

He laughed, suddenly.

"What was that about?" she asked.

"Just a memory. Strip poker," he said. "When I was a kid, I don't know, thirteen or fourteen, we used to play with the girls next door. They'd always load up with *tchotchkes*— necklaces, earrings, scarves, things like that. So when they'd lose, they'd take off one earring or whatever. Ten minutes in, we'd be nude and embarrassed, and they'd still be fully dressed."

"So why'd you play with them?"

"Hope," he said. He reached beneath her dress, began to massage her labia through her white cotton panties. "Hope that maybe we'd get a glimpse of something. Anything."

"And did you?"

He pulled his hand away, rolled on top of her. They kissed. They pushed as they kissed, gently, crotch to crotch. Her hands squeezed the cheeks of his ass. He shook his head. "No. But you can always dream."

"So. What's silly? And why wouldn't I understand?"

"Because it's dumb. Because . . . I don't know what you're thinking."

She pulled down his jockey shorts. Ran her forefinger along the side of his penis. "It's really big. Natalie said it would be."

"Yeah?"

"I'm not the first person to tell you that it's big."

"No."

She lowered her head, kissed his penis at the base, where the spring of golden hair brushed it, then she dribbled a little saliva onto it and ran her tongue slowly up its length. She pulled back after that, stared into his blue eyes with her brown ones.

"You don't know what I'm thinking? What does that mean? Do you normally know what other people are thinking?"

He shook his head. "Well," he said. "Not exactly."

"Hold that thought," she said. "I'll be right back."

She got up, walked into the bathroom, closed the door behind her but did not lock it. There was the sound of urine splashing into a toilet bowl. It seemed to go on for a long time. The toilet was flushed; the sound of movement in the bathroom, a cupboard opening, closing; more movements.

She opened the door and came out. She was quite naked, now. She looked, for the first time, slightly self-conscious. He was sitting on the bed, also naked. His hair was blond, and cut very short. As she came close to him he reached out his hands, held her waist, pulled her close to him. His face was level with her navel. He licked it, then lowered his head to her crotch, pushed his tongue between her long labia, lapped and licked.

She began to breathe faster.

While he tongued her clitoris, he pushed a finger into her vagina. It was already wet, and the finger slid in easily.

He slid his other hand down her back to the curve of her ass, and let it remain there.

"So, do you always know what people are thinking?"

He pulled his head back, her juices on his mouth. "It's a bit stupid. I mean, I don't really want to talk about it. You'll think I'm weird."

She reached down, tipped his chin up, kissed him. She bit his lip, not too hard, pulled at it with her teeth.

"You are weird. But I like it when you talk. And I want to know what's wrong, Mister Mind-Reader."

She sat next to him on the bed. "You have terrific breasts," he told her. "Really lovely."

She made a *moue*. "They're not as good as they used to be. And don't change the subject."

"I'm not changing the subject." He lay back on the bed. "I can't really read minds. But I sort of can. When I'm in bed with someone. I know what makes them tick."

She climbed on top of him, sat on his stomach. "You're kidding."

"No."

He fingered her clitoris gently. She squirmed. "Nice." She moved back six inches. Now she was sitting on his penis, pushed flat between them. She moved on it.

"I know . . . I usually . . . do you know how hard it is to concentrate with you doing that?"

"Talk," she said. "Talk to me."

"Put it in you."

She reached down one hand, held his penis. She lifted herself up slightly, squatted down on his penis, feeding the head inside her. He arched his back, pushed up into her. She closed her eyes, then opened them and stared at him. "Well?"

"It's just that when I'm fucking, or even in the time before fucking, well . . . I *know* things. Things I honestly don't know—or can't know. Things I don't want to know even. Abuse. Abortions. Madness. Incest. Whether they're secret sadists or stealing from their bosses."

"For example?"

He was all the way in her now, thrusting slowly in and out. Her hands were resting on his shoulders. She leaned down, kissed him on the lips.

"Well, like it works with sex, too. Usually I know how I'm doing. In bed. With women. I know what to do. I don't have to ask. I know. If she needs a top or a bottom, a master or a slave. If she needs me to whisper 'I love you' over and over while I fuck her and we lie side by side, or just needs me to piss into her mouth. I become what she wants. That's why . . . Jesus. I can't believe I'm telling you this. I mean, that's why I started doing this for a living."

"Yeah. Natalie swears by you. She gave me your number."

"She's so cool. Natalie. And in such great shape for her age."

"And what does Natalie like to do, then?"

He smiled up at her. "Trade secret," he said. "Sworn to secrecy. Scout's honor."

"Hold on," she said. She climbed off him, rolled over. "From behind. I like it from behind."

"I should have known that," he said, sounding almost irritated. He got up, positioned himself behind her, ran a finger down the soft skin that covered her spine. He put his hand between her legs, then grasped his penis and pushed it into her vagina.

"Really slow," she said.

He thrust his hips, sliding his penis into her. She gasped.

"Is that nice?" he asked.

"No," she said. "It hurt a little when it was all the way in. Not so deep next time. So you know stuff about women when you screw them. What do you know about me?"

"Nothing special. I'm a big fan of yours."

"Spare me."

One of his arms was across her breasts. His other hand touched her lips. She sucked at his forefinger, licking it. "Well, not that big a fan. But I saw you on Letterman, and I thought you were wonderful. Really funny."

"Thanks."

"I can't believe we're doing this."

"Fucking?"

"No. Talking while we're fucking."

"I like to talk while I fuck. That's enough like this. My knees are getting tired."

He pulled out and sat back on the bed.

"So you know what women are thinking, and what they want? Hmm. Does it work for men?"

"I don't know. I've never made love to a man."

She stared at him. Placed a finger on his forehead, ran it slowly down to his chin, tracing the line of his cheekbone on the way. "But you're so pretty."

"Thank you."

"And you're a whore."

"Escort," he said.

"Vain, too."

"Perhaps. And you're not?"

She grinned. "Touché. So. You don't know what I want now?"

"No."

She lay on her side. "Put on a condom and fuck me in the ass."

"You got any lubricant?"

"Bedside table."

He took the condom and the gel from the drawer, unrolled the condom down his penis.

"I hate condoms," he told her, as he put it on. "They make me itch. And I've got a clean bill of health. I showed you the certificate."

"I don't care."

"I just thought I'd mention it. That's all."

He rubbed the lubricant into and around her anus, then he slid the head of his penis inside her.

She groaned. He paused. "Is—is that okay?"

"Yes."

He rocked back and forth, pushing deeper. She grunted, rhythmically, as he did so. After a couple of minutes she said "Enough."

He pulled out. She rolled onto her back, and pulled the soiled condom off his penis, dropped it onto the carpet.

"You can come now," she told him.

"I'm not ready. And we could go for hours, yet."

"I don't care. Come on my stomach." She smiled at him. "Make yourself come. Now."

He shook his head, but his hand was already fumbling at his penis, jerking it forward and back, until he spurted in a glistening trail all over her stomach and breasts.

She reached a hand down and rubbed the milky semen lazily across her skin.

"I think you should go now," she said.

"But you didn't come. Don't you want me to make you come?"

"I got what I wanted."

He shook his head, confusedly. His penis was flaccid and shrunken. "I should have known," he said, confused. "I don't. I don't know. I don't know anything."

"Get dressed," she told him. "Go away."

He pulled on his clothes, efficiently, beginning with his socks. Then he leaned over, to kiss her.

She moved her head away from his lips. "No," she said.

"Can I see you again?"

She shook her head. "I don't think so."

He was shaking. "What about the money?" he asked.

"I paid you already," she said. "I paid you when you came in. Don't you remember?"

He nodded, nervously, as if he could not remember but dared not admit it. Then he patted his pockets until he found the envelope with the cash in it, and he nodded once more. "I feel so empty," he said, plaintively.

She scarcely noticed when he left.

She lay on the bed with a hand on her stomach, his spermatic fluid drying cold on her skin, and she tasted him in her mind.

She tasted each woman he had slept with. She tasted what he did with her friend, smiling inside at Natalie's tiny perversities. She tasted the day he lost his first job. She tasted the morning he had awakened, still drunk, in his car, in the middle of a cornfield, and, terrified, had sworn off the bottle forever. She knew his real name. She remembered the name that had once been tattooed on his arm, and knew why it could be there no longer. She tasted the color of his eyes from the inside, and shivered at the nightmare he had in which he was forced to carry spiny fish in his mouth, and from which he woke, choking, night after night. She savored his hungers in food and fiction, and discovered a dark sky when he was a small boy, and he had stared up at the stars and wondered at their vastness and immensity, that even he had forgotten.

Even in the prettiest, most unpromising material, she had discovered, you could find real treasures. And he had had a little of the talent himself, although he had never understood it, or used it for anything more than sex. She wondered, as she swam in his memories and dreams, if he would miss them, if he would ever notice that they were gone. And then, shuddering, ecstatic, she came, in bright flashes, which warmed her, and took her out of herself and into the nowhere-at-all perfection of the little death.

There was a crash from the alley below. Someone had stumbled into a garbage can.

She sat up, and wiped the stickiness from her skin. And then, without showering, she began to dress herself once more, deliberately, beginning with her white cotton panties, and ending with her elaborate silver earrings.

The Sweet of Bitter Bark
and Burning Clove

Doris Egan

 As always, anticipation was half the fun. Bailey touched his forehead to the window of the sixteen-seat commuter plane and looked down at the white, pink, and apple-green houses of San Cristobel, set around a blue lagoon speckled with boats. He smiled.

He hadn't expected anything to come of his latest e-mail; he'd sent it off on Thursday more in a spirit of keeping to the rules of the game than in any real hope of an answer. Galera Cay was a tropical island, after all; not Lilith's style.

"Galera Cay, arrive San Cristobel February 2. Not sure how long. Bailey."

And three hours later, thanks to the glory of the Internet, he read: "I'm in San Cristobel doing some work. Come stay with me. Lilith." An address followed.

Doing some work? Lilith was an investment banker; her work took her to New York, London, and the Far East—what was she doing on a Caribbean island? But then, the place was notorious for money laundering, and he supposed that not all the clients of Rockville Perkins were spotless in the eyes of the IRS.

So casual: Come stay with me. Like an unexpected

Christmas present. This time it had only been ten months and two weeks. The first time it had been thirteen months, and the next, exactly a year.

And damn, last time it had been almost two years, and he'd been so restless at the end he'd been *that* close to calling Rockville Perkins to find out where the hell she was. That would've been way out of bounds, though, and with good reason. As it was, he'd called and asked for "Ms. Belizaire's number," then hung up, feeling like a jerk. At least she apparently still had an office, she was still around *somewhere* . . .

It wasn't that bad, though. You adjusted.

He remembered that first time—more than five years ago, now. She'd come to his office and explained that she'd heard of him through a friend, and hoped he could help her with a problem. It was so like a noir movie; the expensively dressed goddess in the cheap vinyl chair opposite his desk, the offer of a retainer—he was half expecting to hear she wanted him to murder her husband. Although even then it was hard to imagine Lilith Belizaire with a husband.

But no, it was more prosaic than that. An accountant had dropped out of sight with other people's money—not Lilith's, but a friend's; and she had promised to locate him. Bailey was human, and his first impulse was to seize any excuse to, well, just have this creature return to his office as frequently as possible. But he was realistic. From her story, the accountant would be hard to find, and from his own good sense, Bailey saw no suggestion on Ms. Belizaire's part that the pleasure she brought into his life would be anything but visual.

And visual paid no estimated taxes. He saw this case going nowhere, while there were two others out of town that looked to be more long-term and more promising. He refused, he thought, very courteously; and she left.

That night he stopped at Morell's for a drink.

Jesus. He hadn't been picked up in a bar since he was,

what, twenty-five, twenty-six? He rather suspected that the look on his face in most bars showed exactly what he felt: That he wanted to get a drink and go up to his hotel room—usually it was a hotel room, anyway—and get some damned sleep before the phone calls of the previous day started bouncing back. And how the hell had Lilith found out where he drank when he was in town, anyway?

And then the next morning he'd gone to the mirror to look at the marks, and found a post-it stuck there—like she'd known it was the first place he'd check:

Drink plenty of fluids. OJ's in the refrigerator.

So he'd opened the refrigerator door and found two gallons of it. She must have stopped at the deli across the street before she left. But then, she was always considerate.

That had kicked off a hell of a six weeks, that first time. He'd even managed to concentrate on her case long enough to solve it, unearthing her missing accountant in Sebring, Florida, where he'd bought a condominium in his girlfriend's name.

Bailey had been careful not to find out what happened to him.

There was a faintly British feel to the island, strange in a place of heavy sunlight and pastels. San Cristobel airport was full of vigorous, dark-skinned men and women in crisp, white, short-sleeved shirts, offering information, baggage handling, tour guide cards, and pamphlets on everything from motorbike rentals to scuba gear. Bailey ignored them, till a man in a chauffeur's cap stepped forward and addressed him in a deep, courteous voice.

"Sir? Ms. Belizaire sent me to pick you up." The accent was half British, half lilting. Bailey was not surprised that the driver could identify him; he was the only unattached person on the entire commuter flight of families and couples. It was still winter, prime tourist season in the Caribbean. And Lilith, he thought, always made sure her people were briefed.

Hiring a car for him was efficient, considerate, and expensive—just like Lilith. And pretty much the opposite of him, he supposed.

"Shall I fetch the rest of your baggage, sir?"

"This is it," said Bailey, holding his battered gray duffel. The driver reached for it. Bailey retained the handle.

He smiled at the driver, a smile of blinding innocence he'd perfected through years of work in his chosen profession. The driver retreated, puzzled. "This way, sir."

Bailey did not check his luggage; Bailey was paranoid, and proudly so. There were diskettes in that duffel he just felt better not handing over to people, even people who *said* they were from Lilith.

A long gray limousine was waiting at the curb outside. Bailey grabbed the door handle before the driver could, then shrugged apologetically. *Bailey, those Ford Taurus reflexes are just way too obvious.* As the driver circled back to the front, Bailey looked into the dimness of the interior and stopped short.

Two long, long legs in perfect beige stockings; crossed, shoeless, lapped by a wide skirt of white linen. He felt a huge and stupid grin come over his face: She'd come out to meet him. A sweet gesture—he knew how much Lilith hated sun glare.

His pause of surprise had been noted. A humorous "tsk-tsk" floated from within, the voice detached and friendly. "Don't just stand there. Come in, and let's get you out of all this *nasty* sunlight."

He laughed and tossed his duffel onto the floor, then followed it inside.

Ten months and two weeks since he'd last seen her, and he hadn't been in good shape then, of course. Now he had the energy to appreciate the visuals. She was wearing all white linen, with a thin bracelet of white gold on one pale wrist. Waves of red-gold hair poured over her shoulders. And folded like this into the back of a car seat, even a limo, her tall form translated into legs that went on for years.

"Long time, Bailey."

"Three hundred and twenty days. But who's counting?"

She smiled and he wondered if it would be a little more cool to try and wipe this grin off his face. *Oh, fuck it.* Then she leaned over and kissed him—on his mouth, but just a welcome kiss, a taste; and his grin faded as he found himself trying to pinpoint just what fruit her lips reminded him of; something cool and heavy with summer sweetness. Already his concentration was shot to hell—probably the effect of all this tropical sun.

She shifted her legs, moving further away from the window as the car pulled out. "I take it you're here on a case?"

He nodded. She glanced at the driver, then back at him. "Below the line or above?" She meant, legal or shady? Could they talk about it in front of someone else?

"Below."

"Ah."

They moved out of the airport and all of three minutes later they were in San Cristobel proper; Bailey divided his attention between the wrist just touching his thigh, the bare foot resting against his shoe, and the town passing by the limousine windows. He should really pay more attention to the last, he supposed, but it was always a little disorienting, the first day back with Lilith.

Sunlight, and a two-lane street, and everywhere buildings saturated with color; electric pastels, blue and pink and violet; even the whites were blinding. Was that all really paint, or just the stage lighting of the tropical sun? There was a vague confusion of tourist signs; ice cream, hotels, boarding-houses, bars, dance clubs.

And banks. Lots of banks. No wonder Lilith had business

here. In addition to the National Bank of Galera Cay, there were branches of Credit Suisse, Barclay's, First Tokyo . . .

Money center or not, it wasn't exactly New York. Fifteen minutes later they were out of town, running along a slightly less well-paved road, past one-story houses set among flowers and small blue swimming pools.

"Bailey."

"What?"

She lifted the hand beside hers on the seat, as coolly as if she were lifting papers from a briefcase, and touched her tongue to the center of his palm. *Christ.* It was like a slight electrical charge. He glanced toward the driver, but she'd done it so casually he didn't seem to have noticed. She took Bailey's index and middle finger into her mouth for a moment, sucked, and then nipped the ends in a playful reminder. Then she laid his hand back on the seat.

"I'm glad you could come," she said.

Ten months and two weeks. His heart started jackhammering.

The house was a long, white, L-shaped rectangle, set on a package of neatly landscaped ground on the top of a hill. A vista of blue water curved in the distance. A stand of ferns, elephant ears, and orchids screened the back; there was probably a small swimming pool somewhere behind it. Purple-red bougainvillea surrounded the patio.

And there was a porte cochere. No wonder Lilith liked it.

She opened the door, retrieving a briefcase from the floor as she did. "I had to attend a meeting in town this morning," she explained, gesturing with the case. She fished around for the umbrella she habitually used as a parasol, and Bailey handed it to her, along with the white sandals he found thrust, typically, under the front seat.

"Sure, crush my feeble hopes. I thought you'd come out into all this evil solar radiation for my sake alone."

She smiled. "I hired the car for you, anyway. Teej took the

convertible into town, and I didn't want you wandering around on your own. I'd probably find you sitting here in the bougainvillea when I got back."

"And you figured I'd bring down the property values."

She turned and dropped a kiss from those cool lips on his cheek. *Papaya?* "As a renter," she whispered, and he felt her smile, "it's not a problem for me. But I have a duty to the neighbors."

She got out of the car, all six-feet-four of her, and he grabbed his bag while she dismissed the driver. She looked serene and untouched in the shade of the porte cochere, like some kind of flavored ice impervious to melting; it was the white linen suit with that swirl of a skirt that did it, he thought, and he regretted it. Too bad she dressed for the climate, too bad she couldn't wear that black leather thing she'd worn sometimes in New York, plunging neckline and hem up to there; with her coloring, it was spectacular.

The fact was, thought Bailey, as the car pulled slowly out of the porte cochere and made its way down the gravel drive, you could analyze this relationship any way you liked; but the plain truth was that he was a thirty-five-year-old man who'd never gotten over his crush on Julie Newmar as the Catwoman, back at the age of twelve.

"I like it," he said, skidding his duffel across the floor. Everything was clean and open; terra cotta tiles, white shutters, and the breeze off the ocean running unobstructed over the hilltop through the bank of windows and French doors. He walked through a doorway and found himself in the kitchen. "Nice," he said, looking around at the cupboards and the clean wall of whitewashed stone that held the oven. He opened the refrigerator, grinning. "I guess we better send out for some orange ju—" He stopped.

There were two gallons of Tropicana in there, one of them already opened. Nearly empty, in fact. Being Bailey, he couldn't stop himself from checking the date, from lifting the used carton to see how light it was.

He shut the door. "Who's the lucky guy?" he asked, his voice suddenly gone toneless.

Lilith put her briefcase down on the table. She turned, not hurrying, and looked at him without expression. Bailey said, "Is he still here? Are we going to be bunking together like good campers?"

Still no anger from Lilith; just that careful, judging look. Bailey heard the echo of his own voice hang in the silence and felt like an idiot. Of course there had been someone else, there had been a lot of someone elses over the last five years. It was a necessity. He'd just never run into such timely evidence before.

Damn fine work, Bailey, you've managed to be stupid and offensive simultaneously.

"I'm sorry," he said, in another tone entirely. "It's none of my business who else you choose to see. I'm being a jerk. Can we ignore the last thirty seconds?"

She hitched herself up on the table. "Come over here, Bailey, so I can explain something to you." He came; at the periphery of their personal space, he hesitated, and she wrapped her legs around him and pulled him in. He felt her calves pressing into his ass and her odd, faintly spicy breath on his face, like the wind through an orange grove. "Nobody else counts," she said, "now that you're here." She kissed him then.

Bailey's head started to buzz. No more polite dishes of cool strawberries, lips against alien lips; this was imperative and absolute, a single-minded dipping into the water of the soul. *Christ*, he thought, as he felt her tongue seek him out, *ten months. How could I forget what this was like?*

There was a voice, and he felt a start run through the body holding his. Lilith pulled away and he stepped back, slightly disoriented. He looked for the interruption: a young man, maybe nineteen or twenty, Hispanic-looking, in wrinkled white trousers and a cotton shirt. He stared at Bailey hard, then spoke to Lilith in Spanish, clearly registering a complaint. The marks on his neck showed black against the olive skin.

Jesus! He really is still here, thought Bailey. This was not her style at all.

Apparently it was not her idea, either; now she was answering him in Spanish, curtly, and with the faint discomfort of one who has been forced into a social faux pas. The kid answered her back, gesturing with his arms, a defensive whine in his tone. *I'm sure that'll go over real well.* Bailey leaned back against the refrigerator, folded his arms, and waited to see how the play turned out.

"*Basta!*" said Lilith then. She sighed and looked to Bailey to see how he was taking it. He raised an eyebrow coolly: *Your business, right?*

She smiled, the irony not escaping her. "Perhaps you'd like to throw him out?" she suggested.

He felt a grin break over his face and shook his head in delighted disbelief. *You don't have to do this just to make me feel better. But what the hell . . .*

He advanced toward the problem in their midst, still grinning, and the young man's eyes widened. Bailey was not an enthusiast of brawls, as a rule, but he had a pretty good sense that this would be more like stamping your foot to scare a yapping Peke, and at this moment, boy did that concept hold appeal.

The puppy in question ducked suddenly beyond the doorway and came back with a packed suitcase—evidently he had not had great expectations for this encounter. He made a dash for the kitchen door and was through it in about three seconds, the exit only marred by the fact that in his nervousness working the lock he'd dropped the suitcase inside. Bailey helpfully threw it after him. He turned to Lilith.

"Well, that felt nice. Thank you."

A pleased chuckle, as if they'd been talking about theater tickets. "It was the least I could do."

Before he could reply there was the sound of a car pulling up in the gravel driveway outside, and more voices. The play wasn't over, then. A second later the kitchen door was flung open and another young man appeared, rather breathless and slightly embarrassed. "I'm sorry, Lilith; he said he'd be gone, and then I got stuck at the bank—" The apologetic look was replaced with a blinding grin. "Bailey!"

Bailey's sense of proper melodrama suggested that a wealthy vampire ought to have a retainer who was elderly and European, wearing a butler's uniform, and preferably with a name like Maximilian; not a sandy-haired kid in a Hard Rock T-shirt who seemed so genuinely happy to see you it was impossible not to take his hand, grin back, and say, "Hiya, Teej."

TJ had been nineteen the first time Bailey met him; now he must be twenty-two. Bailey wasn't sure just what the relationship was between him and Lilith, but it obviously wasn't sexual—the fact the kid was still here, and alive, pretty much made that clear.

"Shoot, I wanted to get the room ready before you got here. Don't go in there, Bailey, it's a mess and the sheets smell like bad pot."

Bailey gathered from the tone that the Peke hadn't been popular with Teej.

"Don't worry, I'm not keeping score." *And I probably won't be sleeping in there tonight anyway.* "You're looking good."

There was that wide Teej-smile. Given the kid's natural good humor, the Peke must have worked hard to irritate him. "I've been trying free weights. *You* look tired."

"Gee, thanks."

Teej laughed. "Man, it's good to see you. You had dinner? It's nearly five, and I brought fried chicken back with me. Spicy enough to take the roof off your mouth."

* * *

They ate, or at least Teej and Bailey did, while Lilith sat with them, talking about San Cristobel and the last elections in Washington and whether the London cast of the new production of *Tom Jones* would come to New York. This was custom too, this delicate avoidance of anything personal, like the first steps of a dance. Teej had developed some opinions, Bailey saw, since they'd last spoken; opinions on drama, mostly—he'd fallen into George Bernard Shaw's plays, apparently, with the naive joy of someone who'd never heard of them before, and a dozen library books later he was frighteningly and narrowly well-informed.

It was almost funny when you thought of what he'd been like when Bailey had first met him, scarfing down a bag of McDonalds in Lilith's living room. Teej hadn't been especially promising, back in those days, with a dislike of personal questions, no visible means of support and a tendency to sleep around with older men. He'd come on to Bailey almost immediately. Bailey hadn't mentioned it to Lilith, but the next day Teej had apologized a little sheepishly. It was a tribute to the kid's natural personality—which had been a little squashed, granted, by the life he'd been living—that he'd managed to be so damned likable underneath the bull shit.

After dinner, they carried the dishes into the kitchen and put them in the washer, still talking. Teej made coffee in thin china cups and they sat in the living room as the darkness of the black vista of ocean surrounded them, beyond the open shutters. Eventually Teej excused himself, with one last pleased smile at Bailey, and vanished into his room.

Lilith sat on the white sofa, legs curled up beside her. Bailey was in a club chair on the other side of the unused fireplace. The sound of crickets and cicadas came from outside. To Bailey, who had often imagined variations of this, it was dreamlike; he felt his own blood pulse in time to the rhythm of natural sounds, his own desire, but it held no urgency. It was going to happen now. There was no point in any further effort or anticipation on his part; it wasn't necessary. This was more like daylight coming up in the morning.

After half an hour Lilith rose, took his hand, and led him to the bedroom.

It was light and cool there; another bank of shutters let in the night breeze. The room was uncluttered, and like all Lilith's rooms, neither feminine nor masculine. There were a couple of low bureaus, a table with papers and books stacked on it. The bed was a wide four-poster with clean white cotton sheets and a lemon-colored thermal blanket neatly folded at the bottom. He shivered, and although she knew quite well why he did, she closed some of the shutters and lit a hurricane lamp. The light flickered over her face and his throat went dry.

She pulled him over to the bed, sat down on the edge, and began unbuttoning his shirt. Her fingers caressed his skin as she undid each one, and he stood there, still dreamlike, watching as she bent her head to his chest and placed her lips where a button had been. Her tongue flicked out and back. She looked up at him.

"I never forget your taste," she said. He felt himself sigh.

The shirt went onto the floor. She unzipped his trousers and gave a brief stroke, through his shorts, to the erection already there. "Always so timely, Bailey," she said, amused; and then she moved back in one quick motion, took his arms and pulled him onto the bed with her the way a cat might lift a mouse.

It broke the spell. He laughed and was suddenly aware again, behind the sound, of how long he'd waited. Desire, always breathing down the back of his neck, moved for the reins. It was good that she was against him right then, her thigh between his and her arms curled round him like a leaf, but he wanted her closer still. He tried to roll them both over, needing to press the whole weight of his body into her. She halted the roll while she was on top and pinned him down effortlessly. "We have to be careful," she rebuked. "You know that."

He nodded, breathing hard. He did know. It was dangerous to provoke Lilith to lose control; it was fatal, in fact. Fortunately that had never happened, or he wouldn't have lasted a night, let alone six weeks. He pushed back a handful of her hair and found his mouth conveniently near her ear.

"Please don't leave your tour guide," he said, the first thing that came into his head. "We cannot be responsible for any accidents. Hand in all waivers before boarding the bus."

He felt chuckles shaking her body as he kissed her, and wondered at his own flippancy. How could he want something this badly and still be making fun of himself?

He tasted her then, kissing her face all over, unbuttoning the white blouse, moving his hands under her skirt. Lilith would stop him if he pushed it too hard, if it got dangerous. She gasped and then, abruptly, shoved him back on the bed.

He heard his own breath. Now.

Her lips touched the side of his neck and he felt the familiar tingle that went right down into his brain and his cock. Then came the nick and the first sharp pain. It was brief, just another tease, accustoming him to the start of the dance, then leaving off to let it be swallowed up in the haze of pleasure that surrounded it.

She moved back to see how he'd taken it. He smiled.

She lifted one hand to stroke the side of his cheek and he flinched; then he deliberately took the hand that had reached for him and kissed it.

"I'm sorry," he said. "You know what it's like the first time."

"I know," she replied.

The first time was always the sweetest, before his body's reaction kicked in. And the scariest, in some ways; there was always that sharp blossom of pain, at least in the beginning; and although once his nervous system had relearned its lessons, it wouldn't care, that didn't apply to tonight. The addictive process had to be re-started.

She slid her hand from his and a second later he felt her stroke his cock, as though she were petting a housecat. He closed his eyes.

His breathing became ragged. *Out of his hands, now, literally.*

The rhythm built; he opened his eyes to find hers directly above his, dark and intent. Running an equation while he spiraled out of control. He was panting, on the edge of desperation, and she was judging that edge to a fraction. He felt like a deer after a long run through the forest. He nodded.

The teeth penetrated his skin deeply this time. It was like a tidal pull, lifting out his soul.

He closed his eyes, shuddering. There were no defenses against pleasure like this; go with it, or it would tear you to shreds.

Then he felt his body pumping from both ends, as wave after wave of pure sensation swallowed him, pulling him helplessly down to the ocean floor, and she took him into herself. His soul stretched apart, unable to contain the unbearable sharpness of the delight. His brain told him that nothing human could live through this, or maybe without this; it was impossible to tell.

And then he seemed to be getting weaker. He wondered, vaguely, if he were dying; it seemed only logical. Then awareness left him.

This was tradition, too; to hold each other afterward, then finally to lie apart and talk. It was as though they'd crossed a bridge to some kind of safety, recognized each other at last in a crowd of masked strangers.

Lilith's hair lay like a rainfall over the pillow. Her expression was one of relief—like his own, he suspected. "So tell me what you've been doing in the last ten months," she said, and the prosaic nature of her tone was a comfort.

He decided to go for the danger. "Oh, like you don't know," he said, raising an eyebrow. He sat up on one elbow so they could see each other's faces clearly.

"How would I know, Bailey? All I have are your e-mail addresses. I don't keep tabs on you."

He made a sound in his throat that could have been disagreement, should anyone wish to take it that way.

Lilith sighed and said, "It would be against the rules."

"Yeah, well, the rules are a little more binding on me than they are on you.

She looked at him speculatively, a gaze heavy as a touch. "You say that the way women talk about birth control."

He burst out laughing. She smiled. After a minute he said, "It's a good analogy. So this is what it's like to get the prudent end of the biological stick."

"I don't know how you spend your time, Bailey, you have my word. So tell me. What about that hotel address in Boise? You weren't there long."

"It was an easy case." She was still looking at him. He hesitated, then lay down again, so he couldn't see those eyes. "Parents in Coeur d'Alene, Idaho. Wanted me to find their kid."

Her body made an exasperated movement. "You don't *do* children, Bailey."

"Yeah, well, he was borderline—seventeen."

"When parents are involved, it's never borderline. You told me this."

He pursed his lips, tilted his head slightly, and made half a shrug. She burst out laughing; rolling, affectionate laughter, and he turned to stare at her.

She said, "God, I've missed that."

"What?"

"That thing you do, that gesture. That 'So, I was a schmuck.' "

He felt his own lips curve. " 'He was armed, he was dangerous. He was an agent for the forces of good—' "

"He was a schmuck," she said, agreeing. "Tell me about the kid."

His smile disappeared. "I went through his room. Eight by ten, Ralph Lauren wallpaper—I think his mother picked it out. Desk with a spare kitchen chair. Bed by the window."

Her hand began stroking his forehead, and he took a minute to get his thoughts together again. "I opened the Venetian blinds. You could lie on the bed, look out and see a hill, where a patch of woods started. People like to commit suicide in high places. I knew he was unhappy—"

"How did you know?"

"Christ, talk to his parents for ten minutes. So I hiked up to the hill and searched around in the woods. I found what was left of him." He ran his hand along her arm, cool and re-assuring. "Less than an hour and a half. I told you it was an easy case."

"Yeah. And you told me you found 'what was left of him.' How long were the cops searching, before you showed up?"

"Three months." He shook his head impatiently. "But that means nothing. They were doing all the cop things, like showing his picture and talking to his friends. They did that, so I didn't have to."

"Bailey." She rolled over suddenly and was on top of him, brown and gold eyes a foot away. "One day you must accept the fact you're some kind of perverse genius."

Perverse genius? He was about to make a remark about mad scientists, when she brought down those smooth lips over his, and he lost interest in discussing word choices. When she lifted her head he was thinking: sweet and cool, sweet and cool, like . . . "Watermelon," he said.

She sighed. "This is where the 'perverse' comes in."

His lips felt as though they belonged to someone else, and he was starting to get that dizziness around the edges again. He looked into eyes of warm amber, skin of deadly snow. "I thought I was a schmuck," he heard himself say, distantly.

He felt the laughter against his chest.

* * *

It *had* been an easy case. There were plenty that weren't; plenty that never did reach any kind of resolution, enough to keep him away from children's cases. But he had to acknowledge there were a lot of others where an educated leap could do wonders. Not that they ever felt like wonders; there was always a simple reason behind each one, so it was more like stage magic—the explanation, once heard, was almost a disappointment. *How did you do that?* Well, son, there was a trapdoor over here . . . *Is* that *all*?

His very first case, when Jonathan was showing him the ropes . . . They were looking for an ex-mercenary, recently returned from a lucrative tour of South America; he must have known something was up, for he'd never shown at his New York apartment, leaving one tiny bank account at Chemical and no money trace at all.

No money trace. Fake papers. A three-month head start. "This one's gonna take a while," Jonathan had said. He went out and brought them back two cold cut sandwiches from the deli, and while they ate, Bailey had asked if he could try something.

Jonathan looked at him through those thick, black nerd-glasses and grinned. "Knock yourself out. I'm not paying you for lunch."

Bailey had reasoned that a man can change his identity, but not his *self*; at least, not without years of effort. And why bother to try? You can't trace a missing person's *self*. But in a world based on birth certificates and social security numbers, he thought that the sorcerers of primitive tribes had it right: You didn't send sickness to confound an enemy by way of his zip code. You focused your power on a person, a soul, an inner core.

He'd walked through their target's apartment. He'd talked to their target's ex-wife. She met him at the address, letting him in with her spare set of keys—that surprised him, but she merely said, bitterly, that her husband never kept any-

234 • DORIS EGAN

thing important in the apartment. She took him through each
room, keeping up a continuous stream of information about
her ex as they went. She thought he had some kind of shady
friends in Arizona. Or was it Wyoming? One of those western places. He'd talked about retiring to a cabin there . . .

In the den, above the PC, there was a framed poster of Edward Hopper's "Gas." A lonely road in Cape Cod, shivery in
the gathering darkness. In the foreground a man stood beside the lit pumps of a Shell station; in the background, the
road wove into the dark trees and waving grass. A moment
from the Fifties, frozen in its disquietude.

"I wouldn't let him keep it in the living room," said their
target's ex-wife. "I was sick of looking at it. He had it in the
bedroom in our old place—I couldn't get away from it. I
wanted Impressionists, you know? Was that too much to
ask? I'm telling you—" she paused.

"Bailey."

"Bailey. The man never learned how to compromise.
That's his problem, in a nutshell."

She said a number of other things, but that day at lunch,
Bailey called the fine arts department at Columbia University. Then he called the Museum of Modern Art, identifying
himself as an officer with the fifth precinct. He'd thought it
would be more difficult than that, but the person he spoke
with at the museum simply went away, came back, and told
him that yes, they had shipped a copy of "Gas" to Morant,
Wyoming, three weeks ago. They had the address waiting to
go into the database for future delivery of sale catalogues.
No, only two other copies of that print had been shipped outside the New York area in the last three months—and the
man named a woman in California and one in Texas.

Bailey hung up the phone feeling completely disoriented.
It must have shown, because his eyes met Jonathan's, who
was sitting on the edge of his desk, and a wry grin sneaked
over Jonathan's face. He said, "You didn't think it would be
that easy, did you?"

* * *

Bailey lay there, feeling the late morning breeze ruffle the sheets. Lilith had opened the shutters for him before she left, which probably meant she wasn't coming back to the room. Most likely she was in the study now, working at her computer terminal.

Six weeks. This was February second; he had till mid-March.

"What if she doesn't throw you out after six weeks, Bailey?"

He remembered his friend Marianne's voice, the open window that looked out over the campus, the sound of birdsong and drifting conversation from passing Barnard students. That last crash-and-burn had been particularly bad. He'd needed to talk . . . when he was able to talk.

"She has to throw me out, I told you; I'd die, otherwise." And by the time it got that far, he was no longer psychologically able to leave on his own. Jesus, that got embarrassing, sometimes, that final week or so: *Are you having any symptoms, Bailey?*—Cough, cough. *Oh, no.* As he'd start to shift all his weight onto his hands as he rose from a chair, to try to hide the growing weakness. *Perfectly fine.* Not yet, don't do it yet, I don't want to come home and find the place empty—

"And you just trust her to do it."

"I trust her, yes."

"Does she know how bad it is for you, afterward?"

"I think so."

"You *think* so?"

"We don't talk about it."

"What do you mean, you don't talk about it?"

"You know, it's like personal death or nuclear war. We live in the present."

"*Alcoholics* live in the present, Bailey. Drug addicts live in the present."

"Zen buddhists live in the present."

She sighed. "Bailey, don't you think you should see a therapist instead of an anthropologist?"

He gave her his most innocent smile. "Anthropologists make fewer assumptions."

He suspected the change, whatever it was, went right down to his blood chemistry. He wondered what his cells looked like under a microscope, after six weeks with Lilith. And what if he stopped reverting, afterward? Built up or destroyed some kind of immunity? What if the damage were cumulative?

Yeah, like that would stop you.

Lilith had said she didn't think it worked that way. But he didn't discuss her past with her; what was she basing that on? She didn't let many people come back, the way she did Bailey. In fact, so far as he knew, he was the only one.

So: One day in mid-March, without any warning, she would be gone. And she wouldn't be at the New York address, or any other address he knew about; and if he ever broke the rules and sent her a personal letter, or got her on the phone, he had a pretty good idea that this arrangement would be over permanently.

The soft air through the shutters felt glorious. It could be worse, he supposed, as he burrowed back into the sheets for an extra hour's sleep. There are a lot of ways for people to go missing. One of the things he liked best about Lilith was knowing that he was never going to find her component parts stuffed in a Dumpster in some alley. Just one of the many benefits, he thought drowsily, of sleeping with the most efficient predator he'd ever met . . .

"Check it out," said Teej. "I'm learning to cook."

He brought the pan right out to Bailey's plate, on the wicker table on the patio. The sun was straight up, dead noon, and the wind rippled through the fringe of the overhead umbrella.

And the omelet wasn't bad at all; carefully browned on the outside, with bits of fruit and sour cream within. It was a professional job, though Bailey couldn't help but wonder, once again, when Teej was going to do something with his life besides run Lilith's daytime errands. Although . . . he looked again. The Teej of three years ago had been battered-looking, closed-off; a pinched face and a bad haircut. This Teej was confident, relaxed, consistently charming. Bailey would be willing to bet that *this* Teej used a condom. And it occurred to him to wonder who owned the Columbia College catalogue he'd seen in the bathroom.

"So," said Teej. He pulled out the other chair and sat down, elbows on the table. "You here on a case?"

Bailey smiled. "Yes, Teej, I'm here on a case." He finished up the last of the omelet, wiped up the residue of butter with his croissant, and raised the cup of Jamaican Blue coffee. Damn, the kid was definitely spending more time in the gourmet aisle of the supermarket. Bailey remembered when he'd come home with bags of Cheese Doodles and Hostess cupcakes.

"You're not going to tell me about it?" That slight edge of hurt, as though he couldn't quite believe Bailey would disappoint him.

"It's a missing persons case."

"Well, no kidding."

When he did not seem disposed to go further, Teej sighed. "You're no fun when you're being responsible."

Bailey smiled. Teej probably just wanted to talk for a while, maybe show off a little about the stuff he'd learned in the last year. Bailey didn't mind; the kid didn't seem to have any family to bring home report cards to.

"Are you on a schedule?" Teej asked. "We've got a deck of cards, and I found a Trivial Pursuit game in the closet when we moved in. Or we can play when you get back."

It was tempting in a way, but—"No, I probably shouldn't."

"Why not?" Damn, he shouldn't have phrased it that way—now Teej was looking at him strangely, and Bailey had to figure out how to answer that question.

"I like a nice, friendly game—"

"I play a nice, friendly game!" Teej protested.

Bailey looked at him. "I don't."

The silence held for several beats. Internally, Bailey sighed. If only he were one of those people who *liked* being compulsive. If the cells of his nervous system ever got the vote, he'd be spending that portion of his life not already defaced on his back, lying beside a stream with a cooler of beer. Or he would be, if only he weren't constitutionally unable to walk away from unfinished business.

Of course his clients loved him. He was a fucking neurotic. Change the subject.

"New car, huh?"

Teej accepted it, bless him. "We're leasing it from a local dealer."

"But a convertible?" Bailey inquired. He glanced sunward meaningfully.

"New toy," said Teej, grinning again. "She likes to drive it around at night."

She wasn't the only one who liked to play with it, apparently. Bailey grinned himself. "Great," he said, "it'll save me the price of a rental."

Teej stared at him in melodramatic betrayal for a moment, then laughed and handed him the keys.

It was Bailey's theory that there was always something a person wouldn't give up, even if it was bad for them. He drove the convertible to the north side of the island, up over Buttercream Hill Road and down to the marina, sparkling with fishing boats and pleasure craft. He parked in the lot, as close to the street as possible; fast exits had been imprinted on his mental list of things to do for a number of years now.

He walked out past a civilized little stand with a blue-and-white-striped awning, where iced tea, beer, frozen yogurt, and hot dogs were sold. A mixed crowd, he noted; kids, holiday fishermen, and a somewhat more well-heeled set who probably belonged with those sleek craft he saw in the prime slips just after the refreshment stand.

Nobody who looked like Ron Zygmore, with or without beard.

It was funny how drug dealers fell into the same subgroups the rest of society did. The three men who hired him in Atlanta werc not Miami-Vice type criminal overlords; they were businessmen, members of the Jaycees, the Masons, and the Knights of Columbus. And twenty years ago, when they'd run a thriving illegal business, they hadn't been chic cocaine dealers passing merchandisc in clubs to a soundtrack of throbbing rock; they'd been four college students running marijuana up from Mexico on a secondhand boat, playing Jimmy Buffet and exchanging dreams in roadhouse cafes.

It was the most exciting time in their lives. Bailey heard that, in their voices; Bailey always listened, and watched, and took in everything. You never knew what would work, later.

The most exciting time, and the most pure. Their friendship had been a sacred thing. They believed in it the way some motorcycle gangs believed in the brotherhood of the road, the way officers and gentlemen believed in the concept of honor.

Bailey respected their sincerity. It was the kind of thing he did not consider himself capable of.

"It's not like we really think there's anything wrong," Alan Tillman said. Tillman did most of the talking; he owned a computer supply company and wore his usual business suit when he spoke to Bailey.

"No," agreed the other two men. It was probably a coincidence, they told him. You could hear the embarrassment in their voices at even bringing it up.

It was probably a coincidence that Ron Zygmore, D'Artagnan to the other three, had disappeared just after retrieving the last cache of money from their first, shared business.

"We always planned to retire on that money, you see," Tillman explained. "We'd made about three-quarters of a million dollars, altogether—way too much to explain to anyone how we'd gotten it. And we didn't want to use a bank. So we found . . ." He hesitated. "A place to store it. And we agreed that every ten years or so, one of us would go and retrieve another portion. Well, inflation being what it is—" The others nodded at this. "—this was going to be the last trip. There was about four hundred thousand left. We were going to split it four ways."

It was odd, in a way, Bailey thought. You could listen to these middle-class businessmen talk and you could still hear the country boys underneath, like some kind of skeleton. They'd used their stakes to open supply stores and car dealerships and they'd forgotten about retiring, giving up their dreams to paperwork. But you could still hear the distant clank, under the words, of rebuilt cars and bar brawls where somebody pulled a knife.

"Ron went to pick it up on a Saturday afternoon," said Tillman. "On Sunday he was dead."

"Maybe," said one of the others under his breath. No one commented.

Ron Zygmore, classmate and owner of the *Elly Ann*, the old wooden fishing boat whose hold they'd once stuffed with bags of Mexican Gold.

Two months ago he'd bought a spanking new fiberglass boat, which he'd taken out into a tropical storm off the coast of Florida. Now the boat was gone, and so was Ron. So was the four hundred thousand, and even though the money rankled, Bailey suspected that what rankled more was the possibility that they'd been made fools of by one of their own.

So Bailey had checked: Zygmore had been divorced one

year previously. He had one child in college, with whom he was not very close. Another child had been killed in a car accident years ago. And the boat that had presumably gone down with Zygmore had not even been paid for.

Not Zygmore. *Ron.* Bailey preferred to start thinking of the people he searched for by their first names as soon as possible. It seemed to help the process.

"I'll take it," he said, interrupting another homage to coincidence from Alan Tillman.

Tillman looked at him. "We don't just want the money," he said finally.

"I know what you want," said Bailey.

There was always something they couldn't give up. There were two Monterey Clippers in the marina; one was a newer boat, of fiberglass, and he passed it by to walk out along the last pier to the wooden vessel moored there. He looked at the photograph he'd brought with him, then back at the boat. A new paint job; a new name, obviously—it wasn't the *Elly Ann* anymore. This one was white with green trim, and its name in cheerful green script on the back: *Bastard Luck. Gee, we weren't a little bitter, were we?*

Three months ago, his sources told him, Ron had finally parted with his beloved boat, selling her to a buyer on Galera Cay. Bailey wasn't really familiar with any form of transportation that didn't keep four wheels on the ground, but he'd called the Coast Guard while he was still in Georgia and asked for the hull number. Now he walked around to the bow and checked the numbers there against his information.

Not a match. Well, you wouldn't expect life to be *that* convenient.

He scanned the area; no one seemed to be watching or caring. He stepped over the gunwale and onto the deck.

Someone had taken loving care of this boat, and recently. The deck was clean, sanded, and had a fresh coat of green paint. They were a little messy with their possessions, though; Bailey moved aside a tangle of gear from the back of the boat and found the brass plaque with manufacturer's name and date: Bowman and Sons, 1951.

Also not a match. Damn. Because if it wasn't a match, this wild-card theory was going nowhere, and he really ought to say goodbye to Lilith and fly out of here tonight and see what he could pick up back in Atlanta—

—Which he was about as likely to do as he would be to flap his arms and fly out under his own power. Which meant blowing this case and giving the retainer back to his clients, or at best postponing the fieldwork and jeopardizing the possibilities of success.

Bailey was not happy, and he found himself looking over the evidence again, as though it might suddenly change from the last moment he'd seen it. *Good thinking, Phillip Marlowe.* Except . . . now that he was down on his knees examining the damned thing, didn't those brass screws holding the plaque look bright and shiny and new? Almost unseemly in their contrast to the darkened plaque itself.

He stood up and brushed off his jeans, then headed for the stairs to the hold. A few steps down and he was standing in the dim light of a galley—well, there was a tiny stove and a sink, anyway. A toilet sat on the floor opposite, unencumbered by so much as a shower curtain. Either the owner lived here alone, or the concept of physical privacy was not much regarded. A bunk was set back in the rear of the boat. There was a pile of waterproof clothing, but nothing else in the way of personal possessions. No books or papers saying "Ron Zygmore owns me. And he banks at Credit Lyonnais . . ."

Bailey didn't know boats, but he knew how to research. He pulled out his penlight and examined the overhead beam supporting the deck above . . . hull numbers on older boats were often carved into the rafter. *A library is a useful thing, God wot.* But damn, Mr. New-Paint-Job had gotten here first, too. High-gloss white, applied with enthusiasm. You could see the brush strokes against the rough grain of the wood.

Well, screw that, he refused, he *refused* to go back to Atlanta just because the universe was conspiring against him. There had to be . . .

. . . There was a smooth, shiny spot on the beam near his head, as though a couple of coats had suddenly been deemed necessary. He lifted his hand and ran his fingers over the spot; beneath the paint there was a pattern of inconsistencies in the surface, almost the suggestion of a bas-relief. Hmmm. He'd never done this, but it always seemed to work on television . . .

He took out a piece of paper, held it against the beam, and rubbed with the side of the pencil.

Three . . . four . . . two . . . no, that was it, the rest was too messed up to read. Evidently Ron had filled in the numbers with putty, but he hadn't been very good at it.

Three-four-two were the first three digits of the old *Elly Ann's* hull number. There was a point at which coincidence went too far, and Bailey was sure in his own mind that Ron Zygmore was alive and somewhere on his way to San Cristobel. Certainly Bailey had enough to justify a prolonged stay (sweet, heavy breath, and her heels pressing into his ass, and that tongue on his neck; no, that was for later, let's get off this damned boat first)—he could call his clients tomorrow. They could decide for themselves whether they wanted to move ahead on his recommendation or get a sight confirmation. Now that he had evidence, Bailey felt more than justified in billing them for the time he'd spend waiting for Ron to show up.

As he climbed over the gunwale, a hand grabbed his arm. Bailey looked into the face of a black man, about six feet, well-muscled, in a light jacket and chinos.

"Can I help you?"

Righteousness and threat were in the voice; Bailey decided not to pretend the *Bastard Luck* was his. "Maybe you can. I'm Roger McAdams, with the Bureau of Marine Tourism—"

"The *what*?"

That's what happens, Bailey thought, when you don't know shit about boats. His smile remained unshaken, with a surface confidence that only years of asking strangers for private information could give.

"Marine Tourism. We're trying to promote the use of San Cristobel Harbor among tourists targeted for the Caribbean market. That means making it more attractive for Europeans—"

"Look, I don't know who the hell you are, mister." Bailey noted the bulge in the man's jacket, as well as the simple fact that the man was wearing a jacket on this sunny day. Of course, Bailey had a jacket himself, and for much the same reason. "But I think you better get out of here before I call the police."

"Hey, look, no offense. We're just trying to talk to some of the tour captains—"

"This ain't no tour boat. You see a sign saying TOUR?"

"Not everybody has signs posted—"

"*Out* of here, mister. *Now*."

Bailey went, trying to look aggrieved. He felt the man's eyes on his back, all the way down the pier.

Walking away, it occurred to him that for a forty-five-year-old floating house of wood, the thing was very well maintained, and the paint job was the least of it. It was too bad, in a way; too bad Ron's love for this boat would go unrequited.

Bailey remembered the old Polaroid of the four men in a roadhouse, with "June '73" in faded magic marker on the back. He could see the gangly, dark-haired kid with the beer and bandanna; he could see him lying on the deck here and looking up at the stars, dreaming about . . . about not even the big score; the *moderate* score. About retiring to this boat and never having to chain himself up from nine to five again.

Not a yacht in New York Harbor or a string of clubs in LA; innocent, working-class dreams for working-class drug runners. And what did the decades bring him instead? A divorce, one dead child, and the seduction of a decent 401k plan. The kind of thing that seems bearable until suddenly you look back and wonder . . .

Still, it was never nice when one of the four musketeers dumped the others over the side.

Bailey took his time making his way back to the car, checking periodically to see that his interrogator wasn't following. When he reached Lilith's convertible he was still thinking about it. Okay, treachery, pain, and a failed life; but at least, no bodies in the woods this time.

Well, no doubt there would be a body eventually . . .

It was for his clients in Atlanta to deal with that. Fortunately Bailey had ceased to believe in God some years before he went into this line of work; otherwise, he would have felt terribly betrayed.

When he got back to the house he found Teej lying on the sofa, reading. Lilith was still closeted in her office, no surprise there; she'd brought three phones and two fax machines with her, and took her work seriously.

Bailey took off his jacket; Teej was used to the gun. "Is there a television around here?"

"There's one in my room. You can watch it, if you want."

"Thanks." Lilith was oblivious to much of popular media, but this case looked like a short one, she spent a lot of time working, and as far as Bailey was concerned, he was just glad to know the Queen of Air and Darkness had cable.

"Red Stripe beer in the fridge," offered Teej, making the immediate connection between pay-per-view movies, hockey games, and grain alcohol. Teej was more into oddball PBS stations himself, but he was perceptive about the needs of others.

Bailey opened the refrigerator and pulled out one of the Red Stripes. As he straightened up, he found Teej standing behind the door. "What?" Bailey said.

"Um . . . do I get the convertible tomorrow?" Teej asked.

Bailey sighed. "I should never have taught you to drive. That's the problem, right there." He handed over the beer.

It was a beautiful night; he supposed they were all beautiful nights here. Bailey sat on the patio behind the house, his back against the wall of the kitchen, knees up. A breeze stirred the ferns and orchids that screened the driveway, and the pool lay like a submerged grotto, lit from below. Teej was in his room watching the Discovery channel, or some such thing; Bailey could hear occasional scraps of television, very faint in the distance.

Footsteps tapped on the flagstones of the patio; Lilith deliberately making noise in her sandals, to let him know she was coming. She brought a bottle of champagne and a single glass, which she gave to Bailey.

"I know you like to watch me open these," she said. And without benefit of corkscrew and no apparent effort, she pulled off the wrapper and the cork in one smooth gesture.

"I'm amused by simple things," he said, holding out the glass for her to pour. He didn't much like dry champagne, but he'd drink it anyway. She sat down beside him in her jeans and halter top, skin like snow under moonlight.

He was a thirty-five-year-old atheist sleeping with a Jewish vampire of indeterminate age, and he was drinking champagne because *Lilith* liked the tang. Work that one out, Ann Landers. Or maybe the *Penthouse* letters column would be more appropriate . . .

She rested one hand on his thigh as he drank. This was cozy, like coming home; the closest he'd ever come, anyway. The soft wind that ran up the hill from the ocean was

like raw silk, a few degrees colder than usual. He'd worry
about rain, except the night was so damned clear.

She was thinking the same thing, apparently, because she
glanced upward, smiled, and said, " 'Look, how the floor of
heaven is thick inlaid with patins of bright gold.' "

"What's that from?"

"Merchant of Venice." She poured him more champagne.
Get that blood alcohol level up past .08, where she could
taste it. He smiled; God, he was easy.

"And it means?"

"Come on, Bailey, you never see stars like this in the city."

"Ah, stars. I thought you said 'pattens.' I wondered why
the floor of heaven was covered with shoes."

She looked at him. "You're just asking for it, aren't you,
Bailey?"

He nodded, not even trying to beat back his grin.

She reached up and pinched his neck, suddenly, as
though testing readiness for the oven. "Ouch!" He let go of
the champagne glass. Her tongue followed a second later,
laving the vein, playing with the hollow, tracing its way to
his ear. His breathing become ragged. She touched tongue-
tip to the mapped roads of his ear and began running fingers through his hair, nails trailing the scalp, just above
that ear. He gasped and his body jolted very slightly, as
though a current had run head to toe. He turned into her
touch, then turned further, facing her. He took that hand
and kissed the palm, his gaze steady, leaping deliberately
into those eyes.

Some time later she said, "Bailey . . ."

"What?"

"Why is the floor of heaven covered with shoes?"

He knew this game and smiled through the haze. "Well, it
would make sense, you know." Her lips were playing with
his neck now; and the longer he could spin out this nonsense, the longer the beautiful torture would go on. "The
floor of heaven is painful."

"How do you figure?" Her breath was warm spice in his ear. She ran her palm over his forehead and he sighed.

"It shifts under your feet." She moved on top of him, covering him with cool heat. "You need rubber-soled shoes." Her hair swept past his neck like living silk. "Enjoy it while you can." She'd zipped down his shorts and now she was playing with both ends of him, caressing his cock while she let the tip of her teeth remind his neck what it liked. So much for his concentration.

"Bailey?"

"Umm."

"I liked that."

"Umm." Fortunately, the change in tone seemed to be carrying his response, because it was the best he could do just now.

She'd shifted position, her knee between his legs, just touching his cock, the extra contact making him dizzy. A new breeze rolled in off the ocean, unexpectedly cold, and Jesus, on his sensitized skin it was as erotic as the rest, making him shiver with pain and pleasure. He didn't know the wind could do that.

He clutched her shoulders as the first touch of desperation took him. She held him then, rocking him through it, as his body, reminded now of what it had lacked for the last ten months, convulsed.

Lilith never took him after the first one. She could spin this out for hours, on a good night, and for most of those hours he'd be right there with her, delighting in the ride. Even delighting in the sudden, sickening descents of the roller coaster, because he knew what followed. But these moments, these were the hardest, when his body didn't care about games or what came first or followed after.

Then it passed, and he was breathing hard. The cool, healing lips were on his, as though she could pass that inhuman strength into him, keep him going long enough for a dance humans weren't designed to live through.

He sucked it in, opening his mouth, welcoming her tongue and its invasion. That army was on his side, boys. The cavalry was here for him . . .

There was a sudden change in her body. She pulled her mouth away, pushing him back.

He murmured, confused, "What . . . ?"

She rolled away from him, staring toward the kitchen door. From which Teej emerged, looking as if he were about to be sick. His hands were clasped behind his head and he stumbled as he came through the door. A nine-millimeter automatic was about an inch from the back of his skull, held there by a man in a T-shirt and light nautical windbreaker.

Ron.

Shit. Bailey stared, appalled, as the knowledge cut through the haze in his mind like an icepick. *Someone had gotten the license plate.* Ron had more than one person helping him, and Bailey had missed the second confederate. He'd been careful, sure, just not careful enough to keep someone from putting an automatic to the head of a kid who was silly enough to think Bailey knew what he was doing.

Ron looked grim and nervous. Bailey zipped up his shorts hastily and rose to his feet. Lilith stood too, her eyes not leaving the gun. Ron's gaze went to her and widened with surprise; then he turned back to Bailey.

You're the guy who was on the boat. Let him say that.

"You're the guy from Atlanta," said Ron. "I heard about you."

Death sentence. Ron would have to make sure he didn't report back; it was too easy to trace someone off this tiny island, and Ron would have to change tactics and ditch the boat. And even then—once they knew, people would never stop looking for him.

"You called in yet?" Ron asked.

"This evening," said Bailey.

Ron grinned. "That's a lie. If you'd called in, I'd know about it."

That would be an interesting statement, if the gun weren't such a distraction. And Ron looked jumpy. He was holding the automatic like it might explode if he loosened his grip. Maybe he'd been nervous for a while; he had a few day's growth of beard, and it occurred to Bailey in one of his compulsive empathic jumps that maybe it wasn't just for disguise. This guy looked like he didn't trust his hands around razors.

Teej was starting to shake, and Lilith shifted on her feet, her predator's gaze locked on Ron. *No, she'd never make it. Not even a jaguar could take out Ron's throat before that gun went off. Did she realize?*

She did, thank God. She wasn't moving.

"Maybe I'd be better off with your girlfriend," Ron commented, following his glance. For a second Bailey almost smiled. Ron's eyes shifted back and forth between them, deciding on his best move.

"Okay," he said suddenly, looking at Bailey. "You're with me. Get over here."

So he wants to switch me for Teej, Bailey thought. This was marginally better, but not a stunning improvement. What was the score supposed to be here? Drive Bailey somewhere, put a nine millimeter through his skull, then come back for Lilith and Teej? Because he would want everyone.

No, not convenient, Bailey thought, moving slowly toward Ron. Better to take them all out now. First Bailey, whom he incorrectly considered the greatest threat. Then Teej. Then the unarmed woman in the halter top last. Damn, and they could have done something with the opposite order.

When he was close enough, Ron pushed Teej out of the way and grabbed Bailey.

He heard Teej sob. He felt the cold barrel against his scalp, Ron's way of telling him not to move. It was moderately eloquent. Bailey faced Lilith—good, she was watching him. He threw everything he could into his expression. *Do*

*it. Do it. He's only going to shoot Teej next, there's nothing
to gain by waiting, just do it.*

She looked at him warily. *Lilith, please, just—*

She drew herself up to her full height and transferred her
gaze to Ron with the air of one discarding the irrelevant. A
low sound motored through the night: Lilith was growling.
It made Bailey's hair stand on end. He felt Ron's start of surprise, felt the barrel move from his head.

Her fangs were enormous. Or maybe it was the fear that
sound from her throat created in your guts, making those razors look like what they were.

"What the f—" said Ron.

Then she was on top of him. And the gun went off.

Pain tore through Bailey. He kept his head enough to
move out of Lilith's way.

He retreated against the other end of the L-wall of the
house, putting his hand down to his leg to feel the wetness
there. *"Fuck."* The bullet had gone through his outer thigh.
Nice that it hadn't passed through his torso instead, but it
stung like a bitch, and it was only going to get worse.

And Lilith hadn't torn Ron's throat out after all. That was
mildly surprising. Teej lay on the grass, trying to cry very
quietly. Lilith had backed Ron against the other wall and
was holding him by his collar, several inches off the ground.
His face looked sick in the light of the kitchen window.

Lilith, on the other hand, looked thoroughly inhuman, and
outraged. You didn't need to see fangs to feel the threat, and
the alienness, pouring off her. "Who do you think you are?"
she inquired of the deer, the stoat, the weasel she held in her
grasp. "To come in my house, with a gun. To make someone
here cry."

Bailey heard a pause in Teej's gasps, at that; heard him try
to control his sobs.

Ron made a choking sound. She let his toes touch just the
ground, taking some of the weight off his neck. His feet
scrabbled for purchase.

Bailey hadn't heard that in a long time—that edge of anger and hostility—of death, really—in Lilith's voice. It was not anything he'd ever been on the receiving end of, nor did he want to be.

"Bailey, if there's a reason you need this man alive, tell me now."

Ron Zygmore had been a condemned man for weeks, ever since he cut out his partners; it wasn't Bailey's place to try and resurrect him, especially now that he'd seen Lilith in action. "I need his bank account number."

She glanced back toward him, disagreement in her face. "Bailey, you're bleeding. I can smell it from here." *Let me kill him now.*

"It's not serious. I *want* the account." He met her glance with one of his own. Lilith considered Ron as Bailey's prey, by right of professional courtesy—clearly she wanted to overrule him, but thought it would be rude.

"Christ," said Ron. The voice came out hoarse. "Christ. Dear God." He looked at Bailey in wonder. "How do you control her?"

Control her? What was that, some gender thing, or did he believe Lilith was some kind of demon Bailey'd called out of Hell and needed to be on the right side of a chalk circle to keep from being devoured by?

Shit, that bullet wound stung. "Sheer force of personality," he heard himself saying, with perfect seriousness.

Lilith looked at him briefly. "And purity of heart. You forgot that."

"Yeah, I do tend to forget that one."

Ron stared at them both. "God," he said again, softly. Lilith ran her fingernail gently across his throat, forcing him to turn to her. "Cariad," she said softly. "My heart's desire." There was a kind of passion in her voice, and Bailey didn't blame Ron for the way he paled. She kissed him, the way you'd kiss a seventeen-year-old who was a little shy and charming in his gawkiness. He'd moved his head back, as far away as he could, and Lilith chuckled, deep in her throat. The kiss went on for a moment, then her lips moved over his neck, his chin, up over his cheekbones; she bestowed one on each eyelid, with awful tenderness, as she passed; and then finally his forehead. When she drew back he followed her, trying to regain contact.

Her fingers were delicate, holding the line of his jaw, thumb under his chin. Bailey saw nicks of blood from the skin where her fingernails rested. Ron didn't seem to notice.

She withdrew her hands and waited for his eyes to clear. She said, with that same terrible gentleness, "Bailey tells us you have a bank account number. It would be best to give it now, cariad."

Cariad. A Welsh endearment, Bailey thought; why? Had her first prey been Welsh? Her first surviving lover? He put the question aside with the ruthlessness of practice—he was never going to know; the rules that allowed them to live safely together did not permit questions about the past.

Ron looked at the three people before him in the backyard as though somehow this would all make sense, in a minute. Confusion and fear were plain on his face, but he said nothing, pressing himself further against the wall of the house as though to remove himself from this entire nightmare. She sighed and moved in on him again.

Bailey couldn't stop watching. Her breasts against Ron's chest, her leg between his—as Bailey stared, she lifted her toy's wrists, thumbs rubbing against each pulse-point, and held him outspread against the wall as though she couldn't decide whether to fuck him or crucify him. Bailey was vaguely aware of a choking sound from Teej, kneeling in the grass.

Her tongue played with neck and collarbone and she took her first nick. A gasp of pain; then Ron's expression changed, evening out, letting go. He moaned and sank down an inch or two, and Bailey knew from experience just what that extra bit of his own weight, rubbing his cock against

Lilith's knee, was doing to the man. That clamp of Lilith's hands on his wrists was doing the bulk of holding him up now.

Bailey found his own cock getting hard. Great, he was wounded in the line of duty and he was getting turned on by watching a six-foot-four-inch vampire torture an embezzling drug runner. He definitely had problems. Maybe he should seek therapy after this six weeks were over.

She made a sound in her throat as she kissed the vein in her prey's neck, a sound Bailey had often heard before. His knees weakened sympathetically.

—On the other hand, maybe this was good, maybe he was diverting the flow of blood away from the injured area. Maybe hard-ons were recommended for gunshot wounds.

Then she pulled back again and waited. The return to clarity took longer this time. After a minute or two, Ron asked, bewildered, "What are you doing—"

She spoke to a lover. "Heart of my heart. Tell us what we want to know."

He gasped, half in despair. He still didn't know what was happening, but the fear and loss of control were obvious. "No," he said, like someone who held to a route through enemy territory.

But none of his maps were working. Lilith reached for him again, and tears were running down his face. She caressed his cheek, ran her hands through his hair, comforting him; then she kissed his mouth, long and hard, and when she moved back again to his neck there was blood on his lips. His eyes rolled back with ecstasy, then closed. When she finally let go of him, he sank to the ground, sitting aimlessly for several minutes. Eventually he looked up, trying to focus on her. He reached for her hand. She stepped back and said, "Bailey, come here."

Walking wasn't easy for him, but she was too concentrated to notice that right now. His leg throbbed with the effort, pain meeting each pulse of his blood, a connection he was not unaccustomed to. He was sweating by the time he reached her. He waited. She touched Ron's cheek, getting his attention. "Tell him," she said, gesturing to Bailey.

Ron looked at him blankly. Bailey said, "The four hundred thousand dollars. Where is it?"

Ron continued to regard him as though he were a stranger. Then, after a few seconds, he frowned. "They're not dollars. They're bearer bonds."

"Where are they?" Bailey repeated. It was like talking to a six-year-old.

"A safety deposit box at the Bank of San Cristobel."

Lilith knelt beside him. She didn't know Bailey's case, but she could see where this was going. "Do you have a key?"

He blinked at her, then reached into his jacket pocket and took it out. Bailey didn't know why he was surprised; naturally Ron wouldn't let that out of his sight. Lilith took the key, then held his face in her hands again. "Do you remember the box number?"

He whispered it, hoarsely, and she let go of him. "Do you need to write that down?" she asked Bailey, not looking at him.

He could replay every beat of that hoarse voice. "I really don't think either of us will forget it."

She ignored that. She stood up, lifting Ron with ease. She walked him back against the wall.

He said, "No more, please." She kissed his hair.

Bailey looked away briefly. They had the information, but he supposed it was hard for Lilith not to play with the things she killed.

He barely looked back in time to see her break his neck.

Bailey sank down on the patio, reflecting that shock seemed to be catching up with him. The world around him, stars and breeze and nightbirds, seemed to be unnaturally silent.

They were all beautiful nights in San Cristobel. Except,

he thought vaguely, for the sound of weeping that came from someone unhappy, nearby.

"Teej, stop it." Lilith's voice cut through the thick silk of the night like a blade. There was a catch in Teej's breath. "Bailey needs us now."

Another long gasp for breath from Teej, and then a slower, more deliberate one; he was obviously forcing himself to come down. Ten seconds; fifteen. Then he spoke. "The car," he said, surprising Bailey. "He came in a car. It's down the hill. We can't leave it there."

Good kid, thought Bailey. Maybe it was time to stop underestimating him.

"You're right," said Lilith. "And we can't leave him here, either. I'm not worried about his friends, but I do wonder if the police will come."

She spoke as though it were a hypothetical question in philosophy; nevertheless she came over to Bailey and squatted down beside him. "Bailey?"

"He was never really here on the island, anyway. Good chance he won't be missed." What an epitaph, he thought, belatedly. She was still thinking it through, a serious expression on her face. She turned to Teej.

"Take the car into town. Park it behind one of the clubs . . . Deadeye Dick's, if you can find a spot. It'll be weeks before they notice it there. I'll drive Bailey to the hospital. We'll explain that he was mugged."

Teej's gaze went to the dead man. Lilith said, "I'll take care of the body when I get back."

Teej's eyes were wide and strained, with the look of someone who's heard too many artillery shells. He said, "What . . . what will you do with the body?"

She moved to him, stooped down beside him, and lifted his chin in her hand. "Teej. *Worry about the car.*"

He let out another breath, and nodded.

After a moment Bailey saw him rise and vanish into the

house. Lilith walked over to the pool, cupped some handfuls of water, and began washing blood from her face.

Bailey sank back on the patio, resting. Anything else was beginning to seem too much effort. He was vaguely aware that she'd gone to the driveway and returned. He waited.

He heard sandals on gravel, felt the cold reassurance of it as Lilith's arms lifted him up and carried him to the back seat of the convertible.

"Lilith," he said, "don't ever call me 'heart of your heart.' "

Her voice was amused. "You are," she said, "but I won't call you that if you don't want me to."

She opened the door and helped him to lie down. A bowl of stars hung over him, diamond-edged and painfully clear. He said, "You know, maybe you could do that thing with me, later."

"What?" Lilith closed the door.

"You know. That thing with the wall. Watch out for my neck, though."

"Bailey, you four-star schmuck. You sickest of puppies. Shut up, I'm taking you to the emergency room."

He laughed. The floor of heaven was thick inlaid with patins of bright gold, and March was a lifetime away.

Heat

Melissa Lee Shaw

 Her breath
was what he noticed first,
steaming as she laughed
into a warm summer evening.
A trick of the light? A cigarette?
But no—arms wrapped around two companions, she
    laughed again.
Clouds lifted from her mouth into the lamplight.

Those surrounding her laughed too,
like statues—their mouths did not smoke.
He thought of her hot mouth pressed to his lips, throat. . . .
And other places he blushed to name.

He hungered for such heat.

I have felt your eyes on me,
the letter read.
by the pier, where I gather with my friends
to watch the ships sail into the sunset.
We go there often—but lately
I have felt your eyes on me.

What is it you admire best?
Tell me tonight. Eight o'clock.
It named a mansion cordoned from the world by a spiked
    iron gate.
The letter bore no signature.
I will not go, of course, he thought at seven-fifteen,
taking random streets through the city.
It is madness. How do I know
the letter came from her?
But he knew. And eight o'clock found him pulling up
outside the gates, which opened for him
slowly, soundlessly.
He drove through, down a lane lined with weeping willows
and white stone statues. Marble.
Men, all of them, slim and tall, youthful,
naked.
Their bodies bent in all manner of attitudes—crouching,
    kneeling, standing.
Two characteristics they all shared—expressions of a
    singular passion and grief,
and erections, gleaming in the electric light.
Twenty he passed, then thirty.
And finally, the mansion.

He parked. His nerves made the crunch of gravel beneath
    his feet uncommonly loud.
He thought a servant would meet him at the door—
but it, like the gate, opened for him
silently.
He peered inside.

"Come in!" sang out her voice—throaty, amused.
"I'll be down in a moment. Come in and explore.
No matter where you go,
I shall find you."

He entered, and the door clicked shut behind him.
Nervous, he tried it.
It opened to his touch.

"None enter," came her voice with a laugh,
"who do not wish to be here.
Leave if you like—
but I will not send for you again."
A marble hallway, white pillars limned with angular tiles
    of dark blue and yellow,
a fountain in the middle of a mosaic floor.
More stone men stood ankle-deep in the shimmering
    water.
Naked, yearning—phalluses straining, shining as if
    polished.
His own body swelled toward a similar excitement.
He imagined her soft hands polishing the statues with
    green velvet cloths,
lingering on their cocks,
rubbing them to a high sheen.

"Do you like them?" came her voice. Her breath warmed
    his ear. He jumped—his feet, his skin, his blood.

"I like to look at them," she said. "I imagine them alive."
He turned to regard her
and his breath stopped
like a clock set to rest at the moment of someone's death.
Her eyes, so crystalline a blue they sparked,
her lips wet and red and curved in a teasing, daring smile,
her hair tumbling wild down her back, bright as burning
    coals.

Her perfume, rose and honeysuckle and sweet musk
seared his nostrils and burned his blood.
He stirred, though he stood still. He stirred.

A sarong of sea-blue silk clung to her body,
tied carelessly in a knot behind her neck.
A belt of gold links hung from her hips.
Around her throat nestled a thin gold chain
adorned with sapphires and diamonds.
Sapphires hung also from her ears.

"Are you hungry?" she said.
Her eyes traveled down the length of him,
lingering.

He could not speak. His mouth opened,
tongue and teeth and lips moved,
but his lungs froze.

"Come," she said, laughing. She took his hand (so hot, her
    fingers)
and whirled him, dizzied, through halls and rooms.
Her scent teased at his nose.
She brought him to a dining hall,
chandelier winking overhead,
the long table spread with roast pheasant, rack of lamb,
simmering soups, heaps of rolls,
and an entire pig, skin browned to a ruddy glow.
"Eat," she said, giving him a playful push. "Anything you
    like."

He found his voice. "Anything?" He stared at her,
his hand tingling where she'd held it.

Delighted, she laughed, teeth sharp and white and even.
    "Anything
that doesn't eat you first!"
Her hands curved around his neck,
Her breasts pressed against his chest.
She took his lip between her teeth, tugged—

gently, then like a wolf worrying a bone.
Before he could draw away, she released him, set
her lips to his throat.
"You are flushed," she murmured. Her lips and breath
   warmed his ear.

He seized her, pulled her against him,
his body chilled, craving her heat.
"Where?" he asked, or tried to. It escaped his lips
as a sigh, a moan.
She licked his neck, then suckled hard against his throat.
His breath left him—he could not even gasp.
When she released him, his skin chilled in the absence of
   her touch.

She took one end of the golden belt around her hips,
placed it in his hands.
"Follow," she whispered. Her throat pulsed fast, light and
   shadow.
She led him by the golden chain to a room of midnight
   blues—
walls, carpet, ceiling. A wooden table held a dark blue
   bowl.
A bed with a gauzy blue canopy sat against the wall.
She pressed him down onto cool, smooth sheets.

"Here," she said, turning slowly.
The belt he held unwound from her body, fell to the carpet.
The sarong bellied like a sail in a breeze.
"Here will be our first place.
And our last."
He hardly heard her.

She moved toward him. A tanned thigh peeked
between the sarong's silken folds.
She stood before him, pulled his hands up around her neck.

He drew them down smooth, uninterrupted silk.
She arched against his touch, breasts lifting.

He reached inside the folds of her sarong,
stroked her curved belly, lifted the underside of a taut
    breast.
His thumb brushed a soft nipple, tightening beneath his
    touch.
"How sweet," she murmured, "how delicious and cool."

She untied the knot behind her neck.
The sarong whispered down, curving like a snake,
to her hips,
where it stopped.
A shimmy, and it flowed to the ground,
revealing a nest of embers, of live coals.
He held his hand an inch in front of that auburn cleft.
Waves of heat licked his palm.

"Not yet," she said, pushing him back onto the bed with
    her body.
She wound her sarong around his hands, looped it around a
    bedpost.
"First, you must watch."

She drew back the gauzy canopy to reveal
a marble man, ice-white,
captured in a moment of yearning, straining—mouth
    parted,
hands outstretched,
phallus so swollen it glistened in the blue light.

She moved to the bedside table, bent over. Her buttocks
    curved against her back.
She picked up the dark blue bowl.
"Watch," she said, voice airy as butterfly wings—

"watch, and if you like what you see—why, then,
perhaps . . ."

Her fingers dipped into the bowl, came up glistening.
With deft strokes, she painted the statue with scented oil:
its hands,
its smooth chest,
its thighs—
its cock.

He strained, his groin afire, but the silk
held his hands fast.
His hips, of their own accord,
writhed, grinding against confining cloth.
She stroked the statue's cheek, kissed it tenderly,
suckled its stone nipples, gazed into its vacant, yearning
    eyes.

Kneeling before it, she put her tongue to its navel, then
    down the length
of the shaft below.

He groaned and struggled. His body burned. He cursed,
but she was lost to him, sliding the marble prick
in and out of her mouth.
He could not bear to watch. He could not look away.

She raised up, slid her skin along the statue's oiled chest,
lifted on tiptoe, her buttocks centered over the stiffened
    stone,
and sank down with a sigh.

She gripped the marble arms, wrapped her legs
around its back,
and began a rhythmic dance that revealed
and concealed

by turns
the gleaming stone cock.

He could not breathe. His head thundered. His eyes swam.
He wrestled the smooth silk binding him, but
could not find release.
"Please," he growled, whispered, wailed—"please."
Her arms locked around the statue's neck,
she pressed her red lips to its white ones.
Did she murmur? Did it answer?
She moved faster, faster, until—
she stopped.
Poised on the brink, her skin twitching,
she disengaged from the statue
and returned to the bed.
Scented oil streaked her skin,
and beads of oil glistened
in the auburn nest beneath her belly.

"And?" she said with a smile. "Did you want to be that
    statue?"
Her hands lifted to her breasts, traced circles around her
    nipples.

"Yes," he hissed between locked teeth. His vision blurred red.

She unbuckled his belt, slid his trousers
down his legs,
lifted the elastic of his briefs over his wagging prick.

"Are you sure?" she asked, sliding her hot hands beneath
    his shirt.

"Yes." His breath bucked at her touch.

She tore his shirt from his body,
ripped the sleeves from his arms.

"Very sure? Careful—this one's three,
and that's the one that counts."

Though he heard the warning, his maddened mind
could think no other thought.
"Yes. My God, yes."

She laughed, long and free.
Releasing his hands from the confining silk,
she slid onto the bed, onto her back.
She held a hand to him.
"Well, then," she said, flushed and smiling. "Come to me."

He wanted to drive inside her, to pin her to the bed, but
his body, raised to such a fever pitch, would not last long.
He wanted to prolong his pleasure, so
he kissed her, rubbed against her oiled skin.
The air chilled him.

He drank of her mouth, her throat, her breasts, her belly.
He tasted the oily beads in the nest that opened to his
    tongue, tasted
the oil and tang of the folds within, the hard nubbin
that crowned them.

Her legs locked hot around him, her voice reduced
to animal gasps, primal cries.

His skin grew cold,
his fingers tingled,
his toes numbed.
Craving heat, he slid up her body, her skin like lava,
like sunlight.
He suckled at her warm breath, but grew
colder still,
and his cock, coldest of all.

Blindly, he drove toward heat—
and found it.
Roaring flame engulfed his phallus, fire
fanned at his hips. He drove and thrust
toward that blaze.
Her body grew hotter still, searing his skin,
burning his hands.
Her scalding breath tickled his neck,
sent chills through his legs.

Desperate for warmth and for release, he grunted and
    thrust
till his muscles burned
with cold.
Frostbite.

"The cold," he heard his own voice say. "I need . . ."
"Shall I warm you, then?" she asked, a hot smile
curving her lips.
She bucked once,
and he tumbled to his back, with her astride him.
"Please," he said, unsure if it was heat or release he begged
    for.

His feet grew cold as lead
beneath her pumping thighs.
His fingers chilled to ice.
And yet it built within him, the explosion.
She set hands hot as pokers on his chest.
He groaned, yearning toward ecstasy.
"Please . . ."

His legs grew cold from the bone out.
Her caress on his cheeks was a furnace blast.
She glowed red. Her hair was flame.
His arms grew numb,

but climax tickled at his shivering blood.
"Please!"

She stroked his thighs with fingers like candle-flames.
He shuddered on the brink, the fireburst just before him—
and froze. Solid.
Stiff.

Her hips stilled. She laid a burning kiss upon his lips,
then lifted herself up and off.
He howled silently inside his prison,
balanced ceaselessly
on the brink.

She raised him to his feet, patiently
arranged his limbs—arms outstretched, face
caught in a rictus of yearning, desperate passion.
She faced him toward the door.

Time fled. Her laughter filled the halls, trailed
through the room of midnight blue.
She entered, clad in a blue sarong,
and trailing a tall, slim young man
by her golden belt.
Soon, he lay, flesh and warm blood, tied to the bedpost
    with silk.

She picked up the blue bowl
and came to him, her marble statue.
She anointed him with scented oil.
He could not move, or strain—but her eyes on his
said she understood his hunger.

Ah, such delicious torture, to pierce her again,
when she lowered herself atop his gleaming shaft.

She clung to his legs with hers. Such heat,
to warm his frozen soul.

The hot breath of her murmur as she kissed him
quickened his lips—
"Would you leave, if you could?" she asked.
And his reply, in the moment before the stone
took his mouth again—
"No. I would stay."

For after all this time,
when the explosion he yearned for came at last—
as surely it someday must—
it would set the world
ablaze.

The Eye of the Storm

Kelley Eskridge

I am a child of war. It's a poor way to start. My village was always ready to defend, or to placate, or to burn again. Eventually the fighting stopped, and left dozens of native graves and foreign babies. We war bastards banded together by instinct; most of us had the straw hair and flat faces of westerners, and we were easy marks. Native kids would find one or two of us alone and build their adrenaline with shouts of *Your father killed my father* until someone took the first step in with a raised arm or a stick. These encounters always ended in blood and cries—until the year I was fifteen, when a gang of village young played the daily round of kill-the-bastard and finally got it right: When Ad Homrun's older brother pulled her from under a pile of screaming boys and girls, and Ad's neck was broken and her right eye had burst. The others vanished like corn spirits and left us alone in a circle of trampled grass, Ad lying in Tom's arms, me trying to hold her head up at the right angle so that she would breathe again. It was my first grief.

It was no wonder our kind were always vanishing in the night. "You'll go too," my mother said for the first time when I was only seven. She would often make pronouncements as she cooked. I learned her opinions on everything from marjoram ("Dry it in bundles of six sticks and keep it away from dogs") to marriage ("Some cows feel safest in the butcher's barn") while she kneaded bread or stripped slugs off fresh-picked greens.

It shocked me to hear her talk about my leaving as if it were already done. Ad was still alive in her family's cottage a quarter mile from ours, and I believed that my world was settled; not perfect, but understandable, everything fast in its place. I peered from my corner by the fire while my mother pounded corn into meal, jabbing the pestle in my direction like a finger to make her point. "You'll go," she repeated. "Off to soldier, no doubt. Born to it, that's why. No one can escape what they're born to."

"I won't," I said.

"You'll go and be glad to."

"I won't! I want to stay with you."

"Hmph," she replied, but at supper she gave me an extra corn cake with a dab of honey. Food was love as well as livelihood for her. She never punished me for being got upon her while her man screamed himself dead in the next room; but she never touched me or anyone else unless she had to. I grew up with food instead of kisses. I ate pastries and hot bread and sausage pies like a little goat, and used them as fuel to help me run faster than my tormentors.

One of the childhood games Ad and I played was to wrap up in sheepskin and swan up and down the grass between her cottage and the lane, pretending to be princes in disguise. We were both tall, after all, and looked noble in our woolly cloaks. What more did one need? To be the first child of a king, Tom Homrun said, and our king already had one. There could only be one prince, only one heir. The rest were just nobles, and there were more of them than anyone bothered to count. *What's the good of being a royal if you're as common as ticks on a dog?* my mother would say, with a cackle for her own wit. But I had heard too many stories about the prince. My aunt's third husband went to court for a meeting of royal regional accountants, and told us in his letters that the prince was fair and strong and already had the air of a leader. *And puts me in mind of your Mars, he wrote my mother; something about the eyes.* My mother paused after she'd read that part aloud, and looked at me with a still face. It thrilled me to be likened to the prince, and Ad was rigid with envy until Tom carved her a special stick to use as a scepter in our games, with a promise that he would never make me one no matter how hard I pleaded. I could not care about her stick, about her silence and hurt feelings, even though she was my only friend. My head was full of daydreams of walking through the streets of Lemon City, of being seen by the prince's retainers and taken up into the citadel, marveled over, embraced, offered . . . what? My imagination failed me there, so I would start from the beginning and see it all again. I began giving the pigs orders, and delivering speeches of state to the group of alder trees near Nor Tellit's farm.

They were different speeches after Ad died. At first they were simply incoherent weepings delivered from a throat so thick with snot that I barely recognized my own voice. It sounded adult and terrible, and filled me with a furious energy that I didn't know how to use; until one afternoon when I had run dry of tears and instead picked up a fist-sized stone. I beat the alders until the rock was speckled with my blood. I washed my swollen hand in the village well and hoped that my rage would poison them all. Then I found Tom Homrun and asked him to teach me how to fight.

From the first I was like a pig at a slop pile, gulping down whatever he put in front of me, always rooting singlemindedly for more. He taught me to use my hands and elbows and knees, to judge distance, and to watch someone's body rather than their eyes. It was hard at first to trust him and his teaching: I'd always thought of him as a native, as a danger, in spite of his fondness for his yellow-haired bastard sister. And it hadn't occurred to me that he would have to touch me. Apart from Ad, I'd only touched my mother by accident, and the village kids in desperate defense: but this was new and electric. The first feel of his muscle against mine was so shocking that the hair on my arms and legs stood up. I was desperately uneasy to think that I might be moved by Tom after what I'd begun to feel for his sister, as if it were some kind of betrayal of Ad. But I was fascinated by the strength and the power of his body, the way it turned when he wished, held its balance, reached out and so easily made me vulnerable.

I was just sixteen when we began, and the sky was always gray with the start or end of snow. I learned to move when I was too cold, too sore, too tired. I learned to keep going. All the things I wanted—Ad, my mother, a life of endless hard blue days in the fields, and just one true friend with dark hair and a father still alive—all those precious things became buried under a crust of long outlander muscles. I began to imagine myself an arrow laid against the string, ready to fly. I looked at the village kids with my arrow's eyes, and they stayed out of my way.

By the summer I knew enough not to knock myself silly. I was tired of the same exercises and hungry now for more than just revenge: I wanted to be a warrior. "Show me how to use a sword," I begged Tom constantly, sometimes parrying an invisible adversary with a long stick.

"No," he said for the hundredth time.

"Why not?"

"There's no point until you get your full growth. You're tall as me now, but you might make another inch or two before you're done."

"You didn't make me wait to learn how to fight."

"Swords are different. They change your balance. You've got to make the sword part of yourself, it's not enough just to pick it up and wave it around. It's true that you've learned well," he added. "But you haven't learned everything."

"Then teach me everything."

"Leave it alone, Mars."

I had no idea I was going to do it: I had never given him anything but the obedience due a teacher. But I was so frustrated with behaving. "You teach me, damn you," I said, and swung the stick as hard as I could at his ribs.

He softened against the blow and absorbed it. The stick was dry and thin, but still it must have hurt. It sounded loud, perhaps because we were both so silent.

I stammered, "Tom, truly, I was wrong to do it, I just . . ."

"You're stupid, Mars." His voice was very quiet. "You're not the strongest, you never will be, and no sword will change that. I'm heavier and faster than you, and there's thousands more like me out there." He waved at the world beyond the fields, and when I turned my head, he reached out and twisted the branch away as easily as taking a stick from a puppy. "All you have are your wits and your body, if you can ever learn how to use them."

What had we been doing, all these months? "I can use my body."

A bruise I'd given him at the corner of his mouth stretched into a purple line. Then his smile changed into the stiff look that people wear when they are forcing themselves to a thing they'd rather not do; like the day that he'd had to butcher Ad's favorite nanny goat while she cried into my shoulder. I did not like him looking at me as if I were that goat.

"You want to learn everything." He nodded. "Well, then you shall." And he came for me.

I managed to keep him off me for more than a minute, a long stretch of seconds that burned the strength from the muscles in my arms and legs. But he was right; he was too strong, too fast. First he got me down and then he beat me, his face set, his hands like stones against my ribs and my face. His last blow was to my nose, and when he finally stood up, he was spattered with me.

"This is everything, Mars. This is what I have to teach

you. Become the weapon. Do it, and no one will touch you in a fight. Otherwise it's only a matter of time before someone sends you to the next world in pieces."

I was trying to spit instead of swallow; it made it harder to breathe, and every cough jarred my broken nose.

"I regret this," he said remotely. "But every time we meet from now on will be like this until you win or you quit. If you quit, I'll teach you nothing ever again. That's the lesson. I don't think you can do it, you know. I don't think you're ready. I wish you hadn't pushed so hard." He spoke as if he were talking to a stranger on the road.

He left me at the field's edge, under a creamy blue sky and the alders that were scarred with months of practice; all those pointless hours. After a long time I dragged myself up and limped home, turning my head away as I passed the Homrun cottage so that I would not have to see whether Tom was watching. I let my mother bind my ribs, avoiding her questions and the silence that followed. Then I wrapped myself up in wool blankets and shivered all night, bruised and betrayed, frightened, and hopelessly alone.

He beat me badly half a dozen times in the next year. Between our fights, I practiced and worked and invented a thousand different ways to keep distance between us, to protect my body from his. None of it made a speck of difference.

The day came when I knew I could never win. There was no grand omen, no unmistakable sign. I was milking our goat and I suddenly understood that Tom was right. Someone would always be faster or stronger, and until I learned my place I would always be hurt and lonely. It was time to make peace and stop dreaming of Lemon City. I should be planning a fall garden, and tending Ad's grave. So there, it was decided; and I went on pulling methodically at the little goat's dry teats until she bleated impatiently and kicked at me to let her go. Then I sat on the milking stump and stared around me at the cottage, the tall birch that shaded it, the yard with the goat and the chickens, the half-tumbled stone wall that bounded our piece of the world. If someone had come by and said, "What are you looking at, Mars?", I would have said *Nothing. Nothing.*

Massive storm clouds began moving up over my shoulder from the west. The shadow of the birch across the south wall faded, and the chickens scuttled into their coop and tucked themselves up in a rattling of feathers. The wind turned fierce and cold; and then the rain hammered down. I hunched on the stump until it occurred to me that I was freezing, that I should see the stock were safe and then get inside; and when I tried to stand the wind knocked me over like a badly pitched fence post. I pulled myself up. Again the wind shoved me down. And again. This time I landed on one of my half-dozen unhealed bruises. It hurt; and it made me so angry that I forgot about my numb hands and my despair. I stood again. There was a loud *snap* behind me. It took a long second to turn against the wind: By that time, the branch that the storm had torn from the birch tree was already slicing toward me like a thrown spear.

I took a moment to understand what was happening, to imagine the wood knifing through me, to see my grave next to Ad's. Then the branch reached me, and I slid forward and to the right as if to welcome it; and as we touched I whirled off and away, staggered but kept my balance, and watched the branch splinter against the shed. The goat squealed from behind the wall; and I laughed from my still, safe place in the center of the storm.

I had an idea now, and the only way to test it was by getting beaten again, and so I did: but not as badly. When he'd finally let me up, Tom said, as always, "Do you give in?"

"No."

He was supposed to turn and walk away. Instead, he kept hold of my tunic with his left hand and wiped his bleeding mouth with his right. He took his time. Then he said, "What was that first move?"

I shrugged.

"Who taught you that?"

I shrugged again, as much as I was able with one shoulder sprained.

"I expect I'll be ready for it, next time." He opened his hand and dropped me on my back in the dirt, and set off down the road toward the village. He favored his right leg just slightly: It was the first sign of pain he had ever shown. But that wasn't what made me feel so good, what made the blood jizzle around under my skin: It was the way I'd felt fighting him. I treated him just like the flying birch limb—allowed him close, so close that we became a single storm, and for just a moment I was our center and I spun him as easily as if I were a wind and he a bent branch.

The next time went better for me, and the time after that. It became a great dance, a wild game, to see how close I could get to him, how little I could twist away and remain out of reach, just beyond his balance point. He was heavier than me, differently muscled: It taught me to go beyond strength and look instead for the instant of instability, the moment when I could make him overreach himself. It was exhilarating to enter into his dangerous space and to turn his weapons against him; it was delicious to be most safe when I was closest to my enemy. I didn't notice my hurts anymore, except when parts of me stopped working. Then I would retreat to my corner by the cottage fire, sipping comfrey tea and reliving each moment, sucking whatever learning I could from the memory of each blow. My body and his became the whole of my world.

And the world was changing. I got those last two inches of growth and my body flung itself frantically into adulthood. I suppose it must have been happening all along underneath the sweat and the bruises and the grinding misery. But now that I was noticing it, it seemed to have come upon me all at once, and it was a different feeling from the days when Ad's smile could make me feel impossibly clever. This was the lust I'd seen at the dark edges of the village common after the harvest celebration, the thing of skin and wordless noise. No one had told me it would feel like turning into an arrow from the inside out and wanting nothing more than something to sink myself into. Sometimes it was so strong that I would have thrown myself on the next person I met, if only there had been anyone who wouldn't have thrown me right back. But there was no one. I could only burn and rage and stuff it all back into the whirlwind inside me: make myself a storm.

And so one day I finally won, and it was Tom who lay on one elbow, spitting blood. When the inside of his mouth had clotted, he said, "Well." Then we were both silent for a while.

"Well," he said later.

And: "You'll be fine now. You're a match for anyone, the way you fight. It's okay to let you go now. You'll be safe."

And then he began to cry. When I bent over him to see if he was hurt more badly than I thought, he gripped my arm and kissed me. He did not stop me when I pulled away, and he did not try to hide his tears. I didn't understand then what kind of love it is that kills itself to make the beloved safe: I only knew that my world had shaken itself apart and come back together in a way that did not include me anymore.

I told my mother that night that I would leave in a week. She did not speak, and all I could say over and over was "I have to go," as if it were an apology or a plea. Later as I sat miserably in front of the fire, she touched the back of my head so softly that I wasn't sure if I was meant to feel it. Her fingers on my hair told me that she grieved, and that her fear for me was like sour milk on the back of her tongue, and that in spite of it all she forgave me for becoming myself, for growing up into someone who could suddenly remind her of how she got me. I had traded scars and bruises with the village kids for years, but never before had I hurt someone I loved just by being myself; and in one day I had done it to the only two people left to me. I felt my world hitch and shake like a wet dog, and my choices fell over me like drops of dirty water: none of them clean.

I set off early, just past dawn. Over breakfast, my mother said, "Here's a thing for you," and handed me a long bundle. When I unwrapped it, the lamplight flickered across the blade inside and my mother's sad and knowing eyes.

"Don't look at me," she said. "That Tom Homrun brought it around three days past and said I wasn't to give it to you until you were leaving."

There was no scabbard. I made a secure place for the sword in my belt, across my left hip.

"Feel like a proper soldier now, I expect," my mother said quietly.

"I just feel all off balance," I told her, and she smiled a little.

"You'll be all right, then." She nodded, then sighed, stood up, fussed with my slingbag. "I've put up some traveling food for you. And a flask of water as well, you never know when the next spring might be dry."

I tried to smile.

"Which way are you heading?"

"East. In-country."

She nodded again. "I thought you might head west."

"Mum!" I was shocked. "Those are our enemies."

"You've had more enemies here than ever came out of the west, child," she said. "I just wondered."

I took a breath. "I would never do anything to hurt you, Mum. You've been nothing but good to me." Another breath. "Tell Tom . . . give him my thanks." Opening the door, the damp, gray air in my face. "I love you, Mum." Kissing her dry cheek. "I love you." Three steps out now, her standing in the door, half in shadow, one hand to her face. "Goodbye,

Mum." Four more steps, walking backward now, still looking at her. "Goodbye." Turning away; walking away; leaving. Her voice catching up with me, "I've loved you, Mars. Godspeed." The bend in the road.

I was alone on the road for a week. Every day brought me something new; a stand of unfamiliar trees, a stream of green water, a red-hooded bird that swooped from tree to tree above me for a hundred paces before it flashed away into the woods. I walked steadily. I didn't think about home or the future. I became more thin. I played with the sword. It wasn't balanced well for me, but I thought a good smith could remedy that, and meanwhile I learned not to overreach myself with the new weight at the end of my arm. Carrying it on my hip gave me a persistent pain in my lower back, until I found a rolling walk that carried the sword forward without swinging it into my leg at each step. Ad would have called it swagger, but she would have liked it. There was one moment, in a yellow afternoon just as the road lifted itself along the rim of a valley, when I could hear her laugh as if she were only a step behind me, and I missed her as fiercely as the first month after her death. And I kept going.

On the eighth day I met people.

I heard them before I saw them; two speaking, maybe more silent in their group. I stopped short and found myself sweating, as if their sound was warm water bubbling through the top layer of my skin. I hadn't thought at all about what to do with other people. I had met less than a dozen strangers in my life.

"I think there's something in the wood," one of the voices said brightly.

"A wolf?" A hint of laughter.

"A bear."

"A giant."

"A creature with the body of an eagle and a pig's head and teeth as big as your hands."

I was beginning to feel ridiculous; it made me move again. I came out of the trees into an open place where my road met another running north and south. Just beyond the crossroads, three people sat with their backs against a low stone wall that bounded a meadow. I slowed my step. I had no idea how one behaved, and I'm sure it showed. The woman who called to me had the same glittery amusement in her voice that I'd heard as she'd described all the fabulous monsters I might be.

"Why, it's not a bear. Ho, traveler." She nodded. I felt awkward and I wondered if my voice would work properly after so long in its own company, so I only returned her nod, hitched up my belt, and kept walking. As soon as it was clear that I meant to pass them by, she scrambled to her feet, scattering breadcrumbs and a piece of cheese out of her lap into the grass. "Luck, don't," the man said, and grabbed but missed her. She darted toward me. I turned to face her, my hands out, waiting.

"Ah, ha," she said, and stopped out of my reach. "Perhaps a bear cub after all. I don't mean to detain you against your will, traveler. We have Shortline cheese to share, and we'd welcome news of the world beyond this road."

She was relaxed, smiling, but she watched my body rather than my face, and her knees were slightly bent, ready to move her in whatever direction she needed to go. She looked strong and capable, but I could see a weakness in her stance, a slight cant to her hips. *I could probably take her*, I thought.

I put my hands down. "The place I've come from is so small, you'd miss it if you looked down to scratch. But I can trade flatcakes for a wedge of cheese and your news."

"Fair enough," she said.

She was Lucky, and the man was Ro. The other, silent woman was Braxis. We ate cheese and my mother's cake in the afternoon sun, and they told me about the north, and I gave them what I knew about the west. I was nervous, but gradually their laughter, their worldliness, won me over.

They never asked a question that was too personal, and they gave exactly as much information about themselves as I did, so I never felt at a disadvantage.

"What is it you want from me?" I asked finally. I don't know exactly what made me say it. Maybe it was the combination of the warm gold sun and the warm gold cheese, the bread and the cider from Braxis's wineskin. Maybe it was hearing about the great cities to the north, Shirkasar and Low Grayling, and the massive port of Hunemoth, the way they made me see the marketplaces and the moonlight on the marbled plazas of the noble houses. Maybe it was the looks the three of them traded when I answered their questions.

Braxis raised an eyebrow in my direction. It was Ro who answered.

"Okay, so you know when something's going on under your nose. That's good. Can you fight?"

I tensed. "I've told you how I grew up. I can fight."

"We're going to Lemon City, to the auditions. We need a fourth."

"What auditions?"

"Hoo hoo," Lucky said with a grin.

"Three times a year they hold an audition for the city guard," Ro said. "They only accept quads, they think it's the most stable configuration for training and fighting."

"So," I said. I thought of Tom under the alders, of Lemon City as I'd imagined it with Ad.

"So you probably noticed there are only three of us."

"You came all this way from Grayling without a fourth?"

"No, of course not," Ro said patiently. "He left us two days ago. He found true love in some stupid little town with probably only one bloodline, but he didn't care. He's a romantic, much good may it do him in the ass end of nowhere."

"And you'd take me just like that, not knowing me at all."

"What do we need to know?" Lucky said. "You breathe,

you can stand up without falling over. You're on the road to Lemon City, aren't you? Do you want a job or not?"

"You mean for money?" She shook her head as if she couldn't credit my being so dumb. But I'd expected to have to find honest work, meaning something dirty and bone-tiring, before I could start looking for someone to train with. The idea of getting tired, dirty, and paid to train was so exciting I could hardly believe it was real.

Ro said, "We'll offer you a trial on the road. Travel with us to Lemon City and we'll see if we want to take it any farther."

"Not without a fight," Braxis said. We all looked at her; Ro and Lucky seemed as surprised that she'd spoken as they did at what she'd said.

"I don't take anyone on without knowing if they can hold their own," she said reasonably. "Not even on trial. That's the whole point of a quad, isn't it? Four walls, stable house. We need strong walls."

"They train you, Brax," Ro responded. "All we have to do is get past the gate."

"No," I said slowly. "She's right. And so are you: I do want to go to Lemon City, but it's got to be properly done." They looked at me with a variety of expressions: Braxis impassive, Ro with his head tilted and a wrinkle in his forehead, Lucky grinning with her arms akimbo.

"I can't explain it. But I need this to be something I can be proud of. It needs to be earned."

"Gods, another romantic," Ro muttered.

We climbed over the wall into the field, and laid aside our swords. Lemon City was just behind that cloud, and I was a hot wind. It was such an amazing feeling that I almost forgot that I'd never really fought anyone except Tom, that I didn't yet know if I could. Then Braxis's strong arms reached for me.

When we were done, and Brax had finished coughing up

grass, she said, "Fine. On the way there, you can teach us how to do that."

We began to learn each other: Braxis woke up surly; Lucky sang walking songs out of tune, and she knew a hundred of them; Ro was good at resolving differences between others and peevish when he didn't get his own way. I wasn't sure what they were discovering about me. I'd never lived with anyone except my mother: It was one more thing I didn't know how to do. I watched everything and tried not to offend anyone.

We got into the routine of making camp early in the afternoon, to keep the last hours of light for practicing swords and stormfighting. It didn't take them long to work out that I barely knew one end of my sword from the other. I was ashamed, and halfway expected them to kick me back up the road. They surprised me. "I've never seen anyone fight like you do," Ro said matter-of-factly. "If we can trade learning between us, it makes us all stronger." Then he set about showing me the basics.

Two weeks later it was Lucky who came toward me with her sword. I looked at Ro. He smiled. "I've given you enough so that you can at least keep up with what she's got to show you. She's the best of us."

I expected the thrust-and-parry exercises that I'd worked on with Ro, but Lucky came to stand to one side of me, just out of blade range. She extended her sword. "Follow me," was all she said, and then she was off in a step, turn, strike, block that moved straight into a new combination. She was fast. I stayed with her as best I could, and actually matched her about one move in seven.

"Not horrible," she said. "Let's try it again." We worked it over and over until finally she reached out and pried the sword out of my grip. "Those will hurt tomorrow," she said of the blisters on my palms. "You should have told me." But I was determined to hold my own with these people, so I only shrugged. My hands felt raw for days after; but I was stubborn. And it helped that I could teach as well as learn. It did not matter so much that I was the youngling, the inexperienced one, when their bodies worked to imitate mine, when their muscles fluttered and strained to please me.

And I had a new secret: I was beginning to understand the price for all those months that I'd wrestled my body's feelings back into my fighting. I could scrub Lucky's back after a cold creek bath, see Brax's nipples crinkle when she shrugged off her shirt at night, lie with my head pillowed on Ro's thigh—and never feel a thing except a growing sense of wonder at what complex and contradictory people I had found on my road. But when we met in practice, everything changed. The slide of Brax's leather-covered breast against my arm during a takedown put a point of heat at the tip of every nerve from my shoulder to my groin. Ro's weight on me when he tested the possibilities of a technique was voluptuous in a way I'd never imagined in my awkward days with Ad. Lucky's rain-wet body twisting underneath me excited me so much it was almost beyond bearing: But I learned to bear it, to stuff the pleasure back inside myself so that it wound through me endlessly like a cloud boiling with the weight of unreleased rain. In my days with Tom I had learned to fight through cold and pain and misery; Now I learned to persist through pleasure so keen that sometimes it left me seared and breathless and not sure how to make my arms and legs keep working. I told no one; but I woke in the morning anticipating those hours, and slept at night with their taste in my throat. I was always ready to practice.

"I sweat like a bull," Brax said ruefully one day when we were all rubbing ourselves down afterwards. "But you always smell so good." I smiled and pulled my tunic on quickly to hide the shudders that still trembled through me.

It was a few days later that Ro approached me after supper, squatting down beside me near the fire. We smiled at each other and spent a quiet time stripping the bark off sticks and feeding it to the flames. Eventually, he said, "Share my blanket tonight?"

I'd seen from the first night how it was between them, bedding two at a time but in a relationship of three. I had already guessed at their idea of what a quad should be. I wondered how sophisticated people handled this sort of thing.

"No, but thank you," I said finally. "It's not you, Ro, you're a fine person and I'm pleased to be part of your quad. It's just—"

"No need to explain," he said, which only made me feel more awkward. But the next day he treated me not much differently. By the afternoon I had recovered my equilibrium, and I'd noticed their quiet conversations, so I was only a little surprised to find Lucky at my elbow after practice.

"Let's take a walk," she said cheerfully. "Fetch water, or something."

"Fine," I said, and went to gather everyone's waterskins.

"No need to rush," Braxis said. Ro nodded agreeably.

"Fine," I said again, and off we went.

We found a stream and loaded up with water, and then sat on the bank. I laid back with my head on my arms while Lucky fiddled with flower stems. Then she leaned over me and kissed me. Her mouth was dry and sweet. But nothing moved in me. I sat up and set her back from me as gently as I could. She didn't look angry, only amused. "Would Braxis have been a better choice for water duty today?"

"No, it's not that."

"Don't you know what you like, then?"

"You know what?" I said, "Let's go back to the others so I only have to have this conversation once."

We all sat around, and they chewed on hand-sized chunks of bread while I talked.

"Anyone would be proud to have you as lovers, all of you." It was nice to see the way they glowed for each other then, with nothing more than smiles or a quick touch before turning their attention back to me. "It's not about you."

I stopped, long enough that Braxis raised an eyebrow. It was hard to say the next thing. "If you need that from your fourth, then I'll help you find someone else when we get to Lemon City, and no hard feelings."

We were all quiet for a while. Finally Braxis wiped the crumbs off her hands. "Oh, well," she said. "Of course we don't want another fourth, Mars, we'd rather have you even if we can't have you, if you take my meaning." Lucky hooted, and I went red in the face, which just made Lucky worse.

"No, truly," Braxis went on when Ro had finally put a hammerlock on Lucky. "We like you. We're starting to fight well together. We learn from each other. We trust ourselves. We can be a good quad. The other," she shrugged, and Lucky made a rude gesture, "well, it's nice, but it isn't everything, is it?"

It stayed with me, that remark, while I did my share of the night chores, and later as I lay on my back in the dark, listening to Ro's snores and the small, eager sounds that Braxis and Lucky made together under a restless sky of black scudding clouds. It was strange to think about sex with them so intent on it just a knife-throw away. *It's nice but it's not everything*, Brax had said: But for those moments it sounded like it was everything for the two of them.

I hoped they stayed willing to take me as I was. I didn't know if I could explain that what they did wrapped in their blankets was like being offered the lees of fine wine. I could tell they thought I was still grieving for Ad, or Tom: Let them believe that, if it would obscure the truth of what I had become and what stirred me now. *Keep your mouth shut, Mars,* I told myself, and twisted onto my side away from them. *They'll never understand and you'd never be able to explain. They'll think you're insane or perverted or worse, and they'll send you packing back to your no-name village before you can say "oh, go ahead and fuck me if that's what it takes to let me stay with you."*

I never was much good at cheering myself up: But in spite of it all I finally fell asleep, and I woke to a hug from Braxis and pine tea from Ro, to a sleepy pat on the shoulder from Lucky, and for the first time in oh-so-long I felt the hope of belonging.

It took weeks to get to Lemon City, mostly because we were in no hurry. There was always so much to do each day, so much exploring and talking and the hands-on work of turning ourselves into a fighting partnership. And other kinds of work, as well. In spite of what they'd said, the three of them made a concerted effort to seduce me, and I did not know how to reassure them that they had already succeeded, that they had turned me into a banked coal with a constant fire in my belly. "Damn your cold heart, Mars," Lucky spat at me one day, "I hope someday someone you really want turns you down flat, and then see how you like it!"

"Luck, it's not like that!" I called out after her as she stalked off down a side trail into the woods.

"Leave her," Ro advised. "She'll accept it. We all will." He and Brax exchanged a wry look, and I felt terrible. I must be cold, I thought, cold and selfish. It was such a small thing to ask, to make people I loved happy. But it wasn't just my body they wanted, it was me, and they would never reach me that way, and then we would all still be unsatisfied. And I was not willing to explain. So it was my fault, my flaw. My failure.

I was packing my bedroll when Lucky came back. "Oh, stop," she said impatiently. "You know what I'm like, Mars, don't take it so personally. Just stay away from me tonight and I'll be fine in the morning." And she was; and the next afternoon, when she took hold of me so unknowingly, I gave her myself. I gave to all of them, a dozen times each day.

"The hardest part about all this," Brax said one evening as we all stretched out near our fire, "is overcoming all the sword training."

"Whaddya mean?" Ro mumbled around a mouthful of cheese.

"Well, the sword makes your arm longer and gives it a killing edge, so that you still strike or punch, sort of, but it's with the blade. But the stormfighting, well, like Mars is always saying, the whole point is to become the center of the fight and bring your enemy in to you. So with the sword we keep people out far enough to slice them up, and with the storm art we bring them in close enough to kiss. It does my head in sometimes trying to figure out where I'm supposed to be when."

"You think it's hard for you?" I replied. "You're not the one with half a dozen cuts on every arm and leg trying to learn it the other way around. I always let Lucky get too close."

"So maybe there's a way to do both." Lucky reached out to swipe a piece of cheese from Ro's lap.

"What do you mean?" Ro asked again.

"Pig. Give me some of that. I mean that maybe there's a way to combine the moves. All the sword dances I do are based on wheels, being able to turn and move in any direction with your body and the sword like spokes on a wheel. It's not that different from being at the center of a wind, or whatever."

"Gods around us," I said. She'd put a picture in my mind so clear that for a moment I wasn't sure which was more real, the Lucky who smiled quizzically at me from across the fire, or the one who suddenly rolled over her own sword and came up slashing at her opponent's knee. "She's right. You could do both. Think about it! Just think about it!" They were all bright-eyed now, caught in the spiral of my excitement that drew them in as surely as one of the armlocks we'd worked on that afternoon. "Imagine being able to fight long or short, with an edge or a tip or just your bare hand. They'd never know what to expect, they couldn't predict what you'd do next!"

"Okay, maybe," Lucky said. "It might work with that whole series that's based off the step in and behind, but what about the face-to-face? A sword's always a handicap when you're in that close."

"That's because everyone always goes weapon to weapon." Lucky looked blank. "If you have a sword, what's the other person going to do? Get a bigger sword if they can. Try to beat your sword. But we don't need that. Our weapon is the way we fight. Go in and take their sword away. Go in and do things with a sword that no one thinks possible. In my head I just saw you roll with your own blade and come up edge-ready. Maybe staying low would give us more options for being in close."

"Come here," Lucky said, and scrambled up, and we worked it out again and again until the fire was almost dead and we trod on Brax in the dark. "Stop this idiocy and go to sleep!" she growled; but the next day we were all ready to reinvent sword fighting, and we ate our dinner that night bloody and bruised and grinning like children.

We came into Lemon City on a cold wind, just ahead of a hard autumn rain that dropped from a fast front of muddy clouds. We crowded under cover of a blacksmith's shed inside the city gates, with a dozen other travelers, three gate guards, and two bad-tempered horses, while manure and straw and someone's basket washed away down the water-logged street. Everything was gray and stinking. I couldn't help laughing, remembering my fantasies about the golden streets full of important people in silk with me in the center, being whisked toward greatness.

When the rain had passed we walked in toward the heart of the city. My boots leaked and my feet got wet, and Ro stepped in goat shit and swore.

"So far, I feel right at home," I told Lucky, who cackled wildly and reminded me for one sharp moment of my mother, bent over in laughter with her hands twisted in her apron and flour dust rising all around her.

We found an inn that they'd heard of, and got the second-to-last room left. We were lucky; the last room was no better than a sty, and went an hour later for the same rate as ours. The city was packed tighter than a farm sausage, our landlord told us with a satisfied smile. He took some of Ro's money for a pitcher of cider and settled one hip up against the common room table to tell us where to find the guard house for the coming auditions. The next were in two days' time. "And lots of competition for this one, of course," he said cheerfully, with a glance around the crowded room that made him scurry to another table with his tray of cider.

"What's that mean, of course?" Lucky wondered when he'd gone away.

I shrugged. Brax drank the last of her cider. "I hate it when they say of course," she muttered, and belched.

The next day was sunny, and we went out exploring. I left my sword for the day with the blacksmith near the city gate, who promised to lengthen the grip. From there we wandered to the market, and they laughed at my wide-eyed amazement. And everywhere we saw foursomes, young or seasoned, trying not to show their stress by keeping their faces impassive, so of course you could spot them a mile off. We followed some of them to the guards' training camp, and waited in line to give our names to someone whose only job that day seemed to be telling stiff-faced hopefuls where and when to turn up for the next morning's trials. Then we found a place to perch where Lucky and Brax could size everyone up until they found something to feel superior about: a weak eye, too much weight on one foot, someone's hands looped under their belt so they couldn't reach their weapon easily. Eventually the strain got to be too much, and we went back to the inn for an afternoon meal and practice on a small patch of ground near the stable. Working up a sweat seemed to calm them down; and touching them erased everything else for me.

That night, I laid an extra coin on the table when the landlord brought our platter of chicken and pitcher of beer, and said, "Tell us what's so special about these auditions."

He looked genuinely surprised. "Anybody could tell you that," he said, but he put the coin in his sleeve pocket. "The prince has turned out half the palace guard again, and Captain Gerlain's scrambling for replacements. Those who do well are sure to end up with palace duty, although why any of you'd want it is beyond me."

"Why's that?"

"Our prince is mad, that's why, and the king's too far gone up his own backside to notice."

Lucky put a hand to her knife. "You mind yourself, man," she said calmly, and Brax and I tried not to grin at each other. Lucky could be startlingly conservative.

"Oh, and no offense intended to the king," he said easily. "But well done, the king needs loyal soldiers around him. Particularly now he's old and sick, and too well medicated, at least that's what they say. You just get yourself hired on up there and keep an eye on him for us." He poured Lucky another drink. I admired the skill with which he'd turned the conflict aside.

None of us could eat, thinking about the next day, and the beer tasted off. We sat at the table, not talking much. Eventually we moved out to the snug, where the landlord had a fire going. It was warmer there than the common room, but no more relaxing. I turned the coming day over and over in my head as if it were a puzzle I couldn't put down until I'd solved it. Lucky and Ro sat close together: their calves touched, then their thighs, then Ro's hand found its way onto Lucky's arm and she sighed, leaned into him, looking suddenly small and soft. When I looked away, Brax was there, next to me.

She cupped her hard hand around my jaw and cheek and

left ear. "Don't turn me away, Mars," she said quietly. "It's no night to be alone."

"You're right," I replied. "But let's try something a little different." I felt wild and daring, even though I knew she wouldn't understand. I took her by the hand and led her out to our practice area by the stable. They kept a lantern out there for late arrivals; it gave us just enough light to see motion, but the fine work would have to be done by instinct: by feel.

"You want to practice?" she said.

My heart was thudding under my ribs. This was the closest I had ever come to telling anyone what it was like with me. It was so tempting to say *Take me down, Brax, challenge me, control me, equal me, best me, love me.* But I only smiled and stepped into the small circle of light. "Put your hands on me," I whispered, soft enough so that she would not hear, and centered myself.

They were fair auditions, and hard, and we were brilliant. I could tell they had never seen anything like us. The method was to put two quads into the arena with wooden swords. I learned later that they looked for how we fought, but that was only part of it. "The fighting is the easiest thing to teach," Captain Gerlain told me once. "What I look for is basic coordination, understanding of the body and how it works. And how the quad works together."

It was an incredible day, a blur of things swirled together: crisp air that smelled of fried bread from the camp kitchen and the sweat of a hundred nervous humans; the sounds of leather on skin and huffing breath interleaved with the faint music of temple singers practicing three streets away; and the touch of a hundred different hands, the textures of their skin, the energies that ran between us as we laid hold of one another.

After he saw our stormfighting, Gerlain started putting other quads against us, so that we fought more than anyone else. Most of the fighters didn't know what to make of us, and I began to see that Gerlain was using us as a touchstone to test the others. Those who tried to learn from us, who adapted as best they could, had the good news with us when Gerlain's sergeant read out the names at the end of the day; and Gerlain himself stopped Lucky and said, curtly, "You and your quad'll be teaching the rest an hour a day, after regular training, starting tomorrow afternoon. Work out your program with Sergeant Manto. And don't get above yourselves. Manto will be watching, and so will I."

"Hoo hoo!" said Lucky. "Let's get drunk!" But I was already intoxicated by the day, dizzy with the feel of so many strangers' skin against mine. And I was a guard. I whispered it to Ad as we walked back to the inn through the streets that now seemed familiar and welcoming. *I made it,* I told her. *Lemon City.* I thought of Tom, and my mother: *I'm safe, I found a place for myself.* I saw Ad with her sheepskin and her special stick; I felt Tom's tears on my skin, and my mother's hand on my hair. Then Ro was standing in the door to the inn, looking for me, waiting: and I went in.

It was the stormfighting that kept us out of a job for such a long time. Gerlain and Manto saw it as a tactical advantage and a way to teach warriors not to rely on their swords. Tom would have approved. But many of our fellow soldiers did not. Our frank admissions that it was still raw, as dangerous to the fighter as to the target, and our matter-of-fact approach to teaching, were the only things that kept us from being permanent outsiders in the guard. Even so, we made fewer friends than we might have.

"Can't let you go yet," Manto would shrug each month, when new postings were announced. "Need you to teach the newbs."

"Let someone else teach," Ro was arguing again.

"Who? There's no one here who knows it the way you do."

"That's because you keep posting them on as soon as they've halfway learned anything."

"Shucks," Manto grinned, showing her teeth. "You noticed."

"Manto, try to see this from our point of view . . ."

"Oh, gods," I whispered to Lucky, "There he goes, being reasonable again. Do something."

"Right," she whispered back, and then stepped between Ro and Manto, pointing a finger at Ro when he tried to protest. She said pleasantly, "We came here to be guards, not baby-minders. You want us to teach, fine, we'll teach other guards. Until then, I think we'll just go get a beer." She turned and started for the gate, hooking a thumb into Ro's belt to pull him along. Brax sighed and reached for her gear. I gave Manto a cheerful smile and a goodbye salute.

"All right, children," Manto said, pitching her voice to halt Lucky and Ro. "Report to Andavista tomorrow at the palace. Take all your toys, you'll draw quarters up there."

Even Lucky was momentarily speechless.

Manto grinned again. "The orders have been in for a couple of weeks. I just wanted to see how much more time I could get out of you." She slapped me on the arm so hard I almost fell over. "Welcome to the army."

"Where the hell have you people been?" Sergeant Andavista snarled at us the next morning. "Been waiting for you for two weeks." There seemed to be no good answer to that, so we didn't even try. "Your rooms are at the end of the southwest gallery. Unpack and report back here to me in ten minutes. Move!"

The rooms had individual beds, for which I was grateful. The double-wide bunks at the training camp had made us all more tense with one another as time went on, and I was tired of sleeping on the floor—particularly after a good day's work, when my body felt hollowed out by the thousand moments of desire roused and sated and born again, every time we grappled, when I only wanted to sleep close to one of my unknowing lovers and drink in the smell of our sweat on their skin.

Andavista handed us off to the watch commander, who gave us new gear with the palace insignia and a brain-numbing recital of guard schedules. Then she found a man just coming off watch and drafted him to show us around. The soldier looked bone-tired, but he nodded agreeably enough and tried to hide his yawns as he led us up and down seemingly endless hallways. He pointed out the usual watch stations: main gate, trade entrances, public rooms, armory, the three floors of rooms where the bureaucrats lived and worked, and the fourteen floors of nobles' chambers, which he waved at dismissively. I remembered my mother saying *ticks on a dog*.

He brought us to a massive set of wooden doors strapped with iron. "Royal suite," he said economically. "Last stop on the tour. Can you find your own way back?"

We did, although it took the better part of an hour and made us all grumpy. "Not bad," the watch commander commented when we returned. "Last week's set had to be fetched out."

And so we settled. It wasn't much different from living in my village, except that I belonged. We learned soldiery and taught stormfighting and found time to practice by ourselves, to reinforce old ideas, to invent new ones. It was an easy routine to settle to, but I'd had my lessons too well from Tom to ever relax completely, and the rest of the quad had learned to trust my edge. And it helped in a turned-around way that news of us had spread up from the training ground, and there were soldiers we'd never met who resented us for being different and were contemptuous of what they'd heard about stormfighting. Being the occasional target of pointed remarks or pointed elbows was new for Brax and Lucky and Ro; it kept them aware in a way that all my warnings never could. So on the day we found swords at our throats, we were ready.

They came for the king and prince during the midnight watch when we were stationed outside the royal wing. Ro thought he might have seen the king once, at the far end of the audience room, but these doors were the closest we had ever been to the people we were sworn to protect. And it was our first posting to this most private area of the palace. Perhaps that's why they chose our watch to try it. Or perhaps because they had dismissed the purposely slow practice drills of storm art as nothing more than fancy-fighting; it was a common enough belief among our detractors.

The first sign we had that anything was amiss was when two of the daywatch quads came up the hall. Brax stepped forward; it was her night to be in charge. "We're relieving you," their leader said. "Andavista wants you down at the gates."

"What's up?" Brax asked neutrally, but I could see the way her shoulders tensed.

The other shrugged. "Dunno. Some kind of commotion at the gates, security's being tightened inside. Andavista says jump, I reckon it's our job to ask which cliff he had in mind."

Brax stood silent for a moment, thinking. "Ro, go find Andavista or Saree and get it in person. No offense," she added to the two quads in front of her.

"None taken," their leader said; and then her sword was out and coming down on Brax. She struck hard and fast, but Brax was already under her arm and pushing her off center, taking only enough time to break the other woman's arm as she went down. The other seven moved in, Brax scrambled up with blood on her sword, and then they were on us.

I wasn't ready for the noise of it, the clattering of metal on metal, the yells, the way that everything reverberated in the closed space of the hallway. I could hear the bolts slamming into place in the doors behind us, and knew that at least someone was alerted: No one but Andavista or Gerlain would get inside now. Lucky was shouting but I couldn't tell what or who it was meant for. Then I saw Ro shaking his head even as he turned and cut another soldier's feet out from under him, and I understood. "Go on," I yelled. "Get help! We don't know how many more there might be!"

For a moment Ro looked terribly young. Then his face set, and he turned up the hall. It was bad strategy on the part of the assassins to arrive in a group, rather than splitting up and approaching from both directions; but they'd had to preserve the illusion of being ordered to the post. Two of them tried to head Ro off: He gutted one and kept going, and Brax stepped in front of the other. Three horrible moments later she made a rough, rattling sound and they both went down in a boneless tumble. Brax left a broad smear of blood on the wall behind her as she fell.

Lucky and I were side by side now, facing the four that were still standing. Out of the side of my right eye I could see Brax lying limp against the wall. Lucky was panting. There was a moment of silence in the hall; we all looked at each other, as if we'd suddenly found ourselves doing something unexpected and someone had stopped to ask, *what now?*

"Blow them down," I told Lucky, and we swirled into them like the lightning and the wind.

I'd never before fought for my life or another's. These people weren't Tom; I couldn't drop my sword and call *stop*. And these were our own we were facing, people we'd eaten with, insulted and argued with, and whose measure we had taken on the training field. Some of them were people I had taught, muscle to muscle, skin to skin. Now I reached for them in rage, and my touch was voracious. I went in close to one, up near his center, my arm fully extended under his and lifting up, taking his balance, thrusting my weight forward to put him down. It was sweet to feel him scrabbling under my hands, pulling at my tunic, trying to right himself, and then my sword was at his neck and I cut off his life in a ragged line. His trousers soiled with shit and he fell into a puddle at my feet. My body sang. I took the taste of his death between my teeth, and stepped on his stomach to get to the woman behind him.

I woke in our rooms. Ro was there, watching over me.

"How are you?"

"Don't touch me," I said.

He waited. "Brax and Lucky are going to be fine." I put a hand up to my head. "It was deep, to the bone, but it's not infected. They had to shave your head," he added, too late.

"Sarce came around. Those two quads were hired to win a place in the guards and wait for the right moment. The one they took alive didn't last long enough to tell them who did the hiring. Poor bastard."

I felt empty and dirty, and I couldn't think of anything to say.

He swallowed, moved closer, but he was careful not to touch me. "Mars, I know it's the first time you've killed. It's hard, but we've all been through it. We can help you, if you'll let us."

"You don't understand," I said.

"I do, truly." He was so earnest. "I remember—"

I held up a hand. "Blessing on you, Ro, but it's not the killing, it's—I can't. I can't talk about it." I swung my legs off the other side of the bed, stood shakily, looked around for something to wear. My head hurt all the way down to my feet, but I wasn't as weak as I'd expected to be. Good. I found my tunic and overshirt, and a pair of dirty leggings.

"Where are you going?"

"I need to get out. I'll be fine," I added, seeing his face. "I won't leave the palace. I just want some time to think. I'm not looking for a ledge to jump off."

He managed a tight smile. I did not come close to him as I left.

I really did want to wander: to get lost. I had the wit to stay away from the public halls, and I did not want the company and the avid questions of other guards, so I steered

toward the lower floors: the kitchens, the pantry, and the en-
closed food gardens. I found a stair down from the scullery
that led to a vast series of storerooms, smokerooms, wine
cellars.

I thought about the killing.

The sword work wasn't so bad. The sensations of weapon
contact were always more muted for me than hand-to-hand.
But stormfighting was so much more intense: seducing my
opponent into me, or thrusting myself into her space, or
breathing in the smell of him while my hands turned him to
my will. I'd got used to it being delicious, smooth, powerful,
like gulping a mug of warm cream on a cold night. Until the
hallway, until the man's throat spilled open under my sword,
until I broke his partner open with my hands. With my
hands—and the fizzing thrill through my body was overrun
by something that felt like chunks of fire, like vomit in my
veins. I hated it. It made me feel lonely in a way I'd never
thought to feel again. So I sat down in the cellars of the
palace and wept for something I'd lost, and then I wept some
more for the greater loss to come.

My head hurt worse when I'd run dry of tears. I gathered
myself up and went to find my quad.

They were sitting quietly when I came into the room, not talking; Brax on one of the beds drowsing in the last of the sun
through the west window, Lucky crowded in beside her with
her bad leg propped on a pillow, Ro on the floor nearby leaning against the mattress so that his head was close to theirs.

"Ho, Mars," Lucky said gently.

They were so beautiful that I could only look at them for
a handful of moments. When I opened my mouth I had no
idea what might come out of it.

"I love you all so much," I said. I wasn't nervous anymore; it was time they knew me, and whatever happened
next I would always have this picture of them, and the
muscle-deep memory of all our times.

"Being with you three is like . . . gods, sometimes I imagine leaving home a day earlier or later. How easy it would have been to miss you on the road. What if I'd missed you? What would I be now?"

They were silent, watching me. I was the center of the world.

"That time on the road, when you asked me to . . ." I made a hapless sort of gesture, and Ro smiled. "You thought I was saying no, but what I was really saying was no, not like that." I swallowed. I wasn't sure how to say the next bit; and then Brax surprised me.

"The night before the guard trials, out behind the inn, when I thought we were practicing. We were really fucking, your way."

I felt like a lightning-struck tree, all soft pulp suddenly exposed to the world, ruptured and raw. And I did the thing more frightening than fighting Tom, or leaving home, or losing Ad. I whispered *yes*. Then I crossed my arms to hold myself in, and began to find any words that I could use to hold off the moment when they would send me away. "I didn't know until I met you on the road, and we began to practice, and every time we touched in this particular way I thought I would die from it. That's when I figured it out, you know. I was a virgin when I met you," and I couldn't help but smile, because it was so right. "For me, the touch of your palm on my wrist is the same as any act of love; it's my way of bringing our bodies together. It's no different from putting ourselves inside each other."

"Mars, it's—" Ro began.

"Don't you tell me it's okay!" I cut him off. "You're always the peacemaker, Ro, but you don't understand. You don't understand what I've done. Every time we've touched as fighters, all the teaching and the practice, it's all been sex for me, hours and hours of it with one of you or all of you, or other quads that we've taught. And you never knew. What's that but some kind of rape? It's bad enough with

people I love, and then there's all those strangers. I've probably had more partners than all the whores in Ziren Square.
And I can't help it, and gods know I can't stop because it's
the most unbelievable . . . but what I did to all of you, that's
unforgivable, but I was so afraid that you'd . . . well, I expect
you can guess what I thought and I'm sure you're thinking
it now. No, wait," I said, to stop Brax from speaking. "Then
there's this killing. You were right, Ro, I've never killed before, and it was horrible, it was disgusting because I still felt
it even when I was pulling her arm out of its socket. And I
didn't want to, I didn't want to, but I thought of what they'd
done to Brax and then I was glad to hurt them and then there
was this fierce, terrible wave . . . oh, gods, I'm sorry." I was
panting now, clenching myself. "I'm sorry. But it's there,
and I thought you should know." They were still silent; Brax
and Lucky were holding hands so tightly that I could see
their fingers going white, and Ro looked sad and patient. "I
love you," I said, and then everything was beyond bearing
and I had to leave.

I went back to the cellars because I didn't know where else
to go. I did not belong anywhere now. I sat curled for hours
next to one of the beer vats, numb and quiet, until I heard the
chattering voices of cooking staff come to fetch a barrel for
supper: I did not want to meet anyone, so I unkinked myself
and went farther down the hallway until I found a small
heavy door slightly ajar, old but with freshly oiled hinges
that made no sound as I slid through.

I came into a vast, dim place, heavy with green and the
smell of water. Not a garden: an enormous twilight conservatory in the guts of the oldest part of the palace. Even
through my despair I could see the marvel of the place, feel
its mystery. There were trees standing forty feet tall in
porcelain tubs as big as our room upstairs. Light seeped
through narrow windows above the treetops. There were
wooden frames thick with ivy that bloomed in lightly per-

fumed purple and orange and blue. Everything felt old and unused, sliding toward ruin, with the particular heavy beauty of a rotting temple. The humid air, the taste of jasmine on my tongue, the stone walls that I could sense although I could not see them under so much green—everything collided inside me and mixed with my own madness to make me feel wild, curious, adrenalized as if I'd eaten too many of the dried granzi leaves that Brax liked to indulge in sometimes when we were off duty. The narrow path that twisted off between the potted trees was laid in the unmistakable patterns of desert tile. I followed the colors toward the sound of rain, and the sound turned into a fountain, a flat-bottomed circle lined with more bright tiles. Strings of water fell into it from a dozen ducts in the ceiling high overhead, onto the pool and the upraised face of the woman in it.

She was dancing. From the look of her, she'd been at it a while: Her hair was flung in sodden ropes against her dark skin, and the tips of her fingers were wrinkled, paler than the rest of her when she reached them up to grasp at the droplets in the air. She breathed in the hard, shallow gasps of someone who has taken her body almost as far as it can go. Her eyes were rolled up, showing white, and her mouth hung half-open. She whirled and kicked to a rhythm that pounded through her so strongly I could feel it as a backbeat to the juddering of my heart. Faster, faster she turned, and the water turned with her and flung itself back into the pool. I knew what I was seeing. It was more than a dance, it was a transportation, a transmigration, as if she could take the whole world into herself if she only reached a little higher, if she only turned once more. I knew how it must feel within her, burning, building, until her body shuddered one final time and she shouted, her head still back and her arms clawed up as if she would seize the ceiling and pull it down over her. Her eyes opened, bright blue against the brown. She saw me as she fell.

Bless her, I thought, *at least I'm not that alone.*

Her shout still echoed around the chamber, or at least I could still hear it in my head; but she was silent, lying on her side in the water, blue eyes watching me. I eased myself down onto one of the tiled benches bordering the walkway, to show her that I was not a threat or an idle gawper. There was a shawl bundled at the other end of the bench, and I was careful not to touch it. After a minute she rolled onto her back in the shallow pool and turned her blue gaze up to the high windows. Neither of us spoke. I was relaxed and completely attentive to everything she did: a breath, a finger moved, a lick at a drop of water caught on her lip. When she finally pulled herself up to her knees, I was there with the shawl and an arm to help her raise herself the rest of the way. She draped the shawl around her shoulders but did not try to cover herself; she seemed unaware of being naked and wet with a stranger. I stood back when she stepped out of the pool.

She looked me up and down. She was medium tall, older by a few years, whip thin with oversized calf muscles and strong biceps. An old scar ran along one rib. The skin on her hands was rough. I pictured her in one of the kitchens, or perhaps tending the smokehouse where the sides of beef and boar had to be raised onto their high hooks.

"I hope you closed the door behind you," she said absently, in a dry and crackly voice.

"The door? Oh . . . yes, it's closed. No one will come in."

"You did."

"Yes. But no one else will come."

"They might."

"I won't let them."

She looked me up and down. "You're a guard," she said.

"Yes."

"So you'd kill anyone who tried to get in."

"I'd meet them at the door and send them on their way. If they tried to come in further, I'd stop them."

She drew a wrinkled finger across her throat.

"Not necessarily," I replied. "I might not have to kill them."

"Oh," she said. "I would. I wouldn't know how to stop them any other way. I don't know much about the middle ground."

She had begun to shake very slightly. "You're cold," I said, and pulled off my overshirt to offer her. She peered at it carefully before she put it on, dropping the shawl without a glance onto the wet floor.

"Most people don't talk to me," she said.

"I'll talk with you whenever you like," I said, thinking that I knew very well how people would treat her, particularly if she wandered up to the kitchens with one of the meat cleavers in her hand and tried to have this kind of conversation. Standing with her in the dim damp of the room felt like being in one of those in-between moments of an epic poem, where everyone takes a stanza or two to gather their breath before the next impossible task.

She appeared to be thinking, and I was in no hurry. Then she straightened the shirt around her and said, "Walk me back."

"Of course," I answered. I plucked her shawl out of the muck and fell in behind her with my hand on my sword, the way I'd been taught. She was so odd and formal, like a little chick covered in bristles: She wanted looking after. When we left the room, she watched to make sure that I closed the door firmly, then nodded as if satisfied and led me back up through the cellars. I was surprised when she bypassed the carvery and the scullery, and nervous when she took the stairs away from the kitchen, up toward the residential levels of the palace: I wasn't sure what to do if someone challenged us, and I did not want trouble with Andavista on top of the mess I'd already made with my quad. But she held her head high and kept going, and then we made a turn and almost ran into Saree talking something out with one of his seconds. *Oh, icy hell*, I thought, and was absolutely astonished when Saree gave me an unreadable look and then bent his head. "Prince," he said, and she sailed by him like a great ship past a dinghy, trailing me behind. As I passed him, Saree pointed his finger at himself emphatically, and I nodded, and then followed the prince. We came to the great wooden doors of the royal suite, and the four guards there stiffened. They opened the doors clumsily, trying to see everything without appearing to look at us, and I knew the stories would start a minute after the watch changed when the four of them could get down to the commissary.

The hallway was a riot of rich-colored tapestries, plants, paintings, a table stacked high with dusty books: and silent as a tomb. I wondered if the king was behind one of the many doors we passed. A servant came out of a room at the far end and hurried toward us with a muffled exclamation. The prince waved her off, and I handed her the shawl as she stepped back to let us pass. Then the prince stopped in front of one of the doors and turned to me. Her eyes were hard, like blue stained glass. I saluted and bowed.

"You saw me," she said, and her voice was like her eyes.

I imagined what it would be like to practice with my quad from now on, their knowing what it meant to me every time we touched, their distaste or their tolerance, my most private self on public display because I had not kept my secret. I understood how she might feel; and she deserved the truth.

"You were beautiful," I said. "You were like a storm."

She looked at me for a moment, then she took in a breath and blew it out again with the noise that children make when they pretend to be the wind. Her breath smelled like salt and oranges. The door shut between us.

"What happened?" Saree growled when I found him.

"The prince asked me to escort her back to her rooms," I said evenly.

"Where did you find her? Her servants have been looking for her for hours."

"In the hallway near the armory." It was the farthest place from the cellars that I could think of.

"Oh, really?" he rumbled. "She just happened to appear in the armory hallway soaking wet and there you were?"

"Yessir," I answered. "Honestly, sir, I didn't even know who she was until we met you. I just didn't think that she should be—I mean—"

He relaxed. "I know what you mean, no need to say any more. But we'd like to know where she disappears to." I stayed quiet, and he lost interest in me. "Don't you have somewhere to be?" he said, and I saluted and got out of his sight as quickly as I could. My head was too stuffed full of tangled thoughts to make any sense of anything, and I didn't want to deal with Ro and Lucky and Brax until I felt clear. I took myself off into Lemon City for a long walk and did, in the end, get my wish: I got lost.

It was late when I came back to our rooms. The quad was there, and so was Andavista. They all wore the most peculiar expressions: Lucky was trying to send me seventeen different messages with eyes and body language, but all I got was the general impression that a lot had been going on while I'd been away. Then I looked beyond her, and saw the carrybags we'd brought with us all the way from the cross-roads, packed now and waiting to be closed up.

"No, you idiot," Brax said. "Your things are in there too, we're being transferred. Don't look at me like that, everyone knows what you're thinking, we can always tell."

"Ummm," I said helplessly, and Ro grinned. Andavista stood up from where he'd been sitting, in our only chair. "Very touching. Sort it out later. You, I've just about run out of patience waiting for you but I've got direct orders to fetch you all personally and I suppose I can be thankful you didn't decide to stay out all night. Particularly since this lot wouldn't say where you could be found." He squinted at me. "Well, at least you're not stupid enough to turn up drunk. Now, all of you, get your things and follow me."

He stomped out of the room and we scrambled to shoulder our gear and follow him. I shooed Lucky out of the way and picked up our biggest pack. "Get away from that, you can't carry it with your leg." She grimaced impatiently. "What's going on?" I whispered.

"You tell me," she whispered back. "All we got is some wild story at dinner about you and the prince, and then Andavista saying he's giving us a new home and everyone who's not on watch finding an excuse to wander by our rooms and goggle at us."

"Shut up and move," Andavista snarled without turning, so we did, Ro and I carrying everything between us while Brax braced Lucky with her good arm. Of course I knew where we must be going, but I could scarcely credit it: I'd only been nice, and certainly more free in my manner than what was due to her. But I was right: We went through the by-now-familiar wooden doors and into a room just beyond, where sleepy-eyed servants were busily beating the dust out of a rug and several coverlets, with a new fire in the hearth and a pitcher of mulled wine on a mostly clean table. And my overshirt, carefully folded on the mantel.

Andavista said, "You've been assigned as the prince's personal guard. You're with her wherever she goes, all of you, which means more time on duty than before. She breakfasts at midmorning, you two—" looking at me and Ro— "report to her then. If she forgets to let you out for meals, let me know. I expect a full report every day from one of you, personally to either me or Saree, no exceptions. You'll go back to teaching when you're all off the sick list, at least until you've got others good enough to take over. Where you find the time is your problem. And don't get above yourselves, I'll be watching. And don't let so much as a mouse near her," he added, in a different tone. Then he glared around the room and left. The servants scuttled out behind him.

My three pounced on me with questions before the door

was closed. "Wait, wait," I said, trying to gather my wits while Ro poured us a cup of wine. I told them about meeting the prince between hot swallows, curiously content even though we all knew why I'd been downcellar in the first place, the unfinished business between us.

"Unbelievable," Lucky said. "How do you do it, Mars?"

Brax said, "I wouldn't go planting any gardens here, Luck. She's thrown out more guards than we have ancestors. She could change her mind anytime."

"I don't think so," I said. "She's never taken a personal guard before that I know of, just the shift watches outside the door. Can you imagine some of our mates in the barracks standing outside the conservatory doors while she . . . She'd have been a laughingstock years ago."

"So why now?" Ro said.

"I understand her." They looked at me. "Maybe I'm mad too, I don't know, but seeing her dance—you know what I think? I think she wants someone to share with. I told her she was beautiful, and she was. Maybe no one else ever has. But whatever you think of her, you mustn't—you mustn't hurt her."

"Oh, Mars," Lucky said sadly. "Of course we won't."

"I know, I'm sorry. It's just—"

"We know what it is," Ro said. "And we decided we didn't want to talk about it until you and Lucky and Brax are better. And that's the end of it," he said as I opened my mouth to speak. "Now, who gets the bed nearest the fire?"

We and the prince began getting used to each other. She spent a lot of time watching us; it was a bit unnerving at first. She tested us in little ways. She led us on some incredible expeditions into the belly of the palace. She seemed more and more trusting of us; but she did not dance. She seemed to be waiting for something.

And so was I. Every extra arc of motion that returned to Brax's arm was one step closer to all my worst fears. By unspoken agreement, we did not practice, and the others stopped making love in front of me. There was a particular kind of tension between us that I could not define, but that made me miserable when I let myself think about what it all might mean, and what I had to lose. I wondered if the prince felt it and thought it was directed at her: It made me try even harder to be easy and gentle with her, who'd had so much less than I.

Ro and I came back to our rooms one night to find Lucky and Brax already toasting each other with a mug of beer from a barrel swiped on our last trip to the cellars. "Back on duty tomorrow," Lucky grinned around a mouthful of foam. "Hoo hoo!" She poured, and we all drank. I felt numb.

"Oh, sweet Mars," Ro said, "don't look like that. Don't you know we see right through you?" Then he took my cup away and opened his arms and folded me into himself, and Lucky and Brax were behind me, gathering me in, stripping off my clothes and theirs. "I don't know if I can—" I began to say, and Brax murmured, "Shut up, Mars." Then Ro shifted his weight and sent me backwards into Brax's waiting arms, and she pinned me down for a lightning second while she brushed her breast against my mouth, and then rolled us so that I was on top and Ro's arms came around me in a lock, and I hesitated and he whispered *Go on* and I turned the way we'd taught ourselves and felt his thigh slide across my back and heard his breath hitch, and mine hitched too. And then it was Lucky with her leg across mine, strength to strength, my heart beating faster and faster, everything a blue-heat fire from my groin to the tips of my fingers. They traded me back and forth like that for some endless time, and each moment that they controlled me they would take some pleasure for themselves, a tongue in my mouth or a wristlock that placed my hand on some part of them that would make them moan; and I moaned too, and then answered their technique with one of my own and changed the dance. Then Brax reached for Ro, and Lucky and I continued while beyond us they brought each other to shouts; and then Lucky was gone to Brax and it was Ro with me, whispering *Best me if you can*, and then Brax with her strong arms; until finally the world stopped shuddering and we lay in a heap together in front of the fire. And later some of us cried, and were comforted.

We are the prince's guard. When she sits in a tower window and sings endless songs to the seabirds, we are at the door. When she roams the hallways at night peering through keyholes, we are the shadows that fly at her shoulder. She dances for us now, and we protect her from prying eyes; and when she is ecstatic and spent, when she is lucid and can find some measure of peace, we take her back to her rooms and talk of the world, of the rainbow-painted roofs of Hunemoth and the way that cheese is made in Shortline. She is safer now; she has us to see her as she is, and love her.

And there is still time for ourselves, to teach, to learn, to gossip with other guards and steal currant buns from our favorite cook. Sometimes the prince sends us off to Lemon City for a day, to collect fallen feathers from the road or strings of desert beads from the market; to bring her descriptions of her beggars and smiths and shopkeepers; to gather travelers' stories from the inns. Sometimes we carry back a flagon of spicy Marhai wine, and when she sleeps, we drink and trade wild stories until the moon is down. Sometimes we sleep cuddled like puppies in our blankets. Sometimes we fight.

O for a Fiery Gloom and Thee

Brian Stableford

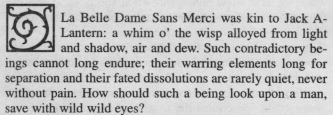 La Belle Dame Sans Merci was kin to Jack A-Lantern: a whim o' the wisp alloyed from light and shadow, air and dew. Such contradictory beings cannot long endure; their warring elements long for separation and their fated dissolutions are rarely quiet, never without pain. How should such a being look upon a man, save with wild wild eyes?

La Belle Dame Sans Merci could not stroll upon the mead like any earthbound being for her footfall was far too light, but she had the precious power of touch which earthbound beings take overmuch for granted. She could not be seen by light of noon, but when she did appear—bathed by the baleful moon's unholiness—there was magic in her image.

Salomé the enchantress knew how to dance, and stir the fire of Hell in the hearts of those who watched, but La Belle Dame Sans Merci knew how to lie as still as still could be, and ignite the fire of Purgatory by sight alone.

La Belle Dame Sans Merci was a daughter of the faery folk, but it is not given to the faery folk to know their fathers and their mothers as humans do. It is easy for faery folk to believe that they owe their conception to the fall of the dew from their father the Sky: from the dew which never reaches Mother Earth but drifts upon the air as wayward mist. That, at least, is the story they tell one another; but what it might mean to them no merely human being could ever understand. Humans are cursed by the twin burdens of belief and unbelief but the faery folk are no more capable of faith than of mass; they have the gift of touch without the leaden heaviness of solidity, and they have the gift of imagination without the parsimonious degradations of accuracy.

The earliest adventures of La Belle Dame Sans Merci were not concerned with warriors or princes but with men unfit for oral or written record—mere passers-by on the rough-hewn roads of myth and history—but she always felt that she was made for the Royal Hunt and for the defiance of chivalry. She always felt that she was made to tempt the very best of the children of the Iron Age, to draw the users of arms and armor from the terrible path of progress. Because she had no human need to transmute her feelings into beliefs she had no human need to ask *why* she was made that way—or whether she was *made* at all—so she followed the force of her impulse with all blithe innocence, her eyes as wide as they were wild.

Like the rough-hewn roads of myth and history, the many roads of England were not at this time wont to run *straight*. The Romans had come but the Romans had gone again; their legacy remained only in a few long marching-paths, and it was more than possible that the few would become fewer as time went by and Rome became but a memory.

Made for men a-foot and horses poorly shod, the older roads of England wound around slopes and thickets, ponds and streams, always avoiding places of ill repute, always preferring the gentle gradient and the comfortable footfall. In poor light such pathways become mazy and treacherous and there is no cause for astonishment in the fact that far more travelers set out in those days than ever arrived at their destinations.

These older ways were the roads that the faery folk

loved—not so much for their actual use, but rather as a means of design and definition: a map of the world whose interstices could provide their home and habitat. The faery folk had hated Rome, and they hated echoes of Rome with equal fervor. They hated arms and armor because arms and armor were the mechanics of empire, and they hated knighthood and chivalry because knighthood and chivalry were the ideals of empire.

When the Romans had gone, there still remained in the population they left behind the idea of a Great Britain and a concomitant cause of fealty and fellowship. The idea that *Great* Britain was the property of petty kings ambitious to be Once and Future Kings, and the guiding light of counselors ambitious to be Magi. There was more than one Arthur, more than one Merlin and more than one Round Table—but they all became one in the labyrinth of myth and history because they were all bound into one by the idea of empire and the notion that all roads should run *straight*, cutting through slopes and thickets, filling in ponds and bridging streams, and frankly disregarding matters of ill repute.

The idea of Great Britain and the dream to which it gave birth would probably have come to nothing, had it not been for the Church, but Rome was replaced by Christendom, and Christendom returned to the England the Romans had abandoned. The actual empire of Rome was replaced by the imaginary empire of God, which was all the more dangerous to the mazy roads of England and myth by virtue of its ingenious abstraction.

Christendom gave the knights of England a Holy Grail which none of them was good enough to touch, and made them mad with virtue as they strove for worthiness. The idea of chivalry had never quite contrived to extinguish lust from their hearts, but the idea of the Grail was all the stronger for its manifest absurdity; it forced the minds of knights and princes into straight and narrow paths, so that their vaulting ambition became ever-more-narrowly focused on broad, straight *highways:* highways fit for ironclad chariots of vulgar fire.

Because of chivalry and Christendom it was not easy for La Belle Dame Sans Merci to follow the force of her defining impulse, but she was a creature of paradox from the very start: an amalgam of elements at war. For folk such as her there is no end but catastrophe, no medium but hazard.

That evening, a knight whose name was Florian had sent his horse to a well-appointed stable and his servants to sleep in the straw. He could have had a bed for himself, a loaf of bread and a cup of mead, and dreamless sleep—but that was not his way. Sir Florian was a chaste knight oft disposed to prayer, to the rapt contemplation of the heavens, and to the frank disregard of matters of ill repute. Rather than dispossess a doleful but dutiful host of the only good mattress for miles around he set himself to sleep beneath the stars, at one of those mysterious crossroads where the winding paths of myth and England intersect in a tangled knot. He had been warned of Jack A-Lanterns and their kin, but he considered his stubborn virtue to be proof against all temptation.

There are those who say that men see most and best when blinded, but the principle of pedantry defines such persons as fools and poets. The prosaic accuracy of the matter is that men see *most* in gentle sunlight, but *best* when they are no more than half-blinded; it is then that light and shadow have the greatest power of conjuration. The stars shone brightly enough that night, but the autumn air was cold and the mists condensed as soon as the sun had set.

Long afterward, Sir Florian thought that his ill-remembered visitor might have come from the direction of the lake, perhaps from behind its rampart of withered sedge. In the beginning, however, all he knew was that she was suddenly *there*, her silver hair hanging loose about her shoulders. She was clad in white—or so it seemed against the darkness of the night—and he might have taken her for a saint, had it not been for her wild eyes.

Even though the faery was more beautiful by far than any human woman he had ever seen, without the least trace of a pock mark on either cheek, the innocent but armored Florian would have thought her good *had it not been for the wildness in her eyes*.

"What dost thou want with me, Lady Fair?" he asked, abridging the final word as half a hundred men had done before, without quite knowing why.

"I'd like a garland for my head," she told him, as she had told half a hundred before, "and bracelets for my arms. Summer's all but dead, and I must mourn her passing."

For a precious moment, Sir Florian hesitated. The lady stood as still as still could be, and his eyes had never beheld anything so marvelous. He felt that if he turned aside from the vision he would never see anything so lovely in all his life—but a man in search of Christendom's Grail is not in search of loveliness.

"I will not give thee anything," the knight replied, with a catch in his throat. "I know what thou art by the hectic wildness of thine eyes." Saying so—and with considerable effort of will—Sir Florian drew his sword and raised it up before him, so that the hilt and handguard were displayed in the sign of the holy cross.

To his consternation, the lady did not disappear. Nor did she move, for she had the art of lying still even when she stood erect. Had she only moved, the spell might have been broken, but she was as still as still could be and her beauty had all the force of sorcery. She waited for a moment before she replied: a moment sufficient to win the damnation of any ordinary man.

"If thou wishest to be rid of me," she said, in the end, "thou hast only to banish me with a threefold conjuration. Do so, and thou wilt never see me again although thou livest a hundred years and more—but I must warn thee that if uncertainty should cause thee to falter or hesitate in mid-injunction, I shall have the power to trouble thy most secret dreams."

Had Sir Florian been as true a knight as Parsifal or Galahad he would have called upon the name of God without delay, and pronounced the threefold curse as easily as any other feat of simple arithmetic, but he was what he was and the thought that sprang to the forefront of his mind was a question.

Can a man sin in his dreams?

Had the question been followed by an answer the knight might yet have been saved, but it was not. He did not know the answer. Whether his ignorance was folly or wisdom, he did not know the answer.

"In the name of the Lord," he cried, "I banish thee! I banish thee! I . . . banish thee!"

When she vanished on the instant, neither recoiling from his curse nor turning on her heel, nor fading into the mists that dressed the shore of the lake, the knight almost believed that he had won. No sooner had the faery gone, however, than he felt an ache in his heart born of the knowledge that he would never see her like again should he live a hundred years and more—unless she came to him in a troublesome and secret dream.

Again the thought came into his mind: *Can a man sin in his dreams?*

Now, alas, he knew the answer. He knew it with a certainty that charmed and terrified him, in equal and by no means paradoxical parts.

La Belle Dame Sans Merci could work her wiles in the world of dreams as easily as any other. She preferred the world of mist and stars and mazy roads, but that was merely her whim. There were those among the faery folk even in those days who thought the empire of the earth far overrated, and not worth fighting for, but La Belle Dame Sans Merci was not among them. She loved the air and the dew, the light and the shadow which made her earthly form, despite that they were elements at war which would, in time, tear her raggedly apart.

She went to Sir Florian in his dreams that very night, as he had all but invited her to do with a moment's hesitation in his speech. She bade him come to her, while she lay as still as still could be—stiller by far than any human woman could ever have contrived at any distance from the brink of death. She was as delicately pale as a wisp of frosty mist, but she had the gift of touch unspoiled by the contempt of familiarity. La Belle Dame Sans Merci touched the knight as lightly as the forefinger of fever; and set the fire of Purgatory alight throughout his kindling flesh.

Sir Florian gave her a garland for her head, woven from prettier flowers than ever grew in the earthly spring, perfumed more fragrantly than any musk of nature or artifice. He bound her hands and waist with vines and she thrilled to the binding, knowing that every circle was a fortress wall imprisoning his heart. He set her upon his horse so that they might ride together, both astride, so that the rhythm of the stallion's gallop might carry them beyond the reach of any roads, to the jeweled infinity east of the sun and west of the moon and the quiet eternity beyond.

And so they rode, imprisoned both by the saddle and harness which contained them, borne by the power of a tireless mount, from the curving roads to the undulant hills and away into the airy wilderness, where the height made them giddy and giddier, until the subtler rhythm of a horse's sturdy heart displaced the clatter of its hoofbeats and they passed at last into the jeweled infinity east of the sun and west of the moon.

Then La Belle Dame Sans Merci took Sir Florian, in her turn, into the warmer and warmest depths of the motherly earth: to those caverns measureless to man that lie beneath the purgatorial realms of Tartarus. There she sang to him, and sang again, and gazed at him with such apparent adoration that he closed her wild wild eyes with kisses, unable to bear the yearning of her stare.

The knight unwound the binding vines from the faery's helpless wrists while she trembled sightless in his arms, drawing every vestige of intoxication from the pressure of his body upon hers and the congruent pounding of their hearts. She took them from him, and opened her eyes again, commanding him to tilt his head and bare his throat.

There was no hesitation this time, no faltering in his resolve. It was not that he was not afraid, but only that he was content to savor his fear as he savored every least sensation which still had the power to stir him, all equalized as pleasure.

La Belle Dame Sans Merci wound the vine about Sir Florian's slender neck, and began to draw it tighter. The pressure she exerted was gentle at first, and it was only by the slowest imaginable degrees that it grew more and more insistent.

Now he closed his own eyes, even though there had not been the least trace of wildness in his sotted gaze.

Still it was not finished, for the sense of touch still remained to Sir Florian's dizzied mind, and for the first time since consciousness was born in his infant brain the knight felt as a faery might feel, taking nothing of that sensation for granted. He could never have done so had he been awake, but he was not. In dreams, sometimes, even humans are privileged to forget the follies and fervors of flesh. For a moment and more Sir Florian was well-nigh incorporeal, yet gifted still with the sense of touch.

Had the knight been truly incorporeal, of course, the strangling vine could not have harmed him; but even in dreams, the follies and fatalities of flesh may reassert their sullen shift upon the human form.

When the delicious moment was gone, Sir Florian fell into the sleep within sleep: an abyssal deep as far beyond the shallows of dreamless peace as quiet eternity lies beyond the jeweled infinity east of the sun and west of the moon.

* * *

The story would have ended there but for one thing.

It did not matter in the least to La Belle Dame Sans Merci that Sir Florian had felt, if only for an instant, as a faery might feel. She knew it, of course, but there was nothing in his momentary revaluation of the preciousness of touch to strike a spark of empathy. When she drew back from him, however, and saw him lying cushioned in the earth, *as still as still could be*, she saw for the first time how beautiful he was.

It occurred to her, in a way that no other notion had ever occurred to her before, that he was unusual among his own kind—and perhaps unique.

When she had appeared to the knight by the lake the faery had only seen him in general terms. The wildness of her own eyes had ensured that when she looked at him she saw nothing but arms and armor, holiness and chivalry, empire and progress. When she had first come to him in his dream she had seen even less, for she had been in the grip of her own passion. There is nothing human about a faery's passion, but it is passion nevertheless, fiercer in its own way than the lumpen kind of lust which oozes in a human's veins. It was she, then, who had consented to be tied about the wrists and waist, knowing that the binder is more securely captive than the bound. It was she who had consented to be placed astride his mount so that the two of them might ride from the earth into the sky, to soar beyond the limitations of the air, knowing that the commanded is more securely in control than the commander. It was she, then, who had been caught between light and dark, as between full sight and blindness, seeing so much *more* as to be convinced that she saw *everything*.

It was she, now, who realized with unaccustomed, appalling and massive accuracy that the *best* sight is not necessarily the *most* sight, and that beauty works most insidiously in misty uncertainty.

La Belle Dame Sans Merci touched her hand to her own

throat, and asked herself whether she rather than he might have been more securely strangled by the knot that she had made. She closed her own less-than-wild eyes in order to wonder whether *his* consent might conceivably have more power than *her* command.

And she did not know the answer.

For the moment, at least, she did not know the answer.

La Belle Dame Sans Merci was afraid, and could not count her fear solely in the common currency of intensity, in which all is equalized as pleasure.

She was afraid for herself, and rightly so. Creatures of paradox cannot abide *doubt*. Doubt is the crack which opens the way to destruction.

La Belle Dame Sans Merci might still have saved herself, if she had searched assiduously for the answer to her question, found it and made it fast—but she did not.

Instead, she murmured the words which came spontaneously into her head as she looked down at the pale Sir Florian, who was lying as still as still could be.

"O for a fiery gloom and thee," she whispered, wishing as the words escaped her that the two of them might be other than they were, further elsewhere and further elsewhen than the jeweled infinity east of the sun and west of the moon or the quiet eternity beyond.

Alas, there is no elsewhere or elsewhen beyond infinity and eternity, for any such place and time would be a blatant contradiction in terms—and neither human nor faery can be other than they are, however paradoxical their natures might be.

Sir Florian awoke with the light of dawn and the warning words of a warrior host echoing in his ears. It seemed to him, although he could not quite imagine why, that kings and princes had come to him, with all their armored knights in train, with the pallor of death upon all their faces, crying: "La Belle Dame Sans Merci! La Belle Dame Sans Merci! La Belle Dame Sans Merci hath thee in thrall!"

He found himself on a cold hillside far above the lake and its miasmic mists. While he watched the silver light of dawn play upon the clouds clustered on the eastern horizon and a few frail sunbeams flickering in the nearby mists the knight felt a flush of fever in his heart and upon his cheek; but when he rose to his feet the fever died like the vestige of a dream and when stronger rays of the rising sun burst through the clouds a moment afterward he saw the golden track it laid upon the still and silent waters of the lake as a great straight road connecting earth with Heaven.

In that instant of revelation, Sir Florian knew that it would not matter how many kings were fated to fall in battle, nor how many knights were doomed to perish in hopeless quest of the Holy Grail of Christendom. He *knew*, without a moment's faltering, that the cause of progress and empire could not be stopped, nor even significantly interrupted, and that Great Britain would one day exist.

He knew, too, that he ought to feel proud of his knowledge, grateful for his certainty. He knew that the gift of this revelation was a token that he had won the greatest battle of all: the battle of right over wrong, of reality over myth, of reason over emotion. Within this knowledge, however, there was the faintest seed of doubt—not doubt that it was true, but doubt that truth was as precious as he had been taught to hold it.

He noticed then that although dawn had broken, there had been no chorus of voices to greet it. No birds sang.

Autumn had not yet given way to winter, but no birds sang.

Sir Florian shivered then, in the cold morning air. A strange thought came into his head, which he could not understand at all but which filled him with a longing more desperate than any he had known before or ever would again.

O for a fiery gloom and thee!

He could not understand at first what it was that he longed for, or why, but the thought persisted nevertheless, as plaintive as the echo of a soul torn apart by damnation, until he began to remember. He never recovered all the memory, but in the fullness of time he remembered far more than enough, with the consequence that the enigmatic thought echoed down his straight bright days—and deeper still in his long and lonely nights—though he lived to be a hundred years and more.

O for a fiery gloom—and thee!

The Light That Passes Through You

Conrad Williams

I was on my way to work when Louise appeared, seeming to peel away from the gray cement walls of the block of flats opposite. She drifted into my arms. I could feel her bones, thin and febrile, poking through the shredded leather of her jacket. As I drew her inside, I noticed it was a jacket I'd given her, five years ago—the last time I'd seen her. She made sticky, glottal noises into the crook of my arm as I led her upstairs. Her hair was matted with dog shit; her mouth pinched and blue.

"What are you on?" I asked, but the question could have been directed at myself. I should have been taking her to hospital. She didn't answer.

I sat her down in the hallway while I ran a bath. My face dissolved in the mirror.

"Can you . . . ?" Clearly, she couldn't, so I undressed her myself, trying to keep my eyes off the breasts I'd once caressed. Unbidden, a memory of me rubbing olive oil into them on a hot beach somewhere made my cheeks burn. "Let's get you into this bath. Come on, Louise." She'd lost weight. The skin around her navel was purpuric and slightly raised, like that of an orange. I hoped her condition was due to vitamin deficiency and exhaustion. I wished I hadn't written to her.

She revived a little when the suds enveloped her. She found some kind of focus, frowning as I no doubt looped in and out of view. Her slight overbite rested upon her bottom lip: something I'd once found irresistible. Now she just looked afraid.

"It's been like—" she began, and coughed a thick clot of mucus onto her chin, "—like I've been drowning. All this time. Just as I thought I was leaving, going out like a candle, you rescued me." She collapsed slowly into the water; her ribs, for a moment, seemed like huge denuded fingers pressing against the flesh from inside, trying to punch their way out.

There was nothing particularly unusual about our relationship to warrant my attempt to contact her. At the time, I was nineteen, she eighteen. We said we loved each other. Although we had no money and still lived with our parents, we believed we were independent, different from anyone else because we were intelligent; we were mature about sex.

We were stupid. We were children.

We holidayed in Wales one summer, borrowing a caravan that belonged to a friend of my father's. We buried each other in the sand and lost sleep, fucking with impunity. It was exciting, hearing her approach an orgasm without fear of a parent barging in on us. She missed a period.

I wanted to go with her on the day she aborted. I'd traveled to Stockport with her to make the appointment, sitting in a waiting room trying to avoid the female faces around me, watching faded vehicles slew across wet, wasted dual carriageways which reached into the dun fug over Manchester. Louise's mother went with her when the time came because she paid for the operation. The private clinic was picketed by pro-lifers that day. Louise told me they pleaded with her to reconsider, that they would help to bring up the baby. It fluttered in her womb. Ink blot eye. Fingernails.

When I saw Louise again, she'd gained something which

made me nervous for a while, something which shone dully in her eyes as if the surgeons had implanted some strange, ancient wisdom at the time of termination. We talked about it and grew very close; smiles and kisses drew a frosting over the bad area, like icing decorates the mold in a cake. I suppose we believed we were richer for the experience. Louise became clinging; I thought it was love. I never believed that we would be together forever but she didn't doubt it, as if this trauma provided a bond we must never break. Sometimes I'd lie awake at night feeling like the carcass of a sheep; she, a dark scavenger of emotions, burrowing ever deeper into the heart of me. That I felt guilty, for entertaining such thoughts shouldn't have brought me comfort but it did.

It was like laying down a bundle of kindling when I tucked her into my bed. I left a window open and glanced at London's center. It seemed strange that I would be working in that glut of noise down there while she slept, a Rapunzel in her tower. I left a note with my number by the bed, in case she should wake up. I had to lean over and smell her mouth.

On the Northern Line, I tried to spot other faces which bore the same kind of expression as Louise. A fusion of vulnerability and assuredness. The look of someone who knows they will be protected and cared for. I couldn't find anything like it here. Maybe it was London which prescribed a countenance of stone; to progress here, you oughtn't allow any emotion to slip.

It was a photograph that did it. A black-and-white shot of Louise staring out of my bedroom window, one breast free of a voluminous cardigan, her body painted white with morning sunshine. She wore a sleepy, gluttonous expression: We'd just made love. I'd placed some crumpled cellophane over the lens to soften her image. When the picture fell out of a book, I wondered what she was doing now. It pained me to think that the partners we felt so deeply for can be allowed to drift out of our lives. We were both five years older than the time it had ended. Old enough, responsible enough to face each other on a new footing and be friends . . .

. . . Ha.

I thought about her all day. I even tried calling her but all I got was my Duo plus: *"Hi, this is Sean, all calls gratefully received, except those from Jeffrey Archer or Noel Edmonds . . ."*

"Lou? Are you there? Pick up the phone."

I left the office as early as I could and caught the tube back to Belsize Park, having to wait an agonizing time at Camden for the Edgware connection, which was late due to I don't fucking know—litter on the line, driver claustrophobia, lack of application.

She was still in bed when I got back. I heated a bowl of celery soup in the microwave and fed it to her, remembering too late that she despised celery. And what else? Beetroot? She didn't seem to mind now though, her belly grateful for anything to mop up the misery in which it was dissolving. The early February sky shuttered out the light in gray grades across my wall; she became more beautiful as darkness mired her features.

She sat up against the headboard, the duvet slipping away from her body. She didn't attempt to cover herself. I gave her a T-shirt.

"What happened?" I asked, lighting a candle—she wouldn't have appreciated the harshness of a bare bulb.

"I don't know," she said. "It's like I described earlier. I feel as if I've been gnawed away from the inside. For a while, I thought it was cancer."

I bit down on my suggestion that it still might be; the candle's uncertain light sucked the gaunt angles of her face and shoulders into chiaroscuro.

"Lie with me," she said.

My sleep was fitful; I was expecting her to murmur something that would shape the formless panic I was barely managing to fasten inside. I lay awake listening to horses clatter lazily up Primrose Hill Road at five A.M., trying to delve for conversations we'd had, or pregnant pauses stuffed with meaning. All I could remember was the sound of her crying.

I nipped outside at around seven, when she was stirring, to the baker's for croissants. I picked up a pot of jam and the newspaper, a pint of milk and headed back to the flat. Only gone ten minutes, it was some surprise to find her showered and dressed, lying on the bed and listening to one of my Radiohead albums. "We'll go out after brekkie," she said. "You can show me around Camden."

"How are you feeling?" I asked, unwrapping the croissants and offering her a knife.

"Better." She broke off a corner of bread and chewed it, dipping her next bit into the virgin surface of the jam, getting crumbs in there. That was something that pissed me off no end when we were together. It didn't bother me now. Maturity, I suppose. She looked at me slyly, as if she were testing me; I ignored it.

"It's good to see you, Louise," I said. "Really."

"It was a beautiful letter. How could I not answer it?"

"I didn't necessarily expect to see you on my doorstep . . . you know, a letter, a phone call or something, to let me know how you were."

"It was an invocation, Sean."

"A what?"

"I said, it was an invitation. You called to me, I was on the brink. Your timing was immaculate." She raised an eyebrow. "It always was."

Camden was pinned down under a grimy, stifling sky. Drawing breath was like sucking exhaust fumes through a burning electric blanket. She leaned against me as we threaded through its unfriendly streets, funneled into passageways and alleys pumping with sound and people.

"This is wild!" she laughed, the plum gash of her mouth halving the pallid remains of her face, once so fleshy and pinkish; at once she looked both like the most alive and the most enervated person and in Camden that was saying something. She looked synthetic, the skin too tight, as if it might split and waft the smell of plastic toys over me. But her eyes had lost their initial vagueness, fastening on individual blurs of color as it all streamed past us, like a hawk tracking its dinner. The whites were so clear they were almost blue.

We tooled up and down the main drag, trying on sunglasses and hats. She fingered jewelry and squeezed the arms of thick sweaters, which made me feel even hotter. I pointed out the egg-tipped folly of GM-TV and she scoffed when I told her it was a listed building. I showed her where I'd seen Adam Ant handing over some coins to a charity collector as we crossed the walkway over the Grand Union Canal into a tight knot of stalls and alcoves. The heat was building up here; candles were sagging on their displays and the drifts of antiques shone dully in a solid mass of bronzed light. Every time Louise brushed against me or held on to my arm, I sagged, as if she were transmitting weight through her touch. At such moments, she would perk up and become animated, trying on hats or mugging in smeared mirrors, laughing as my face grew greasy and pale.

The stream of people was endless. The pavements were so obstructed, pedestrians spilled into the road, slowing the traffic which began to trail back toward Mornington Crescent Tube. The crowds seemed to be swelling, like a single bloated body, inflated by sore tempers and the ceaseless, airless heat. I pulled Louise into a café, worried by a mild panic that had transmitted itself into an hallucination of us crushed beneath a stampede of bodies as they attempted to escape their stifling skins. I bought cappuccino, hoping I could relax sufficiently at the counter before she noticed my discomfort.

When I turned round, Louise was bathed in sunshine. Because of the angle of her chair and the way the sunlight was blocked by the weirdly squashed conglomeration of buildings, only she was favored by its color. It invaded the thick pile of her hair, seeming to imbue each filament, like one of those carbon fiber lamps. It moved across her face like thick fluid and, somehow, seemed of her too, picking out the configuration of her bones slouched inside their fleshy housing, curled into the chair. A comma of wet sunshine touched her lower lip and I found myself wishing I could kiss it away. I still wanted her, even after such a long time had passed. No time at all. Everyone around her seemed to diminish, shadows on the wane, growing sluggish like figures trapped in tar. And then she looked at me. For a moment, I wasn't sure what kind of fire it was that filled her eyes, certain only that it wasn't human, but then the moment passed, and she smiled and everyone was a component of the greater animation around us once more. She just seemed like a willowy girl, lost in the scrum. Unremarkable.

"Get this down you," I said, pushing across her coffee. "It'll put hairs on your chest."

"This place, Camden that is, reminds me of my last few years," Louise said, furring her top lip with the froth of her cappuccino. I don't know why, really. Something about the way everything feels sad and unreal but is all disguised by movement. I bet this place seems more like its true self when the shops close and everyone pisses off."

"What have you been up to these last few years?" I asked that, when all I wanted to know was how she'd turned up in such a state on my doorstep. Now that she looked in some semblance of control, I was finding it hard to believe that I'd seen her like that, *in extremis*.

"It felt like I was being followed. No, that's not right, it felt like I was being hunted. I had to keep moving or I felt

I'd be consumed by something so big I couldn't even see it. Just an aspect of it, I saw, usually in sleep, moving furiously, like an engine part well oiled, pistoning and thrashing around. It belonged to something that was vast and after me. Hungry for me." She took another drink of coffee, then reached over and tapped a man in a vest and combat trousers on the shoulder. Asked him for a cigarette. After he'd lit it for her, she turned back to me and spoke around a mouthful of bluish smoke.

"I left Warrington just after we finished . . . after you finished with me. I got a job with a waste disposal firm in Keighley."

"Keighley? Why Keighley, of all places? Middle of nowhere."

"No, *I* was the middle of nowhere. Anywhere, everywhere else was a grip on something real. I was on Temazepam by this time, for my depression and insomnia but it wasn't working. The doctor gave me Prozac, and that was better, for a while, until I wanted to do nothing other than sit in front of my window and watch the litter being blown across the street. I kicked all that but it was like the feeling had settled into me and wouldn't go away. I slept late, ate less, became constipated. I began to appreciate a particular kind of darkness I found in the loft. There was a cat, Marlon, his name was, that would sleep up there. Made his way over the roofs and climbed in through a hole in the eaves. We'd curl up together, flinching whenever a bird's claws rattled on the tiles. It was almost magical. I felt safe; that thing that was looking for me wouldn't have me here. It was just me and Marlon and the dark. Holding on to Marlon's fur kept me real and sane. If he wasn't there, I think I would have just . . . well . . ."

"How long were you in Keighley for?" I asked, sensing a dangerous moment of self-disclosure if I let her carry on.

"Not long. I hitched a lift to Scarborough and did some work at one of the hotels. Cleaning rooms in the daytime, serving behind the bar at night. I liked it. Days off, I'd walk along the beach up to the amusement arcades. I met boys there. When it got dark we'd go behind the generators and I'd just let them do what they wanted to me. I went with this really gaunt, ill-looking boy called Felix. He was half Croatian. I sucked him off and when he came—"

"Jesus, Lou—"

"—when he came, there was blood in his semen. He blamed it on me, said I'd infected him—some nonsense like that—and he tried to strangle me. I didn't fight him off. I was struck by how beautiful he looked in the thin light rising from the harbor behind us. I think he got scared when I smiled at him. He left me alone. I like to believe you were thinking of me at that very moment. My Guardian Angel, rescued me with some attention."

I laughed nervously. I didn't like anything she was telling me. I was jealous and I was resentful of her for keeping a hold on to me. My letter hadn't been a cry for reunion, it had been a friendly endeavor to find out what was happening to someone I cared about. But I found myself hooked on her story. "And then?" I asked, my voice dead, resigned.

"I stayed in Scarborough for some time. A year or so. Things changed. I found that I seemed to be waking into thick air. Walking, blinking, breathing—it was all such an effort. Things weren't right while somehow keeping a surface of normality. I'd see something odd, but everybody else's reaction would be nonexistent and it might be hours or days before I told myself that no, it was not right but by then I'd suspect that it happened at all."

"What kind of things? What are you talking about, Louise?"

"I'm talking about the skeletons of fish on the beach flopping around, trying to get back into the water. I'm talking about sand castles that didn't dissolve when the tide touched them. A couple kissing under a streetlamp whose heads melted into each other."

"Tcha!" I said, rocking back on my seat and attracting a few glances from the punters sitting nearby. She'd drawn me into her story so effectively that this nonsense had spat me out, like a newborn, unable to cope with the sudden influx of normal sensations. I sighed and rubbed my eyes. She wouldn't give up on it though.

"A dog smoking a pipe. A parrot on a smiling tramp's shoulder picking his brains from a bleeding eye socket. Burning children playing leapfrog on a lawn."

"Stop it, Louise."

"I was there. I saw this happening."

"In Scarborough? I've been to Scarborough. The strangest thing they have there is a ghost train that squirts water at you."

"Yes. But, although it was Scarborough, it could have been anywhere. I was drawing these things to me. I was in some kind of midway. A lost soul."

I necked my coffee. I could feel myself bristling under her expectant gaze. She'd always been like this, pushing the envelope of provocation and gauging my reaction till I exploded. "If you're trying to make me feel guilty for finishing with you, you're doing fine. Not that you're one to hold a grudge."

"I don't blame you for this, Sean. I did at first. I spent all my time thinking of you. Thinking of how our child would have been two, three, four, five. You laughing and having a good time. Fucking lots of women. I played the whole victim thing. I wanted you and hated you in equal measure. I needed you. But then I realized all my misery was externalized too. It got so bad very quickly that I didn't even notice things had changed until I started paying attention to the outside world rather than my puffy face in the mirror.

"The coming of daylight seemed to take longer than it ought to in the mornings. I'd see weather forecasts predicting rain or shine but there was a constant haze, like the sun trying to force its way through mist. It never changed. I'd visit my parents and they appeared to talk through me, looking at my face but somehow misdirecting their focus as if they were talking to someone standing behind me. And then this awful sense of something coming, gravitating toward me . . ."

I noticed that I was holding her hand but I couldn't recall reaching for her. Her casual referral to her pregnancy had shamed me. I couldn't say anything.

"And you wrote to me. It was salvation. There was no longer a sense of me being consigned to limbo. Does this sound silly to you? Because there are others. I saw one or two, drifting like me, pale and withdrawn like flames that can't quite catch upon what they're supposed to be burning. People who were dismissed from somebody's life. People who had an umbilicus disconnected. God knows what would have happened to me if you hadn't written. I think I'd have faded away. Winked out. There's still something missing. Something I need in order to give me a sense of being replete but I'm buggered if I know what it is."

It was a lot to take in. I wasn't convinced by a great deal of what she'd imparted but I had a handle on her dislocation. I'd been gearing up to ask her how long she planned on staying but it didn't really matter if she stayed a few more days, if it meant she'd get back to full speed.

"A party," I said, lightly, trying to dispel the intensity that had drawn in around us. "There's a party tonight. Why don't you come? It will do you good to kick out and relax."

She appeared briefly reticent but agreed, her eyes hankering after some morsel of encouragement as we held each other's gaze for longer than necessary. It was a look I'd once suffixed with a kiss or a touch of my finger against her neck. *Don't get back into that*, I thought, pushing away from the table. I couldn't understand why she'd want to get involved with me again if there was even the shred of threat she might return to the dire illusions of her mind.

The party was at a friend's place in Hammersmith; we

were to meet by the bridge at one of the pubs which snuggled up to the Thames. Benjie was there to greet us, a tall affable lad who didn't care if he was thinning on top as long as there was a beer in front of him. One of those people who needs only the most rudimentary of introductions before getting on well with anyone, Benjie soon had Louise feeling comfortable and interesting; she soon relaxed into the evening. A fine evening it was, the sun losing itself to the strata of color banding the horizon. Great jets would lower into it as they nosed toward Heathrow. We stood and watched them halve the sky till it grew dark and cold.

For my part, I felt better now that Louise was being shared around a dozen or so other people. I could allow my anxieties to shrink within alcohol's massage and see Louise as someone more than a chipped and faded signpost to my past.

Benjie lived in a first floor flat on a wide avenue behind King Street. When we arrived, stopping off en route to buy beer from a twenty-four-hour inconvenience store that didn't sell Beck's or Toohey's, there were already around thirty people stuffed into the kitchen and living room. Overspill meant that the landing and stairs were occupied too, by flaky-looking individuals wadded into sheepskin coats with excessively furred collars. They probably looked furtive because they'd crashed the gig, not that it mattered: Benjie was hospitable to all. I followed him into his room where a hill of coats and plastic bags swamped his bed. A couple was leaned across them, kissing each other with such fervor that it seemed his mouth must engulf the entirety of her lower jaw. His left hand violently kneaded the pliant spread of her right breast. She could have been dead. I sensed Louise stiffen beside me and squeezed her hand, understanding her revulsion. The union was void of any tenderness. Perhaps Benjie noticed it too, because there was a needle in his voice when he asked them to move over. They simply stopped kissing and staggered from the room, lobotomized expressions all round. The woman was wearing six-inch rubber platforms and a black cat suit. An exterior white leather corset battled to keep her chest *in situ*. She hadn't even bothered to take off her heart-shaped satchel with its blunt rubber spines.

"Kids, eh?" said Benjie, plonking his sweater on the pile. I followed suit but Louise refused to take her coat off. "Actually," Benjie continued, gesturing after the zombies, "that was Simon. Top bloke. Known him since school. Spacecat. Does a bit too much of the wacky baccy to keep him compus mentus but you can't hold that against him."

So, the party. Which was as punishing as any party I'd been to before. We drank. And then there was a spot of serious drinking. And a post-drink drinking session and then a long stretch of complete and utter drinking. Benjie's windows in the living room had been sealed shut by whoever had last painted the flat. It grew so stifling that the ceiling eventually shed a thin, bitter rain of nicotian moisture. I ranged around the room, trying to find the door so that I might lose some of my own fluids but it appeared that someone had painted that in too. I started laughing till panic hovered but rescued myself by simply pissing my pants. It proved an excellent sobering technique. I poured what was left of my Budweiser onto my jeans and made like I was the clumsiest arse ever but nobody cared a toss. I found the door where I'd left it and spilled on to the landing. Someone was playing Nirvana—*Drain You*—with the volume turned all the way up to eleven. I yelled a line from the chorus and dived for the toilet only to find a queue which, in all probability, was the longest toilet queue in the history of clenched bladders. I had the last laugh, though, when my brain caught up with the fact that I'd already been.

Simon's disembodied head loomed in front of mine. "Where the fuck is the rest of you?" I almost shrieked, but it was all there, just slow in arriving. God, I was spannered. He grinned, showing off a gold premolar. He smelled of beer,

smoke, and CK One but then, so did everybody else. His
skin possessed a greasy olive hue; up close I could see that
his lips were rugose and discolored. His rubberized partner,
I guessed, was being trampolined elsewhere.

"Highayemsimon," he said. "Hooeyoo?"

"Me no speaka your language," I replied, suddenly cot-
toning on to his flighty Scots burr. I barked laughter and
slapped him on the arm. "Sorry. I thought . . . I thought . . .
oh, cocks to it. I'm Shhhhhuh . . . Sean. Benj told me you
were Simon but it's good to have it confirmed."

"Hoowazatlassyacuminwi?"

"Her name's Louise." I came right back with that one, getting into the swing of it.

"Shizaspankinlassamtellinyi."

"Too right." I sensed he was waiting for me to continue.
"She's not with me, if that's what you're wondering." If I'd
had my brains in properly, I'd have asked him to be tame on
her; she wasn't ready for some fast-talking shagmeister
bundling her into his bed. Talking about Louise reminded
me that she was here. I caught sight of her standing on the
edge of an intense circle, watching the interplay. She
looked—God, strange word to use but it summed up her appearance she looked *ripe*. Her face was jutting and beautiful, her eyes hungry on everyone. Having finally divested
herself of the coat, her breasts hugged the deep collar of her
blouse like loaves in an oven besting their tins. No longer
the *ingénue* I'd staggered into adulthood alongside, she appeared confident and armed with secrets, like a soldier returned from a killing field.

But that could have just been the alcohol, twatting around
with my head.

I started toward her, eager to let loose some of the
thoughts with which I'd been so circumspect that afternoon.
I wanted to draw her into the crook of my arm and tell her
I'd missed her. Tell her I was sorry.

But then Simon was locked onto her, their bodies flush

with each other as they traded words. I watched them flirt, dipping heads against ears so that lips brushed lobes. Yoked together, I watched the tethered jewel at Louise's throat move with each undulation they created. Violence spread through me. I wish I could have let it come. Louise's capitulation and Benjie's hand on my shoulder prevented me. In that moment, Simon was condemned.

Black out.

I surfaced from a terrible dream in which I'd been kissing a woman whose lips were sticky, whose tongue, whenever it emerged to roil against mine, was coated in a clear membrane. She worked my mouth with spidery endeavor, knitting it closed with her adhesive spit. Black eyes burning into mine. When she wrestled with her clothing, to reveal that yawning part of her which would dissolve and ingest me, I lurched away, opening my eyes to dawn as it drizzled the curtains. Bodies were sprawled around me. I hauled myself upright, shuddering with cold and the mother and father of all hangovers. The Fear unzipped its dark little bag and teased me with its contents but I couldn't remember anything beyond Benjie, me, and a bottle of vodka. My jeans felt stiff against my legs. There was a smear of lipstick on the back of my hand.

I negotiated the snoring corpses till I was on the landing. Benjie's door was shut. I remembered. Some time in the night I'd gone for a glass of water, opened his bedroom, mistaking it for the kitchen. Louise was straddling Simon in the bed; the hill of coats had slid to the floor. The first thing I saw was the last thing to follow me back to sleep. Her breastbone, slick with sweat, or his saliva, overlaid with a lozenge of pure white light which pulsed with every languid stroke of their lovemaking. There was light elsewhere on her, solidifying in clusters and then dispersing like minute shoals of fish only to coalesce once more on her thigh, her mons, her navel. But it was that oval of light on her sternum which transfixed me, even as her eyes met with mine and she flew toward a climax that terrified me for its intensity. Simon was paling beneath her, jerking around: a rabbit mauled by a stoat. His hand reached out, almost desperately. Froth concealed his mouth. Louise was keening, slamming down upon him and baring her teeth, eyes rolled back till I could see their whites. The light inside her intensified and gathered at her core, retreating from the surface of her skin till it was but a milky suggestion deep inside her. Then it sank to where he must have been embedded in her. I couldn't watch anymore, not when she drove her fingers into his mouth to allay his scream.

Was that really how it had happened? My sozzled brain painted a detailed picture, but my dream had seemed equally alive. If it had happened, how could I have been so calm as to close the door on them and get back among the dead in the living room? How could I have returned to sleep?

I thought of the first words Louise had mumbled to me after her abortion all those years ago. She'd said: "I was so close to darkness, it felt like I could never again be close to the light."

She'd been chasing it ever since. I'd taken it from her and something as simple as a letter had given it back. A letter that had been as much a cry for help as an olive branch. I thought of the places she'd passed through over the years, alternate lands that had claimed her as she drifted, loveless. I thought of how easy it could be to consign someone to such torment. I tried to imagine the hunger that needed to be sated in order to forge a way back.

My hand on the door. It swung inward. The pile of coats was still there. Beneath them, the bed appeared not to have been slept in. The room was still, its occupants gone. I was happy to leave it that way but found myself entering the room. There was a scorched smell. A cigarette burn, probably. I dragged the covers off the bed. A thin plug of mucus, streaked with blood, stained the undersheet.

"Simon?" I said to it.

A sound drew me to the window. She was standing by the street-lamp, which died at that moment. Subtle light crept through the avenue. I heard a milk float play its glassy tunes far away. She was smiling as she waited, holding her coat closed on whatever it was that burned inside her. I sniffed and dug my sweater out of the pile, went down to hold her hand and send her a plea through my lips when I kissed her.

Private Words

Mark W. Tiedemann

 May, 1936

Conny, he's asking for you."

She blinked in the bright wash of morning light and looked up at Geoffrey. His face was pale, making the scar across his cheek look like a slight fold of skin.

Conny sat forward in the overstuffed chair. It had seemed the most comfortable chair in the house the night before, but now her back ached. She rubbed sleepers from her eyes. "What time is it?"

"A little past seven." He stepped back, hands in pockets. "He's been awake less than half an hour. The nurse is with him."

"How is he?"

"Not good."

Conny stood and her head swam. She remembered dreaming, and a half-real tingle in her abdomen. It startled her and she almost asked if William had been writing. But the images fled as soon as she tried to capture them, like ghosts.

She went to the window, stretching, and gazed out at the slope of land that ended at the river a hundred yards below. No dream. They had returned to the House. Her house now.

She had smelled the traces of her uncle's cherry tobacco when they arrived last night, surprisingly clear after all this time.

"I called Dr. Ludi," Geoffrey said. "I still think we should have taken him to the hospital."

"That's not what he wanted. Is there coffee?"

"In his room."

Conny used the bathroom. Feeling more awake, the dull pain in her back almost gone afterward, she walked down the hall.

William looked like a miniature in the mass of pillows and blankets on the huge canopied bed. Small and bleached. The last few months of illness had etched out his features, robbed him of expression, as if sifting him away. His hair lay matted against his skull and his beard needed trimming and combing.

The room smelled of sweat and soup, the weak breeze from the open window doing little more than stirring the air and mixing the odors. A pallet with pages of marked-up manuscript lay next to him.

Conny gestured toward the door and the nurse left.

"I'm sorry," William said. "Were you sleeping?"

"No. I can't sleep in the sunshine for long."

"Of course not." He coughed thinly and lifted a blood-stained rag to his mouth. "My letters. You still have them?"

Conny sat on the edge of the bed and took his free hand. "You mean 'our' letters, don't you? Of course I have them."

"Of course. They're yours. Yours and Geoffrey's. No one else."

"You were working?" She nodded toward the pallet.

"Last words. Notes to you. Something . . . a closure."

"Dr. Ludi's been called. Geoffrey wants you to go to the hospital."

"Shh. Doesn't matter. The letters. Do you have them?"

"Yes, I said—"

"Get them. The first one, anyway. I want to remember."

Conny peered out the door. Geoffrey stood in the hallway, leaning on a windowsill. "The trunk," she said. "Would you bring it?" He nodded and hurried off. Conny glanced at William. He seemed to be sleeping now. *Only sleeping*, she thought, *I'd know the difference*.

Then Geoffrey was back, carrying the heavy oak box edged in tarnished brass. He placed it in her arms and went back to the window. He spent as little time as possible with William now; he could not bear the smell and taste and waiting of death. Conny tried not to be angry with him—everyone had weaknesses and flaws—but it would not have hurt him just now to have brought the trunk all the way into the room. She wrestled it to the bed and set it at the foot of the mattress.

When she looked up, William's eyes stared at her, brightly feverish. She unlocked the box and pushed up the lid.

Within lay neat bundles of papers, each stack tied with a ribbon. Seventeen of them, one for each year until this last. A few loose sheets lay on top. A rich, musky odor escaped, displacing the sickroom stench for a few moments. Conny licked her lips and dug to the bottom of the box. She took out the oldest bundle, bound in a brittle blue band. The pages showed faint yellowing.

"D'you remember the first one?" William asked. "The first time, really. Here. In this house."

She undid the bow and sorted through the handwritten sheets. "Here. Yes." She read the date. "I'd forgotten it was in March."

"Read it to me."

March, 1919

They laughed about it later, the way she kept saying no and giggling even as she unbuttoned his vest, his shirt, his pants. Not here, she meant, not in her uncle's study, in sight

of his enormous desk and his books; no, while she helped
him undo her girdle and roll down her stockings; no, in a
kind of disbelief, while his hands trembled as they brushed
her breasts; no again, until he kissed her and their mouths
became busy with other sounds in a different language. She
liked the feel of his beard on her skin, the exhilaration of his
belly against hers. Not here, she wanted to say, they could
sneak up to her room and lock the door, down the hall from
where her uncle slept upstairs, morphically coddled by one
glass of claret too many. But there was no question of yes,
not for weeks now.

She had come from New York to stay with her British relatives, to see Oxford, London, perhaps tour the continent.
He had been helping her uncle with a translation of some
Latin texts she had been forbidden to see. The tension between them had not been immediate, but Conny could
barely remember that first week when he had been little
more than part of the furniture.

The leather divan had not been intended for sex—the
lumpy, squeaking surface seemed to grab at them, refused to
let them slide or find comfort fully stretched out, and her
head jammed against the arm, bending her neck awkwardly.
Before she could find a different position, he was inside her.
She closed her eyes and concentrated on each sensation,
drawing her legs up and around him, determined to mine as
much compensation as she could for the guilt she knew she
would feel later.

Too many sensations. The smooth texture of his skin, the
pressure of his hands, one on her shoulder, the other on her
right breast; the rush of his breathing in her ear; the tension
building in her stomach, as if someone were holding her inside, a safe, warm embrace. Far too many sensations. She
realized that she would have to do this again just to count
them all.

His breathing became ragged and he moved faster. Sweat
slicked their flesh. Suddenly all the stress in his body re-

leased, along with five or six sharp breaths. He shuddered, then lay still, panting and damp. Finished. He raised himself up on his arms and smiled.

"We must do that again."

Conny laughed anxiously. "Of course." She felt vaguely disappointed and wanted to ignore it.

He gestured across the study. "We've made a bit of a mess."

Their clothes were everywhere. Conny felt herself blush when she spotted her chemise draped over the green-shelled lamp on the desk. She caught his eye and they burst out laughing, Conny tapping a finger to her lips and making shushing sounds. "Someone will hear," she said.

"Would you mind so much?"

"No." Surprised at her own boldness, she reached for him.

"Wait," he said, catching her hand and kissing her fingers. He climbed off her and went to the desk.

Crossing the study, Conny saw all at once how thin he was. Frail. His shoulder blades protruded and she could count each vertebrae. His skin gleamed like molten wax.

"I want to give you something," he said, sitting down in her uncle's high-backed chair. He searched the drawers till he found paper, then took Professor Carlisle's ivory pen. He ran his fingers through his hair, closed his eyes for a moment, then began writing. "Something more than my exhaustion, anyway."

Conny pushed herself up a bit and watched him. William Heath had written a novel, which he had sent off to a publisher, and he had shown her some of his poetry, published in *The English Review*. He was self-conscious about it, though, as if writing was the wrong thing for him, or that he was inadequate to the challenge.

It amazed her, after a time, how natural became the sight of him naked behind the huge oaken desk, intently scribbling away. Absurd and comic, yes, scandalous, and a little frightening. But while he wrote Conny imagined herself like this every night, watching him write, afterplay of their love-making.

"I love you, William."

He hesitated just before he looked up. "Really?"

"Yes, really."

He seemed to think about it. "Good," he nodded. "Good." And continued writing.

Conny slid a hand between her thighs, toyed with her hair, then pressed her fingers into the moistness. The pressure began rising again. It was like the fear of a child doing something forbidden and expecting to be caught, a nagging fascination, like a warning impossible to heed. She moved on the divan, leather tugging at her, the air cool across her skin. The sound of the pen scritching across the paper, his breathing, the sensation of her own lungs filling and emptying, all seemed enveloped in the stillness outside the room, as if they had separated from existence and were drifting in a nonplace, without time. *If I open the door*, she thought, *there will be nothing . . .*

The experience came like panic. Conny closed her eyes and held her breath against an almost intolerable urge to escape. Her muscles tightened in preparation, ready to send her running. She did not move, held in place by an intense curiosity to know what came next. And next. And next—she shivered at next, her body wanting to fold in on itself and stretch out at the same time.

When she opened her eyes he was squatting before her, a few sheets of paper in his hand. *Everything is changed*, she thought, and touched his knee. He offered the pages.

"I love you," he said.

June, 1920

He jerked his finger away and Conny laughed, grabbing for it. "Come on, ninny! It won't hurt!"

"It's macabre," he objected, waving at the bottle of ink

and candle on the floor of her room, and the needle in her hand. "Your uncle is already furious about this."

"What does that have to do with anything? Uncle Francis would be furious with anyone taking his favorite niece from him."

"And you want to compound it with this superstitious nonsense."

"I don't intend to *tell* him, William." She snatched at his hand again and caught his wrist. He tugged but she held it firmly. "What am I going to say? 'Oh, Uncle, I know you're displeased that I'm marrying a writer, but it's all right, we're signing the certificate with our blood, so everything will work out.' "

"I think it's silly."

"As silly as the wedding itself?"

"Well . . ."

"Come on, open your fist. This will only take a second. Didn't you ever do this with your friends when you were a boy? Blood brothers and all?"

"No, I didn't. I didn't have any friends."

She squeezed his wrist. "Open."

His hand unfolded and she shifted her grip to hold his index finger stiffly. She waved the needle through the candle flame again, then jabbed the fingertip in the center of the faint sworls. He almost pulled free, but Conny held on. Blood beaded and she brought the finger over the open bottle of ink. She pressed both sides of the wound to bring more blood and let it drip into the ink.

"Not so much!" he complained.

Conny dabbed his finger with a ball of cotton soaked in gin and released him. "Ninny," she said playfully, then stabbed her own finger and added her blood to the bottle. She sucked at the tiny puncture while she took a piece of straw she had plucked from a broom and stirred the mixture.

"I don't see what this is supposed to accomplish," William said.

Conny capped the bottle. "What do you mean you didn't have any friends?"

He looked at her with the sour expression he gave to unpleasant topics, a reproachful look that embarrassed her that she had even asked the question.

"I was never strong," he said. "And people mistook my asthma for tuberculosis. I seldom got to play with others."

Conny thought, *I could have figured that out for myself.* She said, "So who is this Geoffrey you've asked to be your best man?"

His expression relaxed. "College. We roomed together for one term." His voice sounded instantly lighter.

"What's he like?"

"Different than me. You'll see. I think you'll like him."

Conny entered the small chapel on her uncle's arm. A few of her friends smiled at her over the backs of the dark pews. They, and a couple of Uncle Francis's colleagues, comprised the entire guest list. William had no family, and, evidently, no friends. Conny's cousin Janet waited, diminutive bouquet in hand, opposite William and the man beside him. Geoffrey.

He had arrived this morning and this was Conny's first look at him. As she drew nearer, she stared, shocked. A deep reddish-purple scar trailed across the left side of his face from the bridge of his obviously broken nose to the hinge of his heavy jaw. William was taller, but Geoffrey possessed a robustness that more than compensated.

She jerked her attention back to William just before she reached her place.

The parson cleared his throat and proceeded through the ceremony. He ended by having them sign their certificate. The parson held out his pen. William hesitated, then pulled the pen from his pocket—the ivory one Conny had talked her uncle out of—and signed. He handed the pen to Conny. She anxiously scrawled her signature and returned the pen to William, who tucked it in his jacket pocket. Conny's cousin took the parson's pen and signed in one of the spaces for witness. Geoffrey bent over the parchment.

"Ah!" he shook the pen, tried again, then dropped it, empty. "Pardon me," he said and snatched the ivory pen from William's pocket. Deftly, he uncapped it and signed on the second line for witness.

Conny felt a brief, giddy vertigo. She blinked at Geoffrey, who frowned for a moment, then gave the pen to William. William looked around as if startled, then laughed.

"That's it, then," he said.

The parson's housekeeper set out scones and punch in the parlor.

"I'm sorry for arriving so late," Geoffrey said. "No excuse. I just lost track of time."

"Geoffrey almost ended up expelled for tardiness," William said with a wry grin. "Never could keep an eye on the clock."

"Don't like them much," Geoffrey admitted.

"Still, you made it," Conny said. "I'm glad you did. I haven't met any of William's friends."

"He doesn't have any but me." Geoffrey frowned in the silence. "Now he's got you," he added quietly. He ducked his head. "Excuse me."

Conny watched him move away. He managed with a kind of artless grace to pass by people at the exact moment they were turned away from him.

"What does he do?" she asked.

"Lately? I don't know. He's been a miner. Worked on the docks in Liverpool. Bargehand on the Thames."

"I meant his profession."

"He doesn't have one, really. He could never decide."

"How did he get his injury?"

"Um . . . a misunderstanding."

William said no more. Geoffrey had disappeared. She did not see him again until she climbed into the taxi her uncle had rented them. Then he was there, leaning in the window.

"Luck," he said, clasping William's hand. He looked at Conny. "I'm pleased he found you."

Conny moved quickly and kissed Geoffrey, first on the scar, then on the mouth. He looked startled. Then his face relaxed into a grin.

May, 1922

Conny watched morning sunlight dapple the walls and furniture, filtered through the thin curtains that shifted across the windows, and thought how it even seemed to get into her dreams, the same color, lucidity. She sat up.

The other half of the bed was neat, unslept in. Conny stared around her and wondered who had waked her. *Who was touching me?* Her nerves rippled pleasantly. She bent over herself, hands between her thighs, and tried to remember what she had dreamed. Men and women with no faces, standing around her, hands outstretched, moving . . .

Gone. She pushed the damp sheets back.

She found William in the next room, the dining room-turned-study. Books piled everywhere. William sat at the long table, still dressed from the night before, jacket draped over the back of his chair. He rubbed his forehead absently, staring at the pages spread in front of him, the ivory pen in his hand. Conny hesitated. Since his last bout of illness he wrote seldom, little besides reviews of other peoples' books and the letters he drafted for her almost every night. Judging from the pages stacked by his elbow and the sensations she woke from, he must have been writing those letters all night.

He looked up. "Oh. Good morning."

"I'm sorry. I didn't mean to interrupt."

He shook his head.

"What are you writing?"

"Dreck, by the look of it. I thought I'd solved a problem

with the new novel, but . . ." He tossed the pen atop the sheets.

Novel? "Then maybe I should let you work. I thought I'd go out. Do you want me to bring you anything back?"

"No." He smiled briefly, then picked up the pen.

Conny dressed quickly, grabbed her bag, and hurried out of the apartment.

The streets of Newport, this near the waterfront, were relatively empty in the mornings. Everyone was either down at the docks or further in. This thin slice of shops and cafes remained quiet till nearly noon. Conny was grateful for the solitude. She strode along the narrow avenues that twisted through the district until the sensations pulling at her ebbed. When they seemed at a safe distance, she stopped in a small café and ordered coffee.

It's never happened with anything but the letters before . . .

They joked about the letters, pretending that their influence was purely suggestive—what was that delicious word from the psychoanalysts?—psychosomatic. That Conny's reactions came from her own imagination while he wrote. He did them after lovemaking—or had, until illness stole his energy and all he *could* do was write about making love. He had missed several days during the worst of it. Afterward, when he wrote, scribbling earnestly to her with the ivory pen, she responded. Perhaps it was imagination, as he said. Perhaps he even believed it. She no longer did. Especially not now. She was disinclined to question it too closely—sometimes it seemed like the only thing they had together.

She looked down the cobbled street, glimpsing something familiar. A few people walked along—workmen, heads bowed, caps pulled low on their foreheads. Conny watched them go by across the street. As they reached the next street, one of them looked her way. A heavy line staggered over half his face.

Conny stood abruptly. Coffee sloshed onto the table. She fished tuppence out of her bag, dropped it, and hurried after the workmen. When she got to the corner they were gone. She continued down the canyonlike avenue, but she saw no one.

Most of the shops were still closed. Conny framed her eyes to peer through the dusty windows. In one, among the assorted bric-a-brac, stood an attractive oak chest with brass trim. When she looked up she saw the shopkeeper, smiling at her. She pointed to the box and he nodded, motioning her to the door.

A musty, decayed odor escaped the box when she opened it. Shreds of felt still clung to the inside. "How much?"

"Oh . . . two pounds."

She surprised him by not haggling. Instead she counted out the notes and laid the sheaf in his hand. She lifted the chest. It was only a little larger than what comfortably fit in her arms.

When she stepped from the shop, Geoffrey was standing in the street, hands tucked in his pockets.

"I thought I saw you," she said.

He touched two fingers to the bill of his cap, then came forward and took the chest from her. He tucked it under one arm.

"I'll carry this home for you," he said.

They stopped in another café, not far from the apartment.

"After he recovered he wanted to leave London," she said. "I suppose he blamed it for making him sick."

"Hm. Well, that's as good a reason as any, I suppose."

"It hasn't helped much."

"He still isn't selling? How are you getting by?"

"He writes reviews. My uncle sends money. We have friends—*I* have friends. One or two seem to find it romantic to help an aspiring writer. William almost never goes out."

"He never was one for socializing." He nodded at the chest. "What are you going to use that for?"

"Oh . . . memories."

Geoffrey smiled. It eased the severity of his scar.

"William said you got that because of a misunderstanding."

"Did he now? Interesting way of putting it."

"Was he wrong?"

"To tell you? No, I suppose not."

"No, I mean—"

"Maybe someday I'll tell you about it."

Conny drank her coffee to cover her disappointment. "What are you doing here?"

"I've got a job working dockside." He lifted his cup to his mouth. His hands were wide, heavy. Conny imagined them holding and lifting, easily, as though born to it. She imagined them then palms out, calloused, flat against her face, her breasts, her thighs—

"I really ought to get back," she said, looking away.

Without a word he picked up the chest and followed her.

"Would you like to come up?" she asked. "I'm sure Will—"

"No. I have to get to work." He handed the chest to her, touched his cap again, and walked off.

William was asleep on the sofa. Conny carried the chest into the bedroom. She took the letters from the suitcase where she kept them and transferred the pages into the box. Two stacks fit side by side as if the container had been made for them.

She locked the chest and slid it under the bed. Listening to William's labored breathing from the next room, Conny sat by the window, absently chewing on a thumbnail, and thought about Geoffrey's hands.

July, 1926

"Don't you want to come?"

William looked up from the desk and shook his head. "I need to work."

In the two hours since he had sat down he had done nothing but stare at an empty sheet of paper, one finger absently rubbing along the hairline at his temple. Conny felt the stir of unease. She had not told William about the invitation from Brian, the man who owned this house and the car they—she—had been using for weeks now. William only knew they were invited to a party.

"Then I'll stay," she said, half hoping he would say yes, please stay, half afraid that he would.

"Don't. You want to go. There's no point in both of us suffering through this."

Despite his open shirt and the cool breeze coming off the Channel, his skin glowed with a fine sheen of sweat. He slouched in his chair. A typewriter—a gift from Brian's wife, who was in Paris this month—sat before him like a model of some improbable temple, but beside it lay sheets of handwritten manuscript, the ivory pen on top of them.

"Are you sure?"

He nodded.

"It could be a late evening."

He shrugged and picked up the pen.

She kissed him quickly on the head and hurried downstairs. She started the car and anxiously pulled away. She had not thought too directly about tonight's party. Brian had given her directions to a house down the coast road east of Brighton and had somehow made it clear that, while certainly William was invited, he would prefer her to come by herself.

Her body told her the moment William touched nib to paper. The villa was two miles away. Halfway there she considered pulling over, but she kept driving.

A mass of cars filled the grounds in front of the house. She could hear the jazz band even before she turned off the engine. She sat in the car for several minutes, pressed against the door, waiting for the rush to pass, imagining the sound of his pen, the faint susurrus of his breath. Tonight's

work, she decided, would be very good and as unsalable as
the rest. It was all for her anyway—he said so, but he did not
mean it the way it really was—it was all he ever wrote anymore. Conny leaned her head back and closed her eyes, letting the tension between navel and anus twist into
completion. If anyone walked by they would hear her small
sounds, and politely veer off to leave the lovers alone. But,
she wondered, if they did not go away, if instead they indulged a voyeuristic impulse and came to see, they would
find her alone, legs drawn up, face bright with pleasure.

Just me and his work . . .

She never asked if he received anything from the connection. They never talked about it anymore; he seemed antag-
onistic toward the subject. That and his illness. He refused
to see a doctor, adamantly declared that his lungs were fine,
the trouble was his bronchials, and then worked himself to
exhaustion and coughed violently half the night through.
They coupled so seldom that it always surprised her when he
pressed against her and explored her. She made it as convenient as possible for him, opened herself, shifted at the
slightest hint of where he wanted to touch her. She had
learned all his wordless signals and more often than not paid
no attention to her own pleasure. Afterward, every time, he
went to his desk, naked, and wrote another letter for her.
Some of them covered less than half a sheet, others went on
for three or four. She woke in the mornings to find them beside her on the bed, William asleep in the next room. They
went directly into the chest.

Her breath shuddered out in a last wave and she felt control return. She smelled pungent and dug out her bottle of
perfume. A few minutes later she walked over the grass to
the gravel driveway to the marble entrance, the music growing louder, now mingled with laughter. She thought as she
walked into the storm of revelers, *I've made a mistake.*

Then she took a glass of champagne from someone and
entered the beast. Hands, hips, elbows, and knees all

touched her, seeming to caress her as she passed along, deeper into the antic folds of expensive clothes and cigarette smoke bluing the air. Everyone seemed on display, but crammed together so no one could get a clear look. Conny drank her champagne and made greeting noises, searching idly for a familiar face, one with a name that she could talk to. The faces all looked so earnest about being casual that they lost all legitimacy and their smiles seemed overburdened with meaning. She recognized no one. It was pleasant, though, to be stroked and petted through the careless gauntlet. She missed it, touching and being touched by flesh. It would, she thought, be pleasant not to miss it. She finished her drink and found another before she made it to the far side of the room.

A bar had been set up, tended by three men in short white jackets. She caught herself on the edge and watched them busily mixing drinks for a space. She stared at their hands, at the quick efficiency of them working with bottles and ice and glasses. She finished her second glass and set it down with a solid click.

"I'd like a Manhattan, please," she said. "Something from home." She laughed.

"Conny! Glad you made it! Where's William?"

Brian stood at her side, grinning, his face a bit red.

"Home," she said. "Working."

"Ah. Dedication. Admirable." He glanced to the side. "I'll have a gin tonic." He smiled at her again. "Any trouble finding the place?"

Conny lifted the glass to her lips and shook her head. Brian picked up his own drink as people jostled against him. Fluid sloshed over his hand and he glared around.

"Crowded here." He gestured with his head that she should follow him, then took her hand and led her through the labyrinth of people. His touch was moist and too warm, but she was reluctant to let go.

She lost her bearings quickly. It was as if the room had

suddenly grown larger now that she was nearing its center. All she saw were people pressed close to her or the ceiling beyond the brilliant chandelier.

There was a second floor and more people standing along the railing looking down. She imagined that they watched her, making quiet bets on whether she would reach the exit of the maze before being eaten . . .

A clarinet screamed against the steady, frantic rhythms, but she could not see the band. Conny saw people bobbing in place, unconsciously following the beat, their bodies drawn into the pulse. She knew that feeling and for a moment it seemed right that she was here.

She bumped against Brian. He had stopped to talk to someone. She heard him introduce her briefly—something about "his writer's wife"—and saw a bright face smile at her. She made herself smile back. She could not hear their conversation, not as words. Except for the surreal sharpness of the music, sounds seemed muffled, blended into a steady drone, like water. She liked the effect. The anonymity of the noise made everyone appear smarter, more sophisticated. They all had something to say to each other and they all appreciated what was being said.

She could hide within it, say nothing, and pretend along with the rest of them . . .

She felt warm. She raised her glass and noticed a faint tremor in her hand. *He's working again.* . . . She licked her lips and filled her mouth with cold liquid.

"Corny?"

She looked up and saw Brian staring at her, a faint crease of worry between his eyebrows.

"Warm," she said. She finished her drink. How many did that make? "I think . . . is there somewhere I could lie down?"

His smile widened almost imperceptibly and the crease vanished.

"Of course," he said.

He pulled her through the crowd until they reached a curved stair that went up to the second floor. She sensed people staring at her—or maybe they stared at Brian and only wondered who she was—and imagined what they might think. She realized that they would be right, too. He took her elbow and helped her up the stairs.

When she reached the top she looked down into the mosaic of people, still unable to locate the band, and tried to picture herself as part of them, one frantically bland face out of hundreds.

Brian tugged her away and suddenly they were in a long hallway and the music seemed abruptly tamer, more distant. Brian knocked on doors and listened. At the fourth he grinned and they entered a room.

She found the shape of the bed by the light from the hallway. Her legs felt uncertain as she stumbled toward it. She reached it just as he closed the door. She sprawled across the soft surface in the darkness and drew her legs up against her breasts.

"I'm sorry . . ." she said. "Just need a little time . . ."

"Of course. I quite understand."

Through the insistent sensations growing inside her, along her thighs, through her stomach, she felt the bed shift. Then someone stroked her shoulder, touched her face. She flinched away and rolled onto her stomach.

"Here now," a voice said, "let me help."

She felt her skirt lifted, a hand against the back of her calf, up to her knee. She began to laugh. He pushed at her shoulder, trying to roll her over again.

Then lips brushed the side of her face, her neck, her ear. She laughed louder, and turned her face away.

"Here . . . now . . ."

His hands took hold of her hips and began rocking her. She let herself be moved, over onto her back, still laughing. She buried her hands between her legs.

He kissed her. His tongue prodded at her lips. She

thought, *I should be polite and let him, this is why I came*, but she could not stop laughing.

"Damnit," he hissed. "What's the matter with you?"

"I'm sorry . . ." She tugged at her skirt, pulling it up, and spread her legs.

After a few moments, she felt his hand against her, fingers tangling her hair, thumb searching for entrance. It tickled and she jerked. He rubbed at her, but did not quite manage to find the right places, the right pressure. Finally she sat up and grabbed his wrist.

"No, like this," she said, moving his hand away. She ran her index finger through her hair. Then she laughed, realizing that it was too dark for him to see. She fell back against the pillows.

"Thank you," she breathed. "I appreciate the gesture . . . just let me rest."

She sensed him, sitting nearby in the darkness, rigid and frustrated. She could almost feel him weighing his options. He tried to kiss her again, one hand on her breast, squeezing. But she rolled away. She did not know when he left. She remembered the light from the door again, the sound of the door closing. Then she was alone. She pulled up her skirt, jammed her fingers in deep, and rolled over onto her side, coiling around the orgasm, again . . . again . . .

"Would you like me to drive you home?"

Conny opened her eyes to the yellowed light of the bedside lamp across a pillow. She blinked and rolled onto her back. Geoffrey's face hovered above her; the glow spilled across his scar, leaving half his face in shadow.

Her head pounded and her right arm had fallen asleep. She tried to sit up. Geoffrey helped her. She bent forward and gazed down at her bare thighs. She tried to tug her skirt down, then gave up and fell back onto the bed.

"Conny?"

"Mmm?"

"You should go home. I'll take you."

"Sure." Her arm tingled painfully. She used her left arm to push herself back up. "Where's the bathroom?"

A strong hand took her elbow. She got to her feet, then across the room to a door. Geoffrey switched on the light and gently propelled her into the small porcelain chamber.

She did not throw up. Her stomach churned, but nothing happened. She washed her face, relieved herself, and emerged feeling more awake. Her arm felt almost normal.

Geoffrey waited on the edge of the bed, a white bartender's jacket beside him, smoking a cigarette. He let the ashes fall to the floor.

"Ready?" he asked.

"Yes . . . you were downstairs?"

He nodded. "Saw you come in, but I didn't get a chance to say anything to you."

Geoffrey held her arm descending the staircase, a pleasant pressure she missed immediately when he released her at the bottom. A few people still lingered in the main ballroom. The floor was covered with debris—streamers, paper napkins, broken glass. One bartender slept in a chair behind his station. Conny did not see Brian.

Geoffrey drove her back to their borrowed house. *Not for long now,* she thought muzzily, *we'll have to move again.* He pulled up by the front door and shut the motor off. A single lantern shined by the door.

Conny stared at him. "You were in Newport. We took a cottage in Swansea near the end of the war and I thought I saw you there, working in a dry goods shop. Then we went to London for a month, after the Armistice, and you were driving a hansom. We moved back to Newport, then to Bristol, now here to Brighton. I always felt you were somewhere nearby and now you turn up. Are you following us, Geoffrey?"

"You should get to bed. It's nearly dawn."

"William doesn't expect me."

"Maybe not."

His arm lay across the back of the seat. Conny looked at his hand, inches from her shoulder, a dark mass of contours, faintly outlined along the knuckles from the lantern light. Between that and his nearly invisible face his white shirt looked like a mass of evening fog.

"I think he's asleep," she said.

She traced the shape of his thumb, the raised tendons, the blunt shafts of fingers. The texture fascinated her. She lifted it and turned it over and touched the callouses that ridged the top of his palm, just below the base of his fingers. The skin was very warm and dry.

Conny undid his cuff and pushed the sleeve back, pressing her own palm against his forearm. She could feel his pulse in the thick vein that ran from tendon to elbow.

"Conny—"

"Shh. Don't."

She slid her lips over his thumb and teased it with her tongue. He did not pull away. She licked his callouses, the center of his hand, his lifeline, the tendons that tented the skin of his wrist.

Conny twisted around in the seat to face him, kneeling, and fumbled for the buttons of his shirt. He grabbed her hand. She tugged once, twice, pulled loose, and continued unbuttoning until her hand came against his belt. She leaned forward. He smelled warm and sharp, as if he had been working out in the sun all day. She pushed aside the open shirt and laid her hands against his chest, surprised at the feel of hair. William's body was nearly bald and the contours of his torso were the shapes of ribs and collarbone and sternum.

She heard Geoffrey's breath deepen. He had not moved to touch her and she realized that she preferred it that way. To touch and not be touched—the idea fascinated her.

His nipples went hard and round under her fingers. She licked his stomach, from navel to solar plexus. Geoffrey's head rolled back.

"Damn . . ." he whispered.

She was afraid he might stop her, that she might stop herself. He tasted salty, skin slippery with sweat. She mouthed his neck and worked at his belt, his button, his zipper. Then she laid one hand on the arm still stretched along the top of the car seat and pushed her fingers beneath the waistband of his shorts. His penis bent down, thick and awkward, and she hooked two fingers beneath it to bring it carefully up, afraid of hurting him. The fabric held it until it sprang loose.

Then she looked down, certain now that he would not prevent her from doing anything she wanted. Her body blocked what little light came from the lantern by the door; she could not see his face. What she saw were fragments—a shirted arm, a yellowish glint off the car mirror, part of the door against which Geoffrey lay—but her mind supplied the missing detail from the hundreds of dreams prompted by William's letters. She pulled back a little and grasped his penis. Touching and not being touched . . . a new experience. She laughed at the idea. Married all these years and so few times—when William wanted her, gathered the energy and the will to fuck her, that was all he did, and she accommodated him. He seemed not to like to be touched, as if embarrassed with his own body, as though he did not deserve it, and over time she had become adept at a kind of encouraging passivity and a congenial access. She squeezed Geoffrey, ran her thumb along the underside of the shaft, and wondered why she had allowed it for so long.

He shifted beneath her and her heart slammed, certain that he was about to say enough and push her away. She let him go and yanked at his pants. He grunted and raised his hips. The trousers slid down to his thighs and she had no more room to back up and get them the rest of the way off. She reached behind her and groped for the handle. The door opened and she kicked it wide. Standing on the gravel of the driveway, she drew his pants down to his ankles, then untied his shoes and flipped them off.

Now the wan light fell across him and she saw his legs, the hair around his penis, the geography of his belly and chest, and, for the briefest moment, the broken quarters of his face.

Conny grabbed him behind the knees and yanked until he came across the seat, out of the car, and sat down on the runner. She gathered her skirt up around her waist and lowered herself onto his lap. He seemed to flow up into her and she gasped. She found his face, his mouth. He sucked at her fingers. Her knees banged the edge of the running board. She wanted to move elsewhere, but she did not want to give him a chance to end the contact. She wrapped her hands tightly around his neck and brought first one foot, then the other, up onto the board. Geoffrey's arms joined across her lower back and held her while she seesawed against him. For a moment she was aware of the harsh sounds they made, counterpointing their thrusting, and then she forgot everything but the exquisite contractions, the taste of flesh, and the panic filling her.

April, 1931

Conny wiped William's mouth and shivered at the thin smear of blood on the rag. Huddled beneath a quilt and two blankets, he trembled, his skin dry and papery. Outside the rain continued, as it had for the past three days, and Conny silently cursed their coming to Norwich. She had not wanted to leave Cambridge. Before that she had wanted to stay in Bedford and before that Reading and before that . . . the place names stacked in her memory, a succession of borrowed houses, lent rooms, trains, and taxis. They always seemed to find a place, someone who thought it was sophisticated or chic to help support an aspiring writer, even one who could not seem to publish anything—perhaps especially one like that. The charity rarely lasted, especially when they realized William would not attend their parties to be shown off. She still missed the house in Brighton, but, as she had expected, Brian had tossed them out.

William coughed weakly. He had been sick since Cambridge, but in the last six days he had grown worse. Conny touched her fingertips to his forehead. Hot. She glanced at the bottle of laudanum on the bedside table. William hated it, but it did help him sleep during the worst of his fevers and coughing fits.

She left the bedroom door slightly ajar and went down to the kitchen. A puddle covered the tiles by the door and threatened to become a stream. She took the mop and listlessly dabbed at the water.

When she looked up Geoffrey stood framed in the door window, rain sheeting off his wide-brimmed hat like a veil. She opened the door.

"I asked at the post office where you were," he said. "They asked me to bring your mail. Said you hadn't been down in a week."

"Five days. Come in, then."

She hung his coat off the back of a chair in the corner and set his hat on the seat. She ran the mop over the new puddle he made and closed the door.

He dropped a bundle of envelopes on the table, then stood back, hands in his pockets. Conny thought he looked just like a boy expecting a scolding.

"We haven't seen you since Reading," she said.

"I'm working at the foundry."

Conny waited. She expected a reaction, a recognition, a response—from herself. But nothing happened. She pulled a chair from the table and sat down.

"In Birmingham," she said, "you worked in a warehouse. Ipswich it was a street cleaner and in Bath a stable. I'd gotten so used to you being wherever we were that . . . it took three more moves to realize that you'd abandoned us. Five years since you and I started. Eight before that. A lot of time and effort to just walk away from."

"I didn't—"

She waited for him to finish. When he said nothing, she continued. "He got very sick in Cambridge. I thought he'd die. The thing is, I forgot all about you then. I didn't think about you at all till just now. Isn't that odd?"

Geoffrey's face twisted in a painful scowl. Conny thought his scar would open. "I wondered . . ." He looked toward the ceiling. "Is he—?"

"Upstairs. Still sick."

Geoffrey sighed. "He hasn't written anything since Cambridge, then."

Conny stared at him, a chill settling in her bowels. He gave her a quick, wry smile, then sat down across from her.

"Did you ever ask him if there'd been anyone before you?" he asked.

"No."

Geoffrey gestured at his face. "William wrote a story in university about two boys who became best friends. He didn't know a lot about friendship. The university journal wouldn't print it but the word got around that he'd written it and that it was about me and him. Some lads took it on themselves one night to exact moral realignment. I don't remember much besides William holding me in his arms, screaming, him with a bloody nose and me with a map of the Suez Canal across my face."

"So had there been?"

"What?"

"Anyone before me."

"Just me."

From upstairs came the sound of coughing. Conny listened, willing it to stop. When it worsened, she stood.

"Stay," she said. He nodded and she went up to William.

His fever broke. Conny cleaned him up and changed his sheets, then cleaned the rest of the sickroom. At one point she looked around to see him watching her, eyes half-lidded.

His face moved as if to smile. Perspiration broke across his cheeks.

Toward evening the rain stopped and she opened his window to let out some of the smell. She finished mopping the floor and went into the next room.

Boxes of books stacked against one wall. A plain table served as a desk. Conny picked items up and put them down, not really straightening anything. He had yet to do any work here. Paper waited on one end, the ivory pen and ink bottle by the lamp, and the bulky typewriter he almost never used on the other end. She picked up the bottle; the same one, all this time. The traces of their blood must have long since disappeared. Perhaps some few molecules had worked into the glass wall. He always refilled it when the ink ran out, the bottle and the pen constant, lifelong companions.

She ran the mop lightly over this floor and took the bucket down to the kitchen. She was hungry but too tired to bother cooking anything. She tore off a piece of bread and poured a glass of wine and went up to her own room, just across the hall from William's. She lay down, wondering what it would be like to stay in one place forever.

She opened her eyes to a wash of brilliant moonlight silvering the walls of her room. The silence around her seemed like the night holding its breath. She was absolutely awake, her pulse fast, as if something had frightened her from sleep.

No light in the empty hall except a dim glow that picked out the stairwell from below. She descended the steps cautiously.

The main room held a bluish light—moon reflected off water—that leached color and detail from the furniture, yet gave the impression of perfect illumination. She paused on the last step, letting the feel of the old wood against her feet register as solid, as real. A faint breeze shifted her hair, tickling her face.

Movement caught her eye. She stared across the room,

against the wall, by the long divan. Another movement—an arm shifted, swimming through the unreliable light. Conny stepped to the floor and threaded her way between chairs and tables, and stopped before the couch.

The arm moved again and a face came up out of shadow.

"He's writing again," Geoffrey said.

Morning light turned the room to dusky gold. *That's how I feel*, Conny thought.

Gradually, she became aware that she was lying belly down on the floor. She pushed herself up, triggering a series of small aches and twinges, and rolled onto her buttocks. Geoffrey lay stretched out on the divan, one arm over his face. Conny crawled over to him and perched on the sofa edge, her hip against his side, and walked her fingers across his stomach.

He snatched her hand and held it, running his thumb up and down her palm.

"Good morning," she said.

"How long has it been?" he asked.

She tried to find a way to misunderstand him—she wanted to keep the golden feelings—but she knew what he meant. "Since Cambridge. A little before, maybe."

"For both of us, then." He lowered his arm and looked at her. "I ran away after Reading. I blamed you. I thought we shouldn't be doing this and it was you kept finding me and insisting. But that wasn't it. I wanted to see if I could live on my own."

"And?"

He shrugged. "Sure. If you can call it living. Tasteless food, stale air, meaningless routine. No reason to get up in the morning except that it's too bright to sleep. You?"

"I've been too busy taking care of him to notice."

He gave her a skeptical look. Then, abruptly, he frowned and sat up.

William stood at the bottom of the stairs, a long nightshirt covering him to his shins, staring at them. He held a thin sheaf of paper in his hand.

January, 1933

Conny's lungs emptied in quick stages as her thighs relaxed. The coils in her stomach released across her ribs, over her back, along her arms, and ebbed away. She folded against Geoffrey. Where their skin touched sweat oiled the contact, let them slide minutely with each inhalation and exhalation; at the exact line along which their skins parted, evaporation cooled. Moisture ran from her shoulders, into the runnel of her spine. In the sudden stillness she heard the faint scratch of pen nib on paper.

"My god," Geoffrey breathed, "the man's prodigious."

Conny nodded, face sliding on damp hair. She opened her eyes. Across the room, by the window, William hunched over the small table, working.

"What do we do if he dies?" Geoffrey asked quietly.

Conny raised herself on one arm. "That's not funny."

"Wasn't meant to be. It's a serious question. We ought to think about it."

She kissed his neck, licked the salt from the hollow of his throat. "Not now." She lay back against him and he ran his fingertips lightly along her sides and over her hips and buttocks. It still surprised her sometimes how gently he could touch her.

Conny closed her eyes but could not sleep. Geoffrey's question nagged at her. In the nearly two years since Norwich, William had never really recovered. His coughing peppered the nights and he adamantly refused to see a doctor. Geoffrey regularly threatened to pick him up and carry him to one, but it never happened. Still, William seemed no worse. Conny imagined him like a stone balanced on an edge, waiting for a sufficient tremor to send it tumbling. He needed to be in a sanitorium, but neither Geoffrey nor she could bear to do it. At times their inertia almost let her believe Geoffrey's occasional delusions that they had no reality of their own away from William, that they existed only in the benevolence of his incessant scribbling.

"We go on," she said.

"Hmm?"

"If he dies. We go on."

"Can we?"

"Shh." She listened to William working for a time. She imagined herself as a pyre sometimes. The fire ate everything down to charred debris. Then he stuck his pen in and stirred the ashes and, phoenix-like, found something more to burn.

June, 1935

Conny trudged up the steep path. The late afternoon light angled through the trees in shafts. Devon was peaceful, she liked this place more than any other. She tried to imagine living the rest of her life here. Possible, she decided. The three of them had achieved a kind of equilibrium. The last year had been the best.

It was nearly dark by the time she got back to the cottage. Geoffrey sat at the foot of the steps. He looked up at her grimly. From the house she could hear William shouting. Something shattered.

"What happened?" she asked.

Geoffrey shrugged. "He threw me out."

She dropped her bag by him and ran up the stairs.

Furniture had been moved around, a table turned over. Ceramic shards littered the floor. William squatted before the fireplace. As Conny came up behind him she saw him shove a handful of pages into the flames. They curled up and blackened almost at once and he threw more in.

"William!"

She grabbed the next stack from him and he fell. He stared at her for a few seconds as if he did not know her. Then he jumped to his feet and took the pages back, pushing her away. He flung them into the hearth.

"Damn them! Damn you!"

Conny tried to get the rest of the manuscript from him. He whirled around and caught her with an elbow. She staggered onto the couch, breathless, and watched as he tossed the rest of the pages to the fire.

"Damn! Damn! Damn it all!"

His face seemed to compress, caught for an instant between rage and hurt. Then the tears came and he howled. Conny held him. His thin body convulsed. He screamed and shook, made motions to push her away, but without any force.

"I'm tired," he said.

Conny led him to his bedroom and helped him undress. She could almost pick him up now. She drew the sheets and eased him onto the mattress.

He reached up and touched her face. "Don't go."

Startled, Conny stared at him for a few moments. Then she took off her clothes. He watched her with an expression of gratitude. Naked, she climbed into bed with him. He laid his head on her breast and idly ran his fingers over her stomach, her hip, her other breast. After a time his hand lay still and his breathing deepened.

Conny watched the last light fade and the room pass into night, not wanting to move. She heard Geoffrey come back into the house. She listened to the heavy tread of his boots to the kitchen, then back into the living room. Finally, he came into the bedroom.

"Conny . . . ?"

"He's sleeping," she whispered.

"No," William said. He lifted his head. "Join us, Geoffrey. Please."

"You told me to get out."

"I know. I'm sorry. Please."

Geoffrey drew himself up.

"Conny?"

"Please," she said.

Geoffrey undressed in the doorway. As he did, William's fingers began moving again. At first Conny was more surprised than excited. But his fingers slipped between her thighs and she moved her legs apart to give him access. This time she did not simply lie open for him. She reached beneath the thin leg he had thrown across her thigh. He sucked his breath between his teeth.

Then Geoffrey stood by the bed. She could not see his face and she doubted he could see her well by the dim light through the open door. She brought her free leg up and kicked the sheets down.

"Please," she said.

William scooted to the far side of the bed. Conny rolled toward him and kissed him. The bed shifted as Geoffrey lay down. She felt his hand on her hip. She raised her leg and Geoffrey's fingers slid inside her. She pushed back toward him and he pressed against her, kissed her shoulders, her neck. Conny caressed William and he bent toward her and traced the shape of her breast with his mouth.

Then William reached across her and grabbed Geoffrey's arm. They all stopped, for the moment making a tableau, a kind of completion. Conny bit her lip to keep from crying.

"I love you both," William said. "I'm sorry it hasn't come out better."

Above her in the dark the two men hugged each other, briefly. She eased onto her back, opened her arms wide, and embraced them both.

May, 1936

She looked up at the sudden stillness. For a long time she did not want to look at him. She held the handwritten page before her, pretending to herself that she was simply appreciating it, that it still meant so much to her that she could find nothing to say. But the silence stretched and she set the page aside and looked at him.

There was no way to divide the time into infinite sections, no way to prevent herself from coming to the point of knowing that he was gone.

At least his eyes were closed. He had always been afraid of dying with his eyes open. He could never explain it clearly to her, the only thing he had ever failed to put into words, but it had to do with dreams and darkness and being caught in the wrong reality.

Conny closed the chest and went to tell Geoffrey that William was dead.

Geoffrey sat staring out the window. The mourners had all gone, few as they were. Conny knelt beside him and touched his hand. Dry and papery.

"What now?" he asked.

"We go on."

"With what? I haven't felt much this last year. A few times." He looked at her with a puzzled frown. "Will it be like this from now on?"

"I don't know." She patted his hand and stood.

The chest was by the fireplace. Conny broke twigs and piled them onto the ashes of the last fire, then set four good-sized logs on top of them. The dried sticks caught fire easily and soon the logs burned, too. She sat on a footstool and watched the flames lick the air.

"Did you ever wonder what it would've been like if it'd been me you met first and married?"

"No."

Geoffrey stood nearby, hands in his pockets, staring into the fire. "I think I'll go for a walk."

"All right."

He hesitated. "Conny . . . do you think when I get back . . . maybe . . ."

"We'll see."

He nodded and backed away. A few moments later Conny heard the door close.

She sighed and opened the chest. It seemed to have grown larger over the years. The pages were an inch away from filling it completely.

She understood Geoffrey's frustration, but it was a frustration they shared. Neither of them had felt any desire for nearly a year. Not since that last night, when William had surprised them both. They talked about that night sometimes, as if it marked history for them. Conny supposed that it did.

In the morning William had been feverish and blood flowed from his mouth. They finally got him to see a doctor. Tuberculosis. As if hearing it made it real—more real than it had been—William grew weaker and sicker. Geoffrey and Conny had done their best to take care of him, but there was little they could do. William still refused to go to a sanitorium. He wrote little. Friends sent cards, a few sent money.

Geoffrey was afraid. He did not want to leave her, but without William—without William's scratching and scribbling—he thought she might leave, or that he might.

She lifted a sheet from the trunk. The words blurred. "This is all we had," she said. "All that's left."

She fed it into the fire.

Too many sensations. The smooth texture of skin, the pressure of hands, the rush of breathing in her ear, taste of sweat . . . the tension now building in her stomach, as if someone were holding her inside, a safe, warm, protective embrace—too many sensations. She counted them all now, after so many times, and counted them again. She slid a hand between her thighs, pressed her fingers into the moistness, and the pressure began to build again, like the fear of

*finding something long lost and wanting never to lose it
again. The stillness around her, as if she were enveloped in
silence, drifting in a nonplace, without time. It came like
panic and an exquisite urge to escape . . .*

She stared into the fire, at the few dark shreds of blackened paper. She was still staring at it when Geoffrey opened
the door and came into the room.

"Conny?"

She looked up at him. His scar, she noticed, was not so
prominent anymore. Over the years it had grown fainter and
fainter, so that now it was only obvious when he became
flushed and excited.

"Geoffrey." She took out another page. "I have something
for us. Something William left us."

> *For many months, and days, joys not a few
> We shared; in our delight, no amorous game
> Was left untried, and, as our pleasure grew,
> I seemed on fire with a consuming flame.*

ARIOSTO
"Orlando Furioso"
Canto V

The House of Nine Doors:
The Man Who Came But Did Not Go

Ellen Kushner

In the heart of the city there is a certain House . . .
The young man had been coming to the House of Nine Doors for several weeks now, asking always for the services of the same man. Tonight, as Carlin prepared himself for his nameless client (and are not all clients of that House nameless by choice and by courtesy?) the Master of the House stopped him.

"You say he never touches you, Carlin."

"That's right, sir."

"And yet he seems to enjoy himself fully."

"I think so. *I* certainly do."

"Do you?" The Master of the House, who was called Eyas for his hawklike qualities, ruffled the dark hair of his employee. "I'm glad. What is he afraid of, I wonder?"

Carlin shrugged his muscular shoulders. "Me? Himself?"

"People pay good money not to be afraid here. What's his secret, then?"

Carlin wished the Master would not play with his hair that way. Attention from Eyas was always piquant, frequently stimulating, and he needed to save his energies for the client ahead.

"I think he is ashamed of his desire."

"As are so many. But, tcha!" The Master ran his finger down to his chin, and the man licked his lips. "You know how to help him get over that, surely."

"He does not want me to. He made that very plain."

Eyas sat up straight. "Does not want you to? Or," he shifted the emphasis to quite another meaning, "does not *want* you to?"

"Really doesn't," Carlin explained.

Eyas fingered his nipple. "I love secrets."

"Shall I find this one out for you, sir?"

The Master of the House said, "I will soon make you fit to find out nothing at all. No, don't be offended. And don't go. I'll be sure you make good money tonight, but leave this one to me. Oh—how does he tip?"

"Too high."

"Not a nobleman, then; their fathers always teach them exactly how much."

At the First Door of the House, anyone may knock and be admitted. The porter did not speak, but made a question with his face, and the client nodded briefly. And so the porter led him, as usual, through the Fourth Door, which is the Door of Joy Unasked For. It opens onto a hall hung with green and gold like a woodland in spring, and always there is the faint scent of jonquils. In that hall waited a girl as fresh and young as dawn, with long hair down her back, but her form girded with silver armor, and a long hunting knife at her side. She knew this client did not want his hat and cloak removed, and so she simply escorted him up to a door bound in brass. She knocked and disappeared, and the client entered the room.

It was the usual room, dark with wood and red velvet, candlelit, cushioned. He began to take his gloves off, but stopped when he noticed the room's other occupant.

"Is there a mistake?" he asked in a low voice. "You're not . . . precisely what I require."

The slender man lying decoratively on the floor cushions wore the simplest of white robes. His close-cropped hair stood up like a brush. Although his eyebrows were dark, his hair was bleached almost to white. "I am not Carlin, of course, sir. He cannot come tonight. If you wish to wait, another man, darker than I, and more to your taste, should be free in a matter of an hour or so. But the Master of the House thought I might serve."

"Oh, he did, did he? What does he know of me and what I want?"

"He would not be Master if he did not know us all." The blond stretched his body back against the cushions luxuriously. His robe opened on a supple set of muscles, but his chest had been stripped hairless: no way of knowing whether he were a blond by courtesy only. "I know it does not please you for me to join you on the bed, sir. With your permission, I'll stay here where you may see me clearly."

The young client perched on the edge of the canopy bed. He removed his gloves, but that was all. He had the smooth white hands of a scribe, a scholar, or a dandy. His face hid in the shadows of his hat, his figure in the heavy folds of his cape. But his voice was a young voice, pitched low, without inflection, to cover its youth. "What is your name?"

"That will be your choice," said the blond. "Will you not name me, sir? For a friend, maybe, or for a lover?"

"You would let me do that?" The client scowled. "Very well," he said maliciously; "I will name you for my dog. You shall be—Fluff."

"As you please, sir. Fluff is my name."

"No, no!" he objected, not laughing. The notion did not amuse him. "I don't care what you call yourself."

"Bliss is my name," the blond said; "if you would have it so."

"I would have it so, indeed." He gestured with one leather glove. "Very well, Bliss, stay. But take off the robe."

The blond stood with a dancer's economy of motion, his eyes modestly cast down. "Quickly, sir, or slowly?"

There was a moment's startled silence, swiftly recovered from: "Slowly," the client purred.

And slowly Bliss slipped the robe from one shoulder, and then the other, letting the soft cloth caress his skin, letting the client see the effect that the performance, and the sensation, were having on him.

The client saw. "Goodness!" he squeaked, by which Bliss knew that Carlin sometimes required more encouragement. He already knew of their relative endowments, and watched to see if the young man appreciated them.

He did. He was looking very hard at the one in question. Bliss took two steps toward the bed, and saw the young man on it freeze as if he'd seen a dangerous animal moving. Bliss converted the movement to a langorous dance with the robe, trailing it over his body until the fine white cloth hung like a scarf from the end of his fingers, stretching out toward the bed—as if he were the trainer, now, and the young man the frightened animal he was trying to coax toward him. And so he remained that way for one moment, for two, the white cloth waving faintly in the stillness of the room . . .

"What?" the client demanded. "What am I supposed to do?"

"It is an offer," said Bliss. "An offer without words."

"You need offer me nothing," the young man said gruffly. "I can have whatever I want."

Bliss's hand held steady, and he met his client's eyes. "And yet I offer it: The robe from my body, still warm, and faintly scented, for you to do with as you please: to smell, to stroke, to tear to shreds—"

"Give it to me!"

"Quickly, or slowly?"

The young man's hands were clenched. "Quickly!"

Bliss flung him the robe; it unfolded in midair, landed against the young man like a spider's web, a gossamer net.

The young man tore it from his face, crumpled it into a ball and breathed in deeply.

"And will you give me nothing in return?" asked Bliss.

"You don't need it. You're already randy as a buck in spring."

"That's not why I'd want it."

"Why, then?"

"So that you might see your hand on me."

Mutely, the client held out one red leather glove. Bliss knelt to take it, and pressed it to his lips.

The sharp intake of breath from the bed confirmed his guess. He ran the leather along his chest, across his thighs. Only then did he raise his eyes, shyly, to the client. The young man's hand had vanished inside his cloak, to where a man might keep his dagger. And further down, to where a man kept other things and kept them well. The hand stirred the cloth steadily, and his breathing was audible. Bliss suppressed a smile. He teased the glove across his nipples, and gasped loudly at the sensation, in tandem with the excited young man.

"Ah, yes!" the client breathed. "That's good. Go on."

Bliss stood very still. His naked body was flushed and hard, gleaming in the candlelight. Only his breathing flashed light and dark. "Go on?" he asked, though he knew perfectly well what was meant.

The client's eyes were bright and feverish. "Yes, yes, go on!" His hand stopped moving. "You must take your pleasure," he added gruffly.

"Alone?"

"You know better than to ask that. Let us each . . ." His hand stirred the cloth.

But Bliss did not move.

And neither did the client. "What is the matter?" he asked. "You must be—doesn't it hurt, your, ah . . ."

Bliss said, "It pleases you to see it thus. I would be a poor servant to release it so quickly. You shall look your fill. And when you have had it to bursting, only then shall we concern ourselves with me."

His client's free hand wrapped itself around the white robe. "You will watch me? You like doing that?"

"Very much. Like candle and mirror, we increase each other's brightness. I like to watch you look at me. I like what looking at me does to you."

"Hmph," said the young man; "Carlin is not so bold."

"He is a different man. You must not think, because we have many skills, that we do not have feelings, here in the House of Delight."

"I'm not sure I believe you, but what difference does it make?"

"None, sir; you are wise. When you enter this House, you leave the World behind. Outside, it is dangerous not to distinguish truth from lies. Here, and only here, the lies are always for your benefit—and certain truths cannot be hid."

"My truths are hid," the young man said.

"Only some of them. Or will you lie and say I do not please you?"

"You please me very much. You're beautiful. Different, but beautiful."

"They all say that when they're excited. See if you think so afterward."

"*You're* excited. Am I beautiful?"

"I've no idea. Your hand is beautiful. Your voice is beautiful."

"Close your eyes."

Bliss closed them. He felt the stir of air, heard the hiss of cloth, and the sputter of wax when the candlewicks flickered.

"You may look."

Both the young man's hands were folded on his lap, encased again in gloves. He was breathing hard, and his voice was mischievous, pitched high with excitement. "I think you will go first after all."

"As you wish."

"Show me."

The blond man put his finger in his mouth, twirled it there and removed it, shining with spit. He ran it down his chest to his navel and through the thicket of hair that was, indeed, dark. It traveled a straight line to the tip of his shaft, and circled the hole where a drop of moisture already shone.

The client moaned deep in his throat.

Then Bliss's hand traveled gently over his own body, touching the places an eager lover touches, sometimes gentle and sometimes rough, using the backs of his nails and the tips of his fingers. His thighs, corded with muscle, began to tremble.

"Now!" hissed the client.

"Not yet," Bliss answered faintly. He raised his arms over his head, curving like the arc of the moon, his whole body and its desire exposed.

The young man growled, "If I say *now*, then it is now!"

But Bliss stood poised upon his toes. "The robe," he whispered.

"I have it."

Bliss held out his arms, like a woman just stepped out of the bath. And the young man stumbled off the bed, unfurling the gossamer robe.

He let it fall on the trembling man's shoulders, and took a step closer. Bliss's heat seemed to scorch the only part of him not covered, his face.

"Ease me," said Bliss, not moving.

"I cannot."

"Keep all your clothes, even your gloves, sir, if you will, but I beg you—"

"How?"

"Ah. I will show you."

The young man stayed behind him. "Lie down, first. On the cushions."

Bliss did as he was bid, hands at his side. His tense body

seemed to lie only on the surface of the pillowed floor, straining upward. The young man stood above him, fold upon fold of cloth falling across his body like a sculpture. But his gloved hands were twisting above the naked figure.

"Feast on me," Bliss said; and the young man knelt clumsily. The brim of his hat brushed Bliss's chest. When the tip of his tongue touched the tip of the other man's member, Bliss breathed deeply and did not thrust.

"How soft your skin is!" the soft lips murmured against him. By which the naked man knew that he had indeed been right all along. He felt the delicate nibblings and trembled as he fought the urge to pull the mouth down over his throbbing cock. The strokes grew more deliberate, longer and more avid, now here, now there, sweet and incomplete. His fingers clenched despite himself. Finally, "I wonder," he said, "if you would find it distasteful to close your mouth around me—no teeth, you understand—and feast in earnest?"

There was no answer but the thing that he desired, wrapping him in a sensation even he could not be separate from. It was as though the layers of clothing above him had turned into a ravening succubus, pulling the pleasure out of him like hunger itself finally fed. And yet he retained enough sense to lift his hands to his lover's head, pressing and stroking the back of his neck, burying his fingers in his lover's hair and one by one pulling the long pins that held it in place—so that as his body arced helplessly up in chaotic ecstasy, the long bright hair came cascading down around them both.

"Oh!" his client cried. "Oh, no!"

Hair clung to his damp face, and tangled in the buttons of his coat.

"Never mind," said Bliss. "It's nothing."

The client wiped his mouth with the back of his glove. But he did not pull back when Bliss kissed the glove, and licked some of the moisture off of it. "Am I still beautiful?" Bliss asked.

"Oh, yes. Very."

"Come, then." The naked blond rose lazily to his feet, drawing the other with him, floating across to the red velvet bed.

He held his patron in his lap. The fine hair got in their way, but he drew it gently back, disclosing one scarlet earlobe. Bliss pulled it, stroked it, raised his sharp teeth to it. The other ear was pierced by a small gold hoop, which could be drawn through the ear around and around in a tiny point of pleasure.

"I feel dizzy," his patron said, fingers clenched. "I feel crazy!"

"Yes." The hands kept up their stroking. "That's what it's supposed to feel like."

The gloves were torn off; one hand reached under the cloak again.

"Together," Bliss said, reaching after it, and was not pushed away.

Their fingers met in the moist hot darkness, where there was no man's treasure at all. For a moment they clung there together.

"Do it!" she said fiercely. "I want you to!"

She pulled at his hand and at her clothes at the same time.

"Sweet mistress." He leaned into her, stilling her hands. "I can do better than that." With practiced hands he unlaced the breeches. "You will go virgin to your marriage bed, and still be satisfied here."

At last he uncovered the fair triangle, damp with sweat and heat. "A treasure for a prince," he said earnestly.

"Don't be impertinent," she snapped, or tried to: to her dismay it came out langorous, flirtatious.

"I beg your pardon, madam," he said, and slid his finger down.

She had been ready for a long time. He felt her stiffen.

"Not yet!"

He stopped. "Not yet," she gasped, "not so soon, I don't want it over too soon—"

"My dear mistress," he toyed with her delicate folds, "with me, it is never over too soon."

He ran his face along the sides of her coat, her ruched-up cloak, down to the soft skin of her naked belly. His lips were warm on her skin. His fingers stroked her arms, her legs, methodically, gently, with a soothing rhythm that said that all was well, all would be well, if she would trust her body and its needs to him, and just as she was beginning to be a little soothed, his mouth moved down to somewhere altogether new.

She cried out in awe. Nothing so living and warm had ever touched her there. His tongue darted like a fish amongst the coral shoals of her flesh, coral waving like fans in the deep sea waves of her pleasure. She could feel him straining with passion, could hardly believe anyone wanted her this way, wanted to do this with her, rocking her up and down, inside and out, somewhere beyond sight and sound.

She had always had to control and tease herself; now there was nothing to control, feeling him slipping long and luxurious there where nothing larger, nothing less slick and supple of a man's might go. . . .

She let the world come apart.

He was hard with excitement, but he channeled it all into her pleasure, his skill burning for her. She was bucking her hips without knowing it, riding him, being ridden by her own strong desire, as hard for him to keep control of as a yearling, he relentlessly working to keep her pleasure coming in waves until she shook with it. And still he drove her, and the pleasure drove her, until she was writhing and pummeling him and crying her way to stillness.

She lay at last at peace, sprawled across the taut-muscled, naked man. With his thumb he stroked her side.

"Thank you," she gasped eventually, feeling something must be said under the circumstances. "I didn't know—that is, I usually like the look of men who are a bit more, ah, more heavily built."

"Next time, you must ask for what you want."

She said, still nervously needing to explain, "I am too young to marry. They tell me. I must be 'finished' first, whatever that means. But every man I see—the soldiers, my dancing master, even the baker's boy . . .'"

"I know." He drew a mass of her hair through his hands. "You will enjoy Carlin. He knows as well as I what to do for a lady of quality." She turned her bright eyes on him, and he laughed softly. "Did you think you were the only one, here at the House of Heart's Desire?"

Born among the great, she recognized authority when she heard it. "Are you . . . ?" she asked.

"I am. And your ladyship's servant, for as long as you require it. Return to us whenever you wish. You are as safe here as in your nurse's arms. You will go to your noble husband as virgin as the day you were born."

"If I can wait that long," she muttered rebelliously.

"If you find that you cannot, there are ways to repair it—but you wouldn't like them, they hurt. And should a mistake call a new soul down from heaven . . . there are many ladies who have found their way here to send it back."

She smiled and drew her hand down his spine. "I will invite you to dance at my wedding"

"And I will come," he answered, kissing her hand, "though it be beyond the farthest sea."

He added, "Your time is not quite up," although it was; and he took her in his arms and kissed her mouth as sweetly as a young boy would do who knew nothing of the many uses of the tongue.

"Now," said Eyas, "I shall summon a very dependable servant of mine named Hannah, who will help you wash all the sweat and moisture off you. She will particularly enjoy washing your hair—which, I'm afraid, has become tangled and rather sticky."

Ellen Kushner writes:

It's an all-too-common experience, that I'm sure most of my fellows in this volume are familiar with. "What do you write?" someone asks me, at a party, say; and when I answer, "Fantasy," they give me what is meant to pass for a sophisticated leer.

Well, now I've finally done it. There is no magic in this short story, but a great deal of fantasy.

Actually, this story, editor Terri Windling, and I go back a long way together. When we were in our twenties, living on New York's lawless Upper West Side and looking for assured income, we came up with the idea of marketing a series of erotic novels set in a generic fantasy-style city, centered around an exotic brothel called The House of Nine Doors. We did the fun part first: figuring out who all the continuing characters would be—and then got down to the distasteful chores of plotting and writing sample chapters. The core of this story was one of those.

Our proposed series was packed with sexually ambiguous people, lots of tortured longing, devious machinations, twisted desires and sublimated passion: just like everything else on the market these days. Back then, our radical vision would have sold like hotcakes. So I would just like to formally and publicly say, to all the pusillanimous editors who brainlessly turned it down: *You're Jerks!*

Oooh. That felt good.

Persephone or, Why the Winters Seem to Be Getting Longer

Wendy Froud

Six pomegranate seeds, as red as rubies, lie on a golden plate. They glow with crimson fire in the candlelight. My lord bids me eat. I can feel his hands upon my shoulders. I can feel his breath hot upon my neck. I eat the first fruit, and as I taste, my lord tastes the skin of my throat, where the scent of flowers still lingers.

In the world above, the daylight fades. The wind blows cold among the trees.

The second seed is eaten, and my lord kneels at my feet. His hands reach for my breasts, and through the fabric of my gown I feel his caress, first soft, then hard. I watch my nipples rise and strain against the thin gold silk. He takes a small knife from the table and, holding it delicately, cuts through the neckline of my dress. The fabric tears, parting from white flesh, and falls away.

In the world above, as night draws close, the grasses turn in the wind. Flowers bend. Petals fall.

My nipples are the color of crimson seeds. The third seed is upon my lips as my lord suckles at my breasts, tracing circles of fire with his tongue. They ripen like fruit beneath his kisses.

The world above is dark. The trees are black and bare. Creatures shiver, and shelter where they may.

My lord explores my body, kissing, biting, tasting the length of me. I need to see him. He will not undress. He will not let me touch him. I know that he is beautiful; I can feel that beauty as my body lifts to press itself against him. Naked now, my thighs tremble and open. The fourth seed is eaten.

In the world above, frost traces white patterns on brown leaves. The last of the summer fruit returns to the soil beneath the sleeping trees.

I catch my breath as my dark lord parts my thighs. His fingers touch me, there, gliding on the juices of my passion. His tongue, questing, thirsts for me, tasting me even as I taste the fifth seed upon my tongue.

The world above lies dormant, frozen. A creature caught by the cold, harsh air curls and sleeps, stiffens and dies.

He looks into my eyes, my lord, and slowly unlaces the robe he wears to taunt and tempt me. It falls to the ground. He stands before me, proud manhood beautiful. I long to take him in my mouth, to close my lips around that hot, strong flesh, taste the milky jewel glistening at its tip. He smiles as he puts instead the sixth seed to my lips. He gathers me to him; I twine my legs around his waist and open to his manhood. It thrusts deeper and deeper, taking me further into my lord's dark realm. The last seed bursts cool upon my tongue as my lord's seed bursts hot within my body.

The world above lies still as death, waiting for the spring to come. Hollow promise. Who can know how hard that promise is to keep?

I have always loved the taste of pomegranates.

Taking Loup

Bruce Glassco

 You study your date's fingers intently when you give her the flowers, because you read in a magazine once that women on loup have unusually wide knuckles. You don't know the exact dimensions of a normal woman's knuckle, though, so you don't learn much. Her fingers are long and slim, and you've heard that's a good sign, but the nails look awfully strong, and they curve downwards a bit at the ends.

You remember when it all started, how men were warned to watch out for hair growing in unusual places. But women had been shaving their bodies for years, so that wasn't much help. Men might not even have known what an unusual place was, back then; they might have thought an armpit was unusual. Linda's hair is as black as the night, and if she changed and it covered her she would blend into the night and you would never see her coming.

The fact is, there aren't any signs. The fact is, if a woman is taking loup you won't know it until it's too late, until she's already ripping your chest open and swallowing your heart. The fact is, as Linda takes your flowers and admires them and goes to the kitchen for a vase, her freezer might be filled with parts from a dozen dates, ready to be thawed out for a late-night snack. The fact is, you thought you were sure about the last woman, and you were wrong.

You try not to think about that as she comes back with her handbag and leads the way to the parking lot. She's small, a lot smaller than you, but mass doesn't count for much anymore. Pete Wilhelm at your new job weighs twice as much as his wife, but all summer he came into work wearing long-sleeved shirts. Sometimes there are bandages on his face, and he claims that he cut himself shaving or fell through a window. Sometimes he doesn't come to work at all.

You were fifteen when you first heard about loup. It started with athletes, you think: some kind of steroid that worked a bit too well. They've studied it for years, but they still don't know exactly how it works or where it comes from. All they know for sure is that it doesn't work on men. Something about chromosomes and estrogen and the phases of the moon.

There is a brief quarrel over whether you're going in her car or in yours, but you give in after some token resistance. She opens the passenger door of a silver Porsche. As you sit down you check the velour seat covers for fur or blood.

Tom Schneider was a kid from your hometown—your age, but from a different school. You'd never met him. He hitchhiked home from an away game one night, and no one ever saw him again. You joined the hunt, moving as straight as you could across a meadow, peering in clumps of grass and bushes, bored and scared at the same time. They found a shinbone with tooth marks on it, and that was all they ever found.

You made sure to tell your roommate exactly where you would be, exactly when you expected to get in, who to call if you were late. You wish you could say that you took no chances, but if that was true you would have stayed at home.

At the restaurant there is an awkward pause. You were brought up to offer to take a woman's coat. That's not the custom anymore, and for a moment it looks like she's going to try to take yours. Finally you each awkwardly shrug off your own, and then you take them both to the coatroom while she sees about her reservations.

New customs are hard. New customs—an oxymoron. On the freeway she was listening to the Cleveland Howlers against the Green Bay Pack. Sheila Breen, Cleveland's best runner, had carried the bag to midfield when the Pack caught up with her, and between them they tore the bag to ribbons. It was the fifth new bag of the game. Sometimes you miss football.

"So tell me about yourself," you say when you sit down, and she happily goes into her story. She's on the fast track at an ad agency—a campaign for those new quadrupedal work-out areas. Your roommate Karl didn't tell you much about her when he set the two of you up. He just said you'd been moping around too much, you needed to get out more. Only a few women do the stuff, he said, and most of the ones who do aren't dangerous. Most of them are nice. And of course you know that, except for deep down in your gut where you remember heavy paws on your chest, where you remember hot hot breath and saliva and pointed teeth grinning inches away from your face.

Still, you let him make the date for you, because you hate it when it gets cold at night and the only warm place in the bed is the place where you are. She seems nice enough, stopping to ask you a few questions and sounding as if she's interested in your answers. On the other hand, she orders the steak. She's carving it up and popping chunks into her mouth and chewing heartily, and suddenly you feel your supper shifting inside you. She catches your look and asks you what's wrong.

The first time you left your wife, you called a friend to come pick you up in the middle of the night. She changed back to her trueform then, standing on the lawn apologizing and begging as you drove off. She was so beautiful that you almost told him to turn around, but you could see your blood

on her fingernails in the moonlight as you held your bandaged arm.

She must have rubbed some of the blood on one of the
tires in the confusion. You can't think how else she could
have traced you to the hotel, later that night. She had to pay
for eight hundred dollars in damages to that room, and you
went to the hospital with a broken rib.

The next time, you planned your exit more carefully. You
left work early, went to the bus station, and never looked
back. No, that's not true. Sometimes you miss her so much
it burns; sometimes you would go back and serve her your
liver on a platter, if only she would eat it and smile and tell
you it was good.

Linda is very kind, she's holding your hand as you tell her
the story, and she's telling you how sorry she is you've been
hurt. She asks if you still want to go to the movie, and you
say not really, you'd rather go home.

She parks in the street behind your car, outside her apartment. Then she leans on your hood for twenty-five minutes
and tries to persuade you to come inside. I won't pressure
you once you're in, she says. Truly I won't. I just want
somebody to talk to. I want to hear your story.

There's something about her that still makes you uneasy:
the way the moon looks over her shoulder, the way her hair
moves when there isn't any wind, the way her nostrils flare
when there is. Finally, though, you give in. She's stroking
your arm, and her voice is gentle, and the bed in your own
apartment is cold.

When you get inside she offers you a glass of wine and
puts on some soft music. There's a dull ache inside you like
a lump of congealed blood, and you aren't sure whether it's
lust or loneliness or fear. You hope it's not just fear. You
want her the way you want air, the way you want your nightmares to leave you alone. A part of you is screaming no, no,
we've done this before, but when she reaches up and strokes
your cheek the lump in your gut dissolves, and there's noth-

ing you can do anymore. You need to touch her, need to touch someone, there's an empty feeling in your fingertips like parts of them are missing. You stroke her arm and she kisses you. Her mouth is as hot as blood.

She pulls you toward the bedroom and you don't resist. She pulls off your clothes and lays you out on the bed, then climbs on top of you and engulfs you. Her hands clutch your shoulders and she cries out as she forces you inside her. For this one moment you're important to someone else; for this moment you're her world. As she rides you and cries out into the night, you are a part of something larger than yourself, for you are hers. Even as her arms stiffen and grow hair, even as the fingers on your shoulders grow heavy and sharp, still you are hers and she is yours, and as you see her teeth shine in the moonlight you climax in ecstasy and fear.

Some women never turn all the way. Sometimes it's just an ear pointing, a claw sharpening, a muscle that tenses suddenly with the strength of wind. "That was wonderful," she says, and you see the loup passing from her face like a shadow; the newly grown hair fades and turns wispy and falls like snow. Her nose is still wide, though, and she sniffs the air above you. "You're afraid, darling," she says. "I'm sorry, I should have warned you. Were you scared that I would hurt you like your wife did?"

Mutely, you nod. She climbs off and lies down beside you, resting her head on your shoulder. "Not all of us do that," she says. "That's not really what loup is about." She strokes your chest for awhile with a thick finger, and then she says softly, "I'll protect you, darling. I'll keep you safe."

"What *is* it about?" you ask, and you turn to look into her deep gray eyes. You think you see the answer inside them: It's something that's strong, and young, and very, very old.

"The night is where we belong," she says finally. "Out where the moon burns white-hot at midnight. The stars go on forever, and the only thing for us to be afraid of now is the sound that the moon makes in our blood. Do you know what that's like?"

I remember, you tell her. I remember.

Later you fall asleep. You dream that you are lying in the moonlight, and dark shapes are gathered around you. They are ripping you open and feasting on your warm insides, but you feel no pain. If anything, you are glad to be a part of them, for it is good to feel needed. Then one of them moves up and kisses you with bloody lips, and you see that the eyes on her dark face are your own.

You wake up and check to make sure you are still in one piece, and you think back to the time when a woman's heart would grow cold at the sound of a man's footstep in a lonely place at midnight. How long, you wonder, how long until both of the moon's twin children will be able to walk beneath her without fear? And without fear, would love still taste as sweet?

She is sleeping behind you, her breasts pressed against your back, her arms around your chest. The backs of her hands are covered with short black down, and her fingernails are as thick as dimes. Her breath on the back of your neck is hotter than blood.

Feeling her hot breath on your skin, staring into the darkness, you lie awake until dawn.

Contributors

Edward Bryant began writing professionally in 1968 and has published more than a dozen books, starting with *Among the Dead* in 1973. Some of his titles include *Cinnabar, Phoenix Without Ashes* (with Harlan Ellison), *Wyoming Sun, Particle Theory,* and *Fetish. Flirting With Death,* a collection of his suspense and horror stories, is forthcoming.

Bryant's stories have appeared in numerous magazines and anthologies, and he's won two Nebula Awards. He has been a guest lecturer, speaker, writer-in-residence, and frequently conducts classes and writers' workshops. He has also been a radio talk host, an internet chat host, and an actor in two of S. P. Somtow's movies. Bryant is working on a feature film script and trying to finish a novel.

Storm Constantine is the author of the Wraeththu trilogy. She has written sixteen novels, myriad short stories, and a chapbook of three stories, *Three Heralds of the Storm.* Constantine is also a Reiki Master/Teacher and reads Tarot. The first volume of a new Wraeththu trilogy is due to be published by TOR in 2003.

"My Lady of the Hearth" is a variant of a fairy tale called "The Cat Bride" (in British folklore), which is part of the larger animal bride/bridegroom motif found in myth and folklore around the world.

Ellen Datlow is currently editor of Sci Fiction, the fiction area of SciFi.com, the Sci Fi Channel's website. She was fiction editor of *Omni* for over seventeen years. She has also edited a number of anthologies, including the annual *Year's Best Fantasy and Horror, The Green Man, A Wolf at the Door* (for middle grades), and the six-volume adult fairy tales anthology series, beginning with *Snow White, Blood Read,* all with Terri Windling. Solo, she has edited, among other books, *Little Deaths, Alien Sex, Lethal Kisses,* and *Vanishing Acts,* a science fiction anthology on the theme of endangered species. She has won the World Fantasy Award six times and the Bram Stoker Award once. She lives in Manhattan. Her website is at http://www.datlow.com.

Doris Egan has published City of Diamond, as well as short stories that have appeared in *The Horns of Elfland, Otherwere,* and *Highwaymen,* all under the name Jane Emerson. Under her real name, Doris Egan, she has written three sf/fantasy novels—*The Gate of Ivory, Two-Bit Heroes,* and *Guilt-Edged Ivory.* She currently lives in Los Angeles, where she has worked as a writer/producer on *Smallville, Dark Angel,* and other television shows.

Kelley Eskridge's short fiction has been published in *The Magazine of Fantasy and Science Fiction, Century Magazine,* and the anthologies *Little Deaths, The Year's Best Fantasy and Horror,* and *Nebula Awards 31,* and has been adapted for television.

Her first story about Mars, "And Salome Danced" was a Tiptree Award finalist, and "Alien Jane" was a Nebula Award finalist. Her first novel, *Solitude,* is published by Eos. Eskridge lives in Seattle with her partner, novelist Nicola Griffith.

Wendy Froud is a sculptor and doll-maker whose art (primarily based on myth and folklore) is exhibited and collected around the world. She worked for renown puppeteer Jim Henson for may years, making puppets and sculptures for film and television. She created Yoda for *The Empire Strikes Back,* Jen and Kira for *The Dark Crystal,* and various goblins, pod people, and forest creatures for *Labyrinth, The Muppet Movie,* and *The Muppet Show,* and for television commercials. She met her husband, the painter Brian Froud, on the set of *The Dark Crystal.* She and Terri Windling have collaborated on *A Midsummer Night's Faery Tale* and *The Winter Child.*

Born and raised in Detroit, Froud now lives in a seventeenth-century Devon long house in rural England with her husband, their son, and a menagerie of animals, trolls, and fairies.

Neil Gaiman is a transplanted Briton who now lives in the American Midwest. He is the author of the award-winning *Sandman* series of graphic novels, and the novels *Stardust, Neverwhere* and *American Gods.* He also collaborated with artist Dave McKean on the brilliant book, *Mr. Punch,* and the charming children's book, *The Day I Swapped my Dad for 2 Goldfish.* His most recent novel, *Coraline,* is meant for all ages.

In addition, Gaiman is a talented poet and short story writer whose work has been published in a number of the Datlow/Windling adult fairy tale anthologies, in *A Wolf at the Door,* and in several editions of *The Year's Best Fantasy and Horror.* His short work has been collected in *Angels and Visitations* and *Smoke and Mirrors.*

Bruce Glassco is an English teacher at Eastern Shore Community College in Virginia. He is married with two children. Shortly after graduating from Clarion, his first story was published in the Datlow/Windling fairy-tale anthology *Black Swan, White Raven.* Since then, six of his other stories have appeared in *Realms of Fantasy* magazine. He is currently working on a novel about dangerous fairies.

Garry Kilworth is fond of baroque music and jazz. He loves to travel. He and his wife Annette live a lakeside Suffolk village in England. Kilworth writes children's fiction as well as fiction in various genres for adults. His latest children's fantasy is *Vampire Voles,* the fourth in a series about a rivalry between stoats and weasels. His latest adult fantasy is *Shadow-Hawk,* a novel set in nineteenth-century Borneo with Dyak and Malaysian folklore and myths at its core.

Ellen Kushner's latest novel, *The Fall of the Kings,* written with her partner, Delia Sherman, picks up one generation after her first novel, the underground "mannerpunk" classic *Swordspoint,* leaves off. Kushner and Sherman attempt to maintain homes in Boston, New York City, Tucson, and Paris. They have no cats, but are very attached to their piles of unopened mail and unread magazines.

Ellen Kushner is perhaps best known in the United States as the host of the award-winning public radio program, *Sound & Spirit* (www.wgbh.org/pri/spirit). The weekly show, broadcast on over 125 stations nationwide and on the internet, explores the myth and music, traditions, and beliefs, that make up the human experience around the world and through the ages. Unlike Kushner's novels, it is seldom erotic, though always stimulating.

Tanith Lee lives with her husband, John Kaiine, by the sea in Great Britain and is a prolific writer of fantasy, science fiction, and horror. Her most recent books include *A Bed of Earth, Venus Preserved,* and *Piratica,* a children's book. She is currently working on *Metallic Love,* a sequel to *The Silver Metal Lover,* and, also, a new fantasy trilogy. Her dark fairy tales have been collected in *Red as Blood, or Tales From the Sister Grimmer.* Other stories have been collected in *Forests of the Night, Women as Demons, Dreams of Dark and Light,* and *Nightshades: A Novella and Stories.* Lee has won the World Fantasy Award for her short fiction and has had stories reprinted in several volumes of *The Year's Best Fantasy and Horror.*

Pat Murphy's thoughtful, literary science fiction and fantasy has won the Nebula Award, the Philip K. Dick Award, and the World Fantasy Award. Her work ranges from scientifically accurate science fiction to psychological fantasy to magic realism.

In 1999, Murphy made a departure from her usual, serious work with the publication of a rollicking space romp titled *There and Back Again.* Murphy claims this novel was written by her alterego, Max Merriwell. She says her next novel, *Wild Angel,* was written by Mary Maxwell, who is a pseudonym of Max Merriwell's. Her latest novel, *Adventures in Time and Space with Max Merriwell,* completes this peculiar trilogy with a tale of Max Merriwell and his pseudonyms: Mary Maxwell and Weldon Merrimax. *Publisher's Weekly* called *Adventures* the "cerebral equivalent of a roller-coaster ride." For more on this strange project, check out Murphy's web site at www.brazenhussies.net/murphy

Joyce Carol Oates is one of the most prolific and respected writers in the United States today. Oates has written fiction in almost every genre and medium. Her keen interest in gothic and psychological horror has spurred her to write dark suspense novels under the name Rosamond Smith, write enough stories in the genre to have published four collections of dark fiction, and to edit *American Gothic Tales.* Oates's short novel, *Zombie,* won the Bram Stoker Award for Superior Achievement in the Novel, and she has been honored with a Life Achievement Award given by the Horror Writers Association. Her most recent titles are *Middle Age: A Romance* and the young adult novel, *Big Mouth and Ugly Girl.* Her short fiction has often been reprinted in *The Year's Best Fantasy and Horror..*

Although she is better known for her darker-toned fiction, Oates's writing sometimes displays a sweetly humorous side—as in "Broke Heart Blues," which is part of her novel of the same title. John Reddy might be compared to irresistible fairy seducers, like the Irish "Love-Talker," or he might just be a hormonally driven adolescent with a bit more than the usual charm.

Melissa Lee Shaw has published short fiction in *Writers of the Future, Volume XI, Silver Birch, Blood Moon, Analog,* and *Il Etait Une Fee.* She is a Clarion West graduate.

Delia Sherman is a writer of historical fantasy who is finally making use of her Ph.D. in Renaissance Studies in "The Fairie Cony-catcher." She is the author of numerous short stories and two fantasy novels, *Through A Brazen Mirror* and *The Porcelain Dove.* With Ellen Kushner, she is the co-author of *The Fall of the Kings,* an exploration of history and sex magic set in the world of Ellen Kushner's *Swordspoint.* She is currently working on a novel set in a brothel in nineteenth-century Paris.

Dave Smeds, A Nebula Award finalist, is the author of the novels *The Sorcery Within, The Schemes of Dragons, Piper in the Night,* and *X-Men: The Law of the Jungle.* His short fiction has been published in the anthologies *Full Spectrum 4, In the Field of Fire, Peter S. Beagle's Immortal Unicorn, David Copperfield's Tales of the Impossible, Best New Horror 7,* and in numerous magazines. He lives with his wife and children in Santa Rosa, California.

Brian Stableford's final volume of the "future history" series of novels will be published by Tor in December 2002. The series consists of *Inherit the Earth, Architects of Emortality, The Fountains of Youth, The Cassandra Complex, Dark Ararat,* and *The Omega Expedition.* His other recent novels include the apocalyptic comedy *Year Zero* and the "young adult" fantasy *The Eleventh Hour.*

Other recent publications are a new translation of *Lumen* by Camille Flammarion and a collection of translated stories by Jean Lorrain, *Nightmares of an Ether-Drinker*. Brian Stableford is currently employed as a 0.25 lecturer in Creative Writing at King Alfred's College Winchester, teaching an M. A. course in "Writing for Children."

Ellen Steiber has written and edited many books for children and is currently finishing her first adult fantasy novel. Her short stories have appeared in the fairy tale anthologies *Ruby Slippers, Golden Tears, Black Heart, Ivory Bones,* and *The Armless Maiden.* She lives in Arizona with a cat and a garden that bear a passing resemblance to Enrico's in the story, "In the Season of Rains."

There is only one mention of Lilith in the Five Books of Moses, but references to her have been found on stone tablets dating back to 2,000 B.C. The lines of poetry that Lilith quotes are from the King James translation of "The Song of Songs."

Michael Swanwick slips between science fiction and fantasy with ease, and has won the Nebula, Hugo, Theodore Sturgeon, and World Fantasy Awards for his novels and short fiction. His stories have been published in *Omni, Penthouse, Amazing Stories, High Times, Asimov's Science Fiction Magazine,* Sci Fiction, and *Starlight,* and been chosen for several Best of the Year anthologies. His books include *Vacuum Flowers, Griffin's Egg, Stations of the Tide, The Iron Dragon's Daughter, Jack Faust,* and *Bones of the Earth.* His eclectic short fiction is collected in *Gravity's Angels, A Geography of Unknown Lands, Moon Dogs,* and *Tales of Old Earth.*

Mark Tiedemann was born and raised in St. Louis. He began writing in grade school but was interrupted by his pursuit of a career in photography for several years. Upon graduation from Clarion in 1988, he made his first sale to *Asimov's Science Fiction.* Since then his work has been published in *The Magazines of Fantasy and Science Fiction, SFAge,* Sci Fiction, and several anthologies. He has published three novels in the Asimov's Robot Mystery series— *Mirage, Chimera,* and *Aurora. Compass Reach,* the first novel in his Secantis Sequence, was published in 2001 by Meisha Merlin and was nominated for the Philip K. Dick Award.

The second volume, *Metal of Night,* is a 2002 release. He lives in St. Louis with his companion Donna and their dog, Kory.

Elizabeth E. Wein lives in Scotland with her husband and two small children. She is the author of *The Winter Prince,* which was short-listed for the 1994 Carolyn Field Award. The sequel, *A Coalition of Lions,* will be published by Viking Children's Books in 2003.

According to Wein, "No Human Hands to Touch" is a prequel to *The Winter Prince.* The novel is aimed at teenagers, so the incestuous relationship at its heart is never affirmed and never mentioned. The short story gave me a chance to unmask the dark secrets that lie behind the novel."

Conrad Williams, British Fantasy Award-winner, has had short fiction published in several volumes of *Dark Terrors, Darklands 2, Blue Motel, The Mammoth Book of Dracula, Last Rites and Resurrections, The Year's Best Horror Stories XXII, Cemetery Dance, The Spook, The Museum of Horrors,* and *Best New Horror 9* and *13.* He is the author of a novel, *Head Injuries* (optioned by Revolution Films), and a novella "Nearly People" (nominated for an International Horror Guild award).

"The Light that Passes Through You" was inspired by the realization that five years had gone by since he last spoke to an old girlfriend of his. It amazed him "that it is possible for people who claim to be soulmates or firm friends to end up as strangers."

Terri Windling is an editor, writer, painter, and passionate advocate of myth and mythic arts. She has won the World Fantasy Award six times and the Mythopoeic Award. As an editor, she has created numerous anthologies, including those edited in partnership with Ellen Datlow (listed above), *The Armless Maiden* (on the subject of child abuse), the "Borderland" series (for teenagers), and others.

Previously the Fantasy Editor for Ace Books, she has been a Consulting Fantasy Editor for Tor Book's fantasy line for sixteen years. As an author, she has published *The Wood Wife, A Midsummer Night's Faery Tale, The Winter Child,* and other books, as well columns on folklore and myth in *Realms of Fantasy* magazine. As an artist, her paintings on folklore and feminist themes have been exhibited at muse ums and galleries in America and England. She divides her time between homes in rural England and the Arizona desert. Please visit her web site, The Endicott Studio for mythic Arts: www.endicott-studio.com.

Jane Yolen is the author of over 200 books for young readers and adults, and she has won most of the major literary awards, including the Caldecott Medal, the Christopher Medal, two Nebulas, three Mythopoeic Society Awards, a World Fantasy Award, the Golden Kite Award (and two honor books), state awards, ALA Notable Book awards, ABA Pick of the Lists, etc. Called "the Hans Christian Andersen of America" by *Newsweek* and "the Aesop of the 20th century" by the *New York Times*, Ms. Yolen is married, a mother of three, grandmother of three, and a dab hand at oral storytelling.

She has been married to an ardent birder named David Stemple for forty years, to whom she gives a brief mention in "Bird Count." Though she has spent her time atop the fire tower platform with him, scanning the skies for hawks during the migration, she has never seen the creature in her story.

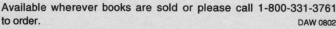

(((((Listen to)))))

AMERICAN GODS
NEIL GAIMAN

Performed by George Guidall

ISBN: 0-694-52549-9 $44.95 / $64.50 Can.
Unabridged 20 hours / 14 cassettes

"Brilliant dialogue and profound insights into
American consciousness show Gaiman to be a visionary and
a master wordsmith. Perfect for a long road trip."

—*AudioFile* Magazine

COMING SOON ON AUDIO FROM NEIL GAIMAN

Coraline

From the critically acclaimed bestselling and award-winning author of
American Gods comes a delightfully creepy tale for children of all ages.

ISBN: 0-06-050454-4 $18.00 / $26.95 Can.
3 hours / 2 cassettes • *Performed by Neil Gaiman*

ISBN: 0-06-051048-X $22.00 / $32.95 Can.
3 hours / 3 CDs • *Performed by Neil Gaiman*

NOT AVAILABLE IN PRINT

TWO PLAYS FOR VOICES BY NEIL GAIMAN

**Two Original Audio Dramas
Produced by the SciFi Channel**

SNOW GLASS APPLES • *Starring Bebe Neuwirth*
ISBN: 0-06-001257-9 • $18.95 / $28.50 Can. • 2 hours / 2 cassettes

MURDER MYSTERIES • *Starring Brian Dennehy*
ISBN: 0-06-001256-0 • $21.95 / $32.95 Can. • 2 hours / 2 CD's

Only Available on Cassette and CD • Available wherever books
are sold or call 1-800-331-3761 to order

📖 HarperCollins*Publishers*
www.harpercollins.com

AGA 0502